THROUGH A
DARKENING
GLASS

THROUGH A DARKENING GLASS

a novel

R. S. MAXWELL

LAKE UNION
PUBLISHING

Published by Lake Union Publishing, Seattle

www.apub.com

Amazon, the Amazon logo, and Lake Union Publishing are trademarks of Amazon.com, Inc., or its affiliates.

ISBN-13: 9781662501067
ISBN-10: 1662501064

Cover design by Faceout Studio, Amanda Hudson

Printed in the United States of America

For Dorothy, Isabelle, and Juliet

Winter 1910

Phineas pulled the cowl around his skinny neck, then started the long walk back to Martynsborough. It was not an ideal night for travel, lashed as it was by December rain, which seemed wilful in its want for warm blood. And while sullen about the business he had just concluded, he was at least grateful for the brandywine in his guts, without which, he was sure, pneumonia would strike before he could cross his threshold.

The grounds of Wolstenholme Park were vast, and as he neared the main gate, he found his pathway blocked by a puddle as monstrous as the Black Sea. With little option, he stepped into a thicket next to the road, a path he knew from boyhood, and perhaps more recently, as a popular haunt for local poachers. It was a lumpish wander, thick with twisted bramble, meandering briefly by the stable, which had not seen a horse in years, before descending again into stands of willow thrusting from snow-covered moss, and middens of dead, papery thistles. To traipse through this place uninvited during daylight was a wish to be shot by the last holdout of the Wolstenholme staff, Mr. Blackwell, a chimeric amalgam of butler, cook, doorman, and gamekeeper. Phineas had tipped his hat to the very man before sitting down earlier that evening with Wolstenholme by the fire, after which the steward had left their company and busied himself with some task or other at the old man's behest. Where Blackwell was at the current moment was not clear, but Phineas took solace in the fact that a gamekeeper would not likely be seeking an uninvited gun at such a time and in such weather.

Ahead, the trees cleared to reveal two perfect circles in the meadow floor—the lime-kiln ponds—apertures in the earth reminiscent of skyward-facing train tunnels, their waters dimpling lightly in the rain. Long abandoned, the subterranean kilns hadn't seen a fire in a decade. With a blocked coal feed at the bottom of the bluff, a particularly fierce storm many years prior had flooded the kilns, transmuting raging furnaces to placid, twin pools. In the summer, they might be pretty, wrapped tightly in a smart ribbon of Victorian masonry. But in truth, they were forty-feet-deep pits of murky water, within which lurked a grim tangle of wrecked farm equipment, horse bones, caustic remnants of quicklime, and God only knows what else.

This particular night, there was something unexpected disturbing the north pond's surface. A white form, like a pleated linen curtain, floated there in the black water. Phineas stepped cautiously through the rain and saw that it was a girl—face down, shrouded in the folds of a pale dress, her yellow hair drifting around her head.

He brought a hand to his eyes. It was the brandywine troubling his vision, it must be, and he looked once more, but the white form remained. As he drew closer, it was clear she was dead. *Oh, how it looked like her . . . Was it her?* No, no, not her . . . it could not be her—this here was some other unfortunate soul . . . some sad girl of whom he knew nothing. He squinted, his vision cloudy, his head a muddle. Did she move? No, no—the wind likely. He then looked up to see a shadowy figure stepping towards him through the leaf litter, wordless and menacing.

Phineas ran in a blind panic. The main road was only a quarter-mile ahead, and he dared not look back, sure that he heard stirrings and the crashing of hedges behind him as he fled through the bramble. He found the river, then the bridge, and scrambled up the embankment and stepped out on to the stone arch. He scanned the river gully to see if anyone followed. He saw no one—only dripping branches and patches of ugly, soiled snow. He lifted his gaze to the escarpment and saw, in the rain-blurred distance, a figure looking down at him. He couldn't distinguish anything beyond a baleful shadow, but it was enough to get Phineas back on the road at a ragged trot. Out of breath, he ran all the way back to the centre of Martynsborough and his terraced cottage close to the mill. He didn't notify an authority or tell anyone about the girl in the kiln pond that night but instead built a raging fire in his hearth. Thereafter, he slipped under his quilts, shivering, and fell into a strange sleep.

SUMMER 1940

- 1 -

Ruth Gladstone heard it before anyone else.

Propped on one elbow and reading by the light of a low-wattage bulb, she became aware of a strange, distant muttering. Both frightened and mildly annoyed, she set her book on the coverlet and listened carefully. It was the droning of a plane propeller. She glanced at the window to confirm the blackouts were fully drawn, then marked her place in the book and stepped from the bed into the hall. She rapped on doors, which soon opened to reveal the distraught faces of her housemates. The sound of the plane outside was quite apparent; questions were few. They pulled on dressing gowns and pushed arms into cardigans, while the designated leader scrounged for her electric torch with the red glass cover. All was done with a quiet sense of urgency.

Past the kitchens they went, and down a flight of stairs, through a dark corridor, towards a room on the lower level, close to the boilers—a grey brick affair with a muddy floor, where coal buckets were kept. They had been told it was a safe place and had visited once before during a drill, but at that time they were fully clothed and distracted with giggles and levity. It was a dank space that was so very at odds with the pale, satin-wrapped creatures within it. And although slightly dulled by the surrounding brick, the ominous burr of the propellers was still audible, along with the fresh and urgent wailing of the air raid warden's signal.

Then, quite abruptly, there was a thundering sound some distance away, and the ground shook. They gasped and huddled closer with stifled cries. Soon the roar of the bomber came even closer, and somewhere, high above, unseen by the young women, a gleaming thing dropped like an egg from the plane's belly. They heard it—a whistle, soft at first, then rising higher to a terrible shriek. They covered their ears and fell to their knees, scuttling on top of one another in a twisted heap of trembling silk and terry cloth as the howl reached its crescendo. Every girl held her breath, but no explosion came, only the sound of a muffled thump. The murmur of the plane receded, and then all fell quiet once more.

After hearing the all-clear, their curiosity got the better of them. They gathered outside near the tennis court, in various forms of night clothing, their gown belts pulled tight, their breath misting in the sharp air. There they found a disturbance in the grass—not a smouldering crater, no; this looked like a furrow dug with a garden spade. The red beam of their torch caught the glint of metal, a fin protruding from the turf.

Two days later, the unexploded bomb remained there like a lawn dart in Girton College's back field. Despite the university constructing a fence around it, tennis was most definitely out of the question. Moreover, it was expected that the girls of Girton's back wing should pack up and move to the Old Hall until that thing in the grass was removed or detonated or whatever it was that they did with unexploded bombs.

Ruth found herself billeted on a sofa in the room of a geography postdoctoral student and assistant professor, who was known for her expertise in English geology. Maude, a tall, pale, bespectacled woman five years Ruth's senior, was not terribly happy about the arrangement, and although unspoken, it was apparent that the guest was to defer to the incumbent's rules. As such, Ruth was no longer allowed her late-night reading—blackout was at 10:00 p.m. sharp. No books, and a room that was deathly silent, like a crypt. Ruth only then realized that she had become used to the rattle of a faulty radiator in her room, and in its absence, the night was bleaker than she could imagine.

In the dark that first night, Ruth's new roommate sighed, and it was apparent that she was not sleeping, either. Ruth rolled over and whispered, "Do you know what would've happened if the bomb had detonated?" The bedside lamp clicked on, and Maude propped herself up on her elbows, her blue nightgown gathering stiffly around her. She looked strange without her glasses on.

"It's a bomb. They explode. That's what would've happened," she said.

"I mean, the building," Ruth continued. "Would our wing have been destroyed?"

"That outer wall"—Maude waved a long arm, indicating the far end of the college—"would have probably come down. The boiler is under there, I think. It might have, you know, *blown*. Papers and books everywhere." She was matter-of-fact, even miming a tiny explosion with her elegant fingers.

"And the basement?"

"They had you take shelter there, didn't they?"

"Yes."

"On our side, we've two Andersons dug out behind the potting shed. You, on the other hand, would have been blown to smithereens by the boiler—that is, if the bomb didn't kill you first."

"That can't be true. The bomb landed by the tennis courts, on the other side of Orchard Drive. It couldn't possibly—"

"It doesn't take an expert to know what a bomb can do to a rickety old building like Girton. You're lucky to be alive. Have you no classmates to talk sense into you? Do you not have a sister or brother to sort you out? Where on earth are you getting your advice, girl?"

"Well, I don't have any brothers or sisters. I suppose I keep to myself for the most part. I do read a lot."

"I see. Well, it's probably best that you get your nose out Wordsworth and find yourself some peers to keep you from trouble. We're on the precipice of an invasion, for God's sake."

"But why would they drop a bomb on Cambridge? We've no industry; we're not building Spitfires."

"I heard from the headmistress that there were two more bombs dropped, some miles away in a sugar beet field. Those two bombs *did* detonate. No one's sure what the Germans are on about, given that all they accomplished in their sortie was to destroy a few bushels of root veg and mar a football pitch, but the headmistress thinks it was *Störangriffe.*"

"What on earth is that?"

"*Störangriffe*—it means 'nuisance,' a way for the Germans to test out their kit and give us a fright. The headmistress said it's the first volley of something coming—something big. It's only a matter of time before they bomb Cambridge in earnest. It will only get worse. I don't intend to stay here. I'm going to Yorkshire as soon as I can. I suggest you gather whatever family you have and think of a place to go, too." She snapped off the light.

Ruth lay on her side and covered her ear with her hand, which she lifted slightly and then brought gently down again. As she eased her hand back and forth, cupped over her ear, she could approximate a rhythmic ocean surf, a sound produced perhaps by the amplification and muffling of her own blood pressure. It was something she'd done since she was a child—filling in the silent void and settling her ever-present nervousness, at least enough to think about Maude going to Yorkshire. This, of course, led to another important question.

If Ruth were to leave, wherever would *she* go?

-2-

Maude's ominous vision of an exploding building with papers scattering everywhere gave Ruth a strong incentive to sort out her affairs quickly. So, the next day, alone, she slunk back into her old room, a place that was off limits and maybe even dangerous. The fact that the new wing was deserted proved to be ideal. She sat by the fireplace and considered a package of letters, mostly all-white envelopes, although a few had green borders, marked with the insignia of the Royal Army Medical Corps. On such a late-summer morning, it might seem odd to burn coal, but it was only a few sooty pieces left over from March. With the way rationing was going, there would likely be less than a daily pail allowed come autumn.

The letters were packaged neatly with a knot of twine, and without removing the string, she flipped through them with her thumb, recalling their contents ruefully, perhaps wishing not to—*trying* not to. She pushed the package into the grate, resting it on the glowing coal until a plume of yellow flame licked out from under the envelopes, and they crackled and popped and were soon engulfed in a diminutive pyre. She held one back, the one that had arrived that morning. The others, she had read only once and then hidden them away among her things. She had envisioned the building blowing up, the letters scattered to the wind and dropped down to earth, picked up and read by any and all.

Watching the flickering glow of the fire, she was now assured that no one would *ever* read Warren's letters.

Some months before, the letters in white envelopes had started innocent enough, but they were soon skirting the edge. Then that first uncensored green post arrived; it was appalling. Several more greens came thereafter, and the third had looked tattered when she received it, as if it had been opened. She later learned from a shopkeeper in Cambridge, whose husband had been in Belgium before the Dunkirk retreat, that the Home Office opened random greens as a deterrent to soldiers being loose-lipped about the division's location or casualty counts. Ruth knew that someone had opened hers; she could imagine this junior corporal reading about her brassiere, her knickers, all those F-words and C-words that Warren casually flung about. And under these frantic screeds and sexual blathering were the dry and deferential initials of the corporal who had audited the letter and a small, red-inked stamp. Warren had revealed no military intelligence, so the letter had been approved and resealed for dispatch. She watched it turn to ash in the grate.

Ruth picked up the most recent letter, the one that announced his return from Dunkirk and his intention to visit her in Cambridge within the month. This one she did not burn; she ought to keep one, and this was the briefest and least sordid. She intended to play-act as if the green envelopes had never arrived—she would be dumb about it. *They'd probably been lost somewhere or censored by the Home Office,* she'd say casually. She couldn't even imagine meeting his gaze knowing what he had written, though, and if he had hoped that his bawdy scribblings would somehow woo or excite her as perhaps they might other women—maybe French women—they were not effective for her. She was no wilting flower, no prude so demure as to not understand the motives and desires of men, or to deny her own desires, which she considered hale and modern. No, that was not so much a problem with Ruth. It was because it was Warren who had written the letters. Warren!

She opened the drawer by her bedside and took out a small gold ring. She had not worn it since her return to Cambridge. It had been last Boxing Day, to be precise, when she had sat at the table for dinner with her family and Warren in London. Warren had invited his parents. He'd worn a military uniform, which looked very smart, and even though war was on the horizon, there were smiles all around. Ruth had not expected what Warren was about to do—not at all—but her mum and dad and Warren's parents—they all seemed to know what was coming. And so Ruth did not refuse, and her mum was so happy. Sitting at that table afterwards, staring into the empty pudding bowl, Ruth had never wished for a sister more. Warren left for RAMC training the next day. Then Ruth's parents left for Canada, where they had some family. There they would take an extended holiday and wait out what they thought would be a very brief war. Ruth stayed behind, alone, to finish her term at Cambridge. The wedding date was yet to be determined, but she knew that even a quick civil ceremony would meet her mother's approval from across an ocean. She shuddered at the thought.

He hadn't given a firm arrival date, but she knew it was only a matter of weeks before he showed up at Girton with prospects of hasty nuptials. She looked out her window, past Orchard Drive, at a pretty line of oaks, the lawns and tennis courts, and a cofferdam in the grass concealing an awful thing. The bomb was not enough to drive her from Cambridge, but it provided her with the excuse she'd been waiting for. It would buy her time to figure out how—or even *if*—she could get out of the mess she was in. She took a pen from the drawer, reached for a fresh piece of paper, and started writing.

Dearest Gran,

I hope all is well. Thank you as always for the biscuits, which go a long way here—they're practically like currency!

If you might believe it, a bomb has fallen on Cambridge or at least near to it—there were two in a sugar beet field not far from Girton, and one within view of my room! Rest assured, I am fine, as are all the other girls. Thankfully, it was a dud, and no person or building has been harmed, but the thing still sits by the tennis court, embedded into the turf, awaiting a deactivation, I suppose. I think I might like to return to London—until this thing is sorted out, at least.

I will write you soon to provide a better idea of my timetable.

Ruth's gran always was very prompt with responses to letters, so Ruth did not wait long before . . .

Dearest Ruth,

Please, thank Mildred for the sugar biscuits. She works her magic as always, even when there is not as much to go around as before.

London is no place to be, either. There has been bombing here, too, I'm afraid—not near to us, but close enough. There were a few bombs in South London last week. Mildred's sister's house was hit, and the poor woman is frightfully injured. Mildred has asked to take her sister and travel to Devon, where she has family, and they can care for her. I have given her my blessing, and so I, too, must leave. Not having Mildred here would be unbearable—I can't be alone, and I believe the worst is yet to come for London. I've evacuated once before, but no bombs fell then. Now I believe it will be the real thing. I know that you've intended to come join me, and maybe Warren, too, but now I'm afraid I will need to leave. Ruth, please, come with me. Come to collect me in London immediately, and we shall leave together. I know a place, a safe place, a tiny village that will likely seem backwards and hay-filled to you, but it is a fine place, and my sister Vera, whom I have not seen in many years, lives there. It is not what we will be used to, but the country is splendid, and as she writes to me, the villages have more to offer in the way of food and luxury than all of London right now, and furthermore, a place so removed will never likely see a bomb unless the Germans manage to invade our island (God forbid).

The village is called Martynsborough and has fewer than a hundred inhabitants. Far north in Lancashire—a long journey, I'm afraid, but beautiful country, I should say.

Write back soon.

Ruth did.

Martynsborough? I've not heard of it. Moreover, I didn't know you had a sister—my great-aunt, I suppose. Why would I not know this? Yes, I am currently making my arrangements to leave and look forward to spending time with you in this Martynsborough place. It will be a silver lining to the troubled times. I will plan to leave within the week and will ring you from the residence telephone when I have received my itinerary.

The chilly reception that Maude had initially displayed for Ruth had thawed a little—perhaps more than thawed. Indeed, on the eighth night in her room, after finalizing her travel plans, Ruth dutifully arranged her rumpled sheets on the sofa, and Maude said, "That piece of furniture can't possibly be very comfortable, my dear." She was perched at the end of her bed, rubbing cream into her hands. "I'd hate to see your spine twisted on account of the horrendously slow progress with that thing by the tennis court. You're welcome to a proper mattress." She patted the bed. "Feel free to use mine."

"That's quite kind of you," said Ruth. "But where will you sleep?"

Maude erupted with a shriek of laughter. "Where? Why, right here, you silly ninny. This is a rather broad mattress—plenty of room for the both of us."

"Oh." Ruth paused. "It's quite all right. The sofa is comfortable enough, really." She shook out a blanket. "We'll be back in our rooms in no time, but thank you for the offer."

Ruth slipped under the blanket on the sofa and waited for Maude to extinguish the light as she did most nights at ten o'clock sharp, but she did not. Maude had gotten into bed and, sitting upright, continued to appraise Ruth with the keenness of a seabird.

"Do you miss your room?" Maude asked.

"Oh, well, yes of course." Ruth rustled about under the sheets, the springs of the sofa creaking and murmuring beneath her.

"You sure you don't wish to sleep in the bed?" Maude had removed her spectacles and was squinting in her direction.

"I'm quite all right, thank you."

Maude snapped off the lamp but spoke again in the dark. "The place I'm going, it's quite beautiful this time of year. Have you been to the Yorkshire coast?"

"No, I haven't."

"You should go. It's lush and damp, and the people are terribly quaint." Then, in a pleasantly long-winded way, Maude told Ruth about Scarborough, where Turner painted his landscapes. Then she spoke about Whitby, which was further to the north and known as a place that manufactured jet for Victorian mourning jewellery and known also for the ruins atop an escarpment mentioned in the story of Dracula—the setting where the beautiful Lucy was seduced by the vampire. Ruth was surprised by Maude's chattiness, thinking perhaps she'd had a nip of sherry from the faculty lounge before coming to bed. Either way, the effect was welcome, the oppressive silence banished by Maude's rambling tales of North Yorkshire. So soothing was the purr of her voice that Ruth was lulled as a babe in a cot, slipping softly into the downiness of slumber while Maude continued to speak to unhearing ears.

Ruth couldn't get out of Cambridge fast enough. Every time she looked out the window, she envisioned Warren walking up the path in his military uniform, a garish bouquet grasped in his hand. She had arranged tickets for London, then she would travel north—but the truth of the matter was that she didn't know much of anything about her final destination.

Martynsborough did not appear in any obvious place among the Girton Library's card catalogue. Many of the maps and surveys of England were already gone, quietly removed by some ministry official or other. Either way, despite a thorough and detailed search of the gazetteers, she found no mention of this mysterious village.

The search was fruitless until Ruth discovered an interesting prospect in a geological survey of northern England having to do with quarried limestone, where the name of Martyn was mentioned. Ruth wandered through the aisles of an unfamiliar part of the library in which she had rarely, if ever, trod. There she found the volume she sought and pulled it from the shelf. Then, over her shoulder, there came the flash of a pale hand, which plucked the book from her grasp.

"An interesting choice."

"Oh. Maude. Well, hello."

"Researching, I see—geology? An odd place to find you. I figured Jane Austen would be more your calling—this is my haunt among these shelves." Maude's brassy hair was twisted up in braids beneath a herringbone scarf, and she wore what looked like a man's sweater over a blouse, and sandy-coloured trousers. Maude was tall, much taller than Ruth. "You'd like to read this one in bed to help with the insomnia, perhaps? Limestone interests you?" She riffled through the pages.

"A place called Martynsborough, actually. Have you heard of it?" Ruth asked.

"No, I can't say that I have, and you'll not have much luck finding any current maps of England in here. There's no sense giving an invading army travel instruction. What's this Martynsborough, anyway?"

"It's with a *y*, first of all, which I found odd. It appears I'll be travelling there. I've decided to take your advice, and I'll be leaving soon."

"Right. Where is it, then?"

"Lancashire."

"Land of the red rose, land of witches."

"Witches?"

"You've not heard of the Pendle witches? I suggest you read up on them. Back in 1612, don't you know, nine of them were executed, hanged from apple trees, so they say. I've only been up that way myself once, near Blackpool. Didn't see any witches, but I recall digging along the coast one summer—acquired some wonderful samples of haematite . . . and a terrible sunburn."

"Well, I don't know *precisely* where it is. I'm to stay with a great-aunt of whom I've only learned, and all of it is a little, how should I say, *peculiar*."

Maude laughed as she grasped Ruth's chin and squeezed her cheeks.

"You're going somewhere you've never been, of which you know nothing about, to stay with a person you've never met? Like a child evacuee with a gas mask and a name label pinned to your jumper . . . and in Martynsborough you'll find what, exactly? Witches perhaps, and, according to this volume, also plenty of limestone." Maude opened the book and examined the index. She flipped a few pages and stopped. "The Martyn quarry, yes, mentioned here, even with your unusual *y* spelling. Limestone, yes, in this case, for the production of quicklime—you know what it is, quicklime?"

"I'm afraid I don't."

"Well, it's not something to put in your gin and tonic. No, dear, it's used to alkalinize clay-rich soil for farming—made by cooking limestone in massive subterranean kilns. Caustic and nasty stuff, but also very useful to the Victorians. They were awash in it. It seems that your Martynsborough is awash in it as well." She handed the book back to Ruth. "Well, see you later in bed, old chap." She strode away, her trousers making a slight swishing sound as she moved down the aisle.

That final night, having readied her bags and her travel clothing, Ruth was lying awake on the sofa when Maude spoke in the dark.

"Did you learn anything else about your Martynsborough?"

"No, not really. It seems I'll be heading blind into the unknown tomorrow. And you? You've made all your plans for Yorkshire?"

"Yes, Scarborough, by the water. I'll collect samples along the estuary until the war is over—or perhaps I'll avoid the sunburn and join the effort. Maybe I'll make bombs in a factory. What will you do in your mysterious Martynsborough?"

"I'll read, I suppose . . . and write. I'm working on a longer piece."

"Interesting. A treatise on limestone?"

"No, it's a novel that I've been trying to write . . . or I haven't really started. I suppose it seems that every twenty-five-year-old girl studying literature is trying to be the next Virginia Woolf, so don't mind me."

"I'll leave you my address in Scarborough. Send me anything you learn about limestone . . . or witches. It could be of interest."

"I'm not sure what I'll learn about limestone," Ruth said, wondering if Maude was being earnest or facetious—it wasn't always easy to tell. "But I'd be happy to write you. If you're curious, that is. Yes, that might be nice. I don't really have many classmates to correspond with as it is."

"Of course, of course. Now, listen here, Shakespeare's sister: I know I've been a bit stern with you since you've interloped into my room. Please, first know that it's not personal. I have to say, you've grown on me during these troubled times. So, let me give you a piece of advice, coming from my heart, as a fellow Girton girl—as a fellow sophisticate, a well-read, city-dwelling modern woman—"

"Who wears trousers . . ."

"Yes, who sometimes wears trousers—glad you noticed. Let me warn you, it's not going to be what you expect in your Martynsborough."

"How do you mean?"

"There's a great difference between town and country—and I'm speaking from experience as someone who has traipsed into some far-flung corners of this country collecting stones. Those differences are often not resolvable. Out there, in the fields and wood, on the moor and in the hedgerows, there are old gods, old ghosts, and old ways. People like us—women who wear trousers—we're not always welcome there. Tread lightly, Ruth, and let's hope this war is over by Christmas." She was silent for a moment, and then said, "Also, wear a broad-brimmed hat when you're out in the sun—we wouldn't want that pretty face of yours to burn."

-3-

They sat in a small private train compartment that was hardly luxurious. It smelled of stale tobacco smoke and unwashed wool, the benches pocked with cigarette burns. They moved through stations in small towns for which the names on the signs were blacked out with thick paint. Ruth removed her headscarf and settled deeper into the bench. Her grandmother eyed her closely.

"You've cut your hair."

"Yes." Ruth touched her bangs, thinking of the last-minute appointment before leaving. Her hair, which was the same chestnut colour as her mother's, was indeed shorter, with a fringe resting above her brow and the back length stopping sharply below the nape of her neck. "I thought being in the country, I'd keep it simple. Shorter like this, it's not so much in style anymore, but it won't require as much fuss—no pomade, or curlers, just a scarf for the wind. You like it?"

"Pretty, yes, and very practical of you, Ruth. You're getting into the spirit."

"And Grandpapa, he's still in Scotland? He won't be joining us at a later time?"

"No, my dear, you'll learn one day that when men get quite old, they tend to lose interest in domesticities and family life. Right now, he's with his precious dogs in the Highlands. I'll write him regularly, of course, but I believe he's quite happy where he is, and I'm equally happy to let him remain there without a bother in the world, war or no war."

"So, tell me about Martynsborough, then," Ruth said. "We've not really had the chance to speak of it. You say you've been many times, but you've never mentioned it before. It's horrible, isn't it? I envision a tiny, two-farm heap in the dead centre of a dank moor."

"Oh, the imagination. It's merely a village, like many others." Ruth's gran smiled wistfully as she spoke of a mill with an unmoving wheel, the green fields, and a tiny village of thatched roofs and terraced cottages gathered about the River Harold. Outside town sat a crumbling estate, Wolstenholme Park, which boasted a once-famous glassed-in conservatory. No trains. No telegraph wires. Not even the guarantee of electric lights. Ruth's gran had grown up in London but spent a lot of time in Martynsborough with her sister when they were young, and they had summered in the village many times. Her sister, Vera, ultimately returned as an adult and stayed in the country, where she married a local man, while Gran made her home in London. Vera's husband had died many years before, said Gran, and she now lived alone.

"Why don't I recall this Great-Aunt Vera? Are you sure we've met?" Ruth asked.

"Yes, you've met her—just once—which is probably why you don't remember her. You were only a small girl at the time, perhaps five years old. It was a brief meeting. I'm afraid my sister and I have drifted apart over the years. She really took to the country and would probably be just as happy to never step foot in London again. It's been many years since I've seen her." She took in a shaky breath. "You'll be expected to lend a hand, of course," she continued. "Vera won't appreciate your cluttered ways. We don't have Agnes or Mildred to clean or cook our meals and do our bidding. It's been an age since I've eaten rabbit." She paused in thought. "But there isn't any need to worry. Before you know it, this silly quarrel with Germany will be over, your mum and dad will return, and you'll be back at Cambridge and with Warren." She looked again to the window briefly as the carriage trundled over a wooden bridge. A reedy, slow-moving creek passed beneath. "And what of Warren's whereabouts? Did he get leave? Did you find a way to see him?"

"Safe from Dunkirk, as I wrote."

"You've seen him, then?"

"No . . . no, our paths didn't cross; I came to you instead."

"I see. I would think you'd have been married, the two of you, when he was near to Cambridge—no matter how short the time was. There's a lot of that going on—you know, *quick weddings*. You might not get another chance. Your mama would have expected it, I think."

"No, no. As you said, the war will be over soon, and then we'll have something proper."

They didn't speak for a long while thereafter, and as much as Ruth had intended to use the vast empty periods of idleness on the train to ponder her books, or jot down ideas for her great novel, she instead stared vacantly out the window as the landscape changed from wood to heath to village and back to wood.

Many hours later, at the Clitheroe train station, they met a member of the local Home Guard who was charged with ferrying the two women evacuees from the train station to Martynsborough proper. He was brusque and unfriendly as he packed the women's luggage into the boot. They then drove down a country motorway completely hemmed in by tall hedges. After some time, the land opened to reveal a vista of quilted agriculture. Martynsborough did not loom on the horizon as Ruth thought it might, but instead crept up meekly, almost apologetically—a collection of terraced stone houses, and beyond some hedgerows were the foreshortened tops of other structures, what looked to be a mill, and, taller still, a church's bell tower, the only proud and formidable thing visible from any distance. Beyond it all was a steep ridge, blanketed in lush green, and the grey corner of a citadel-like building that Ruth assumed to be the manor house on the Wolstenholme Park estate.

Their escort dropped them in front of a stone cottage on the outskirts of the town. Ivy crept up the old exterior, its green leaves flickering like pennants in the breeze, and along the side of the house, clear from the road, was a large and expansive garden.

"This will be home for a while," Gran said, smiling tightly as she stepped from the car with Ruth. The man put their bags by the side of the road, and then sped away towards the centre of the village without a goodbye or good day.

Vera stood at the door waiting for them. She was a slight woman, silver haired with a kind face. The two older women then met at the threshold and seemed to struggle with some unspoken, deep sensibility. Vera made the first move and reached out.

"Edith, it is so, so very good to see you." Her eyes gleamed, and Ruth thought that the woman might cry. They then fell into an embrace and held it for some time, while Ruth stood on the flagstone walk, mesmerized by this strange encounter. There was a mystery here, and Ruth's natural curiosity smouldered hotly. The two older women stepped back from each other but continued to gaze into one another's eyes, until finally Gran spoke.

"Vera, please, look—this here is your niece, Ruth, you might remember her. It's been a long time."

"The darling girl with the rhotacism? My goodness." Vera smiled, while Ruth took a shy step towards her, unsure what to say. Vera appraised her with a warm gaze. "You've grown into such a pretty young woman," she said.

"I no longer have that—the rhotacism. An expensive speech doctor can be thanked. I've got the knack for my *r*'s now. Pleased to meet you . . . again, Aunt Vera."

"No *Woothy* anymore?" Vera laughed, and although she was only making light, Ruth inwardly felt a stab of humiliation, knowing that even as a grown woman, in moments of great excitement, she sometimes lost a firm hold on her *r*'s. She forced a smile.

"No, I'm happy to report that it's Ruth with a capital *R* now."

Vera stooped to take one of her grandmother's bags, and together they entered what would be their home, at least until Christmas.

The inside was exactly as Ruth thought it might be. The walls of the kitchen, the largest room on the main floor, were of the same quarried stone as the exterior, with a deep Victorian washbasin and a jam cupboard filled with a curious array of bottles and jars. Tucked into the cavity of an old unused hearth, like an altar, was a large, cream-coloured Aga stove. A windowsill held a pestle and mortar, and drying herbs and other strange vegetation hung from a rafter in the ceiling, releasing musky and heady smells.

"Leave your bags by the door, please. Unwind a moment from your trip," Vera said.

A table in the middle of the kitchen was laid out with tea for their arrival, a lovely sight. Vera had clearly filled her ration book for the week, and Ruth felt a little badly about it, but they nevertheless pulled out chairs and sat. Vera poured tea, and the two older women continued to assess each other in a way that suggested the long period of time that had passed. Ruth noticed quiet music drifting from a small wireless on a sideboard. So then, yes, Martynsborough had electricity, she now knew. She confirmed this by looking upwards to an electric light in the ceiling.

When they were done, Vera cleared the plates and said, "We've more in this small bit of country than in all of London, with almost nothing shop-bought. When was the last time you had any meat for your supper, ladies? Or should I say any proper quantity of it?"

"A little lamb," said Gran. "Not much else."

"First of all, you'll have eggs, fresh, proper eggs, not yellow dust from a packet but from a hen—*my* hens." Vera untied her apron and draped it over the chair. "Come look. You too, Ruth." They followed her out the back door into a small garden bursting with vegetables: kales, cabbages, and curly parsley.

Ruth noticed with delight the bobbing head of a chicken emerging from a small wooden structure in a pen enclosed by some staves and wire. The bird stepped daintily down a wooden ramp, making low clucking sounds, followed by two other hens.

"This is Lucy, Mary, and Stella—lovely ladies, and our resident layers," Vera said. "Ruth, I think you can be assigned the task of collecting the eggs in the morning. Don't worry, I'll show you how and where." Then she led Ruth and her gran towards a low stone wall, next to which was a weathered wooden table with an indistinct brown form atop it. Flies buzzed lazily about. "Dinner," Vera said, pointing at the table. Ruth saw spots of blood here and there, and rabbits: a great dead heap of them. Vera held two aloft by their hind legs, and a stream of watery blood spilled from their muzzles. Ruth noted on the table, as well, another animal that did not look like a rabbit; she thought with dread that it might be a rat. "A squirrel, too," Vera said, as if reading Ruth's mind.

"Oh dear." It was all Ruth could think to say, and she instinctively held her hand to her mouth. Vera seemed to take delight in her discomfort.

"We'll make lovely slippers with the fur! And Ruth, we'll need to get you sorted with the rifle; you're younger—a lighter step, I'd think," said Vera.

"Really?" Ruth looked at her, dumbfounded.

"Yes. As I said, we all need to pull our weight."

"A gun?"

"We're at war, darling," said Vera. "Tomorrow, we'll teach you how to load and clean it. There are almost no men about to help with these sorts of things. There are no police. No lawyers or judges here. The closest doctor is in Clitheroe. We women are on our own, and we may be for some time." She very nearly beamed with delight as she said it, and then added, "In the meantime, I've a bicycle with a basket. Can you gather some watercress? There's loads of it near the millpond."

"Yes, I think I'll manage," Ruth said. "I'm fairly certain I know what watercress looks like."

Ruth found the bicycle and rode it along the gravelled laneway towards a small, hedge-lined road that followed an old drain towards the main river. The road was hemmed in by trees, and then opened up to deep, undulating rye. She looked out at the expanse and, not far from the road, saw movement that looked unnatural, like the wake of an invisible boat moving through the field. She slowed and stopped, looking intently at the waving sea of green, wondering what on earth was approaching. There was a brief flash of white in the strand; then near to the road, something stepped out from the grass. They were sheep—a ram followed by a ewe. Ruth was fascinated and maybe a little unnerved by the male, which was a large creature with impressive weaponry on display. As intimidating as he was, the ram was indeed a handsome animal, with enormous, ridged, and twisting horns coiling tightly in directions of their own accord, and woolly fleece of a beautiful cream colour. His face, like the female partner's, was bold and jet black with a small smattering of white about the eye.

The two creatures lifted their gaze to Ruth and noticed her. The ram bleated in surprise, and they ambled across the road and disappeared into the wood. Ruth put her foot on a pedal and pushed forwards, towards town, following the marshy drain, feeling gratified by the interesting encounter.

Soon, the drain emptied into Wynan Beck. She followed this new waterway until the junction with the larger River Harold, a wide and gentle, pretty thing with willows overhanging. A stone bridge traversed a lock channel, and it was here that she entered the main village. The road led to a church, which was the tallest structure in view, while sprawling north-west, towards a tangled wood, was a graveyard. Below, down a valley grade of sorts, she could see the mill. Running just to the north was the main river, where it was widest. Along the mill was a secondary, man-made channel, encased in stonework and masonry, where the water flowed uselessly over unmoving rungs and poured into a millpond.

Ruth noticed children here and there, unattended, wandering in loose, roaming packs, running sticks along gates, gathering by the river with stones to throw, all a little rumpled, with unwashed faces. The lost look in their eyes suggested that they were mostly evacuees, but she couldn't be sure. She then passed a pub, the Yellow Rattle—a curious name, she thought—near to which there was a butcher's shop, dark inside and apparently closed.

Before the road turned, she came across a slightly more imposing building, seeming to be a village hall. Flags, pamphlets, and propaganda were posted around the open front door. It appeared that a Home Guard meeting of some sort was being held, as Ruth heard the murmuring voices of men. She leaned her bike on the wall, thinking to read some of the postings, and maybe to peer inside, when someone called to her, "You there, miss." Ruth stepped into the doorway and saw the man who had driven them from the station.

"Me?"

"I was meaning to come around to visit you tomorrow. The magistrate would like a word." Ruth stepped into the foyer of the building and through a corridor into the main space to find a group of people working. Many of the men looked up from their work, but none smiled at her. In fact, she got the distinct impression that she was unwelcome there. She looked around and noted a piano on a stage, which seemed to suggest past concerts or plays. The walls were bedecked with Union Jacks, which fluttered in the weak breeze of an electric fan vainly trying to cool a rather stuffy room. Tables and desks filled the hall, and there was a buzz of administrative activity from older men with pencils, rulers, and rubber stamps. At a desk under the window in the corner was a man who appeared to be their leader. He looked up from a pile of papers. Probably sixty-five years of age, he was handsome in that grandfatherly way, with a waistcoat and rolled-up shirtsleeves. His glasses had slid down his nose as he beckoned her over.

"And who do we have here?"

"I arrived from London this morning, sir, with my grandmother. Ruth Gladstone. Is there something I can help you with?"

He reached out to shake her hand.

"From Cambridge, I hear. Yes, please, come now, I won't bite. Have a seat here." He gestured to a wooden swivel chair next to his desk. Ruth reluctantly approached and sat. He took a seat at his desk adjacent. "I'm called Horgon, but you can call me sir. I fought in the Great War, dug seventeen miles of trenches. I know a thing or two about this ugly business, and the truest test of a country's strength is its ability to organize. I'm not speaking of lining up soldiers in a pretty row; I'm talking about bloody paperwork. We've farm targets to make, weights to track, billets to audit, censuses to take, weather to monitor. We've been hoping for another schooled evacuee." He noisily stacked a sheaf of papers on his desk and then slammed them down. "We're drowning in it, and we need people with a strong grasp of numbers and figures, sums and so on."

"I'm afraid I'm studying English literature—and not much in the way of maths."

"Any schooling is helpful. This is a farming community, God-fearing and such. We're not an illiterate rabble, but we need more people adept at pencil and paper than we currently have—there are many ledgers to attend to. No idle hands during wartime. You will of course receive a biweekly stipend for your work—no indentured servitude here under the Crown. All will be compensated, and a rather good idea at that—you'll have a fine savings by the time this bloody skirmish with

Germany is over. I've already spoken with Vera—I know her well. She let me know you were on your way from the city—no free lunch in these parts. Speaking of which, she's a bloody good cook, so you're in for some fine suppers during your stay, which we hope will be short, like this war. We'll give you a chance to settle in, but this Monday, be here at oh-eight-hundred sharp, and we can start your orientation and training."

Ruth was taken aback by so much information so quickly. She was not expecting to actually work in Martynsborough—she had envisioned writing her novel by candlelight, with the most laborious acts being the shelling of peas or making of tea. She took it as an affront. Who was this man to throw around orders at her? She thought to challenge him, but as was her way, her assertion crumbled the moment it appeared. Moreover, some extra money was never a bad thing. With her parents abroad and the war and so on, she couldn't always guarantee uninterrupted access to her trust. "Yes, sir, I think I can manage that."

"Excellent. And I know you're not billeted too far. Did you walk to the village?"

"Better than that, sir. I've a bicycle—or at least, it's my aunt's bicycle. A lovely route—I saw some sheep on my way in; they ran across my path."

"We call them 'mules' here."

"Mules? Oh, I don't think so. Not a donkey—"

"Hmm? No, no, not like a donkey—I'm talking about mules: mutton, fleece, rams, and such. Our mules are called Lonks."

"Lonks?"

"A type of mule, you see—proud Lancashire heritage. You saw two of them, I suspect? A ram and a ewe?"

"Yes, actually . . ."

"Black faces? White fleece?"

"Yes."

"Castor and Pollux."

"Pardon me?"

"You saw Castor and Pollux—among the last survivors. The Ministry of Agriculture came round last winter, had all the pasture and grazing land converted to sugar beet, flax, rye, and barley, and insisted on a cull of most of the herd for the war effort—a necessary tragedy, as the ministry says. They use flax for parachutes and barley for bread—not for animal feed, so most of our sheep are gone, slaughtered, stewed, and tinned up for the boys on the boats. The finest breeder of Lonk mules, a man called Sutcliffe, he was harassed by the ministry for harbouring that last pair—caught red-handed he was—and before they could strong-arm the slaughter, the two animals mysteriously disappeared into the night. Sutcliffe swore up and down he had nothing to do with it." Horgon moved in closer to Ruth and lowered his voice. "Aye, most of us village folk were convinced he had a secret cache in the back of his cottage with all the choice mutton cuts hanging about waiting for his own pot. That is"—Horgon straightened up and his voice returned to its normal boldness—"that is, until there were sightings of the damn things wandering around Martynsborough, our Castor and Pollux. They're a wily duo—mates for life, I'd think, and too slippery to be caught. It's been six months, and no one has caught up to them, and I'll tell you, with so little proper red meat in my guts, I'd take one down myself if I still had the legs for it." He patted his chest and coughed drily. "Too old, I'm afraid now, to be chasing after errant livestock, and in any event, I'd steer clear. The male can be surly and protective of his mate—has horns of steel. There's a good reason they're called *rams*."

"I'll be careful, sir."

"Well, good day to you, then. See you Monday." He turned and thrust his head into another stack of papers.

Ruth stepped from the hall, her thoughts now more clouded than before. She had imagined herself with masses of leisure time, writing a beautiful novel whilst sitting in the sunshine, pen in hand and a steaming cup of tea nearby. Instead, she was facing the prospect of hunting rabbits, collecting eggs, searching for wild greens, and now performing an administrative job, which would take away much of her daytime hours. When was she to write her novel? She brooded, pushing her bicycle down the road that meandered towards the mill and the River Harold. There around the millpond, as Vera had said, were bountiful smatterings of lush green leaves, which Ruth assumed was watercress. There appeared to be more than one variety of plant, and uncertain which was which, she collected handfuls of two kinds and soon filled the bicycle basket.

Satisfied with her small toil, she sat on a large stone to watch the river for a spell. It slid past with a sort of lazy deliberation that was rather pleasing and beautiful, and she could see how a poet might come to such a place. She thought of Tennyson, who said of a river, "Men may come and men may go, but I go on forever." And like the poet, she wanted nothing more than to put pen to paper herself. It was one of the reasons she'd agreed to come to such a tiny, remote village. And such a lovely place ought to be inspiring, but Ruth could think of no subject, no story. Not even a snippet of original verse came to her mind. The thought of an entire novel was too daunting to contemplate.

Eventually she tore herself from the leafy place and returned with the bicycle, pushing it up the steep incline to the high street and then riding past the lock and on to the country road. Up ahead, where a hedge grew quite tall, Ruth saw a fluttering bit of white, as if someone's laundry had blown from the line and become tangled in the leaves. It then disappeared behind the hedge, only to flit out again, this time on to the road. No, not someone's bed sheet, but a woman in a thin white shift. She seemed a ghost, slipping away once more, silent and insubstantial like the wind, only to reappear. She stopped and looked to the ground, considering something, then squatted and picked up handfuls of gravel and let it fall from her fingers like a child might. She was a woman of perhaps thirty, quite beautiful, but seemingly out of sorts. Her blonde hair was unkempt, and she was out and about barefoot and half-naked.

Ruth stopped the bike. The woman threw her body to the ground and sat in the dust and gravel. She dug into the dirt with her fingers, as if looking for something buried there.

"Hallo. Are you all right? Can I help you, miss?" Ruth got off from the bike and walked towards her, thinking she was ill. The woman didn't respond, and then Ruth heard another voice, that of a man, further down the road.

"Elise? Elise?" From the far end of the hedge, he emerged, his back to them, his hand held to his brow to shield his eyes from the dazzling, low sun. "Elise?" He turned and froze as he saw Ruth. Then he said, this time less loudly, "Elise, please, we've got to get you inside." He walked towards the blonde woman, and Ruth could see that he was about thirty years of age, slim and tall with a strong jaw, and the shadow of a day's stubble on his face. His trouser braces hung at his hips, and his shirt front was unbuttoned from throat to navel, revealing the wiry pelt of his chest and flat stomach, as if he'd left the house midway through undressing. He gathered his shirt closed and said, "I need to get her inside." He slid his hands around the woman's waist and pulled her to a standing position. The woman didn't acknowledge his words, or indeed his presence, but in a docile way, she walked with him back towards the hedge. She had a slight limp, like a child with club foot. As for the man, Ruth could see he, too, had an injury of sorts—his left hand had a small disfigurement. He was missing his index and middle fingers, shorn neatly from above the first knuckle. Ruth felt she ought to say something.

"Is anything the matter? Do you need assistance?"

He stopped and met her gaze. His left eye was a little clouded, like sugared absinthe. His other eye was clear, green, and sharp.

"No," he said tersely. "Thank you for your concern, but if you don't mind, I need to get her inside." He turned with a frown and stepped between the hedges. Supporting the woman, he walked towards a small cottage at the end of a path. Ruth watched as she ambled next to him. Her curiosity alight, she stepped closer, peered through branches, and watched as they approached the door of the house. An older woman emerged and took the hand of the young woman, and the trio disappeared into the cottage.

With the road deserted once more, Ruth walked for a while, thinking about the strange encounter, and then got on the bike and continued down the road to Vera's cottage a quarter-mile or so further along. As she rode, she scanned the grassy dales and stands of trees, looking for any signs of Castor and Pollux, but saw none.

-4-

Ruth brought the pile of green leaves into the kitchen and laid them on the table for an inspection. Vera looked briefly and picked out a bunch of one type and handed them to Edith with a cock of her eyebrow. "You can give these a wash, Edith." The rest remained on the table. "You've been studying philosophy, haven't you, Ruth? You know, Socrates?" she asked.

"Yes, well, to some extent. I'm not sure what that has to do with—" Vera held up the greens.

"Oh. You mean—"

"Hemlock," she said with a wry grin. Ruth's shoulders dropped in embarrassment.

"Sorry, is that what I've picked here?"

"Yes, dear. And no watercress to speak of. All's not lost. These other bits you've picked are wild parsnip. Your gran's giving them a scrub; they'll work for our dinner just as well, but it would be a shame for us all to be poisoned at our first meal together. Can you please take this lot"— she handed Ruth the offending leaves—"and toss them in the wood?"

Over supper, Ruth spoke about her trip into the village and her encounter with Mr. Horgon, her enlistment into the war effort and having to work, and how she felt some trepidation. "Maths, of all things," Ruth said. "I was never very good at sums."

"You'll do fine. Walter Horgon is an old friend of mine and interim magistrate in Martynsborough," Vera said. "He is stern but fair, and you will be paid. Everyone must earn their way in the country. You can then squirrel away your coins for when the war is over, buy yourself some new stockings. Yours look a little raggedy, to be honest."

"Yes, right, well." Ruth looked down at her knees briefly, then brightened up. "Oh, he also mentioned that you were, and I quote, 'a bloody good cook.' And I very much agree with him."

Vera grinned modestly and said, "Perhaps you'll cook the next one."

"Me? I wouldn't even know where to begin."

"You and Edith are spoilt by hired cooks. We don't have staff here in the country."

"Now, now," Edith said. "She didn't ask to be born in the city. But Vera is right. As horrible as war is, this will be an education that no money could ever buy at Cambridge. Come, don't just sit there, Ruth." She handed her a tea towel. "You'll do the drying. I hate to admit it," she said dolefully, "but I've not washed a dish in thirty years. This will be an education for me as well."

With plates clean and put away, Vera pulled a deck of cards from a drawer and offered up a game or two in the last bit of natural light before the blackouts had to go up.

"I wanted to ask about your neighbours," Ruth said to Vera as she shuffled the cards. "I saw a woman acting strangely. She's from the third house from here, I presume, a quarter-mile or so down the road. There was a young man, perhaps her husband or brother? I was surprised to see a young man about—that is, other than some of the farm labour, there are so few. I believe the woman is called Elise. At least that's how the man referred to her. Do you know anything about them?"

Vera put down the cards. "Yes, Elise is her name. The man is called Malcolm. They live with Virginia—my neighbour. Malcolm is Virginia's . . . well, I'm not entirely sure of their relation. Malcolm is her great-nephew or distant cousin, perhaps—much of his family moved to Australia some ten years ago. Elise is his wife; she's French, and they had been drifting back and forth from London to the Continent before war broke out. As Virginia has told me, both of Elise's parents were killed last April, when the Germans shelled their village in France. Elise was staying with them at the time and survived but suffered an injury to her brain, and it's permanently affected her. She was evacuated from France before the fall of Paris, and eventually here to Martynsborough, and as a result of the injury, she acts as a young child might. She was in a coma for some time, and then it took her two months before she could walk again, but she's mute and, as Virgie has said, cannot care for herself as an adult woman should. Quite sad."

"And Malcolm? A young, able-bodied man . . . I mean . . . I'd figure he'd be serving, but I noticed his eye . . . And his hand was—"

"Yes," Vera interrupted. "He was discharged after a shrapnel injury in Norway, and they were reunited under rather unfortunate circumstances. With only one good eye, he was taken out of rotation, with the possibility, I suppose, of being called back up for other duties, perhaps if things become dire. His hand was injured—can't pull a trigger quite as well, you know. A shame, too; he was an artist of some renown on the Continent, so Virginia tells me. A sculptor if I recall, thinking to move to France permanently to teach his craft. Not sure how well he can make pretty statues now with a mangled hand."

"It was his left hand injured. He's his right to pull a trigger at least," Ruth said.

"How astute of you to notice. It's not really our business, to be sure. Either way, it's his wife who requires attention. He came here to Martynsborough to help with her and I suppose heal from his own wounds. This is what I've learned from Virginia. Quite sad, really, but such is the way of the war. It's best they be let alone. Their family's suffered. Now come. One quick hand, then let's get the blackouts sorted. We'll listen to the wireless for a bit."

Ruth noted that the room that Vera provided was fine, really, but a bit stuffy and warm, especially with the heavy blackouts over the windows. It seemed to be superfluous to use the things so far north. What would a German bomber hope to accomplish by blowing up a stone house in the middle of nowhere?

Ruth had thought to write a bit, but as was the case when she'd sat by the river earlier in the afternoon, no ideas for a novel came to her. She then took up a book but found herself reading the same sentence over and over, its calming power not working this night. She snapped the light off and, in the dark, slipped from bed and opened the blackouts. The breeze on her face was a great relief. Her second-floor window looked out on to the road and the small wood there. She could see as far as Virginia's cottage, and further out, across the fields, like a black hump against a midnight-blue sky, she could make out the escarpment. Only a small slice of a moon shone, but the stars were milky and bright; the crickets sang.

She pulled a chair to the window, and with her pillow she settled there, her head resting on the alcove. She moved her hand to cover her ear, to make her ocean sounds, which thrummed happily with the sounds of crickets wavering in and out. She felt she might drift off, till she heard something—an unnatural rustle and slither of fabric. Ruth glanced out at the dark fields and the road, then pushed her head out the window, craning her neck so that she could see Vera's garden, and there she saw a flash of white in the gloom. It moved between the pear trees, only for a moment, then it was gone. Was it the sheep out for a nocturnal wander? She waited, held her breath, and again, it emerged— not sheep, but a figure in some white garment creeping between the trees in the shadows. Had Elise slipped out of the house again? It was such a peculiar thing to contemplate. Ruth watched for a moment, wondering if she ought to do something, perhaps wake Vera. The figure melted back into the shadows, but not before turning towards the window in an eerie way and seeming to look directly at Ruth, the shadows of the pear tree concealing her face. Then she was gone.

Ruth eased back from the window, experiencing a peculiar combination of curiosity and fear.

Land of witches. That's what Maude had said. What else, she wondered, lurked out there? Ruth could only guess. She drew the blackouts once more and climbed back into bed, deep under the covers, praying for the morning light.

5

It was still dark in her room, but Ruth knew morning had come. She could hear birdsong, and a small glow of sunlight leaked around the black fabric. Ruth stared at the ceiling and thought of Warren. It had occurred to her, at some bleak moment in the night, that he might not go abroad. He could stay in England. As a military surgeon, and with the bombs falling more readily on British cities, his expertise might make more sense here, which would mean he could get more leave, in which case, he would want to come to Martynsborough.

Ruth got out of bed and opened the blackouts, hoping to turn the tide on her sour mood. It was admittedly a beautiful morning, the mist on the ground illuminated by the gold and pink of the rising sun. There was much to explore here, a perfect place for someone so curious, someone hoping to write the great novel. But also, it was a strange place. The figure she had seen the night before—had it been a dream? No, no, she had seen something. But who? She assumed Elise—an eerie thought— an invalid woman wandering the night, her damaged brain sending her this way and that. Had she made it home? Ruth could only hope.

She went into the bathroom and ran the water. Only cold. She stared in the mirror. She touched her hair, still not used to its shorter length. She looked over at the tub and realized that boiling pots of water on the Aga would be necessary if she wished to take a bath. She thought of the endless bucket brigade required to bring water up the stairs and felt exhausted at the prospect. It was as if she had been transported back a hundred years.

"Today, you'll help me sort the rabbits," said Vera as Ruth came down to the kitchen. "And we'll have our first rifle lesson. You'll be busy working in the village hall before you know it and will have less time to practice. Come have something to eat, and then we'll get on with it."

They listened to the news on the wireless as they ate, and it seemed that the thing that everyone had been anticipating had finally happened. *The battle of London has begun, and those putting out fires now know that Hitler and Göring have turned their gaze to them. The bombing was indiscriminate, with many civilian deaths.*

Vera got up and turned the machine off. "It's begun now, in earnest. I can't bear to hear it." They finished their breakfast in glum silence, after which they cleared the plates, and as Edith washed dishes, Vera brought out a rifle and laid it on the table. "This, my dear, is a Watson 12-bore side-by-side. You're going to clean and oil it. Then you're going to learn to use it." Ruth stared wordlessly at the gun. "Go ahead, pick it up," said Vera. "It's not very heavy, meant for birds and small game— certainly won't do much for an elephant."

Ruth ran a finger along the wooden stock. "It's a handsome thing," she said. "Old? I don't think they make them like this anymore. There's lovely etching there, along the metal bit."

"Barrel."

"Right, the barrel."

Vera picked up the gun. "It's not loaded, but the first rule with this firearm is that you do *not* point it at anything that you don't intend to shoot."

"I'm not sure I can do this. It's one thing to shoot, it's another entirely to kill."

"You liked the hotpot last night?" Vera said.

"Yes."

"Well then, unless you intend to eat turnips for the indefinite future, you'll be shooting things. Lord knows, child, we may be invaded, and then it won't be rabbits you're shooting, but Germans. Now, come, take it. We'll go out back, and I'll show you how to use it."

After a first lesson in shooting, which Ruth was happy to realize came naturally to her, Vera said, "Now let's put the gun away, and we'll sort some that I shot before." She took Ruth to a small shed in the back in which three dead rabbits hung from the ceiling. "They need to bleed out and to dry a bit, not to be eaten right away—very metallic and unpleasant if you do. I've taken out all the livers and kidneys and such—*my* breakfast the day I shot them. Offal must be eaten right away; meat is to hang for at least three days."

"Three days? Won't it spoil?"

"Ah, that's right—you from the land of the electric refrigerator, you've been told to keep everything as cold as the Arctic, I suppose. Not so. A cool, dry shed and maybe a bit of muslin for the flies is all you need. I've already skinned these, and I'm drying the pelts—they make for lovely slippers or trim about a hat. We'll try to bag a few more, and I'll show you how to skin them." Ruth felt nauseated at the thought but said nothing as they stepped outside.

"Hmm, it seems something's been munching on our fruit." Vera picked up a pear that had been cleaned down to the core with small precise bites. She stooped over and found another on the ground beneath the tree.

"Rabbits? Birds?" Ruth asked.

"Perhaps, but I'm not sure, it could also be a person," Vera said and looked around for further evidence. "I wonder if Elise has had a wander over here. Sometimes she gives Malcolm and Virgie a proper scare by giving them the slip. I remember, a few weeks ago, Elise caught sight of those sheep and chased them halfway to the next village before Malcolm caught up with her."

"Castor and Pollux. Why on earth would she chase them?"

"I couldn't fathom why she's drawn to those animals. Perhaps because there's so little livestock now, they're a curiosity to her." Ruth thought to tell Vera about the eerie figure she had seen the previous night, but some instinct compelled her not to. The blackouts were supposed to remain shut, and she didn't wish to cause trouble on only her second day. "Try it. They're a little tart, but very refreshing." Vera plucked some pears from the tree and handed one to Ruth.

"How did you learn to do all these things?" Ruth asked. "You and Gran both grew up in a house with a cook and other staff, but you've got the country in your veins, so unlike your sister."

Vera had several pears gathered in her apron, which she dropped into a nearby basket. She turned to Ruth.

"Edith and I are very different people," she said. "I've always been drawn to the country—it's like I've always been here, at least in spirit. I appreciate my independence. Come to think of it, my life has changed little with the coming of war, while yours and Edith's have been turned upside down."

"Yes, I suppose so. Is that why you drifted apart? Gran says you haven't seen each other in a long time."

Vera paused, an odd expression on her face.

"There's a bit more to it than that, but I don't care to talk about such ancient history. Come, let's peel these pears. We'll need some sugar—we'll combine our ration books, so I'll have to get you to visit the shop; it is only open a few hours on Saturday. I'll make you a list."

6

Ruth put the ration books and a canvas bag into the bicycle basket and rode towards the village. She approached Virginia's cottage and thought perhaps to stop and introduce herself and check in to assure that all was well with Elise, given that she may have been wandering about in the night. She could see Malcolm in the back garden putting some bed sheets up on a line to dry in the breeze and Elise sitting on the ground near to him. She sat at the edge of a large picnic blanket and appeared to be digging with her fingers in the grass next to the blanket, the same curious way she did during their first encounter on the road. Ruth felt a surge of relief and planned to tell Vera that if Elise had indeed been nibbling on pears in their back garden at some bleak hour, she had somehow managed to return home safely.

Ruth slowed the bike and keenly watched Malcolm for a moment. He stooped over and took up a white sheet and flapped it out, then put it on the line. She had never seen a man doing laundry and wondered in what other domesticities this one might involve himself. In a way, Ruth felt admiration for him, to be injured in the war and to return to a wife—a beautiful woman, no doubt—who could not speak, who could not . . . She let the notion drop away unexamined. She then noticed Elise staring directly at her. Ruth looked away, embarrassed, and pedalled down the road, deeply unsettled by the woman's peculiar gaze.

Ruth crossed the bridge into Martynsborough, and as she passed the church, she heard someone shouting, the voice of a young man, excited and angry. It came from the far side of the building. Ruth got off her bike and strode tentatively towards the sounds to investigate. She heard more hollering, and cursing. Ruth found two boys, teenagers, maybe fifteen years old, down in the dust grappling with each other. A few other boys stood around watching and occasionally bleating verbal abuse. She wasn't sure what to do, never having seen such a fight before, but she knew she should intervene somehow.

"Hallo, you there," she said with little confidence, as she walked towards them, and then, gathering her strength, she called out louder with hopes of sounding imperious. "Stop that, this instant!"

The spectators scattered, and the two boys pulled away from one another but remained on the ground, breathing heavily. One of the boys had a split lip and blood smeared on his chin. Another voice boomed from behind Ruth.

"Johnny! Patrick! That's enough!" A man approached, a vicar with his black cassock. "Johnny, this is the second time today." Both boys stood, dusting off their knees. "Patrick, you go back inside. Johnny, I'd like to speak with you." He turned to Ruth. "I'm terribly sorry you had to witness this. These boys are evacuees and farmhands, and it seems this one is ever looking for trouble." He approached Ruth. "Father Tweedsmuir." He thrust out his hand. "Sorry to meet under such circumstances. You're the new evacuee came in the other day, staying with Vera Catchpoole, are you?"

"Yes, actually. My goodness, word travels quickly here." She shook his hand. "It's Ruth, Ruth Gladstone, pleased to meet you. I was on my way to the shop—my first visit to stamp my ration book in Martynsborough." She pointed to Johnny. "He appears to be injured." Ruth and the vicar approached the boy.

"What's gotten into you, Johnny? What's caused the ruckus this time?"

"They're p-p-picking on me. I can't s-stay here any longer." The boy wiped a bloody lip on his sleeve.

"Now, now, Johnny. Everyone is suffering. You're not the only boy away from his parents."

"I'm no boy, sir. I work five days a week same as any man."

Ruth handed Johnny a handkerchief from her purse. "You work?"

"Yes." Johnny wiped the blood from his chin. "On the flax farm. We've S-S-Saturdays and Sundays free."

"Well, then make yourself useful on your free day," said Father Tweedsmuir. "Show Miss Gladstone here the way to the shop. She's new to the village, billeting here, as you are." He turned to Ruth. "I'm afraid there's no butcher since the cull. It being a small village, I'm afraid you're not going to find the variety here you might find in London."

"I have to say, it's a little to the contrary, Father. I've eaten better in the past twenty-four hours than in the previous month."

"Yes, of course. Vera, she's quite the cook—you are indeed blessed."

Johnny took his hat from the ground, shook it off, and put it on his head. "Right this way, ma'am."

"You can call me Ruth." She turned to the vicar. "Nice to meet you. I'll be working in the village hall with Mr. Horgon. I'm sure I'll see you again. Good day."

"No more fighting, Johnny," Father Tweedsmuir called after them.

Johnny and Ruth walked back to where she'd left her bike, and together they walked down the main street towards the supply shop.

"Do you sleep in the church, Johnny?" Ruth asked.

"Yes, ma'am."

"I was wondering where the children are billeted. I see them about, but I wasn't sure. Are there no houses to sleep in? I've not heard of evacuees staying in the actual church for any length of time."

"Some of the smaller ones got into houses, but there's quite a few of us in the chapel. Seems to be some mix-up. The ministry counted much more sp-sp-space for children here, and it seems to all be on account of the manor house—they counted those rooms, too, but it seems we can't stay there. Not sure why—no one tells us anything—but anywhere would be better'n the church. It's sp-sp-spooky, and I hate it. And the other boys pick on me."

"Why do they pick on you?"

"Well, if you can't already tell, I stammer. I've been taught a little how to not do it so much, but when I get properly upset, it comes out."

"Well, Johnny, you're not alone. I've a problem with speaking, too."

"It doesn't sound like it to me."

"I've a rhotacism. Do you know what that is?"

"I'm afraid not, ma'am."

"I've trouble with my *r*'s. I pronounced them as *w*'s when I was young, and like you, when I get excited or frightened, I sometimes revert to those *w*'s. If you listen very closely, I'm doing it all the time. It's rather subtle—at least I hope it is."

"Well, it's nice to know I'm not the only one with trouble saying things." They walked a bit in amiable silence.

"Have you been here since the declaration of war?" Ruth asked.

"No, I was in a house before, outside Blackpool, with my brother, Jude, but when I turned fifteen, just last month, they didn't want us no more. I, uh, was old enough for farm help, so I came here—all the boys are older than thirteen. We don't have to go to school if we're working, which suits me fine."

"And your brother?" Ruth asked.

"I'm afraid I don't know. He's younger than me. I wish I knew where he was—billeted somewhere else, I suppose. We might never find each other again. Our dad's in Africa. Mum's in a munitions factory in Sheffield." Johnny shook his hat out once more, ran a hand through his shaggy black curls, and stopped walking. "Here's the shop. Only open for another hour, so you better get what you need." He turned to leave. "Nice to meet you, ma'am."

"Do take care. I hope you hear from your brother."

Mist blanketed the grass that morning, and in a way, it provided cover for the elusive animal Ruth sought. Vera kept well back in the garden, watching thoughtfully, hopefully. Ruth stood as still as she could, the barrel of the gun resting on a low wall as she scanned the half acre of deep grass. Then, from the corner of her eye, movement. She looked. Yes, the grass rustled, the mist was disturbed—something was there. Then, two grey ears appeared and vanished into the mist. Then, she saw an opportunity and swung the barrel to the right and fired. The rabbit dropped, and another scattered in the opposite direction. She took aim and fired again, and the second rabbit dropped. She broke open the barrel, and the spent shells flew, smoking and triumphant, from the gun.

"Excellent shooting, Ruth," Vera cried from the garden. "You've sorted out Tuesday dinner!" Ruth turned to her aunt, her face flush with excitement and delight.

"I did!"

"Come, child, let's collect your winnings." Vera took Ruth around the garden wall as the morning sun burnt off the last of the mist. She saw a brown pelt ahead, small and dead. "Go on, Ruth, it's your kill. Pick her up. Not by the ears; take the hind legs." Ruth gathered her skirt around her legs and crouched by the rabbit. A flicker of ugly regret shivered through her. The rabbit's eyes were open and vacant like glass beads, but its abdomen still moved a little, small and weak inhalations, the final breaths. Ruth brought her hand to her mouth, overcome with the finality of it. "Go on then," said Vera with a little impatience.

"It's not dead, look."

"It's surely dead."

"It's still breathing."

"Not now, no, look yourself." Ruth inspected the rabbit, and it was still, mercifully, tragically still. "You'll get used to it," Vera said as she grasped the rabbit by its legs and picked it up. "Here, take her. Pay her some respect; she is now dead so you can live." She thrust it at Ruth, who reluctantly took the rabbit's legs in her hand. It was heavier than Ruth had anticipated, and warm, still so very warm with fur, soft and fleecy. She fought with all her strength to keep her composure but felt her eyes sting with salty tears. "There, there," said Vera. "Soon enough, death will become as everyday to you as birdsong. Let's gather up the other, and this time, I'll skin them. Next time you can skin them. One step at a time, right?"

"Yes," Ruth said quietly, deeply relieved that she would not have to bloody her hands pulling the skins from rabbits that morning.

"Go wash up, Ruth. We'll be going to church after breakfast."

The double doors of the church were thrown open, and it seemed all of Martynsborough had come to hear the sermon. Father Tweedsmuir stood at the door, shaking hands with congregants as they arrived.

"Ah, Ruth, good to see you again," he called as the three women approached.

"You've met, then?" Vera said.

"Yes," said the Father. "Ruth here helped me break up some fisticuffs among the boys yesterday." He turned to Edith and shook her hand. "And I suppose this is Edith. Very pleased to meet you." Edith murmured some niceties, and then the vicar said, "Please come. We've many people today. I think the news from London has us needing reassurance from a higher power."

Ruth stepped past the first few pews, and in the very back sat Malcolm, Virginia, and Elise. He wore a tweed jacket and had a protective arm around his wife. She had on a pretty dress of white, matching gloves, and a scarf tied about her blonde hair. Ruth wondered who had dressed her. She looked rather smart, and a vision flashed in her mind of Malcolm pushing his wife's legs into a pair of knickers while she stared vacantly at the wall, oblivious of what he was doing. And her brassiere? She could see that Elise wore one under her frock. Did Malcolm thread her arms into the straps and close the clasps? Ruth stopped herself and tried to quell her curiosity.

Ruth sat at a centre pew with Edith and Vera. She looked around, and it occurred to her that Malcolm was the only young man in the entirety of the large congregation.

Father Tweedsmuir strode down the nave and stood at the pulpit with a surprised smile on his face. "We've not had this many people to church in some time." Murmurs came from the pews, and then he said, "No doubt you've heard the news from London. Two nights in a row, now. In this dark hour, I find much solace in the fact that it's here that we've turned for comfort, among each other, and more importantly, with the Lord." He paused dramatically, the echo of his bold voice lingering in the space of the church sanctuary. "There was a moment in the last war—the Great War," he continued, "that was the darkest and bleakest, when it seemed that the horror stretched on indefinitely into the future, and that the only logical end was for *all but one* to be killed—*all but one* left standing. That grim and reductive math was wrong, however. Thank the Lord it was wrong." He gazed heavenwards for a moment and then back at his flock. "For there *was* an end. We survived it. We persevered." The Father then guided the congregation to find in their hymn books number 376, "The Saviour Is with Us," and they stumbled through the hymn. Perhaps not since those dark hours of the Great War had so many voices been raised to song in the hallowed sanctuary of the church.

Ruth glanced back at Malcolm several times with great curiosity. His face was fixed with stony resolve the entire time. He, too, was persevering through his own private tribulation, silently, stoically, surrounded as he was by bellowing songs of praise. Unexpectedly, he looked towards

Ruth, and they locked eyes—she saw a note of recognition on his face, and she turned away quickly, embarrassed.

At the end of the service as people milled about, Ruth looked towards the door several times, when she caught sight of a head with shaggy dark locks.

"Excuse me a moment." She pushed her way through a crowd of elderly congregants to find Johnny, standing on the steps outside the church. "Johnny," Ruth called to him. "Good to see you."

"Well, hallo, Miss Gladstone. You've come to church. It seems everyone has today."

"Yes. I suppose so. I wonder, where on earth do the children sleep? They can't possibly sleep on the pews, do they?"

"No, no." Johnny laughed a little. "We're in the basement. There's a kitchen and lavatory and such down there. Would you like to see? It's not very nice."

"I *am* curious, I'll admit."

Johnny led Ruth to a side entrance of the church. "This way," he said, and took her through the door, down some more steps, into a dank and gloomy corridor, until they stopped in a windowless room with a single electric light bulb hanging from the ceiling and about two dozen army-issued cots spread around. It smelled of spoilt apples, muddy shoes, unwashed pants. Ruth looked around in horror. "Children sleep here?"

"Yes, it gets cold at night, but they've given us some blankets. The lavatory's horrid. There isn't really anyone to clean. The good news is that I heard today that most of the little ones will have homes to go to. They've found some places in Clitheroe. There will still be six of us here left—the older boys. No girls."

"I don't think this would be a very nice place to sleep," Ruth said, as she glanced into the church kitchen; it, too, was monstrously dirty. She crinkled her nose.

"The Father does the best he can, I suppose," said Johnny.

"Where are all the children right now?" Ruth glanced into an open closet.

"Wandering about, throwing stones in the river maybe. Getting up to no good."

"Well, thank you for showing me this, Johnny. I should talk to the Father. I'm sure there are ways we could improve this. I'll see if we can help somehow. That's no way for children to live."

"I wouldn't want to cause any trouble." Johnny led her from the room and outside once more.

"No, no trouble, Johnny. You take care."

At dinner that night, Ruth brought up what she had seen in the church. "It's good that they're getting the youngest ones to a better place, but what's there for the boys who are left—it's awful, it really is. They're merely young boys. I was wondering if there's anything we can do. Do we have room? You've a sofa, perhaps. There's a boy, Johnny, a farmhand who's had a terrible time—lost his brother Jude in the shuffle of the evacuation, and he's bullied on account of his stutter, a speech impediment that I can certainly empathize with."

"Perhaps Edith and I can share a room. I've a large enough bed, and this boy can have the free room," Vera said casually.

"Vera, really? I don't think so," Edith said. "That's rather rash, don't you think? I can't share a bed. We're not children. We're too old. No, no, that's nonsense."

"It's a big bed. Like when we were little. We'll be fine, Edith. You've lived alone too long in that empty old mansion in London."

"I don't wish to," Edith said pertly, colour rising to her cheeks.

"Gran, he's been beaten several times by the other boys. Please? Or perhaps I can share a room with you—or . . . or, I'll sleep on the sofa and he can have my bed. I'm worried about this boy."

"No, Ruth, that won't be necessary." Edith sighed deeply and thought for a moment. "Very well. I'll share with Vera."

"See, Edith, it's not so difficult. I know you have your posh life in London, with loads of space to shake out your frock, enjoying life with Mildred cooking for you and trying to keep the soufflés from spoiling on her way up the stairs to your dining room. I won't be any trouble, honest. I'm your sister, for pity's sake."

"It's quite all right," Edith said. "Like old times, yes?" Finally, she smiled, with reluctance at first, then more warmly. Ruth leapt up and threw her arms around her gran.

"Thank you so much. I'm not sure if the vicar will allow this, but I'll speak to him on my way into the hall tomorrow. I really feel so much sympathy for this boy—I do. Perhaps I can help him find his brother."

"Yes, perhaps," said Vera. "There's nothing as horrible as losing a sibling."

Ruth sat in her dark room once more, gazing out the window at the blues and blacks of the Martynsborough countryside. It was that deepest hour of night, around three in the morning, when something—she didn't know what—woke her. As she did on her first night in Martynsborough, she opened the blackouts, wrapped a blanket around her shoulders, and sat by the window, thinking the fresh air might help. The crickets sang, but not as loudly this night, as if they, too, wished to sleep but couldn't. She cupped her hand over her ear and opened and closed it intermittently, creating the illusion of a whistling wind, like the coming of a storm, while she rested her eyes on the ribbon of road that wound from under her window, up past the wood to Virginia's cottage, which she could see in the distance. With all homes blacked out, their glass darkened, Ruth couldn't tell if lights blazed within or if all the inhabitants slept.

She looked again to the rye field and was startled as someone stepped from the shadows into the moonlight on the road. It was a figure in white—a woman wearing a long white shift and a loosely drawn white hood about her head. She stood some distance away, her back to Ruth, and then she crept down the track towards Malcolm's house. Elise—it was Elise; she'd escaped again. Ruth's heart rattled, and she wavered a moment, thinking perhaps to throw on a robe and walk the poor woman back to her house—wondering how such an encounter might play out, even feeling a bit frightened of the prospect, recalling how the woman had stared at her the previous day with such an eerie, empty gaze.

But there was something else, something not quite right. This figure's gait was assured, nimble, graceful even—whereas Ruth had observed Elise to have a limp and a clumsy nature to her stride. Elise rarely stood straight, always leaning on Malcolm or against a wall. But this figure on the road—no, she had no such demeanour. Instead, her stride was steady, so steady, in fact, she seemed to glide over the ground—and she had a certain deliberate intelligence to her movements that was very much at odds with what Ruth knew about Elise. It was unnerving and other-worldly. Had Elise's faculties returned? Or was this something else altogether? Ruth backed away from the window, her heart pounding. The figure turned, startling Ruth, and she pulled the blackouts closed before she could clearly see the woman's face.

After a moment, she steeled her courage and peered out from the curtain. The figure was gone. Ruth stared a long time, looking from the patchwork fields, to the wood, to the road, back to Malcolm's cottage, and then wondered if she had imagined it. Had Maude planted this notion of witches in her head, causing her imagination to run wild? In her half-asleep, muddled mind, it all seemed a dream. She closed the blackouts and climbed into bed, perplexed and too scared to do anything about anything.

-7-

Ruth put on her smartest wool skirt, a tartan of various blues and greens, her only pair of dark stockings, and a pale blue blouse. She had fallen well behind on time that first morning, being unused to rising early, along with being disturbed by her late-night vision of a ghostly woman. She pedalled as fast as she could and burst into the hall in a fluster at a quarter past eight. Mr. Horgon looked up from his desk, tapped his watch, and brought it to his ear.

"Let me show you around," he said, "and we'll get you partnered up with someone so that you can see how we do things here." They passed several desks with older people working at them, approached the stage, and moved up a small staircase.

"A stage? Do you put on plays here?"

"Hmm? Yes, I suppose, at one time."

"And the piano? It looks quite handsome. Does anyone play? Are there dances? I play a little myself."

Horgon scoffed. "Miss Gladstone, we are at war. Dances? Now there's a chestnut. Absolutely not." He pushed aside the stage curtain. "Here on the stage are a few desks we've moved up here. The lighting is not quite as good, so perhaps with you being so young with sharp eyes, we'll have you here. Eat a lot of carrots, do you? If not, you should— it's what keeps those eyes sharp." They walked to the back of the stage, through a door, and down a flight of stairs into a basement corridor. "We've got records down here, everything filed for the ministry, as well as a shelter in case of an air raid. No siren yet—we've yet to get one, but as it is, we've some Home Guardsmen with whistles."

They walked up another flight of stairs and back into the main hall. A few more people had arrived, and Ruth immediately recognized one of them.

Horgon called out, "Malcolm, I've your new trainee right here, Ruth Gladstone."

Malcolm turned, and his eyes momentarily registered surprise. "Hello. Pleased to meet you, Miss Gladstone." He did not smile. "We'll be at the desks on the stage; you can come with me."

Malcolm wore dark pants and a white shirt with no jacket or tie. Unlike the time she encountered him on the road, his reddish-brown hair was swept back neatly, and he was clean-shaven. Ruth followed him up the steps to three desks on the stage, none of which were occupied. The desk in the centre had a monstrous stack of papers, a stamp, an inkpad, several pencils, and a ledger book. He pulled a chair out for her. She sat. He, in turn, leaned against the centre desk and took the first page off the pile and scanned it for a minute in silence. He put it down, then picked up the ledger book, opened it, and looked it over. She watched his eyes, the clear, emerald one and the cloudy one— they tracked simultaneously, and there on the dim stage, it was hard to tell that there was any injury at all. Her gaze moved to his left hand, in which he held the book. He wore a simple gold band on his ring finger—a wedding ring, she presumed—and as she had noted before, his index and middle fingers were missing above the first knuckle. She noted how clean the cut was, how little scarring there was, and wondered about the surgeon who had patched him up. God, would it have been Warren? No, no, it couldn't be—Malcolm had been in Norway. Warren had been in France before the evacuation; they would not have crossed paths.

"Miss Gladstone," Malcolm said quietly. She did not hear him as she stared intently at his damaged fingers, her thoughts twisted up about Warren. "Miss Gladstone," he said more loudly, and she looked up, startled, to meet his eyes. "Yes, I've an injury on my left hand, if that's what you find so fascinating."

Ruth blushed hotly. "Sorry, no, that's not . . . I mean, sorry."

"Torn up by shrapnel in Norway, if you must know. Now, let me walk you through what we're doing here. This pile of paper here represents all the various weights and measures of the allotments. As you can see, there's quite a bit of paper here."

"Yes, I see that. Am I to work out the maths—I'm not sure I follow?"

"I was told you were from Cambridge."

"Well, yes, English literature, not maths." At this new information, his features softened.

"Watch me and see how I do this." Malcolm pulled out his chair and sat. He took a page from the top of the pile and placed it on the desk. "Come in a little closer. Have a look at this." He picked up the pencil with his right hand—the intact hand. "You'll see the name at the top is the owner of the allotment, each of which is assigned a registration number." He stopped for a moment and sighed, tapping the pencil on the desk. He then pointed at the book. "Here is the ledger, and you enter the weights here." He sighed again, frowned, and then smiled regretfully.

"Is anything the matter?" Ruth asked.

"No . . . Well, yes. Would you like to take a walk, Miss Gladstone? Let's leave these papers. I'll show you around the hall."

"Mr. Horgon showed me already."

"Miss Gladstone, please, come with me. We'll go this way." He led her to the back of the stage, down the stairs, and into the dim corridor. They followed it around a corner and another staircase, which led to a door that he opened, allowing in blinding sunlight. She followed him out to a small back court, through a gate, and out on to the road.

"Where are we going?" Ruth hurried to catch up to him.

"Just a little further." He walked on, and then down to the high street. They crossed to the other side, to a bench overlooking the River Harold. He took a seat. "Please sit, Miss Gladstone. Let us enjoy the view of the river."

"I'm not sure what this is all about, and you can call me Ruth, by the way." She sat.

"Ruth, very good. I suppose you should call me Malcolm, although I don't recall Horgon giving me the benefit of a surname." He looked around, then he turned to her. "Ruth, I've been helping out at the hall here on a semiregular basis. I arrived in this village some three months ago, and word travels fast here, and it was learned that I studied at Oxford. It wasn't long before Horgon had me summoned and walked me through the same paperwork that you've just now looked at. For the war effort—a noble endeavour, no doubt."

"I would think."

"Yes, one would think. I've no maths or accounting background. I know nothing of agriculture, of flax or barley. I lived in France. I had a studio; I had commissions as a sculptor. I taught. Before that, I studied antiquities at Oxford. I've never counted weights of grain in the entirety of my life, I don't really have any idea what I'm doing, but I suppose to Horgon, Oxford is Oxford. So, here I am. I've been filling these ledger sheets for some time now, and about a month ago, I'd been talking to another villager with a rather large allotment who was providing a small surplus to the War Ag. I watched as he packaged a small stack of ledgers for the ministry man. I asked him about the papers, and he showed them to me. They're the very same ledgers that we're recording. By the time we receive those vast stacks of paper, they're already completed and submitted—weeks before we process them. I shouldn't tell you this— I really shouldn't. Perhaps I'm telling you because I've known some friends who attended your Cambridge whom I very much respect. Or maybe I've had a hell of a morning and I'm feeling a little fed up with the whole production. The work is pointless—it's redundant."

"I don't understand at all."

"We're repeating what the War Ag already has done—creating it in duplicate. They come around once a month and drop a pile of papers on Horgon's desk that have already been completed. It's make-work—to keep people busy. Shortly after the declaration of war, some of those chaps at the desks—they very nearly shot the butcher dead as he stumbled home from the pub. They were among a pack of men roaming about in the wood, with their ancient rifles, imagining a valley infiltrated by German spies. This work keeps otherwise well-intentioned people busy with paper as opposed to guns."

"Mr. Horgon knows?"

"I think Horgon is aware. Perhaps he likes the thoroughness of doing everything in duplicate—maybe they use it as a cross-check on the numbers. Maybe he is the mastermind behind the whole opera-tion, hoping to keep idle hands busy during the war. I've not the nerve to ask, and I highly discourage you from doing so. The other paper-pushers probably don't know any better. Some of them, the younger ones, fought in the last war, and the oldest among them fought against the Boers. Perhaps they want to feel that they're contributing to this new war."

"So, what does this mean? That there's no point to what I'm doing . . . or what you're doing?"

"Not really."

"Then why do we do it?"

"Why do we bomb cities? Why do we drive children into the coun-try? Why does one do anything? It's a war. We just do it. I like it less than you, but at least we are being paid a stipend. Money is money, and there certainly isn't a queue of villagers outside my door hoping to buy my original works of art, now is there? Either way, now that you're in the know, shall we go back and continue this pointless endeavour?"

They returned to the hall, coming in through the stage door. Horgon continued to work at his desk and showed no indication that he'd even noticed they had left. Malcolm walked Ruth through the procedure, and soon she was filling in ledgers, stamping weigh bills and so on. At no time during the morning did Malcolm acknowledge their first meeting on the road. Nor did he mention anything about his wife, Elise, or Virginia. Either way, she found that once she'd learned the basics of the work, she quite liked filling in ledgers with Malcolm at the next desk doing the same. In a way it was pleasant, and for all the unfortunate circumstances of his life, he was affable enough. He was closer to Ruth's age than nearly everyone she'd met in the village, so there was that, too. They were contemporaries—a nice thing.

At noon, the workers drifted to the pub, including Malcolm, while Ruth took her sandwich to the bench overlooking the river and ate there alone. She thought again of her novel, but no fresh ideas came to her during the half hour she sat there.

After lunch, Malcolm returned, and Ruth could smell the stout and the pub smoke on his clothing. The pint or two that he drank with lunch must have loosened his tongue a bit, and he was more talkative, speaking of a café in Paris that he loved. He then talked about the town and how things must seem strange to the locals, having so many billetees and evacuees about.

"I heard a man in the pub saying that crime is up on account of all us lot invading their village." Malcolm laughed a bit. "Perhaps there's some truth to it. Our cottage was broken into yesterday."

"Really?" Ruth asked.

"Yes, it's the reason I was late this morning. I'm still sorting out what was taken. Someone jimmied open a window while we were at church Sunday morning. I didn't notice at first—not till today. The thief had a light touch."

"What did they take?"

"This is the odd thing. It appears he went through my belongings, even some money and other valuables, which he didn't take. He's only taken clothing and a small wool blanket, maybe more—I will likely discover the pilfered items over time."

"How very odd."

"I can envision the assailant wrapping the works up in the blanket and throwing it over his shoulder like a gypsy."

"Did you report it to Mr. Horgon?"

"Why bother? It's one of the evacuated boys from the church out on a morning lark—I'm sure of it. They seem to scatter whenever there's a church service, and I've seen them up to no good—we can only imagine what they get up to while we listen to sermons."

Ruth quietly hoped that Johnny was innocent in the matter; she could barely imagine him stealing, and it would certainly make his life more difficult to be caught. But knowing the children were cold in the church basement, she thought perhaps he was nicking things for the other boys' benefit—he had a good heart. Either way, she did not mention this. Instead she said, "Those poor children. I can hardly blame them for anything."

"I agree. I'm not going to raise a ruckus about it."

They worked the remainder of the afternoon in amicable enough silence. At half-past four, Malcolm collected his hat and said, "Goodnight. See you tomorrow." She watched him cross the room and exit the hall as she gathered her own things.

She rode her bike past the church and saw Father Tweedsmuir and stopped to speak with him about Johnny's billeting.

"Father," she called. "Hallo. Can I have a word?"

"Yes, good day to you, Ruth." He'd been pulling bits of weed from a small vegetable garden and straightened up awkwardly. He dusted his hands off. "What can I do for you?"

Ruth told him about her idea, about her concern for the remaining boys, especially Johnny.

"I'm not sure it's a good idea to put such a boisterous boy in a cottage with three women, two of whom are elderly," he said.

"Nothing will happen, I assure you, Father. Please, I'm adamant about this. I feel for the boy—his troubles are to do with his stammering, to which I can relate. I also had a problem speaking when I was young. The other boys bully him. And he'll eat well—I can promise you that."

Father Tweedsmuir thought for a moment, and then said, "Does Vera know about this?"

"Oh yes, she does. We spoke last night."

"I'd like to confirm personally with your aunt first, but yes, we can do this on a trial basis. I know that Malcolm lives close by—I'll mention to him to keep an eye on things. He has his hands rather full, so I hope there'll be no trouble."

"No trouble at all, Father. Thank you so much!" Ruth hugged him, nearly knocking the hat from his head.

"Well, all is good, then," the Father said. "So you know, he needs to be up by six for his farm work Monday through Friday. I'll hold you accountable that he's out of bed on time. If he's late, I'll come to you for an explanation."

Ruth's happiness was tempered briefly by the realization that she would have to wake up even earlier than before.

With such a light heart and feeling of accomplishment, she didn't wish to hurry back to some drudgery in the garden. She would reward herself for a day's graft with a small glass of beer. After all, she was now a working woman, receiving a pay cheque for the first time in her life, however small it might be. And despite Malcolm's assessment of its redundancy, work was still work—perhaps a good in and of itself.

The Yellow Rattle's wooden sign hung from a black iron hook. She stepped inside to find a very low-ceilinged Tudor-inspired space with a hearth to the side of the room, wooden tables, and, in the back, a lonely, unused dartboard. Behind a handsome, gleaming wood bar, a woman of about forty, wearing a black striped apron, wiped down the counters. A few older men sat at the tables, smoking cigarettes, glaring at Ruth.

"Hallo there. Can I get you something, miss?" the barmaid asked. She had her dark hair up in a scarf and assessed Ruth more closely with an appraising eye. "It's not every day we get a young woman in."

"Um, yes, I'm putting off the long ride home. Thought I'd get out of the sun for a moment." Ruth stepped up to the bar.

"I'm Ellen. Pleased to meet you. Bitter, stout, or ale? It's all we've got. No claret or cordial, I'm afraid, and port only on Fridays, but I could put on a kettle—that is, if you'd like tea or something else, then?" Ellen spoke very quickly, and it took Ruth a moment to process so many words coming at her at once.

"Tea, yes, I suppose would be nice, but don't go to any trouble. I'm happy with a cool glass of beer for the road, as they say. I'm Ruth."

Ellen took a glass and pulled the tap.

"This war's given women a taste for beer, hasn't it? You're new to Martynsborough—staying with Vera, right?"

"Well, yes, but I have to say, how does everyone in this village seem to know all about me? Is there some kind of communication network I've yet to learn about?"

"It's a small village, miss—hard not to notice things." She handed Ruth the glass.

"Cheers." Ruth took a sip. "You're from here, then? I can't make assumptions with so many people evacuating and moving around."

"Not Martynsborough proper. I've come from a nearby hamlet—or perhaps several nearby hamlets. I moved around quite a bit when I was young. Me dad travelled for business as a sundries man, then settled over in the next town for most of me youth, till I come here some twenty years ago. I married a man who pulled pints for a living, so that's why I came. He's now somewhere in Libya fighting Italians. So, it's now me pulling the pints in Martynsborough."

"The Yellow Rattle, it's an interesting name," Ruth said.

"It's a flower, don't you know—little yellow thing that grows in the meadow, bright and pretty in spring. By late summer, they dry out a bit and grow small seeds within 'em. When the wind picks up, they rattle about like shillings in a coffee tin."

"Fascinating."

"Yes, well, I'm no expert in flowers, but it's what me father called me—a long time ago—his 'little yellow-haired rattle,' a tiny thing that made quite the racket. A fine name for a pub, too."

"That's a lovely story."

"This pub is all about stories, miss. There are many stories to be told here in Martynsborough."

"Yes, well, I have to say, I'm a bit of a writer, or at least I'd like to think I'm trying to be a writer, anyway. And it's a good story that I need for my novel. It's so far eluded me. Hopefully, I'll find one myself here in Martynsborough. Either way"—Ruth raised her glass—"here's to British victory."

"Aye, hold that thought," Ellen said, and pulled a few glugs of stout into her teacup. She clinked it with Ruth's glass. "Here's to victory." They drank and were silent for some time. Ellen tended to the bar, and Ruth continued thinking about the beginnings of her novel, when Ellen said, "You work in the hall, pushing papers, don't you? I'd rather be pulling pints any day." She turned to wring out her cloth and spoke over her shoulder. "Have you seen the chap with the missing fingers—works there in the hall? I've wondered about him. He only arrived a couple of months back. Seems to keep clear of most people. He's a pint and chips all to himself at the back table every day for lunch. Speaks to not a soul. Odd to see a man of such a young age around."

"Yes, I actually worked with him today. He's called Malcolm, a nice enough man."

"Hmm, not necessarily what I've heard."

"Oh?"

Ellen dropped the rag in the sink and turned to face Ruth. "Around here, they say he's rather stern and unfriendly. The villagers like to talk. He and his strange wife are a topic of interest, it seems. I've no qualms with the man meself; I've heard only what others say. These folks aren't keen on so many strangers walking amongst them with the war and all. I'll likely be apologizing on their behalf before too long. Hope they've not given you too much trouble."

"Well"—Ruth lowered her voice and glanced around—"I had noticed a slight, how should I say, coolness to the demeanour of many of the villagers towards us evacuees. As for Malcolm, I think it's doubly unfortunate. He's had a difficult time . . . with everything, his wife, and . . . in fact, he told me his cottage was broken into yesterday and some things were stolen."

"Aye?"

"Yes, and you know, it makes me wonder if there's some connection or other. I'm sure you can tell I've not spent much time so far north in the country, and when I first came to Martynsborough, I was quite startled to run into your resident rogue sheep."

"Castor and Pollux."

"Yes, the very same. Then, oddly enough, my first night here, I saw something outside our cottage. I might have been mistaken, it could have been the sheep—or, well, it was quite late at night, I wasn't sure. I thought also it might have been a person. The next day, my aunt found some of her pears had been nibbled in the garden. By whom, we're not sure. Then, there's this break-in—as Malcolm told me. Then just last night, I . . . I swear . . ." Ruth paused, wondering how much she wished to reveal. She didn't want to appear mad—the villagers already seemed to think so little of her.

"You swear what?"

"Hmm, I swear I saw a woman wander out from the rye field, and then move down the road in the dark—a woman or girl. Very eerie, and it was a bit unnerving, to be honest. I was wondering if perhaps—"

"Dressed in white, was she?"

"Yes, actually—"

"You've seen a ghost."

"What?"

"A ghost. It's quite curious you mention it, because it was a topic of conversation here last evening. It seems that this regular drinker, a war objector who's been shipped in to work on the flax interest—he'd too much the other night, never made it back to the farm barracks, dozed off in the blessed field. He woke and saw someone roaming about, before sunup. Looked to him like a girl, a lady in white, and so he come along to the pub that night and told the men what he'd seen, and it seems that it's not the first time this lady in white's been witnessed. Albert, one of the oldest drinkers at the table, well, he starts telling a tale and says that many, many years ago, before my time certainly, there was a man claims to have found the body of a girl floating dead in the old lime-kiln ponds on the estate. Then, the next day he raises the alarm—'There's been a murder most horrible,' he cries, rapping on doors and such. No one found any girl—dead or alive. No crime seemed to have been done, no need to call up the magistrate from Clitheroe. Then, not long after, it seems the village was haunted by this very same girl in white—seen drifting down the streets after midnight, a wraith, as they're called in the hills, a vengeful girl who's been wronged by someone or other. As he tells it, the town went mad for a solid fortnight, crossing themselves with holy of holies, and denning up in their cottages every sundown. It wasn't till the first snow, around St. Stephen's Day, that the ghost wasn't seen no more. That is, everyone calmed down except for the bloke who started it all by finding the girl in the kiln pond—he went quite mad, they say. Name of Phineas, if I recall. Quite the yarn, yeah?"

"Yes, indeed. I'm actually speechless."

"Another local says to me not an hour before you stepped in here that it's on account of all you city folk coming to the village—that they've woke up the trouble somehow. Like I said, they're not keen on you lot crowding up our quiet village."

"That sounds a little ominous, to be honest."

"Aye, we're generally fine people, and you're a lovely girl—you drink beer, for Pete's sake. What's not to like? So, aye, the children, too; I've no quarrels with them, not even with the chap who's missing fingers, with the queer wife." She paused and pulled some stout into her teacup and knocked it back, swallowing loudly. "But what I can tell you is this," she said, more seriously, wagging her teacup in the air. "I've a way about me. I can soothsay a little. I've a bit of gypsy in me blood. I sense a wee muttering in the ground—something's a-coming. I have a feeling that more people will start seeing that ghost—the wraith—and that's when there'll be proper panic and madness. Fear can be contagious, like the Spanish flu. I think there might be some trouble in store for Martynsborough. Mind yourself, Ruth. Here in the country, things can get strange very quickly."

Ruth shuddered and drained the rest of her beer, and then an amazing thing occurred to her.

She'd found her story.

- 8 -

The second day that Ruth worked in the hall, Malcolm asked if she'd like to eat lunch in the pub with him. She reluctantly agreed, and they took a back table in the Yellow Rattle. Within a moment, two pints arrived. Ellen gave Ruth a knowing smile, then addressed Malcolm. "Chips and brown sauce today then, sir?"

"Yes," he said.

"And you've brought your own lunch along, I see," she said to Ruth.

"Do you mind?" Ruth asked.

"No, not at all. I'm sure you've got something better there than I can cook in me drippings pot, which, I'm ashamed to say, is the very same since last January. But chips still taste fine, aye? If not, I've some powdered scramble if you like—I swear it's better than the real thing."

She disappeared into a back kitchen. Ruth looked around and noticed a gathering of older men who sat in a blue haze of cigarette smoke, eyeing her and Malcolm with even more scrutiny than on her first visit to the pub.

"It seems we're quite the curiosity," Ruth said quietly.

"Yes, we're like strange beasts in a zoo. They sure don't seem to like us," said Malcolm.

"I was in yesterday," she said. "I was chatting with the barmaid, Ellen."

"A first-name basis, now? I'm impressed you can understand her—she talks a mile a minute."

"Well, we certainly get on. I think I've gotten used to the way she speaks. And as a girl who likes beer, it seems I'm usually quite welcome in pubs. Anyway, I was talking to her about Castor and Pollux—you know, those local sheep—and then about how we'd found someone or something had been munching on the pears in our back garden."

"Interesting."

"Yes, then I told her about the theft of some of your clothes, with the break-in—"

"You told her?" His mouth pressed into a frown.

"Oh." She felt a blush rise to her cheeks. "Sorry, I didn't think it would be anything. I was just chatting, you know. I'm sorry."

"Yes, well—as you were saying."

"Anyway, Ellen told me that there is recent talk of a ghost amongst the villagers, a *wraith*, as she called it. A woman in white, drifting through the streets."

"A ghost? Quaint. A ghost that has cold feet, I suppose, haunting the town in a pair of my woollen socks."

"Yes, well, she gave me some advice. I'd even call it a warning."

Malcolm raised an eyebrow, and then Ellen was suddenly there, placing a plate in front of him. He looked up at her. "Thank you."

Ellen nodded and lingered for a moment by their table. "I heard you'd some troubles at your cottage," she said.

Malcolm sighed with annoyance.

"Yes, word gets around fast, it seems. Not to worry too much—nothing valuable taken. The local boys, bored, looking for something to do."

"Well, give my regards to Virgie." Ellen walked away.

"It's as if they're all connected to a telegraph machine," Ruth said. "Everyone knew me before I even opened my mouth. And . . . I have to say, sorry . . . on my part, to add to the gossip, you know, talking about the break-in. I didn't think it would be a problem to bring it up."

"No, it's nothing, really." Malcolm took a sip of his beer. "Before coming here, I'd spent more time in France than in Britain, and now to be in a small village—to have the locals eyeing me suspiciously like I'm a German spy—I suppose, the less attention I get the better. That's all—nothing to fret about. So, what was this you were saying about a warning?"

"Oh right, yes. So, Ellen told me that some of the locals think that we evacuees are stirring up this trouble, awakening the ghost, or the wraith, as she called it, and that there may soon be a panic, or worse." She took a bite of her sandwich.

"Vera baked the bread, too, didn't she?" Malcolm asked, looking enviously at her lunch.

"Yes, actually," Ruth said with her mouth full. "Would you like a bite?" She thrust it at him.

"No, no, quite all right. I've got my chips here, cooked in eight-month-old dripping. Austerity never tasted better." He looked at his plate and sighed. "So, a wraith, you were saying? Yes. Interesting." He shoved a chip into his mouth and said, "God, I hope this war ends soon."

They walked home together as the sun dropped low on the horizon, Ruth pushing her bicycle next to him as they crossed the bridge. For the first quarter-mile, they said nothing, and Ruth felt anxious about the long silence, trying to think of something to say.

"Thanks for lunch. It was nice to have someone to talk to," she said. He smiled but didn't speak. "I should say, I came here to Martynsborough to write a novel. I hope that doesn't make you laugh."

"Not at all." Malcolm had his tweed coat thrown over his shoulder, hooked on his thumb. "I came here in a rather bleak state of mind myself, but I also knew it might be an ideal place to sculpt, being quiet, peaceful. There's local clay here. I had some of my things brought from France before Paris fell. God knows what will happen to my studio—or the small art school where I taught. So, maybe I'm a little like you. I'm here to escape and create."

"According to Wordsworth, a poet is *not* to write his verse during the heated moments of powerful feeling, but later, in a state of tranquillity, remembering those feelings with a clear mind. Perhaps Martynsborough is the perfect place for that."

"Wordsworth? You're better read than I am. And what is it that you've written so far?"

"Well, I've been struggling to find something to write, but this legend of the ghostly woman intrigues me. I thought to do something with that."

"A ghost story? Now there's something I can read by a roaring fire while a gale scratches at the window."

"Really?" Ruth said, delighted.

"Why not? But what you need to do now is research. Get to the bottom of this bizarre legend. I don't believe there's any strange ghost roaming the streets. It's either some form of collective mania, or one of the boys is running about at night wrapped in a sheet, trying to scare the locals—and likely wearing my socks. Maybe these villagers will make our miserable lives a little less miserable if we solve their mystery for them."

"Perhaps you're right," she said, "but I'd certainly like to look into it. And it has all the trappings of a capital novel."

"It beats filling in ledger sheets. I could help—a welcome distraction."

"Yes," she said, then turned quickly. "Look, there by the trees." She pointed to where Castor and Pollux grazed by the edge of the wood, not one hundred yards from them.

"Shh." He brought a finger to his mouth. "I've seen them here and there, but they've never stood long enough for me to have a close look at them." For a long, lingering moment, Malcolm and Ruth silently observed the animals, then he whispered, "The ram is quite handsome. Look at those deadly horns, though. I'd hate to be on the wrong side of those." He brought a hand to his brow to shield his eyes from the setting sun. "Such an ancient-looking creature. They call them mules here—which seemed strange until I realized they're not pure breeds, but cross-bred with Scottish sheep."

"Ah, that makes sense."

"The black faces; they've got white markings about them—eerie. Very curious-looking things, like something from witchcraft."

"Yes," she whispered back. "Do you suppose they fare well without the help of the farmer? They're not wild animals, after all, but they've had to act as them to get by."

"A flock without a shepherd, yes. Well, they're wild now, and by the looks of it, they're not wanting for anything. Perhaps they're better off this way. With the war shuttering the abattoirs and chasing all the butchers away, they're free to get on with it."

"Horgon told me they're mates for life," Ruth said quietly, to which Malcolm let out a muffled scoff.

"Mates for life?" he asked. "They don't have a lot of choice in the matter; there's only two of them. Their courtship is by necessity, not selection. I hope they get on well, given they're all each other has."

"Yes, but still—it's rather nice, don't you think? They've found each other—unlikely survivors, the last of their kind, perhaps. They're not alone."

"Under certain circumstances, being alone might be preferable." Malcolm started walking again, and as the sheep heard the crunch of the gravel, they turned and disappeared into the bramble.

Eventually they arrived at Virginia's cottage. "Well, have a good night, then," Malcolm said, turning to go.

"Goodnight." Ruth watched him as he strode towards his cottage, then she leaned her bike against the hedge and peered through the branches to see him open the door and step inside. Ruth realized she'd forgotten to mention that Johnny was coming to live with them, that Father Tweedsmuir had said he might talk to Malcolm about it. She walked up the path thinking to tell him, but as she approached, she thought better of it. She felt a peculiar discomfort being so close to his cottage, like she had trespassed into some private place. She wavered, lingering there, looking at the flowers in the box, then to the window, whose glass was darkened by the blackouts. She saw movement. The curtains parted, and there stood Elise looking out at the garden with the same strange, unseeing gaze; the two women locked eyes. Ruth froze and saw something in Elise's pale blue stare—not vacancy nor callowness, no. For a horrible moment, she thought she saw something else—*malice*.

She stumbled back to her bicycle and rode home as fast as she could.

AUTUMN 1940

- 9 -

By the end of September, London had been bombed for twenty-three straight days with no end in sight. And whilst the capital smouldered in a black cloud of endless destruction, Martynsborough seemed to swell and glow in the autumn sunshine. Flax reached heavenwards, and blueness abounded. Only a rare and gentle night-time rain fell from a sky that was usually clear and unencumbered, allowing the sun to fall upon the calicoed greens and ambers of the Lancashire farms.

Despite the docile footing of autumn, it was still wartime, and there were some unavoidable probations for the village to endure. More rationing had been introduced that month. Petrol was soon reserved mostly for farm equipment and lorries, so automobiles sat uselessly up on blocks, tires removed and much of the parts recycled for the war. Ellen could not replace her pot of drippings until a shipment of national margarine arrived, so she continued to fry the chips in the months-old, diabolical suet—though few of the pub's patrons seemed to notice. Vera gave up all her aluminium pots and pans to the ministry man. They would eventually become fuselages for Spitfires and Hurricanes, and so she returned to more-ancient, earthen vessels in which to cook their rabbit and duck.

It wasn't just clay-pot cooking. Vera had made some other changes, one being that she clicked off the wireless at the end of the Ministry of

Food bulletin, before the news was announced. In a blissful silence, with no breathless accounts of destruction and misery blaring from the set, she sipped her tea, watching through the window as Edith pruned back the pear tree, or clumsily attempted to pull weeds, or collected eggs. These country chores at first seemed awkward to this city-accustomed woman, but she had eventually started falling into village ways, and this, from a woman who had come from a house with bona fide staff.

Staff!

Vera laughed to herself. She couldn't imagine sitting down on a divan to while away the hours as some bedraggled, overworked woman in a starched apron and frilly cap swept the floor under her feet. She could see the temptation, yes, especially in growing old, to wish for the ways of the city, of wealth, but she felt in her bones that her way was better, healthier, more wholesome, more self-sufficient—and she could already see a new glow in Edith's cheeks.

So, without the BBC news reminding Edith of a home in London that might or might not still be standing, Vera did her best to ensure that Edith wallowed in blessed ignorance of the city and all its miseries. She wondered then, if the war indeed ended by Christmas, would Edith simply pack her bag and return? Vera had no love for the city itself, but not in such a way that she wished destruction on it. It was, in fact, rather horrible what was happening. Vera often thought about the peculiar fatefulness of her life, and how such terrible things can sometimes beget good things. Like this: Edith was right there, outside the window; she was *here*, just like that, here in Martynsborough. It had seemed all but impossible before.

They'd sworn that they would not lose touch, but as their lives diverged from that strange and horrible day so long ago, it had become inevitable. One morning Vera awoke and realized it had been twenty years since they had seen each other. Ruth had been there, too, that last day—a tiny child of five years old at the time, and Vera recalled precisely that the little girl wore a most beautiful dress and spun round and round, delighting in the flow of the taffeta, laughing and calling out for her auntie *Veewa*.

At the declaration of war, Vera had sent a tentative letter to Edith—the first in two decades. In the letter, she vaguely suggested that if Edith needed to evacuate, perhaps she might consider travelling north, to the places they enjoyed in the summers of their youth. Perhaps she would like to come and breathe the fresh air of Martynsborough once more? All was well here—she would assure her—nothing to concern them. Vera would see to everything. Did she not recall their fun by the river during those long-lost holidays? How they laughed and hid until they heard calling for them to come home for dinner without anyone knowing that they had stolen away to places that young girls should never go? Or the river with the rowboat, how they had fallen asleep in the bilge and nearly drifted to the next village?

Vera had not expected a reply, but a letter did indeed arrive within the fortnight—brief but not unfriendly. Edith would be evacuating to Essex, *but thank you for writing, hope you are well.* Then some time passed, and she received another letter from Edith, inquiring in more detail about Vera's life. How was her health? How had the years been treating her? It had been ages since they'd seen each other. Evacuation was superfluous. She had returned to London. The war was phony; it was all bluster. She couldn't stand Essex . . . Perhaps they could correspond with more regularity, like they once did?

Vera sensed the thawing of some dense and frozen thing. Perhaps it was the fear of German invasion, the passing of the days; maybe like Vera herself, Edith wished to make things right before they reached the ends of their lives. Perhaps she wished to grasp for some small bit of the warmth and happiness they once shared before it was too late.

So here she was: Edith in Martynsborough, and they were together once more. All was not resolved; they had achieved only a shaky peace. Vera knew that much remained unsaid. Their history was fraught and complex and needed to be answered to. They had not shared a bed since they were so very young, and now they were old. It was awkward, yes, but not terrible. They slept stiffly on opposite sides of the mattress with a space as wide and deep as a washbasin between them, wearing their sleeping caps, ointments under their eyes, cream on their cracked knuckles, and all the other trappings and habits of growing old, a process that, up until then, they had experienced separately. They would get used to it. It would all be all right.

With a sigh and a tentative flush of happiness, Vera turned from the window and started looking over her recipe books from the Ministry of Food. She contemplated the coming weeks and wondered how on earth she was going to keep a growing fifteen-year-old boy well fed.

Johnny had a tremendous appetite. He'd joined them in mid-September during a busy time with the harvest, so the routine of the cottage was for all to be up before dawn, and then Johnny would go off on a bicycle lent to him by the vicar, with at least four hen's eggs in his belly and a bagged lunch, followed by Ruth, with her bagged lunch, and then Vera and Edith worked to start the whole process over again for dinner.

Ruth continued to fill in paperwork that had already been processed by some other hand, like the cursed Sisyphus pushing the stone up the hill for eternity. Yes, she was scratching with a pencil all day, but it was certainly not the kind of writing she had hoped for. Her gothic novel lay fallow on the desk at home. Nor had she witnessed the spectre outside her window for some weeks. With no new knowledge or activity regarding the local legend, she started to think that the novel might never happen—and after such a promising start, too. Brooding and desultory, she decided to focus on writing of another sort, and Malcolm noticed as she placed her school satchel on the desk.

"Pub lunch today . . . or will you be working on your novel about ghost women?"

"No, I've my correspondence to catch up on. I hadn't any idea of where this place was when I travelled here, and I've some people to contact. There's a desk here, and a pencil, so it seems the best place to spend the next half hour."

"So, who are you writing to, then? Classmates at Cambridge?"

"Hmm?" She glanced at him, distracted. "Yes, well. I have to admit, I haven't really been terribly gregarious at school—I really only have the mailing address of one classmate. She's Maude, a postdoctoral student of geography. Due to a bomb scare, I was evacuated from my part of the building and slept in her room for a short period. She seemed interested in the mysterious Martynsborough."

"Couldn't find it on a map, could you?"

"I couldn't find the *map*, actually." She laughed. "There was little information in general about this place. So much so, I started to doubt its existence. And this Maude, if I were to be honest, didn't seem to like me at first, but she became a sort of friend. She's a tall woman, red-haired, intimidating, like some Amazonian warrior—you know, the type of girl who wears trousers."

"Many women are wearing trousers now."

"Yes, I suppose. So, I was going to write to Maude, because I'm willing to bet that she still doesn't believe that Martynsborough exists. I've an overwhelming urge to tell her of the goings-on here—the errant sheep, an unmoving mill wheel, strange ghostly women in white. She'll love it." Ruth placed her list of addresses to the side and arranged the papers and her lunch. "Of course, there's my mum and dad, across an ocean. I'm not sure if my letter will find them, but I certainly hope it does."

Malcolm picked up the page. "Dr. Warren Somersby? Who's this, then? He's got a military address. Serving somewhere? He's RAMC—a medic?"

Ruth snatched the paper from him. "Surgeon, actually." She placed the page down on the other side of the desk, heat rising to her cheeks.

"Surgeon? So, who? He doesn't share your surname, not family . . ."

"None of your concern," Ruth said, annoyed.

"Well, good luck with your letters. Send my regards to your military surgeon friend. I crossed paths myself with a rather good one in a small hospital in Norway. Now, I'm going to go get some terrible chips at the pub. I'll see you later."

Ruth waited till he had left the building and wrote an awkward letter to Warren at the RAMC HQ and provided her mailing address in Martynsborough. It was certainly overdue by many weeks, and she wondered if Warren was becoming impatient—she wasn't even sure where he was, as the letter would be forwarded to him by the military. Then, she wrote to Maude, saying, among other things,

> *This place is strange, possibly stranger than even you could have imagined. There are two rogue sheep who escaped the ministry cull roaming about, called Castor and Pollux. There is the legend of a ghostly girl in white—a wraith, as they call it here—who is said to haunt the streets at night. The story goes that she drowned in a flooded lime kiln many years before. I must confess, I might have seen this ghost myself!*
>
> *Oh, also, I work every day at a desk next to a sculptor with one eye and eight fingers.*

Ruth, who did not typically like early mornings, left with Johnny at the crack of dawn on bicycles. With a rifle slung over her shoulder, and in the cool, ruby glow of a frosted sunrise, they pedalled towards the pea field. There was a small patch of bramble that the farmer suggested as a blind, so they climbed into a thorny nest and waited; the birds would come in at dawn, so they were told, to gorge themselves on the farmer's peas.

"There," Johnny whispered and pointed upwards. Ruth raised the gun; she unleashed two shots into the sky. Both birds dropped. "You got them both! Brilliant shooting!" Johnny cried.

"Even when I'm half asleep, I still manage to put the lead into anything I point at. Perhaps Aunt Vera is right: it's something you're born with . . . or not."

Once back at the cottage, she hung the birds in the shed and then cleaned up to get ready for church. The four of them walked together, enjoying the morning air.

"Johnny, so nice to see you in your Sunday best," said Father Tweedsmuir as they approached the door. "And a good morning to you, ladies. I trust all is well at the Catchpoole cottage, Vera?"

"Oh yes," Vera said, her arm locked with Edith's.

"And here is Malcolm. Good morning to you." Ruth turned and saw that Malcolm, Elise, and Virginia had arrived. They exchanged an overlapping tangle of hellos and good mornings. Elise stood wordlessly next to Malcolm, wearing a dress of pale pink under a crimson-coloured coat with ermine trim. Her eyes, as always, were vacant. And as she had on a few other occasions, Ruth made direct eye contact with her, searching for something, anything—a flicker of awareness, a sign of sensibility, but found none. She remembered that day a few weeks before when Elise had watched her from the window and given Ruth such a start. She had seen her on more than one occasion since, yet there'd been nothing but a glazed stare. It was something that Ruth at first found unnerving—gazing into those bottomless cerulean pools, expecting to be confronted with a malicious glare as she had that day in the window, but it hadn't happened since then, and she hoped it wouldn't ever happen again.

"We've some birds for you," Vera said to Virginia. "Ruth has managed once again to outdo my shooting ability."

The church bell started clanging loudly, and the villagers hastened into the sanctuary to hear some much-needed assurance, given that the bombs had not stopped falling on English cities since the first week of September. With the success of the RAF and the ack-acks in knocking enemy bombers from the sky, Germany had moved exclusively to night-time raids, which seemed even worse.

At the end of the service, Ruth overheard some older congregants talking about the wraith. She approached them, pretending to study a stained-glass window, and listened to what they had to say. They, too, described a woman in white, lurking among the fields and roads at night—one mentioned seeing her by the mill. They grumbled that it was likely the evacuees waking up long-forgotten ghosts. They were genuinely frightened. Soon they noticed Ruth standing there; they glared, turned away, and lowered their voices.

Had these people seen Elise, slipping from the cottage at night to wander aimlessly, as Ruth suspected? Or was it something else? Ruth had never mentioned her suspicion to Malcolm; in fact, she felt uncomfortable talking about his wife in any way. Elise accompanied Malcolm to church every Sunday, and maybe due to some quaint, well-intentioned sense of courtesy, none of the congregants addressed her and instead generally treated her as an invisible being. Perhaps they simply didn't know what to say, so they chose to say nothing. Ruth had followed this example, too, and she certainly dared not speculate aloud that the woman might wander about at night frightening the villagers.

Ruth joined Vera and Edith as they stepped out into the crisp autumn sunshine. "Shall we walk by the river for a spell?" Vera asked. "The air is fine today, and the birds are all out singing. And for your benefit, Ruth, perhaps I'm putting off the chore of all the plucking we have to do this afternoon with nine pigeons to sort."

"Yes," Ruth said. "A walk is a grand idea."

"I can get things started at home," said Johnny, who began the trip back to the cottage. "See you, then."

"Virginia," Vera called out, "we're having a stroll by the river. Please join us. The air will do you well. Malcolm, you too." Soon, the three older women walked ahead, while Malcolm, Elise, and Ruth fell behind.

"I've heard talk of the wraith in the church today," Ruth said quietly from the side of her mouth.

"Oh?" Malcolm asked, his arm linked with Elise's, who stared ahead with no interest in their conversation.

"Seen by the mill, according to one of the village wrinklies I listened to."

"Fascinating," Malcolm said, turning his head to see Ruth with his good eye.

"The story has now spread beyond the walls of the pub—always a good sign that there may be some truth to it. I sensed real fear in them. A witch? A ghost? Something else? I'm very curious and, I have to admit, maybe even a little frightened myself."

"So, the mystery deepens, it would seem. And your novel? You've lots to write about now."

"I haven't had the time—though to be honest, it's getting started that is the hardest thing to do."

Before Malcolm could respond, Elise violently broke free from his arm and ran awkwardly down the road. She veered towards the path that led to the river.

"Elise!" Malcolm cried.

Ruth saw Castor and Pollux ahead, by the banks. Elise sprinted towards the animals, one of her shoes falling off in the process. Malcolm and Ruth chased after her. The three older women were startled as Elise passed them and made her way to the riverbank, stumbling after the sheep.

"She can't swim," Malcolm said frantically to Ruth as they raced towards Elise. Castor and Pollux were sure-footed and quick, and were well out of Elise's reach within moments. Off they went and disappeared into some deep grasses by the river. But she continued after them, her footing almost lost several times along the slippery stones on the bank, wearing only one shoe. Finally, Malcolm reached her and grabbed her arm as she was about to fall into the river, where a stout current twisted. She struggled with him violently, and the two of them went down in a flailing blur of limbs and blonde hair, falling to the wet clover by the pathway. Ruth eventually caught up, panting. By the time Malcolm stood and got Elise standing, Edith, Vera, and Virginia had arrived.

"Whatever happened?" Vera asked, handing Malcolm the errant shoe she'd picked up on the way. "Is everyone all right?"

"She saw the damn sheep," Malcolm said, breathing hard and brushing off his trousers. "I don't know why, but she's drawn to them and pursues them—fast, too, faster than I thought she could ever run. This is *not* the first time." Elise stood, leaning on Malcolm, and as much as she panted from the exertion, her eyes had returned to their usual empty stare. "If she'd gone in the river, with the current, I don't know what I'd have done. I'm not much the swimmer myself." He brushed Elise's stockings and slid the shoe back on her foot.

"Oh, this is all so terrible," Vera said. "Virginia, Malcolm, I feel so badly for you—it's all such a burden . . . such a burden."

"It's no fault of Elise's," he said through clenched teeth. "We've no idea what draws her to those animals, nor what she thinks, how she feels—she may hear and understand everything you say. She'll hear that she's a burden. To think how that might make someone feel—and this injury prevents her from defending herself. It makes a bad situation worse. What would you have me do? Lock her in the attic and forget about her? She's my wife."

"I'm truly sorry," Vera said, chastened. "It isn't what I meant, Malcolm—I understand it's been hard." She reached out and put a hand on his shoulder.

There was an awkward moment of silence, and then Malcolm said, "No, no, Vera, it's quite all right." He put his hand over hers and took a deep breath and exhaled. "I didn't mean to snap. I know you mean well. Please, let's get her home. It's been a lot of excitement for one day."

They all turned to go, and Ruth looked once more at Elise. For a moment, she thought she saw something in her eyes—a knowing look, a sharp alertness—but Ruth couldn't be sure, as it was gone in an instant.

-11-

As Johnny and Vera plucked feathers, Ruth scribbled notes for her book, trying to assemble a narrative loosely around the story of the lady in white, applying some of what she had heard in the church that morning. But she struggled, crumpling many sheets of her dwindling paper supply in frustration, getting nowhere with the novel she so desperately wanted to write. She thought to return to the pub and talk to the man who'd informed Ellen of the story originally. She couldn't envision herself accosting these men alone with a pencil and notebook. They'd been nothing short of hostile towards her to begin with. It would have to be handled delicately. She would need Malcolm with her.

Johnny called from downstairs that he was walking the pigeons to Virginia's cottage. Ruth dropped her pencil and leapt down the stairs.

"No, no, that's quite all right. I'll walk them over. You can help Vera in the garden." Johnny handed Ruth the birds—three of them—plucked and bound together with twine by their feet. She put on her coat and walked down the road, the sun now high enough that the air had lost its chill. She wavered there by the path with that same unexpected feeling that she should not cross onto the property, but gathered her courage and strode up to the door and knocked lightly.

Malcolm answered with a surprised expression on his face. Ruth held up the birds. "A gift." He stepped outside in stocking feet and pulled the door shut behind him. He'd not changed his clothing from church but had removed his jacket and tie. His top buttons were open, revealing a small tangle of chest hair.

"Thank you." Malcolm took the birds from her, eyeing them curiously.

"You're very welcome. Also, I wanted to apologize on behalf of Vera as well. I don't think she meant anything badly by what she said. I do hope that Elise is all right—not too shaken up by what happened?"

"The heat of the moment," said Malcolm. "I was upset; it was a fright. I didn't mean to snap at Vera. And well, thank you, by the way, for being so quick on your feet." He took a deep breath and looked at Ruth squarely. "I know what this all must seem to people—yourself included." He glanced briefly over his shoulder and whispered, "I act as if there's nothing wrong, yet I arrive at church with a woman on my arm who says nothing and acts half-dead to the world, as if she were sleepwalking. I'm sure you've . . . you've been informed of the situation, what happened to her—"

"As you know, there are no secrets in a small village."

"Yes, well, you didn't know Elise before . . . before the injury. She was full of life, kind, and she was always singing. We had wished to have children." Malcolm stopped speaking abruptly, as if he had said too much, then he sighed. "Even after all this time, it is so very strange for me to see her like this—to you and others who didn't know her before, perhaps not, but for me . . . well . . . perhaps this is why I was so upset with Vera—although I know she didn't mean any harm. For now, anyway, there are some things I'd rather not talk about, I don't think I'm ready to, but I appreciate your concern . . . and the apology."

"I'm glad to help in any way I can." Ruth felt a happy relief to finally discuss this unspoken thing. "Well, I hope you enjoy the pigeons." She turned to leave. "Oh, also I'm struggling with the book. I was thinking of talking to this fellow in the pub, the one who told Ellen the story. I'd like it if maybe you were there with me—some moral support if I talk to this man or any other villagers in general. They don't seem terribly friendly with us evacuees to begin with. You seemed like you might also be interested yourself a little . . . I'd hate to be alone."

"Yes, yes, of course. We can talk about it tomorrow." They stood there for a long, wavering moment, one grasping dead birds, and the other warm and flushed. Finally, he said, "Well, goodnight." He stepped backwards into his house and shut the door. Ruth turned and walked back to the road. She threw her coat over her shoulder and noticed her armpits had half-moons of dark sweat staining her blouse.

At dinner that night, Edith asked, "Have you heard from Warren? You've written him, have you not?"

"Yes, sent away a letter some time ago. There's been no response. I'm not sure what to make of it."

"Perhaps he's been assigned duty abroad—he could be on a destroyer in the Atlantic," said Vera.

"No, no, I don't think so." Edith placed her fork down. "He's a surgeon. He'll not be found in the bowels of a ship. Ruth, you've provided the correct information so he can write you back here in Martynsborough?"

"Of course I have," Ruth said, knowing that she had been tempted to alter the post details, to hide herself in the village, but she could not bring herself to do so. Either way, she had not heard from him, and for Ruth, this was happy news. As much as she did not wish him harm, she did indeed cling to the notion that he was very far away at that moment.

Malcolm and Ruth planned to go to the pub the following Friday evening to ask about the wraith. Till that time, they walked home together at the end of each day, as they'd grown accustomed to. They spoke about this or that, but the subject of Elise did not come up again, nor did they see Castor and Pollux that week, and instead they walked in friendly silence, or, if the mood suited, they spoke of their creative pursuits. Sometimes their conversations became a little heated, as they were both passionate about their chosen vocation, but never unfriendly.

Malcolm brought up the French sculptor Auguste Rodin repeatedly and how, with respect to fine arts, England lacked anything close to what he had seen in France.

"We English aren't so bad," Ruth countered. "At least we've got the writing bit down—fellow by the name of Shakespeare, right? It seems everyone I know who spends a week or two on the Continent comes back crowing about how enlightened the French and the Italians are, how liberated they all are—smoking opium, frolicking on the beaches stark naked, having wild orgies."

"I'm not talking about pale, silly English people on the beach in Marseilles. It's Rodin! Ruth, it's all about him!"

"I've only ever seen one of his sculptures—*The Kiss*, at the Tate," said Ruth. "It was rather unlike the statues from the antiquity sections. No, it's much more, hmm, realistic maybe? No, not realistic, but there's something less idealized, perhaps—modern. I do recall the male figure—his hand, very large, grasping the thigh of the woman."

"No, not grasping," Malcolm said, "merely touching—resting there so that she is free to move where she wishes." He stopped and closed his eyes, visualizing it. "The woman," he said, "she gathers her arms about his neck and seems to pull the man towards her; she's an equal participant—not some demure woman being taken up by the hero, where the act of love is merely dutiful—maybe even repugnant. No, no, in *The Kiss*, the female figure actively seeks the male." Malcolm opened his eyes and brought a hand to his mouth dramatically. "Their lips, incidentally, don't actually touch. A hair's breadth separates them as they linger closely in anticipation."

"A statue titled *The Kiss*, in which the figures are not kissing."

"Yes, Ruth! Yes! Sometimes the imagination of a thing can have more gravity than the thing itself; the promise of a kiss as opposed to the act—between that space, that hair's breadth, one can find truth, Truth with a capital *T*! Either way, it should seem somewhat familiar to you—if you look closely, you'll see the male figure holds a book in his other hand. You might know it, given that this couple are a depiction of famous literary characters—which is more about your studies."

"Really? I didn't know that." They started walking once more, Ruth's bicycle clicking pleasantly as she pushed it along.

"Yes," Malcolm said, "the woman is Francesca, as mentioned in Dante's *Divine Comedy*, married unhappily. She pursues an adulterous affair with her husband's brother."

"Paolo—yes, and they're discovered in the act by the jealous husband, who kills them both."

"You know it, then."

"Oh yes—Dante has them imprisoned in the second ring of the inferno, a place reserved for the lustful, swept up in a whirlwind that circles the underworld." Ruth laughed. "Which is not so bad a punishment, I'd think. They'll spend eternity together."

"And what of the murderer? Will he receive the same punishment?"

"No, no—that's not right," said Ruth. "I think he'll be much further down into the inferno than Francesca and her lover, in ring number seven, I believe, which is so much worse than ring number two. It's where the damned are boiled for eternity in a lake of blood."

"Gruesome. And what's at the very bottom? I recall there are nine rings, are there not? What could possibly be worse than murderers in boiling blood?"

"Yes, nine, I believe—but at ring number nine there's ice; it's cold, and there you'll find Cain, as in Cain and Abel, and of course Judas Iscariot—so maybe the sin of treachery—or betrayal—is for level number nine. Betrayal is the worst of the sins."

"Wouldn't Francesca be qualified as a betrayer, then?" Malcolm asked. "She betrayed her husband, did she not? But she gets to flit about in the second circle with her lover."

"Hmm. Well, there's a moral element to it all; Francesca was compelled to betray her husband, and she'd been deceived into the original marriage. With Paolo, it was indeed true love, which could be seen as virtuous—a different thing altogether than Judas betraying Christ. There is nuance to the inferno, and it would follow that there's nuance to the sins themselves perhaps—something may appear bad but is, in fact, good."

"Oh, such sophistry, Ruth. And I suppose the devil himself would be somewhere at the bottom, among the worst of the damned, sorting out these rules and regulations."

"No, the devil is himself being punished," she said. "I believe it's God who makes those rules." They walked in silence for another quarter-mile and soon arrived at Virginia's cottage. "Well, have a good night."

"Goodnight." He turned up the path.

Ruth stopped, remembering something. "How were the pigeons?"

Malcolm turned and cocked his head so that he could see her with his good eye. "Wonderful, Ruth. They were wonderful—they tasted of peas!"

The days were getting shorter, and the blackouts were up by the dinner hour. They turned the electric light off, and a kerosene lamp on the table burned during the meal—Vera had been told by the Home Guard to use the electric light only when washing up or cooking. It was dim but cosy. With the bite of the autumn chill, the house did not seem as stuffy as when Ruth first arrived, and the flickering flame of the lamp felt romantic in a way. They ate soup made from the bones of duck and rabbit, along with fluffy dumplings.

"I'll be going to the pub tomorrow after my day at the hall," Ruth said. "I'm doing a little research among the villagers for the novel I'm working on."

"A novel?" Edith asked. "Is this to do with your schoolwork? It doesn't sound very scholarly."

"Well, no, this is personal writing. And for the record, Gran, novels can be quite brilliant. Some say that it's the perfect medium for the modern age."

"So," Vera said, the spoon halfway to her mouth, "tell us about your novel, then."

"It will be a ghost story," Ruth said. "Isn't it exciting? I've not really talked too much about it, but maybe you know about this, Vera—the legend of the lady in white roaming the streets of Martynsborough? The wraith? Supposedly, some thirty years ago. The drowning in the kiln pond? You were living here then, weren't you?"

"Oh, well, let me see." Vera glanced at Edith and put her spoon down. "What are we saying, then? In and around 1910, perhaps? Yes, a good question—Edith, what *were* we doing?" She glanced once more at Edith, who did not respond. Vera continued, "Well, that was the year of Halley's Comet. No, I wasn't here but in a nearby town. Didn't come back to Martynsborough to live till after my husband died in, oh, I suppose 1918, yes."

"*Back* to Martynsborough? Returned? So, you lived here before? I don't understand," Ruth said.

"Hmm. Well, no—or . . . yes, or you know . . . we summered here when we were young, that is certain. Yes, and well, later, William and I moved about quite a bit then."

"So then, you wouldn't know about the legend?"

"Legend? I don't think there's really a legend to speak of. Nonsense from the pub. You know how things can be in small villages." She took a sip from her glass and lingered over it, then said, "I'd counter that every village has its ghosts. Word spreads, and something that is once dreamt up becomes real."

"I've heard something or other," Johnny said, sitting at the head of the table, his mouth full.

"Oh?" Ruth turned her attention to the boy.

"Yes, I heard the farmers talking. S-s-someone'd seen something or other. One of the objectors, he'd seen something in the field. I heard him talking about a lady who seemed lost, wandering the flax field."

"Yes, that's what I heard in the pub, too," Ruth said. "It's what's spurred the whole thing. Ellen, the publican, she told me that the man fell asleep in the field and saw her in the morning. Is this the same story, Johnny?"

"Yes, but there was more," Johnny said as he dug about in his soup for another dumpling. "A girl in white was seen in a tree—an apple tree, I think."

"A tree?" Ruth asked. "Well, now it's getting very strange."

"Yes, that's what another one of them workers says to me the other day. He was walking back to the barracks, sometime at night, after being at the pub. There's a path there, and he saw a girl or a woman, wearing a white dress—had a veil or hood of some kind about her head, so he couldn't see her face—coming down from the tree she was, floating like a fairy, like a ghost, you see."

"Or perhaps hanged? Like a witch?" Ruth said, thinking of what Maude had said about the history of witchcraft in Lancashire.

"Well, I don't know so much about that. But he was just telling us this morning about it. The objectors and workers that the ministry brought in, well, they're all laughing at him, said he was drunk and seeing things, but a fellow who grew up in Martynsborough, he wasn't laughing, not one bit."

"What did he say?" Ruth asked. Johnny pushed a dumpling into his mouth and seemed to swallow it whole before he spoke again.

"Nothing. That's the thing. Most of the workers—well, they're laughing all along, but this man, well, he didn't laugh, no. In fact, h-h-he said nothing for the rest of the day and seemed out of sorts—maybe even a little bit scared."

"This kind of nonsense happens regularly in the country," Vera said, with a small but discernible edge to her voice, "especially when the men in the pub are involved, if you know what I mean. I've heard nothing from Virginia. She's not mentioned this to me since I've known her. She's lived here the whole of her life as far as I know. Feel free to write a wonderful story, Ruth, but you'll find nothing of interest here but fanciful claptrap."

"Well, maybe Virginia is a good place to start with my interviewing," Ruth said. "I'd never thought to talk to her."

"Mind yourself, Ruth; they've enough trouble in that household without eager Girton girls asking about some ancient village history," Vera warned.

"Oh, it's quite all right," Ruth said. "Malcolm knows all about the legend from our lunch at the pub—we've been discussing it. He's offered to help me with the research."

Edith, who had yet to add anything, frowned. "Ruth, I'd mind that, too."

"Oh, Edith, ever the worrier," said Vera sharply. "Ghostly legends notwithstanding, they're merely friends."

"She is engaged, Vera . . . while *he* is married. What would Ruth's mama think of her cavorting in the pubs with strange men? I'll be blamed if there's trouble—I will. I'll never hear the end of it."

"Gran," Ruth said, with a small huff, "please, don't. Mama is not here . . . We're only friends."

"You hear that, Edith? *Friends*—friends and nothing more," Vera chided. "Do you not recall how when we were young, unmarried men and women would link their elbows, walking arm in arm without a thought to scandal? Women would dance with men who were not their husbands. Have you gone backwards with your attitudes? My goodness, you've become prim and worrisome with so much time spent in the smoke of London. Whatever happened to my dear old wild-at-heart *Kate*?" Vera reached out and put her hand over Edith's.

"Kate?" Ruth asked. "Who's Kate?"

"I am Kate," Edith said with a kind of exasperation, taking her hand away from Vera. "It's what she called me when . . . when we were young."

"That's right," said Vera, "and I was Doll."

"Must you bring this up?" Edith sighed. "I've not heard that in a long time." She looked down at her bowl.

"Doll?" Ruth laughed with delight. "Kate and Doll? Why did you call each other that?" The two older women looked at one another for a long moment. Vera raised a finger to her mouth, indicating that she would speak.

"Edith and I had small, rather old-fashioned dolls when we were little," Vera said. "I named mine Kate—short for Katherine—a name I've always loved. Edith's was simply named Doll, which I suppose is not terribly creative, but your gran has always been the practical one."

"Hmm, yes, the dolls—that's right . . . we cherished them," Edith said with a smile. "There were very few toys then, even for fortunate children like us, and we were inseparable from the things—loved them dearly."

"We were not so rich that we had the benefit of our own rooms from the beginning, so for a time, we shared a bed when we were very small. There were other bedrooms reserved for guests whom Father had regularly, so it was not unlike our arrangement right now in this cottage."

"Yes," said Edith with wistful eyes, "I do recall. How fine your memory is, Vera."

"We quite liked being close," Vera continued, "but eventually our father told us that we were getting more grown up and needed our own rooms, and there weren't so many guests coming around any longer. We were unhappy about the whole thing, so on the first night we were to be separated, Father had fires put in the hearths of each of our rooms, which made them warm and cosy, perhaps to help us get used to the idea. That evening, standing in the corridor, wearing our nightdresses and gowns, we said goodnight to each other—quite distressed and sad, sad that we had to grow up, sad to be alone, sad that something that was so very fine as it was, something so very good, had to change for reasons that we didn't quite understand. Edith suggested we switch our dolls, so that we could pretend that we were still with our sister. I brought Doll into bed with me."

"Yes, oh yes, that's right—and I brought Kate," Edith said.

"We'd feel like we were still together. Then, in the morning, we would return the dolls to the rightful owner. Soon, we started calling each other by the other's doll name, for fun—Doll and Kate." The two women looked once more to each other, a glance that suggested a thousand untold stories, and Ruth felt a longing herself, to have a sibling, a sister to confide in and love.

They had not noticed that at the head of the table Johnny had stopped eating, and his eyes were glistening a little. Vera looked to him and sighed loudly. "Oh, dear Johnny, what ever are we thinking?" She got up from her chair and went to the boy. "We're blathering on about sisterly love, and I've forgotten that you're separated from your own brother. There, there, this war will be over by Christmas, and we'll all be reunited with our loved ones. Till then, we'll be your family."

Johnny sniffed. "Maybe if we find Jude, he can stay here, too?"

"Of course, Johnny." Vera began clearing empty dishes from the table. "There's plenty of room—you can share your room with your brother, like Kate and Doll once did."

Malcolm looked up as the clock approached half-past four and said under his breath, "I'm still a little unclear on our plan of attack. Are we to walk up to the man in the pub and start asking questions?"

"I'm not sure, to be honest," said Ruth, closing the ledger books for the day. "I'd have thought you'd come up with some plan by now on my behalf."

"Huh." Malcolm paused. "Well, I suppose the first thing we do is go to the pub—perhaps the plan will reveal itself. Maybe if we buy a few rounds for the locals, they'll be more keen on chatting with us. We've received nothing but withering glares up till now."

"Yes, I've noticed." Ruth tied her scarf smartly around her head. "I think it's going to be Ellen who helps us along." She took up her purse and glanced at him briefly. "If you don't mind me saying, it might help a little if . . . hmm . . . if you actually smile occasionally? I know you've got it in you. I myself have seen it. So, please spread a little cheer with Ellen, with the villagers, lest you get a reputation for being a dour, cross townie. They'll not want to talk to either of us."

"Huh." Malcolm forced an insincere smile, which appeared like a rictus of annoyance. "How's this?" he said through gritted teeth.

"You'll have to do better than that, I'm afraid. Come, let's go."

They arrived at the pub, and it being Friday, there were more than the usual men gathered around tables, and given the large group, the clinking of cutlery, and the warm murmurings of multiple conversations, Ruth felt less scrutinized by the villagers than she had on previous visits. Indeed, there were women this night, come with their husbands, older married couples, or, in some cases, women without men—their spouses gone to war, far away in Africa, or Italy, or on a frigate somewhere, maybe already dead at the bottom of the Atlantic. They wore hats and heels, sipping demurely from small glasses—cider and port, which was only available one day a week. A few younger farmhands and objectors gathered at another table, their rough, calloused hands grasping cool glasses, the hard day's work showing in their weary faces and lack of conversation. A collection of older men, the ones most drawn to warmth, sat close to the hearth, and at another table sat one with a guitar resting in his lap and a fiddle atop the table. The smell of suet, boiled potatoes, and crisping toast drifted out from the kitchen door.

"There'll be music?" Ruth asked, as she approached the bar. "There's some instruments, I see."

Ellen looked up from her taps with a smile.

"Indeed, Miss Ruth, 'tis Friday, a day that we like to have supper out of the house—busy for me, and lax for the rest!"

"Will the musicians play?"

"Oh yes, after dinner no doubt they'll be tuning up the strings. Cora Dunn sitting over there, she'll sing quite sweetly for you."

"Oh, it's brilliant," Ruth said with delight. "I hadn't expected this."

"You're having a meal with us tonight?" Ellen asked.

"Yes, I suppose." Ruth lowered her voice a little, "Ellen, may I ask something a little unusual? I would like to talk to this man about . . ." She glanced at Malcolm briefly, who nodded in encouragement. "Like I said before, one of the things I thought to do during my time in Martynsborough was to write a book. I study literature, and I love books; in fact, I think it might be an unhealthy obsession." Ellen slid two pint glasses in front of them wordlessly while Ruth continued. "I'd like to learn a little bit more about this legend we talked about before, the lady in white—do you recall?"

"Ah, the wraith. Yes, I do recall."

"Well, as you see, I've brought some paper and a pencil, and I thought I might talk to the chap who knows the story from when he was young. I've brought Malcolm along, too; he's also interested."

"A couple of townie scholars asking about the village ghost," Ellen said with a wry grin. "I'm not sure how that'll go over with this lot. The fellow you wish to speak with is there by the hearth, the one with the red trouser braces, name of Albert. Your answers are in this room, you've just got to pull them out like so many rotten teeth." She laughed. "Brought good pliers, I hope? But first, eat. A plate'll be 4p. Get something in you, and then later, you can settle around the fire and try your luck."

They ate, and the fire crackled in the hearth. Ellen came around and cleared the plates, and a few empty chairs at the tables by the fireplace provided an opportunity. Ruth and Malcolm approached, intending to sit near Albert and some of the other older men, who had themselves finished eating. They looked up with startled expressions as Ruth and Malcolm sat.

"Hello, I thought perhaps we'd introduce ourselves a little more officially. I'm Ruth Gladstone, this is my friend Malcolm."

"Staying at Vera's cottage," said Albert with the red trouser braces. "You've got a boy staying with you from the flax farm. You're quite the bird shot. And you"—he turned to Malcolm—"in Virgie's cottage. French wife. Seen service. Both of you, proper educations. From the city. You work with Horgon, pushing papers."

"Well, yes," Ruth said. "That's right." She smiled. "Nothing goes unnoticed in a place so small, I suppose. I was wondering if we could ask you about the legend here in the village, about the girl in the kiln pond . . . the ghost, as I've heard."

There was a lingering silence. The men continued with their unfriendly airs and then seemed to turn their attention to Malcolm's left hand.

"We'd like to know about this fellow's hand. In France you were, then, come out at Dunkirk?"

"No, actually. It was Norway," Malcolm said. "The 148th Brigade."

"Aye, tell us."

"There's nothing much to say—shrapnel from a bomb during a raid in a small town. A country surgeon cleaned me up. My eye was grazed.

Discharged honourably." The men seemed slightly disappointed in his war story.

"Let's have a song, then," said Albert, "and maybe we'll talk about the lady in white for a wee bit." The musicians took up their instruments and began to play—a robust, bouncing melody that immediately changed the mood of the room from one of quiet contemplation to gaiety.

"It's getting late," Ruth said as the song ended. "The music has been wonderful, but I can't stay too much longer."

Albert looked up from his drink, and he seemed to remember Ruth and Malcolm sitting at the table. "Aye, I suppose I owe you a story," he said as Ruth readied her notepad. "Now, I'll tell you about a very strange day in 1910."

Albert took an inordinate amount of time relighting his pipe, while Ruth's pencil wavered impatiently over the paper. "So, think back to thirty years prior, for which there dawned a chilly December morn," he began, "the cold-but-good kind, for which the rising sun cut through the damp fields, and the chill air had refrozen that sagging ice and snow from the previous night's rain, making all things clean and a land that seemed to sparkle." He paused, and Ruth was immediately delighted by his excellent ability to set a scene.

"I was already up, puttering about over my tea," he continued, "when there was a knock on the door, followed by a racket of hollering from outside. 'Albert! I've seen the worst thing!' I hear. Then I opened the door to find the sickly face of my old friend. He says to me, out of breath, 'A girl, last night, I seen a girl in the lime-kiln pond. Dead she was—murdered, I think!' I then said to my friend, 'What on earth were you doing up there last night? I'd think it would be the last place on earth anyone would like to be in such horrible weather.'

"Well, it seems Phineas had voluntarily gone to that awful place. He says that he'd gone up to see Wolstenholme, a bad idea if I've ever heard one, but I did confirm, as one always should, that he didn't go anywhere near that awful glasshouse."

At this point, Albert stopped speaking, and there were murmurs amongst the older villagers in the pub, who were now keenly listening to the story themselves. A few nodded their heads, and Ruth heard several of the others mumbling, "Aye" and "Don't go there" and "Stay away from there!" She made a note to follow up on this strange mention of the conservatory but said nothing, afraid she might interrupt Albert's momentum. After the men in the pub quieted down once more, Albert took a draw from his pipe and continued.

"Phineas says to me, 'I did go there indeed. It was most dire; I'd nowhere else to turn. But I must say, I didn't go in the glasshouse, though—don't you worry.' So, then, I say to him, 'Why did you go up there to talk to the old man?' 'Never you mind why I went,' he says. 'What's important is that there was a girl there in the pond. I've not acted quickly enough, I'm afraid. I run home, I did, then into bed, frightened and cold, and I fell into an awful, unrousable kind of sleep. I'd some brandywine the old man had given me from the good decanter. Maybe something else or other—something sinister slipped in the drink. It set me down on the quilt like Sleeping Beauty, and now, now we must go back!'

"I certainly had no idea what he was going on about, and let me say, that sounded all terribly unlikely. 'Back where?' I asked. Phineas was quick to reply, 'Back to the blasted ponds, where you'll find the body of a girl, and then we'll call up the law officer in Clitheroe and haul that damn Blackwell and Wolstenholme himself off to prison.'

"Well, let's just say, I had no interest in traipsing about on the Wolstenholme estate, nor did I particularly believe the spectres of Phineas's confused brain, but nevertheless, we decided to go with two other local men, equipped with coils of rope and guns. Up we went, unsure what we might find and equally unsure of what we'd do when we found whatever that was. So, soon enough, we arrived at the kiln ponds with a cold blue sky above us. To Phineas, it all seemed less terrible with the sun shining bright, and the frozen ground firm beneath his feet. And the ponds themselves? Empty—save for a fragile skin of ice, looking all the world like a sheet of darkened glass. Phineas stood before us dumbfounded.

"'So, where is she, then?' I asked, starting to think I was on a fool's errand. I broke up the thin ice with the heel of my boot and asked him again.

"'She was there.' Phineas pointed. 'Right there in the blessed water, the north pond.'

"I certainly didn't see anything myself. I felt I ought to humour my poor friend. I said, 'Bring the rope, then; let's see what we can find.' The other men brought the rope and tied various knots to make a type of seine netting. They lowered it, and down, down it went, much deeper than we thought a pond could be. The waters grew cloudy as we stirred up the mud at the bottom—browns and greys and blacks mingling together like a pint of stout, like a witch's brew. Then when we were satisfied with the depth, we started hauling. To our dismay, it was quite heavy. We grunted, horrified with the knowledge that surely something—or someone—was within the ropes. But after much work and toil, we pulled forth nothing more than the tangled remnants of a wheat thrasher's front end, its rusted blades caught up with thick heapings of mud. I'll say it was a relief not to see the sad remains of a girl there as we pulled the thing out of the pond and dumped it to the side. 'No girl here, old rubbish,' I said.

"'Again!' Phineas cries to us. 'She's surely there.'

"So, for three-quarters of an ugly hour, and then another hour, then more, we men pulled up broken farm equipment, horse bones, chunks of crumbling limestone, and the tires of an Edwardian motor car, but no girl in white, that's for certain. After a spell, stopping to take a breath, I looked around, and I could see we'd made a proper wreck of the place with our muddy boot prints and all the rubbish we'd pulled from the water. I got to thinking that someone was not going to be pleased with this fine mess, and as if the devil himself had read my thoughts, a stern bark came from the wood.

"'You! What do you think you're doing? This is private land, and I've every right to shoot you all.' And there he was, the infamous steward of Wolstenholme, Mr. Blackwell himself, standing at the edge of the path, as broad as he was tall, like a crooked gravestone dressed in an undertaker's cloak. His hair was thick and inky like a wolfhound's, pushed back from his pale face, square as a die. He held a double-barrelled elephant gun, its muzzle trained directly at this humble narrator's skull. He was most unpleased and roared at us, 'What in the name of Beelzebub are you fools doing?' He turned and saw Phineas. 'And you! You were our guest just this last evening, and now you've brought a rabble of your foolish friends to poke about the ponds—and rifles, I see. It's poaching, then. I'll shoot you dead right where you stand as a poacher, as a trespasser on this land—according to the law, I have the right. I've sent away an entire wagon train of gypsy Travellers two days past. At least a hundred tasted my wrath, so you'll be little trouble for me.'

"So, then I said with the softest voice I could muster, 'Mr. Blackwell, we've come on a rescue mission is all—no interest in pheasants or woodcock, but a girl. Our friend here says he saw such a girl in distress this past evening on his way home from visiting the house as you've mentioned. Here she was, in one of the ponds.'

"So, let me just remind you all here who don't know him that Blackwell is no slouch—he is not afraid to use that great, fat gun of his. And knowing full well that any moment I might be riddled with lead shot, I knew my next words had to be chosen very carefully. So I say, 'He's come to tell us this morning, you see, about the trouble with this girl, and I'm afraid for reasons of haste, we've come straight here without providing your boss the benefit of knowing our plans. We'd every intention of coming to the main house first, as has been the way before, but given the severity of the *situation*, we came to the ponds immediately.'

"To my dismay, Blackwell did not move the rifle from my head for long and nasty seconds, then he swung it over to Phineas, then back at me. He says, 'Well, as you can see, there is no girl here; in fact, all I see is a terrible muddle that you've created yourselves around the ponds. Leave this place now, or else it will be you who are found floating dead in the water.'

"So, we men left, while I scolded Phineas the whole way. He seemed confused and kept his mouth shut. We reached the town and went our separate ways, to clean our boots and warm ourselves by the fire and tend to the things that we would have normally tended to if we hadn't been dragged away with what seemed like good intentions on to the lands of Wolstenholme. At the very least, we'd provided that glasshouse a very wide berth—of that we could be sure."

Albert paused here and tapped out his pipe, seeming to relish his own story and the listeners who were rapt with it. The pub had gone dead silent as he spoke, with only the occasional clink of a mug or whoosh of a matchstick igniting someone's cigarette. Albert then relit his own pipe with a flourish; it was a small ritual that carried the same old-fashioned cadence that his yarn thus far had followed. Finally, he spoke again.

"Later that night, after several settling drinks at the pub, as he told me later, Phineas walked home and saw that girl once more—the girl he assumed dead. There she was, walking along the side of the road on the other side of the lock. She stepped through swaying grass, her hands grazing it. Her face, as white and round as the moon, her hair pale gold. I could just picture him, trying to catch his breath and watching in disbelief—a ghost, surely, a wraith had come to curse the village, to curse Phineas himself for sleeping the night away while a girl lay face down in the cold, black water of the kiln pond. Fearing that no one would believe him—especially after all that happened at that afternoon—he turned, and as quietly as he could, he retraced his steps to the pub. He burst in. 'I've seen her. She's come to life—a ghost, a wraith—come back to haunt me for failing to save her!' he cries. Of course, I'd have none of it.

"'Poppycock. You've got me in enough trouble today,' I said to him.

"'Come, she's not a moment's trot by the field on the road,' he pleads with me. 'She's likely still there!'

"So, I tapped out my pipe and said, 'Very well, I was leaving any-way—if it will set your head straight. Let's go look at an empty field.'

"We walked along, Phineas quickly, with me not far behind. He stopped ahead at a particularly dark bit of road and looked around. 'I swear she was here,' he said.

"'Aye, this is no surprise. Let's get you home; you're clearly not well.' As the last word left my mouth, I saw something. There, back the way we'd come, was a large oak tree, a dark and gnarled thing by the side of the road, and on the trunk of that oak tree there was a thin white hand. It grasped the wrinkled bark, with a bit of white sleeve rustling about the wrist. To whom—or to what—the hand was affixed, I couldn't see, for the rest of the figure lurked in the shadows. 'Shush, shush,' I said, and took my friend by the shoulder, turned him, and drew him down-ward, till we both crouched by the side of the road behind tall grass. 'There, the oak. Look,' I whispered as quietly as I could. The mysterious white hand withdrew into the darkness, and then in all holy truth, that figure herself, in full form, stepped out from the shadows. She took a step or two into a pool of silver moonlight. We could not see her face clearly, as her long, unkempt hair concealed it. She seemed to look our way, then turned, with a ghostly kind of elegance, and vanished once more behind the tree. 'I can't believe it,' I muttered. 'It can't be. We should go investigate, shouldn't we?'

"Phineas's face had gone white as a sheet, and he said, 'I'd rather do anything than go over there.' Phineas started walking briskly away from the oak tree, towards his house. Then, I stood and, looking back once more, saw a shimmer of white pass amongst the shadows, and my heart filled with such dread that within moments I had caught up with my friend, walking quickly, almost at a run, till we arrived at the junction of streets that led to the cottages in which we lived.

"'Phineas, please wait a moment.' I put my hand on my friend's shoulder. 'I'm not sure if we've drunk some ale that's gone off, but I don't think we should draw any conclusions about what we saw till we've had a proper night's sleep. It's been a strange day.'

"'Oh, indeed it has. Goodnight.' And Phineas ran as fast as he could to his cottage while I turned and walked briskly in the opposite direction to do the same.

"The next day, we met in the morning sunshine. It had been an awful night of tossing and turning and imagining vengeful wraiths scratching bony fingernails against the glass. In the comforting glow of day, we walked together, discussing the matter, thinking to go to the guild hall to broach it with some of the village magistrates. When we arrived there, we discovered that others had also seen something. It seemed Phineas's story had spread around Martynsborough, and there was much talk of murdered young women, and in the night, others claimed to have seen a ghostly figure in white prowling about the village. One sighting near to the mill, and others in the field by the Wynan Beck. The following day, more people saw her—only at night—and soon a small panic overtook the town. It had been early December and generally mild, the kind of meek winter weather we'd normally enjoy, but for a fortnight, the pub lay empty, and people locked themselves in their cottages after the sun set, cowering by their hearths. It wasn't until the snow came and there had been no sightings for some weeks that we dared venture outside at night once more. Thereafter, no one reported seeing the strange girl in white—except for Phineas, who saw her many times thereafter.

"Since then, people rarely speak of the lady in white. We here in Martynsborough assumed that whatever she was—witch, wraith, or devil—she was gone for good.

"Of course, we've learned that this is not the case, for here she is once more, thirty years later, stirred up perhaps by the brash voices and clamorous heels of unwelcome outsiders."

- 13 -

Albert stopped speaking and tapped out his pipe. The fire burned low, and for some moments no one spoke. The last sentence hung in the air with a flavour of accusation, and Ruth dared not respond. Eventually Ellen broke through the fragile silence. "Another round, then?"

"I think I am finished speaking for the night," Albert said as he buttoned up his coat. "I don't care to add anything to the tale. You've got your story now, miss, so goodnight to ye." Albert stood and pushed out his chair, while several of the other older men did the same. Cora Dunn glanced at Ruth with an expression of sympathy, before she herself rose, and the village elders left the Yellow Rattle.

"Well, I hope you've found some answers to your questions," Ellen said as she removed empty glasses from tables. "A most peculiar story—even I'll agree with that." She placed a hand on Ruth's shoulder, and quietly said, "Try not to read too deeply into their salty tone. Villagers are always wary of outsiders."

So, with only the dregs left in the bottom of their glasses, Malcolm and Ruth had little else to do but say goodnight and head home. As they walked down the road, Ruth realized that maybe she had drunk too much. Whilst seated, it wasn't so obvious, but on her feet, the horizon swam before her eyes. She looked up to the moon for her bearings.

It was high and fat and glowed in that eerie way of autumn—peering through skeletal tree branches and hiding among slow-moving clouds.

"There's a lot to digest from tonight," she said.

"Yes," said Malcolm. "I've got a thousand and one questions about Albert's tale, including this Wolstenholme estate. What the devil could possibly be in that glass conservatory that frightens them? That's what I'd first like to learn."

"Yes, very curious." Ruth looked down and watched her feet on the ground as they took one step after another. The rocking rhythm of her boots on the gravel lulled her, and she felt that she could fall asleep in midstride. She looked over at Malcolm, who had turned up his collar in the cool night air and appeared to be lost in his own reflections.

"If she's not a ghost, then what is she?" Her voice sounded unnaturally loud to her own ears.

Malcolm stopped, his hands thrust in his pockets.

"I've no idea. Like I said, it could be some collective mania—one person tells a harrowing story, another hears it, someone mistakes one thing for another. The nights are long and dark, and a wraith emerges from the village's imagination. Or . . ." He paused. "There's something going on up there." He spun on his heel, the gravel crunching under his boot, and looked out at the spine of the escarpment rising from the blue-black horizon. "There's something not right about that estate. It's spooky. Even seeing it here on this road, in the shadow of the escarpment, I feel something is out of place . . . It would be quite the thing to visit, especially after dark. At the very least, I'd like to have a look at the lime-kiln ponds. I am curious."

"Yes, as am I." They began walking again, and Ruth stumbled a little bit. He reached out to steady her. "I think I've had a bit too much tonight." An owl hooted from somewhere in the hedge, unnervingly loud. "It would be frightful to sleep out here—it seems a particularly eerie evening, with Halloween and Bonfire Night so soon, and my thoughts are twisted and tangled with the story I've heard."

Malcolm looked closely at her for a moment. "You know, I've never mentioned it before. You've a peculiar way of speaking."

"How so?"

"It's almost as if your tongue—if you don't mind my saying—your tongue is struggling to break free from your mouth. It's rather subtle—I hadn't really noticed before."

"Yes, it's on account of my rhotacism." Ruth blushed.

"Your what?"

"I've trouble with my speech. My tongue—as my childhood doctor told me—it's slightly too large for my mouth. I've been taught habits of saying things a certain way to minimize its effect. So, in a way, yes, I suppose it would seem like my tongue is trying to get away from me. To be honest, it's rather embarrassing. I didn't think it was noticeable."

"No, no, not really noticeable—I hadn't noticed really till now. Perhaps the drink . . ."

"Yes, if I've been drinking, my *r*'s tend to become more like *w*'s. It's true. I'm sorry."

"Don't apologize. I like it," Malcolm said. "I'm not sure why, but I do."

"It's odd that we're speaking so much of my tongue. It seems almost obscene." She laughed, trying to make light of it.

"No, not at all," he countered.

The wind picked up, and the dark rye fields rustled and shivered around them. Ruth wanted nothing more than to be in her warm bed under the quilts, and she momentarily thought what it might be like to be alone on the road on a blustery autumn night with thoughts of eerie wraiths moving about. She felt an overwhelming urge to reach out and take Malcolm's hand, but she didn't . . . she couldn't. As Vera had said, in the distant past, unmarried men and women walked together, arm in arm, as friends and friends alone. Back then, in some early day of yore, they had thought nothing untoward of it. Yet, here in the modern age—1940—to even entertain the idea of sliding her arm around

Malcolm's was unthinkable, although she so very much wanted to. She continued onward, one clumsy foot in front of the other, until they saw the blue shadow of Virginia's cottage.

"Well, goodnight," she said.

"I'll walk you to your door, for pity's sake. I won't let you wander the dark road at night."

"I'm quite fine."

"Even with talk of wraiths? Or surly rams?"

"Well . . . yes, I suppose it would be nice to have company to my door." They continued walking. "Do you recall the first time we met?" Ruth asked.

"Yes."

"On this very road. I'd the bicycle. I'd been in town picking what I thought was watercress for our salad, which for the most part turned out to be hemlock—deadly poisonous, you know."

"Yes, so I've heard."

"Well, when I met you, it was my first full day here in Martynsborough . . . and then I was quite surprised when we met at the hall a few days later—to be formally introduced. I have to say, we've known each other now for some time, and we've never really spoken of that first meeting—not that there's anything terribly interesting about it—only that it was the first time that I also met Elise. She was on her own, you know, wandering on the road wearing only a thin white shift, it seemed, like from under her dress—I suppose she'd slipped out of the house without anyone noticing."

"Yes, that's true. And what of it?"

"Oh, I don't know, nothing really. But she did one thing I found odd, and I've observed her doing it on several occasions." She stopped walking. "She digs," Ruth said. "It seems like she's digging in the earth for something—like this." She squatted and picked at the gravel on the road, then as she did so, she lost her footing and fell over with her skirts all akimbo, losing a boot in the process. "Oh!" She twisted about on the ground, embarrassed, trying to arrange her skirt. "I'm a mess, aren't I?" Malcolm extended his hand, and she took it. He pulled her up, and she slid a stockinged foot back into her boot. "Yes, quite the mess. So sorry. Look how I'm wrecking all my stockings." She laughed nervously and brushed the dust from her knees. "I don't seem to recall what I was saying."

"Elise—she digs," Malcolm said, his voice steady, his face expressionless. "I've seen it also, many times. There's a reason, I think. As I was told afterwards, when they—that is, the French rescuers—found her, she was atop a pile of rubble, and she was clawing at it, in a sort of mania. Her parents, I suppose, were buried under the debris, and although she had the side of her skull practically shorn open, some remaining predisposition told her to dig, to save her parents, and so she dug. She lost two fingernails, and her hands were so bloodied that she wore bandages for six weeks. Now, after all this time has passed, it seems to be a comforting action for her to dig. Somehow this memory has lingered, perhaps only in the most rudimentary way within her broken mind. Maybe it is all that is left of my wife—her determination, her instinct to help, played out in pantomime, however."

Ruth felt her face burn with embarrassment. "I'm so very sorry. I didn't intend for you to . . . to have to tell me all that. I just had noticed her doing it, and I thought . . . I'm sorry, I've had too much to drink, and . . ." She swayed a moment on her feet. "I should probably get home now."

"Yes, let's get you home, Ruth. Don't worry about anything you've said."

They arrived at her cottage, and there was an awkward moment when Ruth felt the need for more than the usual spoken goodbyes. They'd discussed some deeper things. She didn't know what it all meant, and in her drunken mind, it all seemed more critically paramount than it probably was. "Thanks for walking me."

"Yes, as always."

"Goodnight." She lingered by the cottage's path while he made no move to walk away. A cool wind picked up and seemed to bring her to her senses. "See you later, then," she said.

Ruth immediately entered the house, went to her room, shut the door, and peered between the blackouts, to see Malcolm walking up the road. Soon, he reached the path to Virginia's cottage. He stopped and seemed to look directly at her, then stayed that way for a lingering moment before turning and disappearing into the blackness of his doorway.

Ruth did not see Malcolm the following day, nor was he at church Sunday morning. At the end of service, while milling about with the congregation, wondering vaguely where he might be, she heard Father Tweedsmuir call her over, along with Vera and Edith.

"Hello, Father. You've not seen Malcolm today?" Ruth asked.

"No, he doesn't always appear. Sometimes." He paused. "Sometimes I think dear Elise has bad mornings. He'll be around next Sunday, I'm sure."

"Oh, I see." Ruth could only speculate what that meant.

"On another matter, ladies, there's something I'd like to discuss," Father Tweedsmuir murmured, looking around as he said it. "Privately, that is. Would you like to come with me for a moment?"

The three women followed him back into the church along a dim, carpeted corridor and into a small office cluttered with books on every imaginable subject.

"Ladies, please have a seat. I'd like to discuss our young Johnny."

Vera and Edith sat, needing first to remove piles of hymnals from the chairs, while Ruth stood.

"Sorry, I only have the two chairs," said the Father. "Now, first let me apologize for the state of this office. I must confess that the art and science of organization is not my strength. Paper, especially when there is more than one sheet of it, acts as water, and I, a drowning victim. So, this brings me first to say that I've not had a chance to examine Johnny's schooling. He's fifteen, quite literate, in fact, rather well read, I have to say, but there is still a year or two of schooling that would do him well. While he's been brought to Martynsborough as a labourer, as much as they are needed, it is his choice really—he gets a stipend for it and doesn't have to sit in a classroom. He's a smart boy, but a bit wilful when it comes to his studies. I thought I'd ask you, Ruth, if you might take some of these exercise books that I've received from the Clitheroe sixth-form school and perhaps go over a bit with the boy one or two evenings a week. He is so very intelligent. I'd hate for a further casualty of this war to be his ability to find decent employment when it's all over." He handed the book to Ruth.

"Of course," she said. "I'm honoured that you'd think of me."

"There's something else," he said, this time with a more careful inflection in his voice. "As you know, Johnny came alone to Martynsborough, his paperwork was a bit of a mess, and we understand he has a brother somewhere, a boy named Jude. He's quite broken up about the whole thing, so I told him that I would help in any way I could. Given that I am part of the committee that oversees billets, along with Horgon, I thought I might be able to help, but as you can see"—he waved his hands round—"I don't seem to have the organizational propensity, so I've lost my way a bit, and it's taken some time to begin my investigation." He took a deep breath. "It seems, from what I can tell, Johnny has run away from a past billet, as did his brother—but it seems they've run in different directions, and I don't have the papers for either to determine what exactly happened."

"My God," said Vera. "Whatever for? He's such a fine young boy. Why would he run away . . . and without his brother?"

"Well, I'm not making any suggestions about his character. I must say, to you both, there are some issues around the billeting of children that generally go unspoken, awful things that I wouldn't like to mention in front of women. I feel that perhaps he and his brother ran from this billet for reasons of their, um, own *safety*. I was not allowed to investigate beyond the administrative side of things, but I will continue to try. I think if I can get more details about Johnny's original billet, I may be able to get to the bottom of this. What I'm trying to say, I suppose, is that Johnny has not been completely forthcoming about his circumstances."

"Why on earth would he not be as honest as possible, especially if he wants to find his brother?" Ruth said.

"Well, there could be different reasons. Maybe he's protecting someone, maybe he's gotten into trouble somewhere along the way, or more likely, the residents of the house at which they were billeting have been the cause of their troubles. I think perhaps some extraordinary circumstances placed him into a difficult position, and he acted. Please, I wish for you to listen to the boy, engage him, teach him, but do not alarm him. Try to coax some information from him. I think he may hold the key to finding his brother without knowing it."

"Thank you very much, Father," said Ruth. "We care dearly for Johnny and will do what we can to help."

-14-

Ruth was late once more, arriving at the hall in a flurry at almost half-past eight. Her eyes were raw and her face pale from lack of sleep, having heard noises outside her window the previous night—the crunch of gravel, the snap of twigs, and the slither of silk. It was another night filled with spectral dreams for which she stayed away from the window and cowered under her quilts. She still wavered on her theories; back and forth between thinking it was Elise wandering about, or something altogether different. Perhaps Ruth had fallen into the mass delusion herself, and it was nothing but a figment of her own lush imagination. Either way, she had no intention of disclosing her peculiar suspicion about Elise. It seemed very unlikely and strange, so she filed this thought to the back of her mind and had no plans to discuss it with anyone until things became clearer.

She sat down heavily at her desk, and Malcolm looked up with curiosity.

"Everything all right?" he asked.

"I've had a bad night, I'm afraid. Nightmares, restless. You weren't at church Sunday."

"No, sometimes Elise has difficulties. Church is often the last thing I think of Sunday morning." He offered no other information.

"I need to get to the bottom of this legend." Ruth sighed. "It makes for great creative fodder, but it's also starting to haunt my dreams. I'm sure you've also noticed a growing negative energy emanating from the villagers . . . towards me . . . *us*. They are holding us evacuees responsible for some treachery, and it's making me uncomfortable. I think I'd like Horgon's opinion about the wraith. He'll dismiss it as fantasy, but his opinion might be comforting."

Ruth called Horgon to her desk. "Mr. Horgon, if you don't mind me asking something completely out of the blue," she said in a low whisper. "What do you make of the story coming out of the pub? There are villagers now who say it has returned—the wraith. There are eyewitnesses. There's real distress and even animosity. I must admit, the whole notion is starting to haunt my own dreams. I'd like to get to the bottom of it. Were you here in Martynsborough when these things happened all those years ago?"

"I was, born and raised here. Let me just say that not all people who live in villages are superstitious plebeians who jump at their own shadow."

"Yes, I suppose, but to be honest, as much as it is a little frightening, I find the story as fascinating as it is unlikely. I've been asking questions. Perhaps I've rattled some folk, judging by the way they seem to avoid me when I walk down the street now. Either way, I study literature as a subject at Cambridge, as you know, and I found the legend interesting."

"A topic of study? Well, that's a different thing altogether. Perhaps you can also learn a thing or two about collective mania, which this village seems to have in spades. There's a library, I'll have you know, in the lower floor of this very building. It contains journals, every copy of our now defunct village newspaper, pamphlets, annals, legal documents— a veritable treasure trove of Martynsborough history. Please feel free to peruse it. Put an end to this nonsense by learning the truth of the matter. If you'd put this to rest sooner rather than later, I'd be properly thrilled."

"A library?" said Ruth in delight.

"Yes, yes," Horgon muttered, pulling a jumble of keys from his pocket. "I keep it locked, though. Those records are precious, nothing in duplicate. So please be careful with them. I'll unlock it now; you can feel free to pop your nose in at your lunch hour." He stepped out the stage door. Ruth and Malcolm looked at each other with knowing smiles.

At noon, Ruth and Malcolm found the room of which Horgon had spoken. It was a low-ceilinged space with a stone floor. Shelves ran the length of each of the main walls, at the head of which was a lead-latticed window. A few wooden office chairs were scattered about, and there was a large oak desk with a green banker's lamp. Malcolm clicked on the lamp and assessed the room.

"This is amazing," said Ruth, enjoying the smell of old paper. "I could get lost in an old town library like this."

"So, what do we know so far?" Malcolm said. "We've got a dead girl in a pond. A strange manor house and a conservatory that everyone seems scared of, a male steward who sounds like something from a gothic horror novel, some frightened villagers, and a restless ghost wandering the flax field."

"Yes, that sounds about right—and also rather wonderful. It's already a great story—we just need to fill in the blanks."

"There's more than a story here; there's a compelling central mystery right before us. Our lady in white is back now, some thirty years later. Are these sightings of something new, or a continuation of the original incidents? Or something else altogether? There are a lot of possibilities. I think perhaps if we solve this, you'll not only have a best-selling novel, but we'll also reduce, by many magnitudes, the hostile glares that have been trained at us. At the very least, it might be a satisfaction for a great curiosity that I certainly have—I'd honestly like to know what's going on."

"As do I. I'd say that, for me, curiosity can be both a virtue and a vice," said Ruth.

"So, who was the girl in the pond? What happened to her after Phineas left? And the estate? I feel like there are so many unanswered questions there. Who is Wolstenholme? What is in that conservatory? Perhaps we start there."

"Yes, I think that's the best course of action: Wolstenholme." Ruth started on the right shelf, and Malcolm went to the left, running fingers along spines.

"I've found the records of their village newspaper," said Ruth. They were gathered in large green folios, with a series of dates on the heels of the volumes. "Here is October to November 1910." She brought the folio over to the desk. "I think this might be a decent place to start." She laid the large volume on the desk, splayed it open, and turned to the first few editions. "Farming news, hmm, a new wing built on the village hall. Not much here," she said, and flipped to November.

"What's that?" Malcolm said, pointing at the headline. "A collection of Travellers arrived outside of town. Seemed to be of concern." They read silently through the article, which discussed the settling of a large Traveller group with slope-topped vardos, wagons, horses, propositions of "tinkering" and "bodgings" for hire, and offers of semiprecious baubles for the locals in hopes of making a few shillings here and there. The locals, of course, saw them as nothing more than brawling drunkards who spoke an incomprehensible language. Several weekly issues of the paper featured articles that generally dwelt on the topic of "What is to be done with the Travellers?" It was reported that many of the young ones, with unwashed faces and raggedy clothing, showed up near the church after Sunday service with hands extended for coins. The village of Martynsborough was not pleased at all with the situation. Eventually, it seems, the Travellers moved on, without any clear explanation.

"I recall in Albert's story that this Blackwell character had mentioned chasing away a group of Travellers himself," Ruth said.

"My god, Ruth, you've quite the memory—I hadn't even noticed that detail."

"I study literature. Every word in a story can tell a thousand other stories. You'll know as well as I that sometimes our so-called frivolous studies of the arts do have their advantages."

"Indeed. So, what do the Travellers have to do with anything?"

"Well, think about it," Ruth said, tapping her chin with the end of a pencil. "There was an unexpected influx of strangers, and then soon thereafter you've got the wraith. As with us evacuees, the same thing, right? We're an unexpected influx of strangers, and it's happened again. There must be a connection."

"Yes, yes, I see what you mean. Very curious."

"Let's put this aside and see what we can find on Wolstenholme," said Ruth.

"I've found some information on the mill, a small volume." Malcolm opened it up, and together they looked it over. Ruth found she was reading the words, but nothing was getting into her brain until the name *Catchpoole* caught her eye.

"What's this? They speak here of a Joseph Catchpoole, the owner of the mill. That's Vera's surname. You don't suppose her late husband had some interest in this mill? I know she met her late husband somewhere in Lancashire; perhaps he originated from Martynsborough."

"Well, it's curious. It says here that the mill had been owned by this Catchpoole family back to the 1840s at least, until it was taken at auction by Wolstenholme—it seems the family had been called for their loans and had to liquidate all their assets. Wolstenholme—I'm not sure if it was the one who continues to live on the estate or some earlier relative—he took the mill and chose to simply close it to all business.

I wonder why?" Malcolm scratched his head. "According to the notes here, it was the main hub of processing for the surrounding farms. He seems to have shut the business down for no good reason."

"I'm terribly curious if Vera knows anything about this."

"Make a note to mention it to her." Malcolm looked at this watch. "I think that's all for today. I suppose we'll be eating at our desks."

The sun was quite low as Ruth and Malcolm walked home. They crossed the bridge, and the wind blew through the bare tree limbs. There was an icy taste to the air for the first time, hinting at the winter that was yet to come.

"I've been thinking about the hall lately," Ruth said. "Have you noticed that underneath all the desks, Union Jacks, and grumpy old men, there is a floor for dancing and a piano?"

"Yes, I'd noticed that. The piano could probably use a tuning, but it would be wonderful to hear some music instead of the sound of scratching pencils. I play a little—the piano, that is; well, I used to." He held up his left hand. "I'd miss a few notes now, I'm afraid, but it would still be a pleasure to graze the ivories."

"Oh, I play, too," Ruth said. "Horgon seems to have a dim view of music and fun of any kind, I think."

"I've heard in other villages, especially closer to military bases, they have regular parties in their halls, with proper bands playing American jazz and dancing. It keeps morale up, I'd think."

"Yes, yes—we should, too!" Ruth said, stopping on the road. "It might help settle down nerves with talk of the wraith—dispel this idea that we've stirred up a ghost. We'll have a dance!"

"Well, it could be fun. Either way, how on earth would we convince Horgon? It'd be borderline heresy to use the space for anything not completely war related."

"Then we don't talk to Horgon," Ruth said with a sly grin. "We will talk to his wife. She's there every Sunday for the sermon. I'm sure she'll have a woman's sense about things. She'll understand the importance of social cohesion in the village."

"Brilliant, Ruth. You should speak with her at church this Sunday. We'll see how it goes." They walked in happy silence for a bit longer. "And how *is* the story going? Have you got anything written?" Malcolm asked.

"I've started a few chapters—but it's hard going. I'm tempted to make up some of the areas for which I don't know the answers. There's another part of me that wants to attack it from a historical perspective and try to stay true, so I dither on, writing a few words a day, but I think once we've learned a bit more from this library, I will be able to move more quickly. And you? Any sculpting lately?"

"I've been doing some small things, largely inspired by Rodin— again. I blather about him a lot, don't I?"

"Ha, yes, you do. Like I said, I only know the one sculpture."

"*The Thinker*, too. I'm sure you've seen that one." He mimicked the famous piece by rolling his fist under this chin and crouching over with a look of studious detachment. "Like this—I'm sure it looks familiar."

"What on earth are you doing?" Ruth laughed.

"*The Thinker*, Ruth! Oh, for heaven's sake, I have a small copy of it. I've got to show you. It drives me nearly mad that you act as if you've not seen this famous artwork." They stopped by the path to his cottage. "Come up. I'll get it so you can see. I know you'll recognize it."

They walked up the path, and he opened the door and stepped inside, closing it partially, leaving Ruth to stand on the flagstone stoop. Within a moment, he was back. "Elise and Virginia are upstairs, having a lie-down; sometimes they do this." He looked around nervously. "I have a few Rodin copies to show you. There's no sense trying to carry them all—they're breakable. You might as well come in, as long as you're quiet."

Ruth stepped into the house, her heart racing for reasons she couldn't quite understand.

In many ways Virginia's cottage resembled Vera's—the quarried stone, the plank wooden floors in the sitting room, a hearth. It was quiet, save for the ticking of a grandfather clock in the corridor. Ruth crept along in stockinged feet, her shoes held in her hand, frightened that the women upstairs might awake at the sound of her heels. Malcolm opened a door into a back room with a flagstone floor and large windows, like a covered sunroom. A stream of white, overcast light poured into a space much different than the rest of the house.

A pottery wheel sat in one corner, along the large stand of broad windows under which were diminutive sculptures. They were human forms along with animals—a horse, a lion, and some similar in style to Rodin, with rough, unfinished-looking edges. In the centre of the room was something rather larger, life-size, in fact. It was made of forged bronze, mottled here and there with blue-green verdigris, and as Ruth stepped closer, she realized it was a startlingly accurate likeness of Elise, an unexpected sight that was both shocking and unbearably intimate.

The nude figure was reclined partially on her back, propped up by her elbows. Her hair cascaded to the floor, and her legs were drawn up slightly and ajar, revealing more of her female anatomy than Ruth had ever encountered in a sculpture. She found it not so much obscene, but modern and honest—beautiful in a way and so very at odds with the stark, sexless Aphrodite of the classical world to which she was accustomed.

Either way, her discomfiture was unexpected, and a blushing heat crept up the back of her neck. She cleared her throat and looked away. Malcolm threw a drop sheet over the statue without comment, then led her to the other side of the room, where a bookcase held a few small sculptures. He picked one up to show her, but she was distracted anew by a military-style cot on the floor under the window. It looked recently occupied, with a tangle of white sheets and a rolled blanket at the head, which seemed to suggest a pillow. She stepped forward and, without really realizing what she was doing, picked up the wrinkled bed sheet and brought it to her face. Beyond the familiar laundry soap, it smelled of a man, a hibernating den—she realized that this was not a craftsman's studio, but a private sanctum. She dropped the sheet back to the cot.

"You sleep in here." It was a statement, not a question.

"Yes, sometimes," he said. "Well, yes, I sleep in here mostly."

"It can't possibly be comfortable. It'll be cold come winter . . . and Elise? She sleeps upstairs . . . without you?"

"There are two rooms upstairs. One is for Virginia, one is for . . . There's a chair in Elise's room; I sometimes sleep in the chair—when she's had a bad night. Either way, this studio is a lot more comfortable than the sleeping arrangements I left behind in Norway." He turned slightly, fixing his clear eye on to her. "I'd rather not discuss this. I'm sure you're curious about my marriage—how it works under the circumstances; maybe other people are curious—but it's not anyone's business. I'll talk about these things when I'm ready, and now is not the time. I think maybe I should have planned this more carefully. Perhaps it was a mistake bringing you into this room."

"No, no," Ruth said. "I'm sorry. Please, show me this Rodin. Is this it?" She pointed to the sculpture in Malcolm's hand. "Yes, it's handsome, but also unusual, like it might be unfinished."

"That was what people have said, but this is most definitely finished." His words hung in the air. Neither of them seemed to be able to recover and hold on to the original reason for Ruth entering the cottage. Instead, it felt like they had trod over some important line drawn in the sand. She felt anxious and strangely vulnerable, standing there on the cold stone floor in her stocking feet.

"Maybe I should go," she said. "I'm sorry, I'm overly curious. I ask stupid questions. You didn't have to cover the statue—it's beautiful, I'm just not used to seeing . . . well . . . and I didn't mean to poke around. I didn't mean to take up your bed sheets—to be honest, I can't believe

I just did that. I don't even know what I was thinking." She turned to leave the room. He reached out and gently took her wrist.

"I don't want you to think I'm strange," he whispered. "I want to continue as we are: doing ledger sheets on a stage, and talking about ghosts, eating lunch in a pub, discussing sculpture and Dante's inferno. I don't want to see pity in your eyes tomorrow. I want it to stay as it is. The fact of the matter is I don't have anyone else to talk to." He continued to grasp her, but she didn't resist, realizing it was the first time that he'd intentionally touched her—they'd never even shaken hands before. She could feel the warmth of his palm and thought of the pottery wheel in the corner, of his fingers slipping into soft clay, his hands moulding and shaping that likeness of his wife's body. He pulled her a little closer, and she acquiesced, now close enough to hear his rattled breath. "Please . . ."

"Yes, we can do all those things, and they'll not change," Ruth whispered in reply. "You sleep on a cot in your studio because your wife has been injured and is unwell. This is not strange, and *you* are not strange. Nothing is wrong with you . . . or with *us*. I look forward to walking home with you each afternoon. I also feel sometimes that you're the only one *I* can talk to about certain things." He released her wrist, stepped back, and turned to look out the window.

He said, "Let's get out of this room. I'll walk a bit with you back to Vera's cottage. I think I need some air. It's warm in here."

Ruth took up her shoes, and together, they crept out of the room. They didn't speak much as they walked, but the strange tension seemed to ease, so that by the time she arrived at the cottage, things between them had returned to normal, and soon Ruth found Edith sitting alone at the kitchen table peeling carrots. Ruth then recalled what she had learned in the library.

"Gran, before I forget, I was looking through the library in the hall today. I found something in one of the books. It said that the original owner of the mill was a family called Catchpoole. I don't know of any other Catchpooles here in the village—it's certainly not a common name—so I was wondering about Aunt Vera's late husband, William. I'm thinking that perhaps his family owned the mill at some point?"

Edith's face blanched, and she turned away, towards the window. "Ruth, I'd rather you not dig around in places that are best left undisturbed. Go ahead and write your story about ghosts, but I ask that you don't look too deeply into the ancient history of my sister's marriage." She turned back and looked squarely at her granddaughter. "It would be best for all if that history is allowed to rest peacefully where it is." Ruth was speechless and surprised by this sudden reaction. "I know you're naturally curious about the business of others," Edith continued. "If anything, do it for me—let it go." The door swung open, and Johnny entered, interrupting the moment.

"I've got some wood for the fireplace—a dead tree at the end of the allotment." A branch fell from his arms to the floor.

"Thank you, Johnny," Edith and Ruth said in unison, the awkwardness dissipated, the moment past. Ruth picked up the branch and placed it back on to Johnny's bundle as Vera entered with a flurry of breathless hellos and started washing green leaves in the sink.

"I forgot to tell you, Ruth," Vera called out over the sound of running water in the washbasin, "you've received a letter."

"Oh, wonderful!"

"It's right there in the hall," said Vera. Ruth skipped to the small table and leafed through the mail that had arrived that day, hoping that Maude had written her from Scarborough, or perhaps there was word from her mum and dad. The military envelope made her heart sink.

"I think it's from Warren," Edith called from the kitchen. "I do hope he's well. Perhaps he's still here in England. Wouldn't that be exciting?"

Ruth took the envelope upstairs to her room and sat on the bed. No. She wouldn't open it. Her mind was so very clouded with what happened with Malcolm—that nude statue of Elise, his cot in the studio—and then this strange behaviour of Edith's around the mention of the Catchpoole mill. The very thought of Warren felt like a gross invasion of a small and private world that Ruth had no intention of sharing with him. She placed the envelope unopened on the bedside table and returned to the kitchen to help with dinner.

"Well, how is he doing? Is he well?" Edith asked.

"Hmm? Oh, I've not opened it. I'm saving the letter for later— something to look forward to reading after the blackouts go up."

"Well, it is your mail. Do as you wish. But do let me know once you've read it. I really would like to know how Warren has been doing. I can't believe you've the patience to wait to read it."

Later that evening, she was in her room, her window glass darkened by the ever-present black curtains. Ruth sat on her bed in her nightdress, brushing her hair, which had gained a few inches. Her bangs had the habit of going into her eyes now, so she took to using two small barrettes on each side.

She glanced over at the letter; it was turned over without the RAMC insignia visible, appearing as any old white envelope might. And despite receiving his letter, she'd hardly thought about him all evening. No, Ruth had been thinking about Malcolm, about his studio and the smell of his white bed sheets. God, why had she picked them up and thought to bring them to her face? She cringed a little at the memory. She then thought of the sculpture. What would Elise think if she learned that Ruth had seen her body in such an intimate way? That Ruth and Elise's own husband had stood together gazing on a likeness of her bared flesh? Would she even be able to understand? Ruth then imagined such a sculpture depicting her own naked form and shivered with a curious mixture of revulsion and arousal. She opened the letter.

Dearest Ruthie,

I am well! I was on a short leave and was rather sad to learn that we couldn't meet at Cambridge. I have remained on English soil and have been working in a military hospital near Aldershot, dealing with various duties. The good news is that I will be getting a decent amount of leave come January. I should think I'd like to visit. I will—I will be there in January!

I'll confirm the dates of my leave and will likely be able to get a train up there sometime after Christmas. It will be perfect to be together once more, and in this charming little village—a place for a honeymoon, maybe?

I wonder what you wear as you read this? Are you in bed? In a nightdress? Or in a hot bath with soapy pink skin, running a sponge along your leg? I'd like to think you're in the bath. Don't drop the letter, or the ink will run!

Oh, Ruth, I don't really know what to write, only to tell you that I cannot wait to be with you once more. We'll be married! We can wed there, can we not? Is there a vicar? I'm sure—there's no village in all of England that doesn't have a vicar. You've your own room there? Soon OUR room? Oh, it will be positively capital. Please write—please tell me how you feel. You miss me? Are you frightened there, on your own with old women? It should be fine. I'll come, I will, and all will be right. If this war ends by Christmas, I swear, I'll come there on foot and carry you back to London myself!

Many, many kisses—no, not just kisses, so much more. You know what I speak of, I know you do. So much more for my sweet Ruthie. Please write back!
W.

15

Maude Sedgwick looked out at the sea and gloried in its vastness. There was the sound of gulls, a saline taste on her tongue, and with such a wide, unencumbered vista, she could detect the curvature of the earth itself. By all rights, she should have loved the coast of Scarborough.

She hated it.

Her gaze turned back towards land, across the mudflat, where her uncle and aunt, swaddled in woollen pullovers, watched from deck chairs, along with her cousin Victoria, a girl of fourteen, sitting on a blanket with a book of word puzzles provided by the local Anglican Sunday school.

It was a warmish autumn day, perfect for the beach, and for Maude's aunt, uncle, and cousin, it was the kind of outing that included the safe anchorage of hired folding chairs, a blanket, a basket of apples, and *Dandy* comics. The water was to be looked upon but never approached under any circumstances.

Maude herself would not set foot on a beach without thoughts of science, and in order to seek the truth that only investigative inquiries could offer, it was necessary that she wear appropriate apparel—comfortable and practical—allowing for much bending and squatting whilst collecting bits of quartz or haematite. She had donned a pale blue, one-piece, pinafore-style trouser outfit with a bib and broad shoulder suspenders. Wide and generous pockets allowed for the carrying of her mallet and magnifying glass. A frock simply would not do. "This war has got women wearing trousers," said her aunt that morning. "If you're not in a munitions factory, you've no excuse. A lady is still a lady, and ladies wear frocks. You look like a lavatory cleaner in that thing."

Maude had tried a compromise for her village relatives. Unlike the girls on the Continent, for example, Maude assured her aunt and uncle a sense of English modesty by wearing a blouse under the apron of the outfit—this eliminated the possibility of a scandalous bare shoulder, or worse, an exposed female armpit. Over it all she wore a buttoned cardigan. She had tied up her strawberry blonde hair in numerous small buns under a wide-brimmed hat, and the only other flesh she bared was revealed through the leather straps of beach-appropriate slingback sandals on her feet. She did not spend an hour painting her toenails ruby scarlet so that their glossy beauty might be secreted bashfully under the veil of patent leather saddle shoes. It would be colder in the coming weeks, and thereafter the wellies would come out—so she ought to bare the toes while she could. God forbid these people ever visit a French beach where women wore actual swimming suits that revealed enough flesh to blind a harp polisher—or they wore nothing at all.

It was a small consolation that Maude made some discoveries on the mudflat. She had found both a sizeable piece of jet and later a near-perfect ammonite of some coiling prehistoric invertebrate or other. She adjusted her spectacles and then squatted in the low tide to rinse her find in the salt water, sighing ruefully, hoping that the war would be over by Christmas.

They returned to the house, and moods had brightened somewhat as Maude had changed into an ankle-length, floral-printed autumn dress. She offered to go with Victoria to the shops to get some fresh bread, which as yet had not been rationed, and soon the debacle of her blue pinafore pantaloons seemed forgotten.

"You've a letter here, Maude. Come this morning with the post," said her aunt, sitting at the dining table with a steaming cup of tea.

"A letter?" Maude picked up the envelope and turned it over to see the return address. She was startled and delighted to see the village of Martynsborough written in the neat and girlish script of one Ruth Gladstone. "A classmate has written me." Maude took the letter and escaped to the small office that had been converted into her bedroom to read her letter in private.

Maude enjoyed every slanted bit of cursive that Ruth had provided. Roaming rams and ewes, ghostly legends, one-eyed artists with less than ten fingers, and lime kilns filled with water and possibly dead girls—it was wondrous and inviting, and a very unlikely thought crossed her mind.

Perhaps she would like to go to Martynsborough.

She'd need a lay of the land first—what was to be expected there? Was there a place for her to stay? She envisioned Ruth living in some manor house of a country squire relative. Surely there would be room for a Girton colleague looking to escape the bombs (and her puritanical assemblage of blood relatives). Oh, what a wonderful trifle it would be—Maude and Ruth, detective inspectors solving the case of the lady in the white. She took up a pen and paper.

Dear Shakespeare's sister,

Greetings and salutations from beautiful Scarborough! Just today I have pulled from the primordial muck of low tide a pristine ammonite. What is that, you ask? Envision a twisted apple strudel, except it is not a pastry, but a seven-million-year-old millipede. Horrible, yes? But also: wonderful! Additionally, I've found many bits of jet on the beach—the black stuff that glistens about the necklines of Victorian funeral dresses.

Thus far, I've generally enjoyed this seaside place. They have peculiar geographic terms here in Yorkshire—for example, there are widges and holes, many types of hole . . . and becks, and there are fosses—also spouts—which are forever gurgling and spewing. The land is sodden. I soak my feet wherever I step, with some places having the babble of sweet water flowing over fringe and maiden fern, while others are the salty eruptions from the sea, soaking my hair and lips at the most inopportune moments.

I've enjoyed reading about the goings-on in your Martynsborough. I particularly like a ghost story, if anything, as a challenge for my scientific mind to confront head-on. What say you on this? Do you dabble in the occult? Seances? Witchcraft? It is Lancashire, after all! I'd need to set you straight. Say, I wonder, is there room for an old friend perhaps to come for a visit to your Martynsborough? Just between us Girton girls, I have to admit I'm growing somewhat tired of the soakings and becks and fosses and holes here—or I suppose if I was to be more truthful, I'm tired of my aunt and uncle. I sleep in a converted office on a bed the size of a boot box, surrounded by liturgy books on the shelf. There's an honest to goodness crucifix on the wall here. My family are not Catholic, so I've no idea why it's there—perhaps a souvenir from their trip to Barcelona? It's unnerving, I feel as if the tiny Christ hanging there on his cross watches me as I undress for bed.

I've thought of trying my luck by returning to Cambridge for my own sanity, but I think it would be even more delicious to make a stop in Lancashire, land of the red rose, and visit the notorious Ruth Gladstone—you know, to make sure that she's wearing her hat in the sun, avoiding village controversy, and minding her manners. Pray, can you spare a bed for the first week of January? I don't mean to be presumptuous, but I'm practically packing already.

All the best,

Your fellow Girtonite,

Maude

WINTER 1940–41

16

As the sun dipped low on the first day of December, the mist moved in over the flax fields, and the moon rose in the deepening purple sky, while the residents of the Catchpoole cottage sat around the table, cosy and warm.

"Has Ruth been working you like a cruel schoolmaster?" Vera asked Johnny, with a hint of mischief.

"I'm getting on a bit better with my sums." Johnny looked over at Ruth. "I can't say I've had a better teacher."

"You're both making me proud." Edith smiled.

"Oh indeed." Now Vera spoke. "And these partridges, Ruth, I have to thank you again. I'm in disbelief that you took a pair—it's not easy. Often a hunter needs an army of volunteers beating in the hedge to flush the birds out into a valley. Very moneyed men with all the advantages you can imagine, teams of beaters and dogs at the ready, and rarely does a gun take more than a single bird without spending the better part of the day out in the rain."

"I'm starting to enjoy it, to be honest; it's the thrill of the hunt, as they say," said Ruth.

"And you, Johnny, you still like my cooking?" Vera asked.

"Oh yes, ma'am," he said with his mouth full.

"And how was the cooking back home? Did your mum cook?"

"Yes, she did, though I have to say it wasn't like this—I'd never tell her myself, of course. She boiled much of our food, to make it safe to eat, I suppose. I've learned that it doesn't seem necessary to do that now."

"And your mum is . . . ?"

"She's in Sheffield, in a factory, making munitions. She wanted me and Jude as far from the cities as possible. Dad's in Italy."

"Right. And your brother, Jude, he liked your mum's cooking?"

"Well, I suppose as much as I did."

"Tell me," Vera said, "what was the cooking like at your billet—not with Father Tweedsmuir, but you know, before, at the place you stayed with your brother." Johnny paused, the fork halfway to his lips, and looked from woman to woman in silence. He pushed the food into his mouth.

"Not very good, I'm afraid. Not very good at all," he said with his mouth full. "It was an older woman, a widow. She told us she had once had a son who had died of the Spanish flu many years before. She longed to have boys in the house again, to help out, wanted to fatten us up, as she would often say, but no, her cooking was not so nice as this—nobody was going to get fat on it, either. She wasn't so bad a woman, I suppose, not as bad as the billet before."

"Oh. There was yet another billet? Before this last one?"

Johnny looked at Vera with a small amount of alarm, as if he had revealed something he hadn't meant to.

"Hmm, yes, I suppose."

"Well, I didn't know this," Vera said. "We're learning so much more about you tonight, Johnny. And where was this billet? How was the cooking there?" He didn't answer right away.

Instead, he chewed on the side of his cheek for a moment. Then he said, "Not g-g-g-good at all, no—that one was not s-s-so good. The old woman was much better'n that."

"Whatever do you mean?"

"If you don't mind, ma'am, I'd rather not t-t-t-talk too much about the billets. Like I said, they weren't so good, and it puts me out of s-s-sorts to think too much about it."

"And you've no idea where Jude is now?" Vera asked gently.

"No"—Johnny paused, looking down at his plate—"I don't. They t-t-told him, though—t-t-told us—we didn't even know the name of this p-p-place at the time, only that it was up the river at the next lock. No, I don't know where he is, like I said before. But I knew he could tell someone that he has a brother, he'd have some idea where I am, I would think, and c-c-could send a letter, at least to Father Tweedsmuir. That's why I check with him often—always hoping there'll be some word."

"I'm sorry, you're not making a lot of sense, Johnny. I don't understand why Jude didn't come with you to Martynsborough," Ruth said. "It's a bit confusing. I'm sure we could help you, I mean, now that we're on the topic, with gathering some clues, like a detective might when they solve a mystery. We could find Jude, I think, with some more clues perhaps *you* could provide."

Johnny had taken all he could take about the subject and put his fork down.

"Really, I'm quite sorry, but I'd really rather not, you know, s-s-speak too much of it. It p-p-puts me out of sorts."

All three women seemed to physically back away simultaneously until Vera said, "Well, of course. It's quite all right, Johnny, we're only trying to help. Tell me, how was the farm work today? I'd think it was slow now with much of the harvest having been done." Johnny perked up with the change in subject and took a bite from a partridge leg.

"Oh, there's always work to do," he said. "Although we'll be cutting back to four days a week soon, which is nice, in time for Christmas and such to have more free time."

"Yes, indeed, Johnny. I'm quite looking forward to having a full house this season," said Vera.

A couple of hours later, with Johnny and Ruth gone up to their bedrooms, Edith and Vera remained at the table.

"It's been several times we've tried to get some kind of useful information from the boy, but he's rather resistant," said Edith quietly. "You'd think he would be keen on finding his brother."

"Oh, I think he wants to find his brother all right," said Vera, "but it is a matter of trying to discover one thing for himself, while concealing another from us."

"What do you suppose he's hiding?" Edith poured tea.

"As the vicar said, there was probably some trouble at his billet, and it seems that he left of his own accord, and from which billet, I wonder—from the old woman he had mentioned or this new place that we've just learned about tonight? How many now? Three different places before this cottage, if you include the church?" Vera asked.

"Yes, it would be three. So unfair for someone so young. Perhaps we should take this into our own hands. The Father means well, but I feel he may actually lose track of the whole thing with the tiniest distraction—he's frightfully disorganized."

"Yes, indeed he is. You know, I've been acquainted with Walter Horgon for ages. If anyone can track down this missing boy, it is he. I'll have a word with him. I'll stop by the hall on the way to the shop." Edith agreed, and both women felt a little better knowing that at the very least, they had a plan.

Upstairs, Ruth brushed her hair in the dark, the blackout shades open to the cool glass of her window. She looked at her nightstand, in the gloom, at an opened letter. She had been thrilled to see Maude's name in the return address and mused about the unusual turn of events that would have Maude visiting. It was rather perfect. If she had Maude staying in her room, either on a cot, which she knew she could borrow, or she supposed they could share a bed if needed, Warren would have no choice but to take the sofa when he arrived, or maybe to not even stay with them once he learned of the new house guest. Yes, the Catchpoole cottage was about to fill up like an overhired inn. And while her aunt seemed to think that the more people in her house, the better, for Ruth, it also provided a way to take cover and buy time. This good grace fell from the heavens like a gift from the gods: Maude Sedgwick, here, here in Martynsborough in four short weeks, to keep Warren from Ruth's room and maybe—God forbid—to even have a little fun.

Yes, it was fun that had become her focus as her mind then turned to events that morning at church. Ruth had planned to intercept Mrs. Horgon and ask about a dance in the hall. But as the congregation milled about after the service, she had missed several opportunities until finally she had managed to get Mrs. Horgon alone and mentioned it. "A dance?" the woman asked. "How absolutely lovely. Yes. I'm not sure what Walter would think of such a thing, but please let me work on him. Morale is often as important as ammunition during a war, and I can't think of anything that would help build morale better than a dance."

The next day, Vera walked to the centre of Martynsborough alone, deep in thought. With Ruth often doing the shopping, she had not been out in some time by herself. She couldn't remember when she'd last had a moment to call her own—a moment to do some thinking.

She and Edith had been talking more lately of their collective history, about that one horrible day many years before, and all the things that followed, along with the potential dangers that lingered. Just yesterday Edith revealed that Ruth had discovered some ancient history related to the mill and the name of Catchpoole. No, not just "the mill," as some might say; to Vera it was so much more. She often avoided walking near it or even looking at it. She had once regularly picked the watercress there, but with the arrival of Edith and the re-emergence of so many memories, the mill had taken on a life of its own in her imagination, and she felt she could not bear to ever go there again.

This day, however, being the first she had stepped into the village alone since Ruth and Edith had arrived, she *would* go there.

It took a long time to walk from her cottage to Martynsborough's high street on her aging legs. Down the cobblestone path, she minded her footing at the parts that got a bit steep, and soon she approached the building with its unmoving wheel. There were two buildings in actuality—one, the bowed and cracked living quarters made of crumbling, salmon-coloured wattle and daub. Its thatched roof had not been replaced in years, or more likely decades, and the pink colour seemed a result of wet rust and other stains sullying the once cream-coloured plaster. Much of the roof was rotten, blown away, and inhabited by starlings and crows.

The water washing over the seized rungs made for a muttering sound, and Vera noted that the level in the race was much lower than it had once been.

Stepping to the heavy oak door at the front, Vera knew it was locked—it had been locked for fifty years. She knew another way in, though, a place where mischievous girls might sneak to evade their parents. She went around the side, to the bottom of a brick bulkhead in the wall, where she found a low, wide plank hatch, an aperture meant to move large metal items in and out for repairs. She reached in for a bolt, just under the jamb, and tickled it just the right way—her fingers slid into the dark confines behind a brick and searched. Yes, there it was, a click and snap of a release. The hatch then eased inward slightly. Vera looked about to make sure she was alone, and then pushed the wooden hatch open wider, stooped over, and stepped inside.

The smell was the same, a wet smell, and a mixture of grease, damp burlap—and also a new scent, something feral. It was quiet, save for the dull mumblings of the river running over the wheel outside. And although weak sunbeams pushed through dusty windows up high, Vera didn't really need the light; she knew her way around. *Just a quick look,* she thought.

Further into the shadows she noted the rickety ladder that led up to the hidden place above. She was too old to even contemplate climbing the thing and approached it tentatively. The ladder disappeared into a dark square at the top. She sighed and looked around the gloom, then back to the ladder. Should she attempt to climb it? Oh, how she wanted to, so very badly. She'd break her neck, though, or at the very least her shoe heel.

She touched the ladder rung, and it came away sticky. She held her hand up to the meagre light of the space. She touched it with a finger and smelled it closely. Jam. It was raspberry jam, and relatively fresh—still sticky and sweet. How strange. She pulled a handkerchief from her pocket and wiped her fingers and looked around again, curious, wondering who had dripped raspberry jam in the mill—and rather recently at that. She startled at a sound from above, dropping her handkerchief to the floor. Abandoning it, she stepped carefully towards the exit and listened another moment. An animal perhaps. Then she heard footfalls just above her. Frightened, she fled the mill, closed the wooden hatch as slowly and quietly as she could, then stepped towards the pond, where she caught her breath. Out in the sunshine, she didn't feel as afraid. Surely it was her imagination . . . or she had awakened a large barn owl. Nothing to concern herself with. She adjusted her collar and turned back to the road, onward to the shop so that she might have her ration book stamped.

With her shopping done, she stopped by the hall, where many of the workers appeared to have left for lunch. "Vera!" A voice boomed from within. "You wish to contribute to the war effort?" Horgon smiled, a smile so very at odds with his tone. "Pray, what brings you here, old friend?" he said, this time quietly.

"I've come to employ the power of that tremendous brain of yours, to help us with our young Johnny," Vera said.

"What in heaven's name would I know about this boy?" Horgon asked as he stacked a sheaf of papers. "As it is, I'm up to my ears in War Ag and Ministry of Food."

"Yes, but you've a knack for organization, let us just say, a better knack of organization than other elders of our community—others who may or may not be on the committee that oversees billets."

"Ah, yes. Tweedsmuir—slovenly."

"Precisely. This boy Johnny, who's staying with us, he's lovely and hard-working, and it's been a rather tragic turn for him throughout this evacuation. He's got a brother somewhere—they were separated. We've also no idea how he ended up in the church basement. What of his papers? He appears to have none. Are children not accompanied by important information? If he'd run, one would think that Father Tweedsmuir would have been contacted somehow, that he would have been informed of all this, that locating the boy's brother wouldn't be so difficult."

"Yes, I see what you mean. The evacuees do indeed have paperwork, but it is minimal. I've already heard stories of children lost in the shuffle, living with some farmer or other in the middle of nowhere with parents' information lost to the wind, no idea of forwarding address—and even if the war ends, little ones who've not the ability to describe their homes or parents, or recite their addresses, may be lost forever to their mothers."

Vera brought a hand to her mouth. "Dear God, that's awful."

"Yes, as is war, I'm afraid. And you can now see why I am so adamant about good record-keeping. The stakes can often be high to get it right. Now with your boy, I think I may be able to help some. I can contact the clerk I know. Someone owes me a favour at the Clitheroe office. Some weeks ago, I caught a critical error they'd made with the numbers and saved them a great deal of embarrassment by flagging it."

"You are a wonder, you truly are, Walter," Vera said.

"No, not a wonder, just focussed and organized." He took up a notepad and a pencil and handed them to Vera. "Write down all that you know, the boy's full name, including surname and middle name or initial, original parish—if he knows it. Of course, age, height, physical description, current billet, and as much information about the past billets as you can muster. I'll see what I can do."

"Thank you so much, old friend." Vera stood and leaned over to kiss his cheek.

"Yes, yes." He shooed her away. "No need for melodrama. I'll have this boy found in no time." He leaned back in his office chair with a sigh of resignation and said in a softer voice, "Also, on another subject, it seems your niece is working in the shadows on nefarious schemes."

Vera looked up from the notepad.

"Oh?"

"Yes, she's been speaking with my wife, rather on the sly, hoping to take advantage of her weak disposition."

"Whatever for?"

"A *dance*, Vera. Your niece wishes for a dance, in this very hall if you can believe it."

"Well, I think it's a wonderful idea."

"Yes—yes, you would, wouldn't you? I was a master corporal in the Great War. I dug seventeen miles of trenches. What are my chances of squelching this small uprising between my own wife . . . and friend?"

"Zero, Walter, the odds are zero. We'll have a dance. You need not worry about it—you don't have to come or even look at it. The dance will be created and dismantled in the time it takes for you to put up your feet Friday evening and return Monday morning. You'll not even find a drop of rum punch on the floor. I'll tell Ruth the good news tonight."

Horgon allowed for the dance to be held on the third Saturday in December, so Ruth decided it would be a Christmas-themed dance—something happy and comforting that would calm fraught nerves and distract villagers from matters of war and hopefully from thoughts of ghostly wraiths as well. "There's so much to consider," said Ruth as she jotted down ideas. Vera and Edith sat with her at the kitchen table. "But so very good for morale."

Vera looked over her shoulder, to make sure that the three women were alone. "And, I might add," she said in a bare whisper, "with Johnny upstairs, I ought to mention that Walter is helping us in other ways— he's agreed to help locate Johnny's brother. Isn't it wonderful?"

"Yes, oh yes," said Ruth.

"And if we were to find this boy," Edith said, with some deliberateness to her voice, "where is he to stay? Here?"

"I should think so," said Vera. "Why wouldn't he?"

"It's getting a little crowded, don't you think? We've got two more joining us after Christmas. There's this classmate of Ruth's, and as for Warren, I would say he is most definitely a priority—all the others . . ." Edith tapped her finger on the table. "We'll be like a boarding house. Do we have enough food to go around?"

"Oh, Gran, we eat like royalty here," said Ruth. "There's more than enough to go around—it will also mean more hands in the garden, more help."

"Yes, I suppose," Edith said. "I'm just not used to sharing my space with so many people. We've only one bath."

Vera placed her hand over Edith's with a reassuring expression on her face.

"Dear sister, in a war, I'm sure we girls can weather the adversity of a crowded dinner table and the occasional queue for the lavatory."

17

"The conservatory on the estate fascinates me," Malcolm said as he flipped through an almanac in the village library. "I've not had the wherewithal to approach that man, Albert, again and ask. It seems no one else wishes to talk about it—you know, what mysterious horror lurks in that conservatory? The very wraith herself could live within its glass walls for all we know. I asked Virginia, and she doesn't seem keen on discussing it. 'Ancient history stirred up in the pub,' she says to me—not worth her breath. I've no intention of interrogating the poor woman. Have you asked Vera?"

"Yes, I mentioned it briefly at dinner last week." Ruth dropped a stack of books on the desk. "She said it's something discussed among the Martynsborough men only—men who were once boisterous boys. She thinks it's nonsense they rustled up when they were young and overly imaginative and continued over the years."

"Either way, there must be something here. I have a feeling that the conservatory and the wraith are somehow connected."

It was their quest for the day—to discover more about the Wolstenholme estate. "Here's something. It is a journal written by a town magistrate, from the 1880s. There's something about the estate." She took it to the desk and placed the book under the light of the banker's lamp. "There's a gold mine of information here." Ruth flipped through pages. "Here's talk of the lime-kiln ponds. Oh, and here is some of the family history, and there's information about the conservatory—it says here, one of the finest in northern England."

"I've heard of these books—it's a vanity piece, commissioned by some past lord of the manor to bring a sense of myth and occasion to what were probably a gaggle of insufferable fops sitting in their palace on the hill." Malcolm looked at his watch. "We've no time to read this now, though."

"I'll take it," Ruth said quietly, her eyes wide with mischief. "Don't you think? I could hide it in my bag, I can make notes tonight in bed, and I'll return it Monday."

"If Horgon catches wind of this, we'll not only lose our privilege to poke around in this collection, he'll probably cancel your dance out of pure spite. There's no other copy of that volume, as he said."

"I realize that, but I think it's worth the risk. An hour a day isn't enough to really delve into this material. It's Friday—I'd have all weekend. I could while away half the night in my bed reading and taking notes. You want to know what's in that glasshouse, don't you?"

"Oh, indeed I do. I'm starting to think your acute sense of curiosity has become contagious."

"Unfortunately, it seems we've become partners in crime." Ruth slipped the book into her school satchel. "Not a word, or we'll both be in it."

In bed that night, Ruth pulled the book from her satchel. She took up a pencil and notebook and started looking through the pages. The Wolstenholme Park estate had been there, so named since 1791. Before that, it was a more modest manor house, owned by an Irish mercantile family by the name of Martyn—which, of course, Ruth realized, explained the origin of the village's name and reminded her of her research in Girton Library. This Martyn family had some mysterious fall from grace and had sold the manor house to an up-and-coming family, the Wolstenholmes, who had made a fortune in the wool trade and limestone, which they converted to agricultural quicklime with the kilns the family had dug in the 1840s. They built on the original house, making it larger and more beautiful. The lands of the park were vast, and soon the Wolstenholme family purchased several properties in the village, including several handsome houses for which they collected rent, along with the acquisition of the mill. They also leased out much of their land to local farmers and continued to accumulate wealth.

Here was this information about the mill once more. There was no mention of who had previously owned it or, more importantly, perhaps, why Wolstenholme had allowed the mill to fall into disrepair instead of operating it or leasing it to a milling family. It was all very unusual, and a ticklish curiosity nagged at Ruth, especially considering her gran's reaction when she had raised the topic of the Catchpoole family. Her gran knew something, possibly something important about that mill, and Ruth was most curious to learn what that might be. She would need to look more closely at that topic and would have to do so with great discretion.

She read a bit about the family that resided in the manor house at the time that book had been published. There was a Randolph Wolstenholme with a wife, Mary, and a brief mention of a daughter, one Charlotte Wolstenholme. As far as Ruth knew, now only one man currently resided there, along with his steward, the mysterious Blackwell, but no women. Where was the wife? Long dead? And the girl—she would be in her forties or fifties now. Where was she? Described as blonde and pretty in the text, she provided another tantalizing clue that would require further investigation.

Ruth continued to read but soon felt her eyes drooping. The book, if she was honest, was rather boring, and it was written in a fawning, overwrought style. Malcolm was likely correct that it was a vanity project commissioned by some Victorian landholder who wished perhaps to join the peerage. She scribbled a few more notes, and then flipped ahead, looking for something that might be of more interest. She finally found a section written about the conservatory.

Built in 1840, the conservatory covered almost one-quarter of an acre. Built of wrought iron and glass, it had become a minor local landmark for a short period in the nineteenth century. Randolph Wolstenholme, the patriarch who commissioned its construction, was an amateur naturalist. He had travelled to Southeast Asia, collecting samples of plants and animals, and with the help of three subterranean boilers and veritable miles of pipes, he heated the conservatory to match the climate of French Indochina. A team of expert gardeners cared for the exotic plants. An Oxford-trained naturalist managed the fauna of the conservatory, which housed a whole menagerie of strange and exotic birds and insects.

Now this was more interesting. Birds and insects from the jungle? She read more and learned that this Randolph Wolstenholme had a great interest in zoology, and Charles Darwin had once visited this conservatory. The summary, though, maddeningly lacked detail.

The estate's halcyon days were long past, and as far as she could tell from the stories of the men in the pub and what Vera had said, only one staff member remained, this Blackwell person, along with some Wolstenholme or other who had not properly been identified. Why had Phineas gone up there in 1910? What was his connection to this estate? And who and what was there now? Was the conservatory left in ruin, its palm trees long dead, the birds flown the coop, the estate itself fallen like the House of Usher? And what of the wraith? Surely it was all connected—the girl in the pond, the ghost in the field, but how?

Ruth leafed through more of the book and realized she wouldn't find the answers in the text. She'd have to visit the manor house and somehow get into the conservatory. An unlikely thought struck her just then. She *would* go there. She'd take Malcolm with her, of course, and they would walk up the road, through the gates, to the top of the escarpment, and personally deliver to the Wolstenholme letter box an invitation for a Christmas dance.

18

After church, walking home, the three older women, Vera, Edith, and Virginia, lagged, while Ruth, Malcolm, and Elise walked in front. Elise, bundled in a handsome coat, her beautiful face pink with the cold, stared glassily ahead.

"I was thinking," Ruth said to Malcolm, "our clandestine book has not provided much in the way of detailed information about the Wolstenholme estate. In fact, I think it's only tickled my curiosity more. I'll be returning it tomorrow." Ruth went on to describe some of what she'd found in the book. "This conservatory becomes more interesting by the minute, though."

"Yes, I agree. We've now got an exotic menagerie of animals thrown into the mix."

"So, what I was thinking . . ." Ruth's voice trailed off.

"I sense some mischief is about to fall from your mouth."

"Yes, well, you're probably right. I was thinking—perhaps the best excuse to knock on the Wolstenholme door, you know, is to invite them to the dance."

Malcolm laughed. "My God, Ruth, you've outdone yourself. The man in that estate is probably no more than a breathing fossil. How on earth would he manage at a dance?"

"Well, I wouldn't expect him to come. I only want to, I don't know, get a look at the place with a plausible excuse for being there should someone confront us."

"And by someone, you're speaking of this Blackwell character with his elephant gun? The men in the pub have painted him out to sound like the devil himself."

"Yes, I'll admit, there is something unnerving about him, but it was thirty years ago! He'll be old now—if he's even alive."

"Well, what do you propose?"

"I propose that I make a very special invitation, provide adequate RSVP information, and we walk up to his door and perhaps knock so that it could be a personal delivery."

"You expect me to go with you?"

"Of course I do."

The next day, on their lunch hour, Malcolm and Ruth walked along the road to the north, then up the escarpment. It was steep going, and halfway up, Malcolm said, "We'll be late getting back from lunch. I'm soaked in sweat. This hill was worse than I thought."

"We're almost there. Look. I see the corner of the gate." They continued onwards, following a bend in the road, around which the trees became quite thick and dark, and then found their way blocked by a tremendous wall with a great iron gate. Affixed to the gate was a sign, in stark black and white:

PRIVATE PROPERTY—NO TRESPASSING—BY INVITATION ONLY

"Well, this is an unhappy development," said Ruth. She rattled the gate lightly and then stooped over to investigate a gap in the bars that she might fit through.

"Don't even think about it. The sign is enough deterrent for me. Look here, though." Malcolm pointed to the side of the gate. "A letter box. Perfect."

"It's a bit disappointing. I was hoping to see the house. Perhaps our invitation to the dance will result in an invitation to the manor. I'd really like to get a look at the conservatory."

"As would I. But let's not risk life and limb for what is probably a crumbling wreck. We'll be patient and methodical and get there in the end."

"I suppose you're right." Ruth dropped the invitation into the box. "We could wait around here until someone comes to collect it . . . say hallo?"

"We need to go. Horgon will be through the roof if we're a moment late, and we've almost a half hour of walking to get back."

Ruth peered into the letter box, then through the rungs of the gate, her curiosity boiling fiercely.

"Yes, right. Back we go," she said reluctantly.

The day of the dance had arrived with no RSVP from the Wolstenholme estate—a disappointment for Ruth. She would have to determine another way to investigate the conservatory, but for the moment, she had another crisis to tend to—her hair.

She stood in front of the mirror and felt the need to tear it out. It had reached an awkward length, and as much as she had pretty pins on each side to keep the bangs from her eyes, the back of her head had done some strange thing that day, of all days. She could not tame it, like a wild, witchy bramble. Worse, the dress she had intended to wear—the only nice frock she had brought from Girton—no longer fit. It seemed she was eating so well that the zipper refused to move as it did when she had dined on rationed peas pottage at Cambridge. There followed a small but violent grapple with the garment, as she tried to cram her body into the stubborn thing, ultimately employing a wire coat hanger twisted into a crude hook to slide the zipper up her spine. She eventually proved victorious with a great holding of breath and then she stepped into Vera's room, which had a full-length mirror. The dress appeared a bit immodest. Her figure strained and stretched the fabric, and an obstinate bit of white lace from her slip insisted on peeking out from her neckline. Either way, she was stuck with it—it would require kitchen shears to get the bloody thing off, so it was best that it stayed on.

The night of the Martynsborough Christmas dance arrived cool and misty, and much of the valley lay shrouded in a thick fog, what a Londoner might call a pea-souper, which in fact was a low-lying cloud almost fifty miles wide that had blown in from the Irish Sea. The mist gathered heavily about the ragged land of the Bowland forests and the valleys of the River Harold. Despite the eerie weather, spirits were high.

In the hall, some of the Union Jacks remained, but there was also bunting, and streamers made from old linens, dyed green and red. A tiny tree had been produced via a pruned-back bramble bush decorated with garlands made from horse chestnuts, the petals of Chinese lanterns, and red yarn. Under the tree volunteers had stacked the children's gifts, wrapped with old newsprint and twine—blue bows for boys and red bows for girls. Someone had also made Christmas crackers from butcher's paper and filled them with lemon sweets. The musicians, having just arrived, tuned up their instruments—a fiddle, a squeeze box, a guitar, and the pub local, Cora Dunn, as a singer.

Ellen had set up a bar in the window wicket and rolled over a keg from the Yellow Rattle. She also brought jars of cider, and punch made from rum that she had been hiding for months. Villagers laid out small, glistening baked things on a table, more butter and sugar used than normal, but as it was with Christmases through the years, it was a time to splurge, not ration. So, although all blackouts had to be drawn, including a large black curtain at the entrance foyer to prevent light from bleeding out as people came and went, the inside of the hall was as jolly and bright as any Christmas party could hope to be.

Ruth welcomed people as they arrived, mothers with children whose husbands were away at war, older couples who missed their sons on frigates or their daughters, some of whom were now joining the Land Army and working in factories. Albert and his wife, Emma, came through the door; they had sons in the RAF. Yet more came. Johnny was there, and some of the older boys came along with Father Tweedsmuir. All were mingling and talking, and soon some were singing along with Cora Dunn to "Hark the Herald Angels Sing" and "Here We Come A-Wassailing." The beer and punch flowed, and the villagers became louder as they drank; the hall soon filled with a haze of cigarette smoke.

Malcolm hadn't arrived. He'd said he would come but had not specified whether he was bringing Virginia and Elise. At six o'clock, the children were given their gifts and told they could open them before Christmas. They tore off the wrapping, and all were thrilled with the various homemade gifts provided by villagers. Girls hugged dolls, and boys ran about with their tin planes, crying *vroom, vroom*, and yet Malcolm was still not there. Soon, the mums and billetees said goodbye and took happy and excited children home to play with their new toys.

The band returned to the stage and played louder music, meant for grown-up dancing, and Cora Dunn offered to do the calling for a traditional folk dance. Ruth looked around, wondering if Malcolm had changed his mind about attending. She realized then, in a rather alarming way, how very much she wished to see him, and how very much she hoped he would arrive *without* Elise on his arm. Shaking away the thought, Ruth joined the group and eventually lost herself in the fun of dancing in a round. It seemed that her dress had drawn the attention of some of the younger men from the flax farm, one of whom she recognized from the pub. Avoiding his gaze, Ruth passed on the next dance and stood to the side, sipping a glass of beer, her eyes regularly going to the blackout curtain in front of the door. She heard it open and close and, expecting to see Malcolm step through the curtain, instead saw Walter and Martha Horgon. Ruth greeted them. "Mr. Horgon, I'm very surprised to find you here, and dressed so nicely with your military suit and your medals. I thought you weren't interested in dances."

"I am not," he said, kissing Ruth on the cheek. "But Martha here is very much interested in dances, and she's insisted I come along, at least that I might have one glass of rum punch, given that it will likely be a long time before we taste rum again."

"Malcolm's not here?" Martha asked Ruth, looking around at the crowd of dancers.

"No, I'm sure he'll come along soon." Just as she said it, the door behind the curtain banged open once more, and after a moment, Malcolm stepped through the blackout curtain. He wore a suit with a waistcoat and a tie of red. Ruth noted he was alone and could hardly hide her glee. Perhaps because she'd already had a few glasses of beer, she skipped over to Malcolm, flushed and hot from the dance. "You've made it," she cried, and without realizing what she was doing, she fell into his arms. He stiffened for a moment, but then relaxed. He stepped back from her, a smile finally appearing on his lips.

"Where've you been hiding this frock?"

"It was a battle to get into it," Ruth said. "Come, have a drink."

"It appears I have some catching up to do." Malcolm took a glass and drank it in one go. "How many has it been for you?"

"Me? Oh, I don't know, three of these maybe." She held up the glass. Malcolm took the beer pitcher, refilled his glass, and downed that one, too. "My, you are thirsty tonight," she said.

"I'm not sure if thirst has anything to do with it. Does that punch there have something strong in it?"

"Rum."

"Perfect." Malcolm walked to the bowl and poured a ladleful into his empty beer glass. He took a sip, this time going a little slower. He seemed distracted. The band had just started up again, and a large crowd of people moved, shoes and heels thundering on the floor.

"Is everything all right?" Ruth asked loudly, trying to compete with the racket.

"Yes. Well, no. It was a discussion about coming, about Virginia . . . and Elise. I wasn't sure what to do. Virginia said she could stay to mind Elise, but I felt that maybe she would rather have come, so I said that I would stay with Elise, and then there was briefly the prospect of bringing Elise, which didn't seem like a very good idea, and so back and forth we went. I left in an odd state of mind."

"Well, you're here now, right?"

"Yes, I'm sorry if I'm a bit dour—it's been some time since I've done anything 'normal' like this. The last time I went to a dance was before, when . . . when Elise was . . ."

"I see what you mean. Surely you can try and have fun tonight? It's not at anyone's expense, is it?"

"No, Virginia was not as keen as I to come, as she said. She thinks it will do me good—and Elise doesn't even seem to know where she is at any given moment." He drained his glass.

"Have some fun. I think you've earned it." Ruth took his hand. "Come, just one dance." They went out on to the floor and clumsily moved through the calls, and soon Malcolm was smiling. Dancers bumped into one another, grabbed for wrong partners, and it seemed the worse they danced, the more fun they had. The song ended, and Malcolm and Ruth returned to the punch bowl, panting and rosy, to find Horgon standing alone.

"Malcolm, glad to see you could come out to sully our war office with rum punch."

"Good to see you, too, sir. The village seems quite pleased once more with us townies. In fact, it seems they've forgotten about the horrible wraith for at least one night."

"Indeed," said Horgon. The band started a new song, a particularly boisterous number, and Horgon appraised the musicians with distaste.

"They're old-fashioned songs, aren't they? Most parties in the south are dancing to jazz, I think," Ruth shouted over the music.

"Yes, perhaps." Horgon stopped, a peculiar look on his face. He carefully placed his punch glass down on the table and cocked his head, seeming to listen. "Wait, wait." He held a finger up. "Wait!" Then he scrambled with his suit jacket, yanking at the buttons, and pulled from around his neck a string, attached to which was a whistle. He placed it in his mouth and blew, the shrill blast cutting through the music. People shrank from the sound, some startled in shock. The music staggered once or twice until the band stopped playing altogether. "Listen!" Horgon cried. Then, from outside, at some distance, they all heard it. Another whistle, a long intense blast. Then, more ominously, they heard the distant drone of a propeller. "Proceed to the lower level," Horgon shouted. The band set down their instruments, and the revellers quietly moved down the stairs and towards the two designated rooms on the lower level.

"I've heard enough Henkels in Norway to know those aren't our birds up there," Malcolm said.

"Martha, please go with the rest downstairs," Horgon said to his wife. "I've got to step outside to assess." He opened a closet door and pulled a helmet from it, which he put on. He fastened the chinstrap and handed another helmet to Malcolm. "Take this. Get the lights out. I'll need your ears. We need to find the guard on duty." Malcolm took the helmet, while Ruth lingered by the stairwell. "You, Gladstone," Horgon ordered. "You get down, too!"

"I can help."

"With that dress on? You can hardly walk!" Horgon took a red-glassed electric torch from the closet and snapped it on. Malcolm meanwhile turned all the overhead lights off; Horgon sighed. "Right, Gladstone, get your coat on. Take this." He handed her a third helmet. "That's regulation to wear if you want to be part of this." Ruth took the immensely heavy helmet and placed it on her head, closing the strap under her chin. Her hair clips pinched uncomfortably as she did so. She then put on her coat, which thankfully was black. As they stepped outside, it seemed the fog was even thicker than before.

The sound of the planes grew louder. "A whole squadron," Horgon said, looking skyward into the mist.

"They've not had any challenge from our boys, either," Malcolm whispered. "I only hear Henkels and some Stukas, but no guns, no Spitfires. They're headed south-east."

"Yes, a rather curious route. We've not been on any flight paths here in Martynsborough; rarely have we heard a propeller for the whole of the war. Out here, it's a rare sound. What the devil are these Krauts doing out there?"

"Look at the fog," Ruth spoke. "My guess is that they're lost."

"Yes, probably returning home from a raid in Aberdeen and they've lost their way." Horgon started walking down the road. "Let's find our guard for the night." The three of them walked down the street with the ominous sound of planes up there somewhere in the mist, invisible. "It's a bit reassuring," Horgon whispered, "knowing that as much as we can't see them, nor can they see us through this murk—I'd wager that you could tear down the blackouts and have every light on in the village, and they'd still see nothing. Moreover, my guess is that they've already dropped their payload. If we're lucky, they'll circle aimlessly in the fog and run out of fuel by the time they get to the North Sea and dunk, or crash head first into Ward's Stone."

By the time they had found the guard, the planes had moved away without incident. Horgon blew the three-blast all-clear signal and was answered by the other Home Guard on duty at the north end, near the church. They walked back to the hall, with Horgon occasionally blowing the all-clear so the whole village eventually knew that the trouble had passed. When they got back to the hall, the lights were once more glowing inside, but it seemed the gaiety had subsided, and people stood about, smoking cigarettes and laughing nervously.

"It's an all-clear," Horgon announced. "Just a small squadron that seemed to have lost their way heading back to the Fatherland." Martha stood next to him and took his arm. "Well, what are you waiting for?" he roared. "You can strike up the band once more."

"Darling, I'd like to go home. It's all been a bit much," said Martha. A few others nodded in agreement, and soon people said their goodbyes, thanking Ruth for a lovely party and so on.

"We can still dance," said Ruth as she removed the helmet. "Can't we?"

The musicians put instruments back into cases; all seemed gracious, but largely finished for the night.

"We'd like to go home as well," said Edith.

"Right," said Ruth with a little disappointment. "Goodnight, then." Vera and Edith said their goodbyes, and Johnny walked them home. Most people drifted from the hall, happy at having a nice party, but wishing to be near home and hearth after the air-raid scare. A couple of farm labourers hoisted up Ellen's keg and carried it back to the Yellow Rattle.

"I suppose we should start cleaning up a bit." Ruth looked around and realized that she and Malcolm were alone.

"It's a quarter past eight," Malcolm said, looking at his watch. "Hardly a late night."

"But no party," said Ruth.

"Well, you've got a lovely dress, and we've got drinks, and we've got music." He walked over to the piano and lifted the fallboard.

"Yes, of course." Ruth poured two glasses of beer from the remaining pitcher and placed them on top of the piano. Malcolm sat down and rolled through an arpeggio and then stumbled a bit, the notes bouncing happily and chaotically from the reticent, slightly untuned piano.

"It might be more difficult than I thought." He smiled, abashed. "I don't have a complete complement as I once did."

"Well, *I* have a fully functional left hand. Perhaps I can help." Ruth slipped in next to him and opened the book that someone had left on the music rack.

"Can you read this?"

"It's been some time, but I'll see what I can do."

She flipped through the pages. "What about this, 'Stay as Sweet as You Are'? It's a little old, but I know it."

Malcolm squinted at the notes, then started playing the right-hand melody. Ruth soon joined in on the bass part with her left hand. "Let's go through the first few bars a couple of times, to find our tempo. And you know"—he turned to look at her with his good eye—"this is really rather fun."

They stumbled through those first measures, their fingers endeavouring to move in tandem, the piano, slightly out of tune, responding to their tentative touch. After some attempts, they felt confident enough to move through the song in earnest. Malcolm played the melody rather adeptly, his dexterous fingers feeling for the correct keys, but Ruth could sense that he was fighting the instinct to do as the notation instructed— to move his alternate hand to the lower register where Ruth's own small hand played with slightly less confidence. Inevitably, he did so; his left hand crossed the middle C, his forearm pushed into a soft velvet bodice, and his fingers fumbled over hers, resulting in a brief galvanic spark. He quickly withdrew the offending hand then leaned forward, smiling, then laughing, likely the first time he had laughed so naturally in a very long while. "Sorry, my left hand has a mind of its own. But that *was* sounding good; let's try it again."

They did indeed improve, with each of their hands playing their part as if they belonged to a single body, while the other, vestigial fingers were gathered chastely in each owner's lap.

Malcolm said, "Go back to the start. Maybe I'll sing."

"You won't," Ruth said in disbelief.

"Oh, I will." True to his word, Malcolm opened his mouth, and he sang.

"I'm so impressed. You have a beautiful voice," Ruth said.

"There's the next verse; it's yours."

"I don't think I'll be very good, but I'll try."

"You've a lovely voice, too." Malcolm then attempted to improvise something fancy in the upper octaves but tripped himself up and slammed both his hands down on the keys, producing a sharp and dissonant muddle. They both laughed raucously. "Oh, Ruth, I may not be able to play as I once did, but I've not laughed like that in a very long time. That was wonderful. I think we sounded rather good." Malcolm got up to rummage about the table to see what was left to drink. "I guess we should probably start to wind this party down. We can finish the cleaning tomorrow." He poured the dregs of the cider into a glass. "You'd like a bit more? There's no sense wasting it."

"Why not?" She stood and pushed out the piano bench, and as she did, her dress ripped from hem to waist. "Oh." She looked down to see her sheer white slip spilling from the rift, revealing her garters, and scandalous ladders running up her stockings.

"Looks like we've got a casualty," Malcolm said.

She hopelessly tried to pull the red velvet together, to cover her undergarments, but gave up. "Oh, no matter. I'm quite drunk, I just have to say." Ruth tipped her drink back and emptied the cider. "Yes, very rather drunk."

"As am I—a prerequisite for a fine party. I'll probably be letting myself in the back door and using the hedge as my toilet tonight."

"It's easier for chaps to do so," she said. "I've a queue for our lavatory on most days." Ruth collapsed in a chair and looked at her knees. "Damn, I've wrecked another pair of stockings . . . *and* a dress. I've almost no stockings left." She yawned. "I'm afraid I might just sleep here."

"I wish I could—I'm hoping the drink helps, but I've had so much trouble sleeping lately." Malcolm sipped at his final drink.

"Oh?"

"I'm not sure why. Before, when it was warmer, with the windows open, the wind and the crickets, I guess it helped. It's much too cold now, and the room is so silent, I jump at every sound, thinking it might be a German bomber."

"Have you tried this?" Ruth brought her hand to her ear and cupped it there, then moved it back and forth. "It's good to calm the mind."

"What on earth are you doing?" Malcolm asked with an amused grin.

"I'm creating ocean sounds, like a crashing surf, or the whistling within a seashell."

"I don't hear anything," Malcolm said as Ruth fell into another laughing fit, her dress ripping some more as she did, which she didn't seem to notice.

"Well . . . no, you won't, only *I* can hear it," she said. "Come try it. Like this." She demonstrated once more. Malcolm looked at his hands.

"I suppose the right hand will have a better effect given that I've got all my fingers there," he said. Then, like Ruth, he cupped his hand and put it over his ear.

"Then move it up and down slowly," she said, "like a scallop shell opening and closing. Be really quiet. Go. Can you hear it?"

Malcolm did as Ruth asked, and in seeing his surprised expression, she knew that he could indeed hear what she had always heard—the air, the rattle of the radiator, the buzz of the overhead light, his breathing, her breathing, perhaps even his beating heart. She imagined the sounds moving through his hand and swirling about in his palm, and as he lifted his fingers, the sounds spilled away and allowed more in, which he then caught by closing his hand once more over his ear. Such a small and silly thing, but also so very wonderful. He glanced at Ruth, smiling, and she realized that they both looked mad, flapping their hands about their ears, but she could see how he liked it so very much.

"Why do you do this?" he asked.

"I've done it since I was little. We took a train once, an overnight train, and I couldn't sleep. I was frightened, having never slept anywhere other than my own bed. By accident, I discovered if I cupped my hand over my ear and moved it slowly up and down, it's like I could capture a sound, in that case, the sound of the train engine, and then I could turn it into a rhythmic, lulling thing quite easily—like I had taken a frightening sound and made it my own. I still do it, at times when I'm nervous, or scared. I find it can be comforting."

"You're not nervous now, are you?"

"Of course not." She laughed. "Quite the opposite, can't you tell? I've got half my thigh on display. I have to say, I've never told anyone about my little trick—I reckoned they'd think me odd."

"Not odd, ingenious." He looked closely at her drooping eyes. "My God, you're putting yourself to sleep right now. Amazing."

"Yes, I suppose. There's also the fact that I'm quite drunk."

"Let's get you home. My cot calls for me, and I'll try your little trick tonight," he said. "I've had a marvellous time. I needed this. I can't remember the last time I laughed so much."

"Yes, it's been grand." Ruth sank deeper into the chair, barely hearing him speak. Her thoughts then drifted to a faraway place—a place with no inhibitions, somewhere around the second ring of the inferno. *You could have me right now*, she thought. *Right this very instant. I'll come to your studio, and we'll squeeze together on to your little cot. All you must do is say the word, and I'll give you no resistance. Come take me,*

*Malcolm—we'll be Paolo and Francesca, the lustful, and damn the conse-
quences. I'll drape my arms around your neck and draw you to my mouth,
but unlike that statue you spoke of—your precious Rodin—our lips will
indeed meet, they will, oh and more, so much more. We'll be punished for
our sin and be sentenced to float about in the whirlwinds of hell, tangled
up in our adultery, our lust. Just say the word, just say the word.*

But Malcolm did not say the word. Instead, he took her wrists
and pulled her to a standing position, gently pushed her arms into
coat sleeves, buttoned her to the top, turned her collar up around her
neck—all done adeptly with a practiced hand, as if by second nature.
Then he led her outside, snapping off the last light and locking the door
with the key that Horgon had provided him.

He turned her in the right direction, and she responded raggedly,
like a doll, as he proceeded to walk her directly to her front door. No
thoughts of wandering sheep or ghostly wraiths crossed her mind that
foggy night. Instead, in a state of warm intoxication, she stumbled
along, hanging from him, her face buried in the hollow of his neck, her
lips warmly grazing the underside of his jaw, desperately seeking his lips,
which—in her mind, at least—were just out of reach.

19

With all the excitement around the Christmas party, the day itself was a quiet, anticlimactic affair. Snow fell gently, crusting the fields in hoar frost, while the residents of the Catchpoole cottage passed a pleasant morning exchanging modest gifts, mostly handmade things. They ate a sparse but rich breakfast that involved honey and golden syrup and things both buttery and sweet. Then they donned their Sunday best, which, for Ruth, with her unfortunate habit of destroying nylon stockings, was becoming rather threadbare. They went to church to hear the Christmas service, leaving Johnny behind to break up some deadfall for the fireplace.

The hall had been closed—at least for some of the workers—from Christmas day and through to the second week in January, so neither Ruth nor Malcolm had sat at their regular desk in some days. She had not seen him since the dance. Nor had she seen him when they arrived at church, and after some niceties with Father Tweedsmuir, they took the pews close to the front. Throughout the Christmas service, Ruth dared not look back, lest he had arrived—she couldn't imagine making eye contact after her behaviour the night of the dance. She wasn't sure if she was more embarrassed by slopping her mouth all over his neck or her undergarments spilling from a rift in her dress. Nevertheless, at the end of the service, she turned and noted that he wasn't there at all.

Walking home, the three women passed Virginia's cottage, and Vera turned towards it. "I'd like to invite them over for a New Year's lunch. Don't you think it would be a lovely idea?" she said. "Come up, let's say hello. They've not come to church. I'd like to say happy Christmas."

"I should get back," said Ruth, walking ahead briskly. "Johnny's probably doing all my chores for me."

"Now, now, come say hello. It's your friend Malcolm—you must wish him happy Christmas," Vera said.

Ruth reluctantly turned and followed the women up the path to the cottage. Vera rapped gently on the door. Malcolm appeared in his housecoat over pyjamas and a pair of navy slippers—and as he often did, he stepped on to the threshold and partially closed the door behind him. He crossed his arms, shivered slightly, and said, "Well, good morning, ladies. Happy Christmas, Vera, Edith . . . Ruth, I see you're up with the lark." He smiled. His face was stubbly, and his breath caused small wisps in the cold air.

"We've attended the church service, and we missed you," Vera said.

"But it's not Sunday—oh, yes, I suppose they do something on Christmas. Virginia was a bit slow this morning, seems to have a small cough. We've stayed warm inside. I hadn't thought of church."

"It's quite all right," said Vera. "I was hoping that the three of you might join us for a New Year's Day lunch."

Malcolm looked over at Ruth, then glanced back briefly at the closed door behind him, a thoughtful expression on his face. He said, "We'd love to," and his eyes fell on Ruth. "I hope you're all well, and happy Christmas to you, too, Ruth. Lovely to see you. I've not seen you since the dance. Where've you been hiding yourself? We should have another patter on the ivories, no?"

Ruth could feel colour warming her cheeks.

"Yes, that would be grand," she said chastely.

"Well then, it's set," Vera said. "Happy Christmas, and we'll see you next week."

By one o'clock New Year's Day, Vera's cottage was spit-clean and festive. With a jolly fire in the hearth and the smells of delicious cooking throughout, there came a gentle knock at the door. "Ruth, go ahead and welcome our guests," Vera called from the kitchen. Ruth stopped and briefly looked in the hall mirror to adjust her hair. She couldn't help but shudder in trepidation.

"Welcome. Please come in," she said with a smile as she opened the door. Virginia entered first, wearing her usual gravy-brown dress. She handed her coat to Ruth and moved to the kitchen, saying hello and happy new year. Malcolm followed, wearing a sweater over a shirt and tie and a smart hat, while Elise, as always, was wrapped in stylish French clothes, a winter frock of deep violet and a cream-coloured cardigan over her shoulders. She wore fresh-looking dark hose with no ladders; her hair was tied back in a simple braid. Johnny joined them in the corridor to greet the guests.

Malcolm removed his hat and handed it to the boy with a wink. "And how is the man about the house? You're well?"

"Yes, sir," Johnny said.

Once coats and hats were hung on hooks, Malcolm led Elise into the kitchen and pulled out a chair, in which she sat without being asked. She folded her hands in her lap and sat quietly. Edith and Vera exchanged glances.

"Some drinks?" Vera said. "I've some cordial, and also some other things I've squirrelled away." She opened a cupboard and brought out a bottle of sherry and another half full of Scotch.

"Well, well," Malcolm said. "You've saved the goods for us. I would love a splash of Scotch—it's been a long time."

"And for Elise? What would she like to drink?" Vera paused. "Malcolm, any suggestion?" Edith and Ruth held their breath, deeply curious what would happen next. Malcolm looked around at the inquisitive faces of his hosts.

"Oh, I suppose Elise quite likes tea—not too hot—with milk. Or a glass of cordial perhaps—whatever's easiest." There seemed to be a collective sigh of relief.

"I can put the kettle on," Vera offered. "In the meantime, here's something to quench your thirst." She placed a glass of cold water in front of Elise and then poured an inch or two of Scotch for Malcolm.

"Cheers," he said, clinking his glass to Elise's glass, which remained untouched on the table. He took a sip of his own, and again, the hosts watched with great curiosity to see what Elise would do next. She did not disappoint them. Glancing at the drink in front of her, she took it up and sipped from it, then put it back. There was an exhale of satisfaction—so now they knew: Elise did not require help to sip from a drink.

"What is that delicious smell, Vera?" Malcolm asked. "I can't wait to see what you've fixed for us."

"I thought I'd try my hand at some French-inspired food, for you and Elise. I've a few cookery books from the Continent."

"Lovely, and thoughtful. Do you hear that, Elise?" She did not respond. Malcolm took another casual sip from his Scotch and rested his arm on the back of Elise's chair. There was an awkward pause. "Can I help with anything?" He looked around at the three wide-eyed, speechless women.

"Oh, please, ladies, have a seat with us at the table," Virginia said impatiently. "If no one will be plainspoken, I will be. You likely have a thousand questions, so I'll save Malcolm the trouble." She took a deep breath and clasped her hands together. "Elise will sit and eat and enjoy the cooking. She can manage a fork and spoon. She can manage herself in the lavatory, possibly with my help, if necessary—and you need not stand about as if you're observing a strange animal in the forest. She'll not speak, but she may listen. At least we'd like to think she listens—we're not entirely certain—but we ought to speak with the assumption she can. She may need help with some small things, but Malcolm and I will see to that. Does that set all your minds at ease?"

"I'm sorry," Vera said. "We only want you to feel welcome."

"And you have, dear Vera. You've made a lovely effort, so let's enjoy the fruits of your labour and not worry ourselves with Elise here. She is more than capable to manage through lunch." Virginia smiled. "Now, how about a small glass of sherry? I've not had any in an age."

"Yes, yes, of course." Vera poured her a glass. "Come, Johnny, come sit." They gathered around the table for devils on horseback and savoury biscuits made with thyme leaves and a terrine of chicken liver—a most un-wartime-like spread. They nibbled and chatted about this and that, the dance, the air raid, the state of the war, and so on. Eventually, Vera served lunch and produced a bottle of French claret.

"My word, dear woman, wherever did you find that?" Malcolm asked.

"Would you do the honours?" Vera handed him the bottle and a corkscrew. "I've been saving this for some time. I'm neither going to confirm nor deny that I have more wine down in the cellar—but just know that you ought not to pour us mere thimblefuls. Be generous." Malcolm held up the bottle and inspected the label, then opened the wine with a practiced hand and poured.

He lifted his glass. "Happy 1941 to you all. Here's hoping this war is over by Easter."

"Hear, hear," Vera cried with delight. They clinked glasses while Elise continued to sit silently, staring at the plate in front of her. They ate, and as Virginia had intimated, Elise took small bites of food with her fork. Malcolm had shredded her duck leg with his knife, but generally she managed, although she ate little.

"Don't take her appetite as a reflection of your cooking," Malcolm said to Vera. "She's always eaten like a small bird. I, on the other hand, would ask that you spoon another lovely leg of duck on to my plate."

The alcohol had its intended effect, and voices grew louder, as did laughter. With dinner complete, Vera cleared plates, and Johnny got up as well.

"I'll get some more wood; the fire's dying down."

"Yes, thank you, Johnny. We can have our pudding in the sitting room. I've saved butter and sugar for two weeks and made a pear cake," Vera said.

"I can help him." Malcolm stood. "A breath of fresh air might be nice."

"I'll come as well," Ruth said. The three of them got up and gathered their coats and stepped outside to enjoy the January air, breaking down a pile of deadfall and gathering it into several bundles. Soon, they were back in the warmth of the cottage.

"Where's Elise?" Malcolm asked as he removed his coat and stepped into the sitting room.

"I thought she was with you—she got up when you went out." A look of concern crossed Vera's face. Something thumped above them, and they glanced upward.

"She's upstairs," Ruth said. "I'll get her." She ascended quietly to the second floor and found Elise in Vera's room rummaging through several open dresser drawers. "Elise, what are you doing?"

The woman turned to Ruth, her face unreadable, then returned her attention to the drawer and withdrew a scarf and tried to stuff it into the pocket of her cardigan. Ruth reached out to take the scarf.

"Let's put this away, all right?" She tugged at the scarf, but Elise would not relinquish it. Ruth searched her eyes, looking for meaning or intent, and saw only ambiguity. One moment, there was nothing, a vacuous gaze, but then the next, there was intent, maybe even intelligence, determination, like a duality—a struggle occurring within the woman's brain. Elise violently grasped Ruth's wrist with surprising strength and made small huffing sounds, while her face remained unnervingly passive. Ruth tried to twist away, but Elise's grip was like a vice. Ruth felt afraid for the first time.

"Elise, that's not yours." Malcolm appeared at the door. "Please put it back, and let go of Ruth." Elise turned her head towards Malcolm, then released Ruth's wrist and the scarf. "That's it. Now come along,

Elise. Do you need to use the lavatory? No? Then let's get downstairs. Vera is serving the pudding." Elise left the room and descended the stairs wordlessly. They heard Virginia speak from below.

"Well, here she is. Elise, come sit. We'll have our pudding."

"Sorry about that," Malcolm said, lingering in the doorway. "Her injury prevents her from understanding some of the rules of social interaction, and if she sees something she likes, she takes it. Has she troubled anything here? Did she hurt you?" He stepped towards Ruth and took up her wrist, examining it for a moment. "She sometimes grasps things with firmness, but she's never been violent to anyone."

"No, nothing to concern ourselves with—I'm fine."

Malcolm held her hand for a moment longer, then released it.

"And what has she done here?" He looked down at the chest of drawers.

"She seemed rather taken with Vera's silk scarves and handkerchiefs," Ruth said, rubbing her wrist absentmindedly. "They are quite beautiful. I don't really blame her." She folded the scarf and returned it to the drawer while Malcolm stepped back into the hall and looked at the door near the stairwell.

"Is this your bedroom here?"

"Yes, it's not much."

"A lovely view." He walked up to her bedroom window and looked out. "You can see clear up to our cottage."

"Yes." Ruth followed him into the room.

"Comfortable?" He turned to inspect the iron-framed bed that was neatly made up with a white coverlet.

"Nothing to complain about."

"Better than an army cot, I suppose." As Malcolm sat on the bed, it creaked under his weight. "And this." Malcolm picked up a messy sheaf of papers on the bedside table. "Is this the infamous gothic novel? *The Wraith of Martynsborough*?"

"Yes. Please, don't read it. It's only a rough draft. I'll let you look at it when it's better."

Malcolm put the papers back on the table and said, "Ruth, you've been acting strange around me. Is there something the matter? Is it Elise? Is it not all right—that I brought her here?"

"Oh God no, it's not that at all." Ruth eased her door shut a small amount and turned to him. "My gran will probably be calling for me any moment, knowing that I'm in a bedroom with a man who's not my husband. I quickly wanted to say something about the night of the dance. I . . ."

"You don't have to say anything if you don't wish to. We had fun, that's all."

"Yes, but I . . . I was—on the walk home, I recall that my mouth might have been affixed to your neck like a horrible leech."

"Huh." He smiled. "I don't recall anything that worries me." He stood and took a step towards her. "Nothing to worry about, not one bit."

"Ruth?" Edith called from downstairs.

"As expected," Ruth said quietly. She eased her bedroom door open.

"Yes, Gran," she called down. "I was just showing Malcolm our paraffin heater. We're coming down now." She turned to Malcolm and whispered, "So . . . nothing to worry about?"

"Nothing to worry about."

They spent the rest of the afternoon around the fireplace, chatting and enjoying themselves. Elise remained close to Malcolm on the sofa, and Ruth observed her keenly from a chair opposite, watching her reactions to things, noting how she stared blankly at the fire, the flame's light reflecting and dancing in her blue eyes. While other times, Elise would look with birdlike attention towards the sound of Malcolm's voice and hold her gaze briefly there, as if she were indeed listening. As Ruth watched, she couldn't help but consider the woman's eyes, like the two kiln ponds themselves—once filled with light and fire, they'd been transmuted into something starless, cold, and watery. They were enigmatic, fathomless, and whatever lurked within them was now unknown, like trying to peer through a darkening glass.

Ruth then started to wonder: What went on in this woman's head? Was she really in a catatonic state due to some brain injury, or . . . She realized how outlandish the notion might be, but nevertheless considered it. What if Elise was completely lucid and sane and simply chose to behave this way? She'd purposefully found a way to retreat from reality, to close herself off from the world and allow someone to care for her, to dress her and bathe her. She'd never have to perform any wifely duties, never have to tend to her husband's needs. She could simply while away the days, her every need catered to. What if, as a cure for boredom, she slipped out at night, taking things that she fancied, like a magpie, nibbling from gardens, fooling everyone, pulling the wool over her own husband's eyes? What if she wasn't simply wandering aimlessly, led astray by her brain damage and somehow finding her way home at night, as Ruth had sometimes suspected, but was doing it all *purposefully*? What if she was, in fact, knowingly playing the part—the part of the Wraith of Martynsborough?

It was an extraordinary thought, but as these notions jostled around in Ruth's mind, she was ever watchful of Elise, and it was almost as if the mute woman was, in turn, considering her. Ruth could sense cogs and wheels turning somewhere underneath that pretty blonde hair. Her pale-blue eyes slid over and met Ruth's, and as the rest listened to Vera recount some story, Elise looked at her intently with an unusual, knowing stare that contained . . . humour? A challenge? Ruth saw the glimmer of a smile—not the type that pulls on the corners of one's mouth, but the type that gleams in the eye. It was there, but then gone, then it returned. Ruth had to look away, to collect herself, because for a brief and frightening moment, she was convinced that Elise had read her mind.

-20-

Well past midnight, with Maude due to arrive in two days, Ruth sat in a chair at her window, staring at a startlingly beautiful moon. She lifted the sash, knowing it would be cold, but she craved the fresh air. The oppressive silence of the windless night confronted her. It was winter; there were no crickets or nightingales, not even owls this night—just cool silence. She rested her chin in her hand on the alcove of the window, and along with a pillow she had taken from her bed, she thought to sleep there, with the cool air, delightful and tranquil, flowing over her face and through her hair. It was not the first time she had slept this way, near to the window. She would often wake with her cheek on the glass and a small kink in her neck at some dark and lonely hour. Yes, something compelled her to be near the window at night. She looked out at Virginia's cottage, at the black windows of the studio with its curtains darkening the glass, where Malcolm was sleeping, or perhaps reading, or moulding a sculpture with his damaged hand. She had to suppress a thought of her own that bubbled up roguishly. No, not a thought—more of a feeling, one that was becoming difficult to ignore. She shook her head, then emptied her mind of thoughts until she eventually fell asleep.

Sometime in the middle of the night, Ruth awoke. Immediately alert, she heard a metallic sort of clatter. It came from the cottage between theirs and Virginia's, where an old, reclusive man named Jeffrey lived. She could see much of his back garden from her window but struggled to peer into the shadows that lurked further back. She rubbed her eyes and looked more carefully. There, in the gloom by his shed, she saw a figure moving in a curious way. It was the wraith—it would have to be—but Ruth could see only the rustle of white fabric in the shadows and little else. The figure disappeared into the gloom. Ruth held her breath and listened as she scanned the moonlit gardens and hedges, but saw nothing more, and could only hear the fierceness of her own pulse.

Ruth was confident that it was Elise who lurked around Jeffrey's garden. There was a certain logic to it—she now knew that Malcolm slept in his studio, and Virginia was, herself, sound asleep upstairs. It would be simple for Elise to creep out through the front door. Blackouts prevented any witnesses. Their New Year's Day lunch proved that Elise was not some helpless invalid but that she could navigate her way through a meal, use the lavatory, and likely even dress herself. As Ruth had started to suspect, based on her careful study of Elise's behaviour, there was every possibility that the woman was not only *not* catatonic but relatively sound and sensible and concealing this fact. The deeper question of course was why. Why would Elise take such trouble to carry on this charade? How was it connected to the larger mystery of the wraith? There was something sinister about the whole enterprise that Ruth found deeply unnerving, but curiosity proved to be a strong motivator.

Ruth crept into the hall and down the stairs, hoping not to wake anyone. She slipped her bare feet into a pair of Johnny's boots and draped her coat over her nightdress before stepping quietly out into the night.

The bravado she felt whilst safe in her room quickly disappeared as she stepped out of the cottage. The moon appeared to be a great frightening face in the black sky. But it was only Elise—gentle, beautiful Elise. Nothing to be frightened of. Although Ruth thought briefly of the vice-like grip on her wrist in Vera's room. No, maybe not so harmless. Either way, she would need to inform Malcolm. She needed proof if she hoped he would ever believe her. She would have to see with her own eyes. It was worth the risk.

Ruth walked up the path to the cottage and into Jeffrey's back garden. She saw a shed with a chain lock that perhaps had been the source of the rattling sound. Then a noise came from the tangled hedgerow that separated Jeffrey's cottage from Virginia's—the snapping of branches and the sound of a catching breath, followed by a soft, female gasp. A cry of surprise emerged from the gloom, but since Ruth had never heard her speak, she couldn't be sure it was Elise's voice. The figure in white stepped away quickly between the brambles.

"You!" Ruth whispered sharply. "I see you. Is that you, Elise?" She followed, clomping along in Johnny's boots. She entered the bramble, and the branches grabbed hold of her coat and hair. Further in, a twisted, covered path led back to Virginia's cottage, which would involve much bending and scraping. Ruth couldn't bring herself to go any further—the gloomy, thorny tunnel was a step too far—and very spooky. She stopped, unsure what to do, and then decided to return home. She stepped through the thicket, back towards Jeffrey's garden, and noticed something hanging from a low branch—a piece of fabric. She took it out into the moonlight and held it up. She recognized the pattern. It was one of Vera's scarves! Ruth knew Vera was asleep in her bed at that moment, having looked in on her mere minutes before leaving the house, so *she* couldn't have dropped it there.

It could only mean one thing . . . it *was* Elise in the bramble—it would have to be. She must have managed to nick the scarf from Vera's drawer during their visit on New Year's Day and had now just dropped it on the path. Ruth had confiscated one scarf, but clearly Elise had secreted a second and smuggled it out of the house without anyone being the wiser. Ruth shoved it into her coat pocket and walked back to her cottage, wondering how on earth to broach this strange discovery with Malcolm.

The next morning, she walked directly to Virginia's cottage after breakfast, the scarf in her pocket. Before knocking on the front door, she thought to first check the studio, where there was a back door that she knew Malcolm sometimes used. This way, she could talk to him privately without alerting Virginia to her presence. The blackouts had been taken down from the studio windows, and she could see him inside. He sat on his cot in his dressing robe, his back to her, leafing through one of his art books. Ruth wavered. Perhaps she shouldn't tell him. She couldn't help but wonder how this information might alter things—between husband and wife, between their families . . . between him and her. Maybe—maybe it was best that she not tell him. She took the scarf from her pocket and inspected its pretty pattern of teal, green, and gold.

"Ruth? What are you doing?" Malcolm stood in the doorway of the studio.

"Oh." She looked up, startled. "Hello."

"What have you got there?" he asked.

"It's one of Vera's scarves." She looked at his earnest expression and decided that honesty was the best approach—they were friends, were they not? Friends should be honest with one another. "Can I come in for a moment to have a short word?"

"Yes, please come in." She entered his studio, and he pulled a chair from the desk for her to sit, while he sat on the edge of his cot. The Rodin book lay open on the blanket, and she glanced at the photo of *The Kiss*.

"What's this all about?"

"I'm not sure how to say this," Ruth began, "so I'll just come out with it. I think Elise has been mistaken as the wraith by the villagers. I believe she's been walking about at night while you sleep. I've wondered before, but now I have proof." She held out the scarf.

"What on earth are you talking about?" Malcolm's face went dark.

"Well, I've seen the wraith from my window. I've never told you, because I've always wondered . . . well, I've wondered if it was in fact Elise, out for a late-night wander. I've wavered about this, thinking one moment it's ridiculous, but then thinking again that it must be true. Even Vera wondered aloud about it when she found her pears nibbled in the back garden. You yourself have had some things taken, and on New Year's Day, as you recall, we found Elise rummaging in Vera's drawer. Just last night, I saw this figure once more in Jeffrey's back garden. I confronted her. It was a woman, clearly. I heard her, I saw her, and she left this behind." Ruth held up the scarf. "It's Vera's. And since I knew Vera to be asleep in her bed last night, it was certainly not her wandering about. So, I figured it was Elise; she must have slipped the scarf out that afternoon when you were at our house. I know this all sounds very odd, Malcolm, but I thought for her safety and for your information, I ought to tell you."

"What you're saying doesn't make sense."

"Well, there's something else. I don't quite know how to put this, but I think perhaps she's more able than she's letting on." Malcolm said nothing. His face coloured, and he frowned in a way that Ruth had never seen, but she stammered on regardless. "You see, I've looked at her, and she seems to maybe be . . . um, exaggerating her symptoms, but then she looks at me, she—she seems not to like me. Perhaps she's jealous, or—oh God, that's not really what I mean, what I mean is . . ."

"You don't mean anything, Ruth. In fact, I don't think you know what you're talking about at all." He stood. "Now, if you'll excuse me, I have things to do."

"I'm sorry, I—I didn't mean for you to get angry. I was worried a little—that's all."

"I suppose you'll inform the villagers that you've solved the mystery of the Wraith of Martynsborough. That would work out for you rather well—the local hero and sleuth solving crimes, with the best-selling novel to follow."

"No, no, that's not what I meant." As Ruth stood, she felt her throat clasp and her eyes well. "I wouldn't say anything, I . . ."

"I think you've said enough, Ruth. Elise is most definitely not the Wraith of Martynsborough, she does not wander the streets at night, nor is she play-acting the effects of her injury for sympathy or jealousy or whatever reason you've cooked up in your head. It is a notion that is not just ridiculous but, honestly, somewhat cruel of you to even ponder. If you don't mind, I'd prefer you go now."

Ruth clenched the scarf in her hand and then brought it to her face to wipe a tear.

"I'm sorry," she said as she stepped from the studio. "I'm very sorry I've upset you."

He shut the door without another word and drew the blackouts.

Ruth walked back down to the road, numb and confused, and then found herself at her front door. She stepped into the kitchen. Vera turned from the basin to greet her.

"Ruth, where have you been? Oh my, are you not well? You look distraught."

"No, Vera, I'm not well." Ruth sat the table and buried her face in her hands.

"What's that you've got there? Is that my scarf, the one I use as a hanky?"

"Yes, it is."

"Why on earth do you have it?"

"I must confess something," said Ruth, with glistening eyes. "I snuck out of the house last night—I didn't want to alarm anyone. But I saw Elise—or at least I'm relatively sure it was Elise—outside. I've started to suspect that there is no ghostly spectre haunting Martynsborough, but in fact, it is Elise, much less mentally deficient than she is letting on, nicking things here and there for reasons I can hardly fathom. I caught her in the act last night, and she left behind incriminating evidence—this." She held up the scarf, which had become damp with her own tears. "Malcolm and I caught her in your dresser drawers when they were here for lunch on New Year's Day. She seemed interested in your things, and it appears she got away with this one. She dropped it last night when I confronted her in Jeffrey's garden."

Vera sat at the table and took the scarf from Ruth's hand. She examined it a moment.

"Dear girl, I've not seen this scarf in weeks, at least since the beginning of December. I believe I lost it when I . . ." She paused. "When I went into the village for shopping, the day that I visited Walter at the hall. I often use this scarf as a hanky; that's how I remember it so clearly."

"This wasn't in your drawer when Malcolm and Elise were here?"

"No, it wasn't. I lost it some time ago. So really, anyone could have found this in town and taken it. In fact, given that she rarely goes into the village unaccompanied during the day, I'd say Elise would be the *least* likely person to have this."

"I'm so stupid." Ruth brought her hands to her face. "I've confronted Malcolm this morning. I told him that I was sure not only that Elise was the wraith but that she might even be . . . play-acting—that she's not really mute."

"Oh, Ruth, you silly girl. Your curiosity is ever getting you in trouble. Was he cross?"

"Oh, more than that, Vera." Ruth sniffed, thinking she might cry again. "He was very, *very* cross with me. He asked me to leave. I've done something awful, haven't I?"

"Now, now. Give him a day to settle, then you can explain everything. I'm sure it will work out. You've also got Maude coming tomorrow afternoon, and Warren the next day—quite the social calendar, it would seem."

"Yes, I suppose." She got up and put her arms around Vera and rested her head on her shoulder. "I'm so angry with myself," she said.

"There, there. It will all work out fine. Now, let's get on to other things. I've managed a cot for Maude. Let's arrange accommodations for our first guest."

Ruth slept terribly. She spent a good portion of the night staring out the window but saw neither sheep nor mysterious girls in white—Elise or otherwise—only the darkened studio, within which was a dear friend who might never speak to her again. She still wasn't sure what to think. The scarf was a confusing detail, but who else could that woman in the bramble have been? There was still every possibility that Elise was the wraith, but she couldn't fathom any detail beyond this wavering suspicion. Either way, it might not matter in the end if Malcolm was angry with her.

Even her attempts to create ocean sounds over her ear failed that night. Instead, she replayed the conversation over and over in her head, and each time it came around worse, with Malcolm's face angrier. He was right, she realized—Ruth didn't know what she was talking about. She'd spent one afternoon with the man's wife and decided that she could make an accurate prognosis about her condition, a prognosis so very at odds with her own husband's, her caregiver and the person who lived with her day in and day out. Wraith or no wraith, Ruth was no doctor. It was arrogant of her to even think she knew anything about Elise, and Ruth cursed her own self-confidence for trotting up to him and making accusations.

In desperation, she thought to write some verse, to get her mind away from her troubles. She drew the curtains and snapped on the lamp and took some paper. And in a such a strange state of mind, by some source unknown, strands of lovely verse fell easily from her pen—a poem that spoke of darkening glass, deep water, reflections, and our own vanities. It was gothic and numinous—the stanzas flowed, and the meter easily found itself. Surprised by how much she liked the verse, she slipped the single page into her bedside drawer to examine at another time—a small consolation for a horrible night—and once more she got into bed.

She lay awake for what felt like hours, the blackouts thrown open, until she fell into a fitful sleep, and she did not rouse until the sunlight scraped her grainy eyelids. She lay like that for some time, ignoring the sounds of the kitchen downstairs, the clatter of forks and knives, the sound of the wireless. Vera, perhaps using some sixth sense, knew to leave her alone that morning, and soon Ruth heard Johnny pulling a chair out and sitting down to breakfast.

She'd go talk to Malcolm—immediately. Ruth sat up and decided that she would march over there and apologize. She got up and had a look in the mirror. She looked awful.

"You've missed breakfast, and no lunch, either?" Vera asked as Ruth gathered her coat and headscarf. "Maude is due in a few hours."

"I've something important to do. I'll be back soon." Ruth started towards Virginia's cottage. She decided to walk around back and check the studio first. She found the blackouts open, but Malcolm was not there. She pressed her face against the glass and could see the cot folded up and leaning against the wall with no linens near it. All the worktables and the pottery wheel had drop cloths and tarpaulins covering them, as if Malcolm had closed things for a long time. Ruth walked around to the front and knocked. There was no answer. She knocked again, impatiently, and then looked through the window next to the door, whose blackouts were also partially open. Everything appeared neat and orderly. She squashed her cheek against the glass and strained to look over to where they kept their coats—nothing hung on the hooks, nor did she see Malcolm's hat or shoes. They were not home. All three had gone somewhere. She walked back to the road and noted that no smoke came from their chimney. She went home and sat in the kitchen.

"Tea?" Vera asked.

"Yes, that would be nice," Ruth said.

"Vera tells me you had some kind of row with Malcolm," Edith said as she came to the room, unable to hide her delight about the whole thing. "It's just as well. Warren will be here in two days."

"He's gone," said Ruth. "They all are. They've left."

"Gone? Whatever do you mean?" Edith asked.

"They're gone. All three. Virginia. Elise. Malcolm. No smoke in their chimney, no coats by the door. Gone."

"There was a motor car this morning," Vera said. "I heard it—a rare thing. Maybe it came to collect them. Virginia has told me nothing. I've no idea where they can be."

-21-

Vera sat at the table, her teal-and-gold scarf spread out before her. She scraped at the raspberry seeds with a thumbnail.

"What's this?" Edith asked as she entered the kitchen. "That bit of cloth looks like it's been through the war itself."

"This is *the* scarf, the one that I used as a handkerchief." Vera looked at Edith with a worried expression. "The one that I dropped in the mill after finding the jam on the ladder, the one that I told you about—like I said, when I went there, just to see."

"And you went back to retrieve it?"

"No, it's seemed to have made its way back on its own."

"What on earth are you on about?" Edith sat at the table.

"I've talked to Ruth today; the row she's had with Malcolm had something to do with this. She seems to think that Elise stole this scarf and has left it as a calling card whilst lurking about Jeffrey's garden shed."

"Well, this is all very unlikely. Did you tell her that it came from the mill . . . that you were in the mill? Did you tell her about . . . did you tell her why you were there?"

"Of course not! Instead I told her I'd lost it somewhere in the village but gave no detail."

Edith reached out and grasped Vera's hand.

"I . . . I would like to go there. I would like to see it—it's been thirty years since we saw the comet, and then . . . and then . . ."

"I'm not sure I want to go back; it's not the same."

"But I do—I do want to see, one more time, it will likely be our last chance. Who knows what will happen with this war. The mill may be torn down—perhaps, perhaps even what is happening now in Martynsborough, this apparition people are seeing, perhaps it is in some way *our* doing? It isn't the same as before, is it? I've not brought this on by coming here, have I?"

"Nonsense. And you'll never get up the ladder," Vera said, folding the scarf carefully. "Nor will I. You'd risk breaking your neck?"

"Yes—yes, I would, I would risk it. I dream about it, I still do."

"Yes, I dream of it, too." Vera dropped her gaze. "Let's do nothing rash right now. Obviously, someone was in the mill, and they've taken this scarf, and they've been lurking about near our cottage at night. I'm not sure what to think of that—or if someone might know something they shouldn't know. Either way, I'd be lying if I said it didn't frighten me a little."

Ruth was poking the fire in a dejected mood when she heard the clopping of hooves and creak of wooden wheels. She went to the window, and there indeed was a horse and carriage. A woman with a pale blue headscarf covering coppery hair, wearing a bright-orange, three-quarter length peacoat, sat with the driver.

"Maude is here," Ruth cried, momentarily forgetting her troubles with Malcolm. She stepped out into the cool morning air to greet her.

"The infamous Ruth Gladstone," said Maude, as she walked up the path. "So very good to see you, and *this*"—she waved her arms about—"your natural element, I suppose. I hope you don't mind the dramatic entrance—it seems there is no petrol nor automobiles left in all of the North." Maude embraced Ruth, pulling her into the folds of her coat and smothering her with a perfumed bosom. She stepped back and assessed the cottage. "Well, Shakespeare's sister, this is not what I had in mind, but it is really rather quaint and lovely, and I think we will have a grand time."

It took several trips to get Maude's large contingent of luggage from the flagstone path into the cottage. Introductions were made, and Vera had laid out an excellent tea for their new guest.

"Now *this* is impressive," said Maude. "I feel as if I've just arrived at the Waldorf Astoria."

The four women chatted, and Ruth caught Maude up on all the goings-on in Martynsborough: the wraith, the dance, the air raid.

"And we'll have one more joining us tomorrow if all goes well," Edith said.

"Oh?" said Maude.

"Yes, Ruth's fiancé, Warren. He's on leave from Aldershot, a military surgeon."

A grin tugged about Maude's bright red lips. "Fiancé? Well, my, my, young Ruth Gladstone, there is so much I have yet to learn about you. Oh, and who is this?"

Johnny entered the room, and his eyes went wide at the sight of Maude.

"I'm Johnny. P-p-p-pleased to meet you."

"There's no need to be frightened of me, young man."

"No, no, not f-f-frightened, just a s-s-s . . ."

"A minor stutter," said Ruth.

"Yes, that's it." Johnny approached shyly.

"Well, lovely to meet you." Maude stood to shake his hand.

"He works several days a week on the flax farm, so he's not in school," said Ruth. "I've been helping him with his studies in the evenings. Perhaps you could help as well, Maude." Ruth turned to Johnny. "Maude is an assistant professor of geography at Cambridge. Unlike me, she is an actual bona fide professional teacher."

"Well, well, young Johnny," Maude said. "I'd be quite happy to take you under my wing, teach you about moraines, hills, becks, mounds, fosses, chutes, and holes? Yes?"

"I would like that v-v-v-very much, ma'am."

After tea, and with Johnny's help, they got Maude's luggage up the stairs and into Ruth's room. They arranged the cot, and after a small freshen-up, Maude was eager for action.

"So, we'll go into the village, then? It's barely four o'clock. We've got a couple of hours of daylight left." Maude tied a fresh scarf about her hair. "If anything, I'd like to walk for a bit with my head down, eyes on the turf, to get a feeling for the local gravel, the rocks, the strata—you know, that kind of thing. Maybe have a look about for the local ghost."

"We could go to the Yellow Rattle. Do you drink beer?"

"Yellow Rattle—now that sounds like a lark. I'm not so much about the beer, but I'll drink what you drink, as they say."

Ruth walked with Maude, pointing out Malcolm's cottage, the drain, the first place she'd seen Castor and Pollux, and soon they crossed the bridge into Martynsborough. They went directly to the Yellow Rattle, and on entering, it seemed every face looked up from their drink—the old men, the Land Girls, the young objectors, dirtied up by their own graft, as well as Albert and his friend Cora in their usual arrangement near the hearth. Ellen welcomed the two women from behind her bar.

"Ruth, good day to you, and you've brought a friend, I see."

Maude strode confidently towards the bar, with many pairs of eyes following her.

"Maude Sedgwick, very pleased to meet you." Maude untied and removed her headscarf and placed it on the bar.

"I'm called Ellen. Ruth, would you like your usual pint?"

"Your usual pint?" Maude asked. "Gladstone, you've become a regular? Let me have what she's having. I'm not usually one for beer, but with the war and so on, as they say . . ."

"Yes, women have got a taste for it now, I know." Ellen slid a glass towards Maude with a coy grin. "Beer, that is."

"Cheers," said Maude and clinked glasses with Ruth's. "It looks like it's just us girls."

"Aye, I'll join you as well—have some stout in a teacup. I'm sure Ruth has caught you up about our interesting village."

"Oh, indeed." Maude sipped from her beer and squinted an eye. "Yes, this will take some getting used to." She placed her glass down on the bar. "I've heard about your resident spectre and a dance that was interrupted by a German air raid, the goats roaming about . . ."

"Not goats." Ellen laughed. "Sheep, actually."

"Right. Sheep. I'm not terribly good with animals; it's geography for me. I spend my days gazing at stones and pebbles, peering into holes in the ground. The only animal life I have any familiarity with is thanks to my beloved Siamese cat, Rumples. May he rest in peace." Maude removed her spectacles and polished them with the sleeve of her blouse. "While for you, Ruth, I envision you with a little dog, the kind of thing that sits on a girl's lap like a trained rat with a bejewelled collar."

"No." Ruth laughed. "I also had a cat—a long time ago."

"I'd a cat once, too," said Ellen. "That makes all three of us. When I was little. She was the palest ginger you can imagine—a little like your hair, miss. She ran away." Ellen poured more black stout into her chipped teacup. "I lost the cat in some village or other for which I'll never recall the name—in Yorkshire perhaps. I wandered for days look-ing for her. Funny, I don't recall her name. Perhaps she never had one."

"A tragedy." Maude placed her polished spectacles back on to her nose. "Well, look at that, we three already have something in common—quite the trio." She raised her glass. "To the majestic house cat—may they be batting about balls of yarn in some happy circle of hell."

It was a small disaster of timings to get everyone in the Catchpoole cottage ready for bed that night. With an overworked bath and paraffin heaters blazing, the upstairs had become steamy, smelling of rose water and talc from the various rituals of four different women. Johnny, avoiding the rush, took to the hedge outside for his needs and was soon in his room, sound asleep. Maude and Ruth, meanwhile, puttered about, preparing themselves for bed.

"You didn't introduce me to your cycloptic artist friend today—the sculptor with one eye and eight fingers. He sounds positively monstrous. Tomorrow, perhaps?" Maude perched on Ruth's bed. Wearing a pale nightdress, she brought one leg up over her knee to casually file at a toenail with a small emery board.

"No, no—not monstrous at all," Ruth said. "He's Malcolm—he's really rather nice and, if I were to be honest, quite handsome. But I don't know where he is. He's left the village. I've no idea why, but perhaps he left because of me."

"Oh?"

"We had a row. Then he was gone. Just like that. They left early this morning, apparently picked up by a motor car."

"A car? You don't see many of those around now. And who do you mean by *they*? Had he people with him?"

"Yes, his wife. She's French, quite beautiful, but an injury has left her mentally deficient, like a child, somewhat helpless. The two of them stay with an older woman, a relative of his. All three disappeared this morning, and I fear it may be because of our falling-out."

"A wife with brain damage and a sculptor with missing fingers, you say? I've half a mind to accuse you of a lurid imagination."

"It's all true, I'm afraid. His wife—well, with her, the circumstances are all very strange . . ." Ruth stopped herself from saying more.

"You seem distraught by the whole thing," Maude said without looking up from her toe filing. "What did you have going on with his chap? Something seemly and inappropriate? Do tell." Maude moved to the next foot with her filing.

"No, no . . . well, I don't know, to be honest. It's complicated. It's probably best if I just put it out of mind. My fiancé will arrive tomorrow. How ridiculous is that?"

"*Very* ridiculous, because it's clear to me that you don't wish to marry him."

"Is it that obvious?" Ruth asked.

"Blindingly so, my dear girl." She put down the emery board and then took up a small tube of cream. She squeezed a single white pearl into her palm and started rubbing it swiftly about her pale hands. She looked up at Ruth. "The thought alone of any marriage makes me shudder."

"You don't want to get married?"

"Do *you?*"

"Well, I suppose that's what I always assumed I'd do—although not necessarily with Warren."

"Well, you clearly don't want to go through with it, nor should you. So, the larger question is why." Maude slipped her legs under the quilts and lay back on Ruth's bed with her chin propped up by an elbow.

"Warren—he's a friend of our family. I've known him for years, and I've always seen him as a kind of cousin. When I was thirteen and he fourteen, we kissed in the closet, and . . . well, I let his hand roam a bit. He was curious."

"Ah, kissing cousins."

"Yes, well, I thought nothing of it, but he seemed to carry this fire from back then, for many years, actually. Perhaps he spoke of me to his parents, mentioned his intentions—I don't really know. And I suppose his family are well-to-do, and our marriage might have a certain kind of logic to my mother—who has a very old-fashioned understanding of class. You must know with Mama, if she wishes something, it happens. I was ambushed in a way. I never saw it coming—my parents, his parents, sitting at a lovely dinner table. My parents, preparing to travel to Canada for who knows how long, while he, wearing a military uniform, was about to go off to France, possibly to die defending our country. How would anyone say no under such circumstances?"

"Elizabeth Bennet refused the vicar," said Maude.

"And the refusal made her all the more desirable to him." Ruth paused. "And how would you know about such things? Jane Austen? You? You're a student of geography."

"And a woman who likes books of all kinds. I can walk and juggle croquet balls at the same time, you know."

"It's funny," Ruth said. "You mention a novel written more than a hundred years ago. I like to think we live in some modern era—we build airships and motor cars and listen to the wireless. We've abandoned corsets, we wear trousers, we've had suffrage, we work in munitions factories, and yet my gran has heart palpitations if I'm alone in the room with Malcolm, I suppose to assure my virginity before marriage. And, and . . . she seems quite pleased to have me marry Warren, for whom I've never showed a moment's romantic interest—like I'm a child, despite being twenty-five years old and a student at Cambridge. I've no idea what to do." Ruth sighed.

"When he arrives, make him some tea, and tell him you don't wish to marry him," Maude said. "Your mama is not here, and your gran will have to honour your wishes, given she has no choice in the matter." Maude fussed with the various ties and clips on her head, until her pale, coppery hair came tumbling around her shoulders. "I'll help you, my dear girl." She shook her hair out with her fingers and said, "We'll get you out of this mess. Is this Malcolm someone you wish? Should that be our next step, that we arrange that you two share a bed? With his wife's condition, I'm sure he's not been enjoying married life very much. He can be your Pygmalion. Now *that* would be delicious—and perfectly ethical, I think."

Ruth fell back on the pillow next to Maude.

"Nothing makes sense to me right now."

"Come then, let's cuddle like our favourite dollies and sleep away our worries."

"I've prepared the cot . . . I could sleep on it if you'd prefer the bed."

"I prefer you right here—you're like a tiny furnace keeping me warm." Maude arranged the blankets around them. "It's positively cosy in this old-fashioned country bed." She removed her spectacles and handed them to Ruth. "Be a love and get my glasses on the table, and snap off that blinding lamp, will you? This country air has just hit me like a horse tranquilizer."

The next day, Warren did not arrive. As the women sat for dinner, they contemplated what it could mean.

"Clearly he's been delayed," said Edith. "Communications are not terribly reliable right now, although I would have expected a telegram if he were to be late, and there's a telephone at the village hall where he could have left a message with the administrator—either way, it should be fine. He'll likely arrive tomorrow."

No one seemed to have any answers for Warren's absence, so the Catchpoole cottage went about its evening routines as usual. This included Johnny's lesson, which had been handed over to a guest lecturer, who sat alone with him at the kitchen table after the dishes had been cleared.

Maude produced a small box. She removed the lid and extracted various stones, which she laid in a row on the table. She picked up the first, a metallic specimen of pale yellow.

"Pretty, isn't it?" She placed the stone in his palm. "Precious, you wonder? No, not really. It's pyrite, otherwise known as iron sulphite. Do you know another name for it?"

"No, I'm afraid I don't," said Johnny.

"Fool's gold. Which is pretty, but not rare—quite common, in fact. Gold, on the other hand, is pretty *and* rare, just like you, Johnny, which makes it more valuable."

"I suppose."

She plucked the stone from his hand and placed it back on the table, then picked up another. "And this? Quite black, right? Have you ever heard the phrase *jet black*?"

"Yes."

"Well, this is the jet they speak of, which is *really* quite black, isn't it? It's a little like coal—consisting of carbon, but it's much denser. We can cut it and polish it into lovely bits of jewellery that won't rub off on your hand. It's from Scarborough. I found it myself, on a beach." She turned it over in her hand with a sort of reverence. "A long time ago, jet was used for funeral dresses, for mourning, and death. It's a bit ironic, don't you think, that one of the few semiprecious materials that come from a living, organic thing is so associated with death? Because you know, Johnny, this jet was once a tree, many millions of years ago, a living thing." She handed the black stone to Johnny, which he cradled in his palm as if it were a precious egg. He frowned.

"Perhaps I shouldn't be speaking of death and grieving—it seems to be making you sad," she said.

"Yes, maybe. I'm feeling grim today, thinking of . . . of my brother. Sometimes I think . . ." He trailed off and carefully placed the jet back on the table.

"What do you think, Johnny?"

"I think that maybe everything was my fault." His eyes shone with the threat of tears. "He . . . he would probably be here if . . . if . . . I'd done things differently. I did a bad thing, maybe, but I m-m-meant well."

"Your fault? What is? That you've lost your brother? That can't be the case. I can't say I've ever met a boy . . . ahem . . . a *man* as kind-hearted and helpful as you, Johnny." She cradled his chin in her hand. "Come have a look at this one; it will make you happy."

She picked up a stone that was deep green on the edges, with a seam of bright oxblood red running through the centre. "This is heliotrope," Maude said as she placed the stone in Johnny's hand. "Sometimes it's called a bloodstone. The red bit is a sort of haematite that is embedded in the green of the quartz—one thing within another, blood within our body, like the blood within our families. Just like your brother, who I am confident will arrive in Martynsborough before you know it. Also, this stone is known to have magical properties, right?"

"Right." Johnny looked at it with renewed interest.

"This was once a land of witches, I'll have you know. They were called the Pendle witches. Well, some say such witches used the bloodstone to beguile men to do their bidding, but for someone so handsome as you, Johnny, no magic stone is necessary for you to attract the girls. This stone was also used to dispel melancholy by those same witches, so I hope it helps you in this regard. Furthermore, with all the charming power it has, let us make a wish on this bloodstone—let us wish that your dear brother sends you a lovely letter saying that he's well and will be coming to Martynsborough *post-haste*."

"Yes, that would be nice." Johnny sniffed. "Very nice."

Ruth was to start work again in two days' time at the hall, which would open after the holiday. Malcolm had not returned from wherever he had gone, and Ruth tried not to think too much about the possibility that he might never come back. She decided that on her last day before returning to work she'd go hunting.

"You'll come, too?" Ruth said to Maude as they sat for supper.

"Ruth is likely the best shot in the village," Vera interjected. "She's been largely responsible for all the meat we get in this household. In fact, the rabbit we're having tonight was one she shot two days ago."

"My, my, what would the headmistress think of this?" Maude said. "Our meek little Ruth—out in the woods with her rifle, hunting and skinning animals like a heathen! I'm in love!"

It was still dark the next morning when Vera tapped on Ruth's door. "Girls, I've got the kettle on. You've to get out before sunrise." Maude stirred and threw a leg over Ruth.

"Is it not the middle of the night?"

"Yes, it is," Ruth answered sleepily as she extracted herself from the warm ensnarement of Maude's limbs. "If we're to hunt, we must start early."

At the breakfast table, Ruth took out the rifle. "A handsome thing, is it not?"

Maude's eyes widened. "Indeed. And you'll wear that." Maude pointed at Ruth's outfit.

"Yes . . . Why?"

"You've got a skirt on. How are you going to traipse about in the hedge with a skirt?"

"It's a wool skirt—warm enough. I've got knit stockings. I'll wear Wellington boots. This is what I've always worn when I hunt."

"Ever the traditionalist, that's you, Gladstone. Hardly practical, though, but it's *your* hunt." Maude tied on her headscarf and slipped into a cardigan. "Look at these, you really should try them." Maude did a one-quarter turn in her blue dungarees and lifted her leg gracefully into the air like a dancer. "Complete comfort. My aunt hated them, by the way, said they made me look like a lavatory cleaner."

The road was dry and firm enough that Ruth and Maude could take the bicycles. They rode towards the village, but then turned onto a small, hemmed-in bit of path with hedges like the vaults of a church ceiling. From there, the land opened to fields, still dark and misty. Ruth stopped her bike.

"The pea farm is the next one over." She pointed, then turned to the north. "Although, I was wondering—I've never been on the escarpment. We're not supposed to hunt there, given that it is private land, but I've heard there's very good bird shooting. I've often thought of it, to be honest. I've been itching to get on to that property for some time, to have a look around and figure out how the local legend might tie into the place. Perhaps your cocksureness is rubbing off on me. What do you think?"

"Poaching? Gladstone, you're shaking me to the core with your recklessness."

"So . . . no, then?"

"Are you mad? Yes! Yes! Yes! I can't think of anything I'd *rather* do. There won't be any gamekeepers roaming about, will there?"

"As far as I understand, the only human residents of that vast acreage are two old men, who are likely asleep in their beds in the manor house, which is more than a half-mile from the place I intend to shoot."

"And what of your wraith? It seems the perfect place for her to haunt. The Pendle witches roamed these valleys in some distant history. Does this not frighten you even a little?" Ruth had not thought of this, but either way, she was still of the mind that the wraith might be Elise, who, at that moment, didn't seem to be in Martynsborough.

"I suppose it is a little spooky—although . . . although the wraith is probably just some mass hysteria." Ruth paused, thinking maybe to tell Maude about her suspicions, but changed her mind. "The scariest thing we'll encounter is a woodcock."

"Right then, lead the way, Gladstone, we should do so while we can. I've heard the ministry is converting country houses into war offices and growing sweet corn in their once pristine woods."

The road wound further to the foot of the escarpment, where a small bridge passed over the Wynan Beck. There they left their bicycles, and Ruth took the rifle and their satchels along a sheep path that wound its way to the top of the bluff. Ruth stepped from the trail and was surprised to see two pools of water up ahead. "Maude, I can't believe it. The lime-kiln ponds—there."

Maude appeared behind Ruth.

"So they are. The ones you spoke of in your letter, where the girl supposedly drowned? Eerie."

"Malcolm would love to see this," said Ruth. "It was part of our research into the wraith, for the book I was writing." She stepped towards the pond. "They're quite murky. Supposedly the men looking for the girl pulled up horse bones and other rubbish from this one, the north pond—but no body. Perhaps she's still down there. What do you think lurks in that black water?" Ruth squatted by the pond and dipped a finger in.

"Nothing good, I'd say. It looks like witches' brew." Maude glanced around and whistled a little bit. "Yes, this is a properly spooky place. I can barely see my hand in front of my face. When will the sun be up?"

"There is light already on the horizon, see? It's on its way, which means if we want a bird, they'll take to the sky the minute the darkness lifts. In fact, they're starting to wake up. Can you hear their song? I suppose we should see if we can shake a pheasant out of this bush. They'll take to the air; I can get a shot."

The two women traipsed about in their wellies. Maude had unofficially taken the role of beater, and with an air of boredom, she hit about the bushes with a fallen branch, while Ruth, some hundred yards away in a dale that ran along the edge of the escarpment, stood at the ready to take any bird in flight.

After an hour, with the sky glowing pink, they had found nothing, neither bird nor wraith.

"I suppose it's all bluster that there are birds here. I've not seen anything bigger than a sparrow." Ruth sat on a tree stump, dejected.

"Can I have a go with the rifle?" Maude asked. "Just a couple of shots, see if I can hit that tree?" She pointed at an ancient oak.

"Right." Ruth stood up and broke the rifle. She hung it on Maude's forearm, barrel pointed downward, stock open. "The cartridges go in here, and you get two shots before you have to reload. I've a pocket full here. This is already loaded, so close the gun, like this, till it clicks, then you need to take aim, a stable stance, yes, like that." Ruth stood behind Maude, adjusting her arm, bending her hip, turning her shoulder, and walking her through the same motions that Vera had taught her.

"This is so very exciting," Maude whispered. "I can barely contain myself."

Ruth stepped behind her to get out of range.

"Right, try to hit the dead centre of the oak tree. This is a bird gun; it's not terribly loud, so I'm hoping it doesn't scare away every pheasant within a mile or bring the old men out to visit us. You won't make a great hole if you hit it, but many little ones—the cartridge is filled with small metal bits—that was news to me admittedly. I had always assumed guns shot one bullet at a time."

"Interesting," Maude said. "I'm going now. Here I go." She fired, and the report rang out, while Maude had barely moved, standing solidly in the thin, smoky wisps of burnt black powder. The tree was unscathed. She fired once more, and the patter of the lead shot shredded the side of the tree trunk. "I've hit it, Ruth, how exciting!"

"You did. Now, break the rifle and reload."

"Do you think . . . well, do you think I might try to take a bird? Maybe you can do the beating for a bit? We haven't tried up near that other ridge there. I'd love so much to boast that I killed our dinner. It would be momentous."

"All right, but we can't waste too much of the shot. Vera will be cross." Ruth took a handful of cartridges and slid them into Maude's coat pocket. "Reload. I'll do the beating over there." She pointed. "And for God's sake don't point the gun at me! If there's a bird, let it take flight until it's well over the gully, then follow with the barrel, and aim *in advance* of the bird by a small distance—it will guarantee a hit."

Maude reloaded the rifle and walked further into the dale to take her position, while Ruth stumbled up to the next rise in the bluff. She walked along a narrow path towards a promising collection of dense thickets. She looked down to see Maude standing smartly with the gun ready. Then, taking the branch, Ruth began beating the brambles, stirring things up the best she could. She heard a violent thrashing a few feet ahead, and a bird burst from the foliage, taking flight over the gully with an annoyed twitter. Maude swung the barrel towards the ridge and fired. Ruth dove and rolled, a patter of shot rustling the undergrowth not five feet from her body. Lying on her back, she watched the bird fly off unhurt, then stood.

"You nearly shot me!" she called down to Maude.

"Sorry! I'll try to control my impulse to shoot," Maude called back sheepishly. Ruth took a deep breath, moved up a bit further, and started beating again among the bushes. She was about to give up when she heard the gun go off somewhere below her in the dale. She shrank for a moment, expecting to be filled with lead shot, then straightened up to see Maude, pointing the gun at a thick bit of wood. "I've got something!" she cried. "There was a bird there."

"Don't move. I'll be right down." Ruth stumbled down the ridge, tripping up in the twigs and roots in a mad rush to see what Maude had shot. When she caught up to her, the smell of cordite hung heavily in the air. "Where is it?" Ruth said, out of breath.

"I saw the head of a bird—some feathers . . . I think. I'm not sure what kind of bird. I fired there." She pointed at a tangle of dead bracken and other thick brush.

"I don't see anything," Ruth said as she walked up to the wood. She poked around with the end of her beater branch. "It's very thick in here, hard to see . . . oh God."

"Oh God, what?" Maude joined her by the edge of the wood. She, too, peered into the thick vegetation. "Oh my . . . What is that? It looks like I've shot an evening gown."

"That's not a dress. You can't see what it is?" Ruth said. "It's a pea-cock—I don't know whether to laugh or—"

"Peacock? Oh. I didn't think they were native to Lancashire."

"They're not."

"I suppose it belongs to the estate, then. Damn. Not a game bird, is it? A pet, I suppose? Can we eat it?"

"We need to leave now." Ruth looked around nervously. "This is very bad."

"What about the bird?"

"We have to take it. Let's get out of here." Ruth reached in and grabbed the bird by the neck. "It's enormous. Oh my God, its tail feath-ers must be six feet long. Take the rifle. I'll get the bird."

The two women hustled down the sheep trail, dragging the tremen-dous bird behind them, and in their haste, Ruth's heel slid in the mud, and she stumbled, causing Maude to fall over Ruth. With the slippery, unsettled nature of the path, neither could regain their footing, and they rolled inelegantly down the mucky incline—a graceless tangle of girls, gun, and bird—until they came to a rest in a muddy heap at the bottom. Ruth's skirt was completely inverted, her stockings once more ruined with ladders, one torn completely from the garter, and covered in mud.

"Quite a state we are in." Maude stood and dusted off her knees. "Your grandfather's gun is quite fine, though, probably the stoutest of the things that just muddled down that bluff. Are you well, Ruth?" She reached out a hand, which Ruth took, and stood, smoothing out her now muddy woollen skirt.

"No, I can't say I'm well. Look at me." She then noted Maude. "And look at you! You've got mud all over your face. Did you wear lipstick today, too? Whatever for? It's all smeared."

"Yes, but my dungarees have done their job. I've no mud on *my* knickers. And your stockings are in tatters. Hope you've got more. I couldn't find a pair in any shop last I looked."

They limped back to their bicycles just as the sun crested over the tops of the highest trees. Ruth did her best to bundle the bird into her game bag. "I can't get these feathers in, they're too long. We'll have to cut them." Ruth reached into her boot and produced a field knife.

"Oh, Ruth, that's top form. You won't wear trousers, but you'll carry a knife in your damn boot."

"Pull the tail feathers straight for me. I'll cut them at the end so we can get the bird in the bag." Ruth hacked through the long feathers, whose quills glistened like fresh wax in the morning light.

"We've neutered him—taken away his lovely plumage, his train. A small tragedy." Maude held up one of the feathers, which tapered demurely into an eye-like ellipse with its brilliant corona of blue and amber shimmering like a petrol slick. "We shouldn't just leave the feathers here. They're far too pretty."

"No, best we take them." Ruth had managed to stuff the remains of the bird into her game bag. "Gather them up and get them in your satchel. We ought not leave evidence." She stopped to inspect the bird before fastening the buttons and mumbled, *"The peacock has a score of eyes, with which he cannot see, the codfish has a silent sound, however that may be."*

"A lovely bit of verse. Bravo, Ruth."

"The words aren't mine, I'm afraid, but I can't say I've seen anything quite this colour in all my life." She grasped the neck of the bird and turned it slightly. "I'd go as far as to say that words truly fail me—*blue* is a poor word to describe this animal." She stroked the peacock's plumage. "Cobalt, indigo, azure . . . sapphire. Not blue."

"I would think his plain-Jane female counterpart would probably have avoided my shot."

"Either way, let me give you some advice about bird hunting in England." Ruth huffed a little. "Don't . . . ever . . . shoot anything that is *this* colour." She held up the bird's neck. "Next time it might indeed be an evening gown that you've shot—not a pretty bird, but a human being. I don't think we're ready to be murderesses."

"Ha! A scolding—I deserve it. But I have to say, even though I am covered in dirt and on the run from a poaching incident, I am so very glad I came to Martynsborough." She grinned, a smudge of lipstick running up her jaw.

They got on to their bicycles, and Maude took one of the feathers from the bag and thrust it into the side of her headscarf behind her ear. They rode along the country roads, taking back ways and brambly cow paths to avoid being seen, and soon they were on their own road at the start of elevenses. Ruth stopped her bike in front of Virginia's cottage.

"Look." She pointed, and her face split into a girlish smile. Maude stopped, and they both gazed over the hedges to see Virginia's chimney. It piffled happy grey smoke. "Malcolm is back!"

"Perhaps we'll invite him to dinner to eat this rare bird," Maude said. "I'm so very excited to meet this mythical creature you call Malcolm; I'm starting to wonder if he even exists."

They continued to Vera's cottage, left their bikes in the garden, and burst through the front door.

"Vera, we're back," Ruth called out as they peeled off muddy coats and boots in the corridor. "You'll never guess the adventure we've just been on." Ruth pulled the brilliant bird from her bag and held it by the neck, and the two women stepped into the kitchen, muddy and triumphant. Ruth's smile fell from her face.

At the table sat a man in military uniform, clean and smart, his eyes widened in confusion. "My word, Ruthie, what in heaven's name has happened to you?" Warren stood up in disbelief. "Is that a peacock?"

The Catchpoole cottage had never seen such chaos. Warren leapt up to smother Ruth with kisses, while she in turn dropped the exotic carcass to the table and fled up the stairs into the bath, where she locked herself, while Maude, with mud and lipstick smeared on her face and a peacock feather behind her ear, attempted vainly to introduce herself to the newly arrived guest, who ignored her to chase Ruth up the stairs, where he rattled violently on the bathroom door. Edith rushed into the scene, shrieking in confusion, thinking that there had been some great embarrassment unleashed in the kitchen, while Vera inspected the shimmering dead bird closely and recalled a Turkish recipe that might do it justice. She mused vaguely of a dinner party. Meanwhile, Johnny chopped wood outside, oblivious to all.

After more riotous action, indiscretions, and unfortunate tracking of dirt and peacock blood throughout the cottage over the course of the next quarter hour, eventually all were assembled around the table, faces and hands wiped clean, dead bird removed to the shed. While nerves were still somewhat frazzled, a fraught and tenuous peace had been established.

"Tea?" asked Vera ridiculously.

-23-

Walter Horgon enjoyed the solitude of working without any subordinates to distract him. He sought no recognition for his attendance in the lonely and rather chilly hall during the high days of holiday and didn't think of himself as anything above the line. He only understood his attributes in terms of duty. He found a knock at the door that morning, however, unexpected and most inconvenient, given that the documentation had finally arrived regarding the billets of a young Johnny Hedley, and he had been eager to get to the bottom of the boy's missing brother. He stood, leaving the ministry envelope unopened, smoothed out his trousers, and went to answer.

Through the frosted glass next to the door he saw a dark, monolithic shape, as if a gravestone itself had strode up to the threshold. "What in heaven's name?" Horgon unlocked and opened the door and was considerably surprised by who stood before him.

Horgon had not seen or heard of Blackwell stepping foot into the village of Martynsborough for years, certainly not since the declaration of war, and it crossed his mind that some strange doings must have occurred to warrant this unlikely visit.

"Blackwell? Here's a surprise. What brings you to the village hall on a quiet Saturday morning?"

"There's been poachers; took one of our ornamental birds just this morning."

"Well, you certainly do get to the point. What makes you think you've had poachers?"

"Heard the shots. Found evidence." Blackwell's face barely moved when he spoke. His eyes were black yolks in rheumy whites, his face sallow, parchment-like and yellow tinged. He wore a coal-coloured greatcoat, and an equestrian dressage hat of uncertain vintage.

"Are you well? You look a little out of sorts; would you like to come in and have a seat and tell me about this?"

"No, I'll stand here just as well. The poachers were of the female type, they were, they took a peafowl—a cockerel—the last one alive on the estate."

"A peacock? For pity's sake, and why women? How on earth would you know that? Did you see them?"

"Didn't see. It happened under the cover of early morning. But they left their boot prints, small ones, not too heavy—not men. Two of them. I could see they took a tumble about the bluff. Tail feathers were cut by the road. Escaped on bicycles, used a twelve-bore, took a swipe at a fine oak tree, too." Blackwell retrieved something from the pocket of his jacket and held it out for Horgon to take.

"What's this?"

"They left it behind. A lady's thing. Made of jet, I see." He dropped it into Horgon's hand. It was a hair clip that had a good amount of earth stuck into the clasp. Horgon couldn't immediately place it, but he then thought of young Ruth Gladstone; he seemed to recall her wearing a hair clip—but who this other woman might be he could only speculate.

Horgon said, "I'm not sure why you bring this to me."

"You are the magistrate! The only representative of the law this village has right now, and you must set this right."

"The war makes things different, I think," Horgon countered. "This is not the Victorian age. I'm not sure what, if anything, I can do."

"The Enclosure Acts. The Night Poaching Act. These are laws that remain on the books—war or no war. If you don't enforce them, I shall, and I've every right to."

"Right, hold on a minute." Horgon retrieved a pencil and notepad, hoping to give the impression that he was doing something to help—anything to prevent Blackwell from haunting the village on a vigilante mission. "Now tell me everything," he said. "I'll open an investigation."

"As you should." Blackwell repeated his accusation and the facts associated with it. Then he turned, without another word, and disappeared into the mist. Horgon shut the door and locked it. He dropped the notepad on the desk, thinking to bring it up with Gladstone the next time he saw her. He sat, trying to shake off the disquieting, almost sulphuric impression that Blackwell had left, and instead turned his attention to the letter from his contact in the billeting office that had just arrived the day before. He tore it open and extracted two neat sheets of typewritten paper. He read them through twice, then set them down, tapping his pencil on the oak desk. "Very curious," he mumbled to no one in particular. "Very curious, indeed."

The members of the Catchpoole cottage and all its respective guests carried through with a peculiar half hour of tea drinking and small talk. Ruth made every effort to appear as if all was normal but had yet to interact with Warren in any way other than a chaste hug and some how-do-you-do's and introductions to Maude. Subsequently there followed a long, meandering discourse on the state of the geography department at Cambridge, led largely by Maude, who could distinctly perceive an awkwardness that Warren's untimely arrival had caused. In a way, she was fascinated but also could sense the anxiety of her friend, so she did her utmost to maintain a spate of words flowing from her mouth regarding any topic that veered her listeners away from the unspoken thing that sat in the middle of the room like a great stinking elephant.

Vera seemed to watch it all unfold with bemusement, whilst Johnny, as per usual, ate much and said little.

"So, Warren, tell us about Aldershot," said Edith in a direct attempt to steer the conversation right back to the glaring fact that Ruth's long-absent fiancé had just arrived, and she had said almost nothing to him.

"It's grand, all very grand," said Warren. "Since I returned from Dunkirk—on the first boat, I have to say—we've been mostly in surgeries, dealing with training accidents and the returned wounded that have been cleared out from casualty hospitals in London. They come up our way for longer recovery. We determine if they're fit to return to the front. Some of them, I can see they don't want to go back, but it's the boss's job, so they see him, the boss, as I call him—me and him, the only chaps in the whole of the hospital. Other than that, it's all young nurses. So, as I was saying, these injured fellows—we mostly deal with RAF—they come in, smoking their cigarettes, all rather brawny and amorous among the nurses, fatherless cockneys most of them, flexing their arms and flashing their brass pins. Then they come in and see the boss, and as soon as the door's closed, they weep like little babies for a discharge. They don't want to get back in the Spitfire or man the ack-ack or, worse, get sent on to Italy. But the boss sees that they've only had a nick on their elbow, lost a tooth, or had a few stitches here or there. Smack on a bandage, and back they go to fight the Hun." Warren roared with laughter. "Some, yes, I suppose they ought not go back. Just the other day, I had to repack a man's viscera into his abdominal cavity. It's very odd, I should say, that one can survive rather well for some time with one's tubes and pipes hanging in a pile outside of one's belly. Quite the thing."

"Yes, very fascinating," said Edith with distaste. "And how long will you be staying?"

"I'm afraid I only have three days, so . . ."

"Right, then." Vera stood. "More tea? No? Tonight, we'll have a hotpot, which will use the rest of the rabbit, and tomorrow I reckon we'll feast on the bird that Ruth and Maude have provided."

"Given our state on your arrival, I think that Ruth and I would like to have a proper wash-up and change, if you don't mind," said Maude. "And by the way, it was I who shot the bird, just for everyone's information, that is, in case you were wondering." She stood and took a bow.

"Yes," said Ruth, standing also. "I'm terribly sorry, Warren. Perhaps we'll sort ourselves out and we can maybe start over again fresh—as if you've just arrived? Let's get clean and some proper clothes, then we can show you around."

"Of course, Ruthie. That's grand." Warren rose. "Yes, have a clean-up. I see that there's still some peacock blood on your sleeve. I'm happy to settle over there by your nice fireplace." Edith led Warren into the sitting room.

He whispered under this breath, "Peacock? One can't eat peacock. I'd think it would be revolting."

"You'll be surprised. Vera's cooking is exceptional." They sat alone while Vera puttered in the kitchen, and Johnny went to his room.

"I've only three days," Warren said to Edith. "What on earth is the matter with Ruthie? She's not been very nice to me. I'd think she'd be beside herself with joy that I'm here, and your sister as well; she must know that this little cottage is bog standard, certainly not what I had in mind. Where am I to sleep? What would Ruth's mama think of all this?"

"Warren, you've been in the military for more than a year. What are you sleeping on in Aldershot? A feather mattress?"

"I've a room . . . actually. My own. I'm with the RAMC officers. It was arranged, you know, the old man. All above the grade, of course, you must know—a favour called in. Papa is very helpful, keeping the riff-raff away from the doctors."

"I see. Well, as it is, Vera has been most accommodating; I'd hate for you to seem ungracious."

"It's like a boarding house here," he whispered fiercely. "Why are there so many people? Surely you knew I was coming. Why were accommodations not made?"

"You'll have to take that up with Vera." Edith was losing her patience. "In the meantime, you must understand, Ruth has not seen you in a year's time; many things have changed. We're at war; she's been uprooted. You must be patient with her."

"Was she hunting, then? With a gun? Just now? Whatever for? I can't imagine . . . moreover, I think this other woman, she's putting the wrong ideas in her head."

"Hmm. Maude. Yes, well, she's an odd bird, but please don't start any more rows. It's been a stress since you walked in the door. We've all had tea and settled down; now let Ruth and Maude sort themselves somewhat, and maybe they can show you around Martynsborough."

"I'm not to sleep in her room? We were to be married. I understand there's a vicar here."

"For heaven's sake, Warren, slow down."

Vera entered the room, cutting off their whispered conversation. "I'm glad to see peace has been restored." She perched on the ottoman. "Mr. Somersby, if you'd like, there is Johnny's room. He has graciously offered to take the cot on the floor so you can have a proper bed; he's at this moment preparing things. As long as Maude is here, as I understand it, we can really only work with this arrangement. The bed is fine enough; I'll think you'll be quite all right."

Warren flashed an insincere smile. "Yes, I suppose. There's not an inn in the village, is there? Perhaps Ruthie and I could . . ."

"No inn, I'm afraid, only a pub, and all rooms accounted for—it is wartime, after all," said Vera pertly. "It should be fine, Mr. Somersby. I'm sure it will be luxurious compared to what the military has offered thus far."

Down the road, Malcolm removed the drop cloths from his pottery wheel and placed his suitcase on his neatly made cot in the studio, realizing rather ruefully that he was glad to be back in Martynsborough.

The letter from the doctor the previous week had been a surprise, and he had thought to talk to Ruth about it before hurrying off in a car to the train station—that was, until Ruth talked to him about her own pet theory. Ruth had been wrong about Elise in many ways, very wrong, but perhaps not all wrong.

Either way, despite the gravity of this trip, he had truthfully thought of little else on the train, there and back. Ruth never left his mind. He envisioned the small barrettes on either side of her head that kept her unruly chestnut bangs from getting into her eyes; her wool skirts and raggedy stockings; her ability to quote English poetry by rote; the unique way she spoke—a rhotacism as she called it. He watched sometimes with wry amusement—no, no, not amusement. It was never at her expense. It was about being charmed—yes, that was it. He was charmed as he watched her wrestle with her own tongue. It was both endearing and strangely arousing to see her grapple this way, then for the most eloquent and well-spoken, sharp, humorous, and amazing words to form on her lips. He could not imagine anyone with whom he'd rather converse.

Sitting in the rocking train cabin on their way back to Martynsborough, he had looked across at Elise, her face, once familiar, beautiful, placid, and now utterly foreign, vacuous, a tragic question mark. The doctor had taken some hope away. Her condition was mysterious. It was no longer just a physical injury—no, that part had largely healed. Now, it could only be a psychological issue, like shell shock suffered by soldiers and poorly understood. It was potentially a lifetime affliction with no known cure. She might float to the surface occasionally, the doctor said. Perhaps to someone who didn't know Elise from before—like Ruth—these brief moments might be more noticeable, but not to Malcolm, given that he had grown accustomed to these mannerisms. He knew she was well intentioned; for Ruth, and Vera and everyone really, Elise was something very unfamiliar and unknown. It was natural to misinterpret such things, perhaps even to fear them. Malcolm wished he'd been more patient.

Nevertheless, the doctor said such surfacings were also poorly understood in a medical sense, and it was rarely more than a flicker of consciousness that would disappear as quickly as it appeared. The doctor had told him of a case in which a young man in the Great War had suffered a similar injury—a combination of physical brain damage and profound shell shock. This young man never emerged from the fog of catatonia. The doctor told Malcolm that he should count his blessings that Elise was mobile—she could walk, she could sit at a dinner table, attend church. She was far more able than the young soldier of whom the doctor spoke—for that poor soul required someone to regularly wipe the drool from his chin. In fact, Elise's situation was unusual in just how *able* she was. This doctor said he had never seen a case of a mute, nonresponsive patient who could also walk, feed themselves, and so on. He admitted it was curious but could offer little advice.

The trip had provided no answers. The woman he had fallen in love with and married, as he had known her anyway, was gone, it would seem, and there was little hope of her returning. But in a way, she was also *not* gone—she was there, breathing, her heart beating, blood flowing, flesh warm with life. He could not grieve properly, for she was not dead, but nor could he comprehend what it was to go on living. It was baffling, and he felt caught in a strange twilight. Nor could he bring himself to get into depth and talk candidly about all of this with Ruth, about the conflicting nature of his marriage or, indeed, about his more recent . . . feelings. Possibly it had been wrong for him to be so opaque. While Ruth, in turn, was so open, earnest—always smiling, curious. She had breathed life back into his lungs—awakening him from a lonely, hopeless place that seemed insurmountable and everlasting.

In the meantime, he had to return the key to Horgon, which he had held on to for much longer than intended. He stepped out onto the road and looked back towards Vera's cottage. Smoke drifted from the chimney. He couldn't see if the blackouts were drawn in Ruth's room—the glass was stark grey in the glare of the overcast sky. Did she stand there watching him, veiled in the reflection of day's light? He now knew that it was her bedroom window. He had been in her room, sat on her bed. He recalled her scent. It lingered on her bed and pillow—talc, elderflower, crisp laundered linen, and something else, a smell that was different than that of Elise, not so much sweet but saline, warm, like the ocean.

He continued walking to the village, and as he passed the Yellow Rattle, he thought to go in and have a pint, to clear his mind, to say hello to Ellen. He stopped by the pub door and looked up the road, to the village hall, and there at the entrance stood a strange man he couldn't recall ever seeing. He wore all black, like a liveryman from some past era, and Horgon stood there in the doorway speaking with him. The man handed something to Horgon, who frowned and said some more things, then the man turned away. Although Malcolm had never seen him before, he knew it was Blackwell. Albert's description in his tale was vivid enough that identification was not difficult. Malcolm watched as the man disappeared into the mist, and then, his curiosities alight, he walked to the hall.

He didn't use the key and instead knocked. Horgon answered. "Malcolm, I see you're back. What news?"

"Not much in the way of news, good or bad. I've brought the key that I'd forgotten to return. Have you, by any chance, mentioned to anyone that I was in Manchester?"

"No, I've not seen a soul but my wife these past few days."

Malcolm handed Horgon the key. "Well, one *other* soul, at least—there was a man at the door I saw on my way in."

"Right, Blackwell, yes—he'd come down to say that some poachers were on his land and had taken a peacock."

"A peacock?" Malcolm laughed, surprised. "Well, that's unlikely."

"All the more so, I might add, he claims that the interlopers were of the female variety."

"Women, hunting on his land? Well, that's rather . . . oh . . . you mean . . . you think it was . . . ?"

"Well, who else could it be? Vera is a fine shot but only leaves her cottage for Sunday church. Ellen doesn't hunt. There are some Land Girls who've come in, but they've no rifles. It could only be young Gladstone, and it seemed there was a second woman with her, according to Blackwell."

"Is there not a wall and a gate? How would she even get in?"

"There's a lot of land there; that gate's all bluster—it's not a fortress, you know. The southern flank of Wolstenholme Park is open to the woods, near the kiln ponds. She probably just went up the sheep trail."

"She'd be thrilled to find a way in." He smiled to himself. "Do you know, it's rather ridiculous, but some time ago, Ruth invited Wolstenholme to the Christmas dance? She dropped an invitation directly into his letter box and was vexed by the gate keeping her out."

"The invitation likely didn't get past Blackwell's hand—he oversees everything. When we need to contact them directly, one has to arrange an appointment—there's a certain process that is rife with eccentricities. The man is still mired in the age of Victoria. It's not easy to get to Wolstenholme in person—and now this complaint about poaching."

"What are you going to do about it?"

"What can I do? I may have a word with Gladstone, but at the same time, I've no love for that estate or the men who inhabit it. I also have learned that they've been importing contraband coke for his boilers. I've not the resources or authority to do much about it without proof, so I'm in no hurry to help miscreants such as them. I am looking forward to seeing it ultimately converted to an officers' barracks."

"Contraband?"

"Yes, I suspect he keeps his conservatory hot as Hades to protect his queer jungle plants while we lot down here in the valley freeze in our cottages. They have a *man* helping them with their illegal fuel, and I have discovered it's Sutcliffe, the breeder of Lonks. He has no love for the ministry after they culled his beloved mules. By this spring, it will all be moot anyway, as that crumbling old manor house will be propped up by the army and filled with high-ranking members of His Majesty's Royal Military. I've gotten the unofficial word already that it's to be commandeered. It's the reason I've let things lie for now—I'm just biding my time."

"How very interesting." Malcolm glanced back at the escarpment.

"Now, you listen here, Malcolm. I don't care for that look of curiosity. Don't go off on some wild chase for your friend's research—her tawdry novel or whatever reason. You've won back the villagers' trust with a Christmas dance, and their mass illusion of a ghostly wraith seems to have finally dissipated somewhat. There's no need stirring trouble up once more."

"Don't you worry, sir." Malcolm turned to go. "I've no interest in following up with any of this nonsense." Horgon did not see the grin on his face.

Ruth and Maude showed Warren around the garden, then took him down the road, to the river lock and the chute and the millpond and the church. They told him about Castor and Pollux, but they did not see the animals anywhere, and then they told him about the legend of the wraith, and he seemed not to believe any of it. They offered to go to the pub, but Warren was not interested. They offered to show him the village hall, but he was not interested in that, either. He acted sullen and childish, and whined about the weather and the cold and the fact that he'd be sharing a room with a common farm boy with dirty fingernails. Ruth and Maude led him around like two schoolmarms, speaking in a chipper tone, almost mockingly, but Warren didn't notice their inflection.

Soon enough, they returned to the cottage, and there they ate hotpot around the table—all of them, a group that had grown to six strong. Edith asked about war medicine, but Warren had lost his interest in conversation. Maude rambled on about something called the Boggle Hole near Whitby, and almost everyone was relieved that she could so astutely fill in the awkward voids of silence that hung heavy over the dinner table. With plates cleared, Warren retired to the sitting room, where he slunk into the large chair that Vera usually favoured and brooded in the blue haze of his cigarette smoke, waiting for someone—anyone—to inquire about his well-being, but no one did.

Eventually they all went to bed. Warren spent an inordinate amount of time in the bath, then ungratefully took the bed while Johnny, readying his cot, asked what else he could provide for his guest, as if he were a bedraggled member of a hotel staff. Warren told him that if he were indeed asking, he could use a room to himself, his own bath, and a place that wasn't as cold as an icebox. He then rolled over to stare at the wall.

Meanwhile in the next room, Ruth hid under the blankets with Maude. "This is a nightmare," Ruth whispered. "I've been in quite the state for the whole of the day—I don't even know what to say or do. He's quite cross with me, isn't he?"

"Oh yes," Maude said. "He's not happy one bit. You can't continue to string him along like this. I've even noticed that your gran is losing patience with him. He's a spoilt little baby."

"Oh, he's just who he is. I've known him forever—he was a darling when he was a boy. He used to make me laugh with his mischief. I'm sure he means well. Maybe the war has put him out of sorts."

"War? He's enjoying his station in life. Carousing with another surgeon in a building filled with pretty, hard-working nurses, deciding the fate of young fighting men? It's repugnant. He's probably bedding those Red Cross girls by the dozen—as much as he's not much of a thinker, I'll grant that he has a fine-looking face that will do him well under such circumstances, but he's only reaffirmed my opinion of marriage."

"Yes, I can't disagree with you. And Malcolm is now back. I've been itching for an excuse to walk over there, to somehow find a way to be friends once more."

"As you should. I'm quite looking forward to meeting your Pygmalion, or should I say, your favourite monster."

"He's blind in one eye and is missing a couple of fingers—hardly a monster. You might even find him handsome. You'll see. In the meantime, what's to be done about Warren?"

"Tell him to go away. Tell him that you're not going to marry him."

"How on earth do I do that? We'll be sitting down, all of us together at a table with this dramatic revelation boiling away, unspoken in my mind. I'm dreading the whole thing. It's ridiculous, though, when you think of it. We're to have a proper dinner tomorrow—to eat a peacock, for God's sake." Ruth sunk back on the pillow and sighed. "I wonder how it will taste. I've never eaten peacock."

"Nor have I, Gladstone." Maude rolled over and whispered in Ruth's ear, "Nor have I."

Warren spent the better part of the afternoon in the sitting room, filling the cottage with foul-smelling cigarette smoke, while Maude and Ruth tended to things in the kitchen.

"Be a love, Warren, and help Johnny, will you? There's some potatoes we can take in the garden; the ground shouldn't be too frozen." Vera stood in the doorway of the sitting room. "A man's help around here is always appreciated."

Warren tossed his cigarette into the fireplace and stood. "Right, where's that?"

"Just out back, thank you so much."

Johnny was already out in the garden. He took a spade and pushed it into the earth, which was firm from a morning frost. He broke the clods up a bit, then thrust his hand into the chilly soil and rooted around until he found his quarry, a Maris Piper potato. He dropped it into the basket next to the furrow and moved up a step.

"Hallo there. I'm to help you with some potatoes . . . or something." Warren lit another cigarette and strode over to the boy, his hand thrust in the pockets of his greatcoat. "Is that what you're doing here?" He puffed on his cigarette. "It's freezing out here."

"Yes, sir. The potatoes won't grow in the winter, but they keep quite well in the dirt. It's just like an icebox—the dirt."

"Yes, it seems this place *specializes* in dirt." Warren looked around the garden with distaste and took another pull on his cigarette. "So, you like being ordered around by a bunch of skirts, then? Being the resident dogsbody?"

"I'm just helping, I think."

"You're not helping, lad, you're enslaved." Warren walked over to the shed and peered in. The recently plucked blue-and-green feathers of the peacock remained scattered on the floor. He frowned and turned back to the boy. "I've noticed all you do is work, work, work, while they put up their feet and slurp tea all day."

"Oh, I don't think that's true. Everyone helps."

"And what do you think of Ruthie? We're to be married, you know. She'll be coming to Aldershot with me."

"Oh, I like Ruth very much." Johnny frowned a little bit. "I didn't know she would be leaving. Well—I'll certainly miss her; I'd think we all would. She helped me get out of the ch-ch-church basement. Helps me with my lessons. Helps Vera and Edith by shooting b-b-birds and rabbits. It was she and Malcolm who surprised the whole village with a nice C-c-christmas dance." Johnny stooped over and pulled out another potato, a fraught expression on his face.

"C-c-christmas dance?" Warren mocked Johnny's stammer. "And Malcolm? Who's this Malcolm?" Warren flicked his cigarette end towards the road.

Johnny looked up from the dirt, wary of being bullied, and hoping to help perhaps, he said, "Malcolm—he works with Ruth at the hall; they're friends, I suppose—they certainly spend a lot of time together. He came around just this past New Year's Day for a nice dinner. Vera even brought out the Scotch—a grand time for all. He lives over there." Johnny turned and pointed towards Virginia's cottage. "He served in Norway, so I've heard."

"Huh. Interesting. Well, it's been a peach doing chores with you, Johnny. I'm going to go inquire about the prospects of a drink. I'll see you at dinner."

Warren hung up his coat to find the women all gathered in the kitchen. "I've heard that there might be a drop or two of Scotch hiding about somewhere." He grinned smoothly. "Your young Johnny's been spilling all the secrets."

"Yes, if you'd like," said Vera. "Ruth, would you fetch the Scotch and the sherry. Maude, you're welcome to some." Ruth brought the bottles to the table. Warren reached out and grasped the bottle from her, his hand lingering on hers. His face held a questioning expression. Ruth presented a pert grin and went back to her task at the washbasin.

"Only a quarter bottle left." He sloshed the brown liquid around a bit. "It seems *someone* has been enjoying this." He poured himself a glass and drained it.

"Dinner will be ready in a half hour," said Vera. "You've got the potatoes?"

"Hmm? Oh, yes, Johnny's sorting that out." He poured another splash. "Just give me a ding-a-ling when it's time to eat." He strode out of the kitchen, bottle in hand.

At half-past four, they sat for the peacock feast. Vera had cooked it to a turn, succulent, and carved it with deft skill. She had managed to coax a gravy from the neck and giblets, which she flavoured with mushroom and a rare bit of black pepper. There was mash, and sweet carrots, and lightly wilted kales, all bejewelled with the dark-green smatterings of curly parsley. Warm bread steamed from a basket, and a week's worth of butter ration sat squarely on a saucer like a challenge to be had. Warren—yes, even Warren—looked on this spread with disbelief.

"Well, I have to say, I'm rather impressed." He pulled out his chair and set his glass down. He was a bit drunk, having consumed most of the bottle of Scotch. "I can't say I've seen anything laid out like this since the war started. I can imagine that by some impossible magic, you'll also produce a bottle of fine French wine to go with all this."

"Now that you mention it," Vera said, and placed a bottle of 1938 Bordeaux on the table. Warren's eyes widened.

"We're eating better than Churchill! And I have to say, I never thought I could stomach a peacock, but that does look fetching." He sat, as did everyone else. There followed a period of serving, passing dishes around, murmuring, clacking of knives and forks, and chewing and grunts of pleasure from Warren, and accolades from Maude, and the boyish haste of Johnny. Food and wine, the great gifts of Bacchus, performed their duty and brought a kind of warm amity among the diners, which was very welcome but not necessarily anticipated, nor lasting. All knew that it would not hold, and something would happen, and it was no surprise that when something did happen, it came from Warren's mouth.

"So, Ruthie, who's this Malcolm chap?" The knife slipped from Ruth's hand, clattering to her plate loudly, throwing up a small eruption of gravy onto her blouse.

"Hmm? Malcolm, you say? Oh, I believe that's Vera's neighbour."

"You believe?"

"Yes." Ruth dabbed at her blouse with a napkin. "Lives with his wife there, just across the way."

"He served in Norway."

"So I've heard." The other women watched her carefully, waiting to see what might happen next. "Norway? Yes, possibly—I'm not certain," Ruth said after a horrifically awkward pause.

"Not certain? Hmm . . . it would seem odd given that he's been a guest here, has he not? You work with him every day, no?"

"Oh, well, yes." Ruth looked around the table for an escape. Johnny didn't seem to have any idea of the trouble he'd wrought by providing Warren so much information and continued to eat like nothing was the matter. "Yes, he came by for lunch, I suppose."

There was another long, awful pause, and just before Warren could continue his interrogation, Maude loudly announced, "This peacock is quite delicious." She imperiously held up her fork, with which she had just speared a large hunk of meat. "You know, Mr. Somersby, I shot the brute myself. He attempted to hide amongst some bracken but couldn't elude me. I've got sharp eyes, I do—don't let these spectacles on my nose fool you. I'm far-sighted—can count the leaves on an oak tree ten miles out. I spotted him quite easily, then boom, boom." She mimed the firing of a rifle with her fork, which she then popped into her mouth. "You go shooting, Mr. Somersby?" She chewed loudly. "I mean for sport?"

"Yes, I do indeed shoot. I've a place in Scotland that I go to with the old man—that is, before all the war nonsense fouled us up." He poured the last of the Scotch into his glass and tipped it back. He swallowed noisily and challenged Maude with an ugly, drunken grin. Then, just as it seemed there would be a joust of some kind between the two, a gentle knock came at the front door, startling everyone.

Vera took the napkin from her lap. "What on earth . . ." She stood, and all the eyes at the table followed her as she stepped out into the corridor. As she opened the door, her voice echoed quietly into the kitchen. "Oh. Why, hallo, Malcolm." Ruth dropped her knife again, this time splashing gravy on to Maude's blouse. Vera continued, "Wonderful to see you, we're just having an early supper. Yes, Ruth is here." Malcolm spoke, but his voice was too quiet to be heard beyond a gravelly mumble. "Oh please, do come in," Vera insisted. "Come in this instant. We'll pull up a chair."

Maude turned to Ruth and whispered gleefully under her breath, "Well, this is about to get interesting." She pulled out her blouse. "And you've got gravy all over my udders, you silly woman."

Then, Malcolm was standing in the doorway of the kitchen, himself looking surprised by the large crowd at the table. "Oh. It seems you have some guests," he said, a little embarrassed. "Well, hallo. Good evening to you, Ruth, and Edith, and Johnny—and, well, hallo, um, well, I'm Malcolm, I just live over the way there."

"So very pleased to meet you." Maude leapt from her chair and offered her hand to him, which he shook lightly. "It's Maude, Maude Sedgwick, a fellow Girton girl—a classmate of Ruth's. I've heard so much about you, and, and . . ." She glanced over at Warren; whose eyes narrowed. "I mean . . . I mean, Vera here has been telling me about you, um, yes, pleased to meet you." She took a napkin and squashed it onto her left breast. "Don't mind me, Ruth has been splashing gravy everywhere." Vera returned with a small folding chair and wedged it between Johnny and Maude.

"This all looks rather nice," Malcolm said. He sat, finding he was much lower than everyone else in his out-of-place chair.

"Peacock, actually," said Warren too loudly. "And I'm afraid there's none of your favourite Scotch left, my man, but plenty of this French claret." Warren stood and thrust his hand across the table. "Pleased to meet a fellow military out here among the women and the straw. Heard you were in Norway. It's Warren Somersby, RAMC—I'm Ruth's fiancé, from London, if you didn't know already, that is." Malcolm went slightly pale as he reached out to shake the man's hand. A thousand tiny emotions passed over his face, before he steadied himself and forced a shaky smile.

"Fiancé . . ." He looked over at Ruth and met her gaze, her eyes wide, like a frightened animal. He turned back to Warren. "Well, congratulations, I guess." Malcolm settled back into his chair. "You said there was some claret?"

The peacock feast continued shakily, with conversation steering this way and that, sometimes avoiding controversy, and other times delving into it, usually with Warren to account. He played up his history with Ruth, spoke of their first kiss and the many times they'd gone to eat in nice restaurants and how close Warren was with her parents, and about the lovely ring he'd given her. He then noticed she was not wearing the ring, which led to another deeply distressing conversation, at once dripping with contempt and terribly evasive and rife with falsehood.

During the meal Ruth had decided quite unequivocally that she would break off the engagement immediately after they'd eaten the pudding (which involved candied apricots and a very indulgent sponge cake). However, with Malcolm at the table and Warren seeming to know so much about everything—learned from some source that Ruth could not identify, though she suspected Johnny—the situation had become untenably complicated.

After a single plate of food, Malcolm stood. "This has been very lovely, thank you, but I should go now and leave you alone to enjoy your guests." He took up his napkin and placed it next to his plate. "Congratulations, Ruth, it's wonderful news." He reached across and shook Warren's hand. "I'm sure you will all be very happy. Goodnight, everyone."

"Malcolm, you don't have to . . ." Vera looked up from her plate.

"No, it's all right. I can see myself out." He awkwardly shimmied behind Maude's chair and through the crowded kitchen. He stepped into the hallway to get his coat. He called out one more goodbye and then went out into the night. A long, strange silence settled over the table, until Ruth abruptly scraped her chair backwards and stood. She seemed to want to say something, opening and closing her mouth, but no sound came from her lips.

"Ruthie, are you not well?" Warren slurred.

Her eyes turned towards him. "No, actually. I am not well. I've not been well for a long time." Ruth threw her napkin down and left the kitchen; she took her coat from the hall and exited the cottage. The cool air hit her, and she looked up the road to see Malcolm, a dark silhouette walking ahead in the light of a dazzling moon. She ran, not knowing what she would say. He heard her footfalls on the gravel and turned.

"Ruth?"

She stopped running and slowed to a walk. She caught her breath for a moment, which misted in the cool air, then said, "Well, hallo."

"What's the matter?"

"With me? Nothing. But you're back. Where did you go?"

"Manchester. An appointment with a doctor. It's a long story. I can tell you another time."

"A doctor? Are you ill?"

"Not me, for Elise, for, for—look, I'm sorry about, about—"

"No, I'm sorry. I can't believe I said those things, I—"

"I was very mean to you; I shouldn't have spoken that way. I was—"

"Why did you go to the doctor? Elise . . . is there something that's happened?"

"No, no—it was an expert I had corresponded with about her condition. He was to be in Manchester briefly and wrote to me, and I saw it as an opportunity to meet in person, to determine what, if anything, we could do for her."

"Oh. That's good, right?"

"Not really. His assessment was rather grim. I don't really wish to get too much into it."

"Of course." They stood in silence for a long moment. Then Ruth said, "I'm glad you're back."

"You're getting married. I didn't know till just now."

"I'm not getting married."

"But that chap, Warren, he said—"

"I agreed to it a long time ago, under duress, I should say. I've not seen him in a year's time."

"But he—"

"And now I'm wondering what on earth I'm going to do. I don't wish to go back in there. He's drunk and sullen and awful, but I can't possibly leave him to terrorize Gran and Vera. What should I do?"

"God, Ruth, I don't know. It's quite the mess. You'll have to go back there and tell him what you've told me. He seems to think you're getting married."

"Yes. Yes, he does. I'll have to do that. Yes. I'm going to turn around and march back into the maelstrom and fix this." She turned to leave, but then stopped and stepped closer to him. "I just have to say—while I still have the courage to do so—that I was afraid you'd gone for good. I even peered in your windows like a madwoman after you'd left. I'm embarrassed to say I checked your chimney, to see if it had smoke, for three whole days—like I was waiting for the election of a new pope."

"Oh, Ruth. I do regret running off like that. I suppose I was upset, but once I was on the train and calmed down, all I could think about was . . . well, I'd wished I'd done it differently."

"I missed you terribly. I couldn't imagine chasing this wraith by myself."

"Yes, yes, Ruth." He stepped closer. They heard the clatter of the door at Vera's cottage and Warren's distant, drunken voice. "I think you're being beckoned," he said. "He won't get violent, will he? Should I come back with you?"

"No, I think we women will have no problem sorting him out for the night and bundling him away first thing in the morning. Do you mind helping us arrange a car?"

"No problem." Malcolm laughed a little. "And a peacock? Really? We've got to have a talk about that . . . later. Good luck. I'll see you tomorrow at the hall." He took one more step towards her and leaned forward to perhaps kiss her cheek but apparently thought better of it and instead squeezed her shoulder. "Goodnight."

"Welcome home." She turned and walked back to the cottage.

Warren left in a car the next morning, on to the station, then back to Aldershot. Ruth was not there to say goodbye, as she had already left for work at the hall. Their cancelled engagement was a messy, fractured process, and there would be explanations demanded from Ruth's mama at a later time—but it was assumed that once Warren had found someone else and settled down, and the damnable war had finally come to an end, the families wouldn't have too much strife between them.

Edith, who had originally championed the arrangement, had changed her opinion—drastically. Her time in Martynsborough had opened her eyes to certain things and would prove to change her in many ways to come. But at that moment, she had a war to consider, and closer to home, a deep and enduring mystery continued to haunt the village of Martynsborough.

-25-

Ruth and Malcolm spent the entirety of their lunch in the Yellow Rattle catching up on all that they had missed. Ruth spoke of Maude, and the killing of the peacock, and the discovery of the lime-kiln ponds, while Malcolm informed her of the unsettling visit by Blackwell in search of the poachers and the new information that Sutcliffe, the sheep breeder, was also a coke smuggler who regularly visited the Wolstenholme estate.

"Mr. Horgon knows it was me on the escarpment?" Ruth asked.

"He seems to suspect, but he's not terribly interested in pursuing the matter."

"Well, that's a relief. It was a comedy of errors, let me tell you."

"The peacock was delicious."

"Yes, I suppose it was. Maude took the kill, not I. She's interesting, this Maude. I've grown quite attached to her."

"It's getting crowded in the Catchpoole cottage."

"Yes, indeed it is."

They walked home that evening, pleased that this small ritual had been restored. There was still much that went unspoken—such as the details about Elise's appointment with the mysterious doctor, and Ruth's theory that she was not truly catatonic, along with the broken engagement to Warren. As before, their conversation meandered like a river, around stones and circumventing obstacles, ever placid and temperate.

The subjects they avoided had a certain gravity, like an invisible force that repelled them, pushing them into alternate realms, safer spaces like the rings of Dante's inferno, erotic sculpture of the late nineteenth century, poetry, myth, and all things Martynsborough. No, they didn't discuss those other, sticky topics; instead, they returned to familiar ground. They walked on a crunching gravel road, they bantered, and they enjoyed each moment.

"Do you not find it odd that the ram and ewe are named Castor and Pollux?" Ruth asked.

"Oh? Well, they're creative names, to say the least. A little odd, I suppose," said Malcolm.

"No, I mean odd in a particular way. This ram and ewe are mates, so says Horgon. Judging by the way nature organizes itself, I wouldn't disagree . . . but there could be more. As I was saying, *Castor and Pollux*—the names, what do they mean to you?"

"From Greek myth, I suppose. There's a seventeenth-century Italian bronze of the subject that I quite like, and an awkward canvas by Da Vinci depicting them with their mother, Leda . . . *Mother*—oh. I see what you mean."

"Not mates—not lovers."

"No. Siblings. Twins. Yes, odd names for a ram and ewe that are supposedly mates."

"Yes, Castor and Pollux—twin brothers, sometimes called the Gemini, though not really twins in the true sense, as they shared only a mother, Leda. One brother was mortal, having a Spartan father, the other was divine, having Zeus as a father. I don't recall which was which."

"You're well read in your antiquities."

"My first term was thick with it. Also, I quite enjoy myth. I love how these ancient stories seem to emerge again and again, even in the most modern writing."

"It might all mean nothing—we might be overthinking this."

"Yes, but I like overthinking things. I suppose their previous owner, Sutcliffe, would know better."

"He may also be our ticket to getting on to the estate, into that manor house and into the conservatory. Sutcliffe, smuggling coke to Wolstenholme—he likely has a direct audience with the man himself."

"Brilliant. So, will we be paying a visit to the mysterious Mr. Sutcliffe?"

"Oh yes, but we must do it with some discretion. Horgon doesn't want us stirring up any more trouble—there's only so far he's willing to go to tolerate scholarly research."

"No, we wouldn't want that."

They arrived at Virginia's cottage and stopped. Ruth said, "Well, goodnight, Malcolm. I suppose we can pick this conversation up tomorrow."

"Yes, indeed, Ruth. Have a good night." He put his hands in his pockets and smiled. "You know, it is really rather good to be back."

"And it's good to *have* you back."

Ruth returned to her cottage to find that Maude had spent the better part of the late afternoon in the pub with Ellen. She was a little drunk and very lively that night at dinner. Soon after, yawning prodigiously, she excused herself early to prepare for bed. Ruth found her in their room later, examining a single sheet of paper.

Maude looked up and said, "Well, hallo there, Shakespeare's sister. I was under the impression you were suffering some horrible writer's block, but this is quite good."

"Oh. You've found that poem. I was rereading it this morning, and I must have left it out on the bed."

"Should I not have looked at it? Is it private and sordid, about your one-eyed man?"

"No, it's quite all right. I actually wrote it the night that Malcolm left. I was so distraught, it just seemed to fall from me. I'm still working with it a bit, though I can't really see what I can do to improve it, although I wasn't expecting anyone to read it quite yet. I've mostly been focussing on my novel, as it were."

"Oh, enough with your modesty, dear girl. This is quite good. I think it's about Martynsborough, isn't it? Would you read it to me?"

"Aloud? Oh, I don't know, I don't think . . ."

Maude thrust the page towards her. "Please? It's really lovely, and maybe you can explain what it means after. I'm no literary genius, you know."

"Right. Well, it's called 'Through a Darkening Glass.'"

"Like the blackouts in the windows, right?"

"Well, yes, among other things."

"Go ahead and read it, then." Maude sat upright expectantly, her hands in her lap. Ruth read:

> *A son of river, his eyes doth keep*
> *Himself alone in view*
> *For eyes, like ponds, are fathoms deep*
> *While mill streams can't imbue*
>
> *Blackened veils conceal our deeds*
> *Hidden o'er mantle quilt*
> *Ne'er at night, we dare sow seeds*
> *Nor hearth-light gold be spilt*
>
> *She haunts yon flax and sundered field*
> *White shift and hair of wheat*
> *Tender stalk, e'er wise to yield*
> *In moonlight's winter fete*

Through a darkening glass, none can see
We blunder forth in callow
For dusk and starless our eyes be
Reflecting our own shadow

Maude clapped her hands raucously. "Bravo! Bravo!" Ruth sat on the bed next to her and sighed.

"I admit, I am well pleased with it. I just think between the blacked-out windows, the dark ponds on the estate, and so on, there is so much that we cannot see, and it got me thinking about darkening glass and mirrors and such. We often try to peer into a window, only to have our own reflection served back. The nature of light can seem contradictory, you know. So, you really like it?"

"Of course I do, you silly girl. You'll be published in no time. But enough reading for now; it's time for bed."

Later, curled up under the quilts with Maude, Ruth said, "I've sometimes wondered—and haven't really thought to ask till now, I guess—but why did you come to Martynsborough? We didn't know each other very well. I slept on your sofa for a few days because of an unexploded bomb. As someone who doesn't have a lot of close camaraderie at school, I felt . . . maybe you didn't even like me at first. Why did you travel the length of northern England to visit me?"

"You're not happy that I've come?"

"Oh, I've had great fun since you've come. I was just wondering, that's all. I was quite surprised when I received your letter—and quite happy, to be honest. I think you saved me from Warren. It's wonderful to have a friend."

"Well, I suppose you've grown on me, Gladstone." Maude's breath was warm and jammy, sweet with alcohol. "If you haven't noticed, there's a war going on. I may swagger about, with all the airs of someone oozing confidence, but these are strange days indeed, and even *I* feel the deep fear of uncertainty. While *you*, on the other hand, have an incredible talent for easing that fear. I mean, that lovely verse you just read, that alone set my heart a-twittering. Indeed, while the rest of us worry about German invaders, you write poetry and chase a ghost. I love it. You're very curious, and earnest, and not only very sweet but very strong—perhaps you're not even aware of how monstrously brave you are." Maude slid her hands around Ruth's waist. "You've stolen my heart, you silly girl, that's all. Now be a dear and get that blinding light off. I'm deathly tired."

It took a bit of digging to determine where Sutcliffe lived. Ellen had informed them of his whereabouts, saying that he had a lorry for deliveries—supposedly for the ministry—the only nonmilitary lorry left near the village. Sutcliffe brought in the legitimate flow of coal and coke supply and, Horgon suspected, also the *illegitimate*. They didn't wish to raise any unnecessary suspicion, and given Sutcliffe's possible criminal activities, they needed to take caution. His defunct Lonk farm was far enough away to require bicycles, so Malcolm borrowed Johnny's, and on the first Saturday since Malcolm's return from Manchester, they rode out. It was another dry, mild day for January, allowing for easy travel.

"You've got the letter?" Malcolm asked.

"Yes indeed; wrote it last night."

After they passed by several flax farms on the outskirts of the village, the land rose to reveal the calicoed fields, once dotted with the white forms of wandering sheep, now furrowed with burgeoning new crops dug from this former pastureland. They could see a rough-looking stable and small cottage down the next hedge-hemmed road. They rode up to the house, which had all its blackouts up. It seemed deserted except for the wisps of smoke drifting from the chimney and the lorry parked under a stand of leafless trees. Ruth took a deep breath and said, "Well, here we go." And the two walked to the door.

Malcolm knocked, and within moments, they heard a jangle of locks being disengaged, and the door opened to reveal a man of about sixty years of age, with salt-and-pepper mutton chop sideburns and a dirty undershirt. A warm waft of cigarette smoke and frying bacon drifted from the house. He looked surprised for a moment, then wary. He scratched his unshaven chin and said, "What can I do ye for?"

"Hallo, sir," said Malcolm. "We're interested in getting some information to Mr. Wolstenholme on the estate, and we understand that you deliver there on a semiregular basis, and we thought you might be able to get a message to him."

"He's rather hard to contact, we've found," Ruth added. "We're hoping to do some scholarly research on the history of his estate."

Sutcliffe's eyes narrowed. "What's this about, then?"

"Like I said," Malcolm stammered. "We understand that you make deliveries there, and—"

"Who told you that?"

"Well, the publican told us that you deliver for the ministry, and—"

"And what?"

"That you sometimes deliver personally to Wolstenholme. We don't want any trouble. This is an academic exercise, and we would really like to deliver this letter . . . to Wolstenholme—to him directly. We understand his steward tends to his mail, and the post is not guaranteed to reach him directly . . ."

"Steward?" He laughed under his breath. "Blackwell, yeah. But what's in it for me? I'm not some private delivery boy—I work for the rotten ministry because I have to, not because I want to. Why don't you just piss off? I've got things to do." He started to close the door.

"Your sheep, Mr. Sutcliffe," Ruth pleaded. "I've seen them—*we've* seen them. Castor and Pollux." The door remained open, and an ugly grin played about Sutcliffe's face.

"You've seen 'em. Yeah, to hell with the ministry." He spit on the ground. "See how beautiful those animals are? Fine, fine stock. The rest, all gone."

"Yes, yes. I saw them near the cottage where I'm staying, Vera Catchpoole's cottage."

"Huh. You know Vera?"

"Yes, she's my aunt, my gran is her sister. I'm surprised you don't know that. It seems everyone in this village knew about me before I even got here."

"I'll be damned—didn't even know she had a sister." He opened the door a little more. "Vera was a good friend," he said, his tone softer. "She looked out for me when I was small. She's good people. Her family owned the mill, you know—that bastard took it away. I was only a wee boy when it all happened. Terrible, terrible."

"Really?" Ruth was surprised at this information. "I thought it was her husband's family that owned the mill."

"No, no—her family. I don't know nuthin' about her husband. I only know it was all very awful, what the old man did."

Ruth frantically tried to process this information. She would have to broach it later, but now, having got the attention and possibly a small measure of amity from Sutcliffe, she proceeded with the matter at hand. "Well, for Vera and for me, it would be of great importance if we could get this letter to Wolstenholme. Perhaps just for her, for Vera, you might consider . . ."

"Yeah, give it here. I'll make sure it's placed directly into his wrinkled old hand. I'm going to do me rounds in two days' time. You didn't talk to the magistrate about any of this? Horgon?"

"Oh no," Ruth said, shaking her head. "He'd be cross with us if he knew we were trying to send letters to the estate. We would of course require your, um, discretion, and in return, we too would be discreet about . . . about . . ." Ruth left it unsaid, and Sutcliffe seemed to understand.

"Aye." He turned the envelope around in his hand a few times. "Well, good day to ye." He turned to close the door, but Ruth thrust out her hand to keep it open.

"Can I ask, Mr. Sutcliffe, was it you who named them Castor and Pollux?"

"Yeah, that was me."

"I have to wonder, why did you choose those names?"

Sutcliffe smiled a weaselly smile, his right incisor tooth missing.

"I stole the names. Stole 'em from Wolstenholme hisself. He's got some, um, *pets*, up there in his glasshouse. He names 'em, he does. I heard 'im say those names, and I liked 'em, so I got these two, the ram and ewe. They never 'ad names before—jus' numbers. They're me finest breedin' pair, and after a while, I named 'em that. Just before the cull, I named 'em that, and then I set 'em free."

"Wolstenholme has pets?"

"Haw. You'll see."

Ruth and Malcolm glanced at each other, then Ruth said, "Do you know what the names mean? Their origin—Castor and Pollux?"

"What they mean? What does *any* name mean? Nothin'. It's jussa name. Now, if you'll excuse me." He closed the door, and the sounds of the lock reengaging rattled behind the wood.

Malcolm turned to Ruth. "Will he deliver it?"

"I think he will."

Once they'd returned to the main road, Malcolm and Ruth went their separate ways. He returned home, while Ruth headed into the village centre to have her ration book stamped—this was the story she had cooked up for her gran in case she inquired where they were going that day. She would need proof that she'd been to the shop.

Her mind was still alight with the strange things that Sutcliffe had said about Vera. As far as Ruth understood, her great-aunt had only ever visited Martynsborough with Edith on holiday when she was young. She'd never lived in the village until she moved here in her later years, after the death of her husband. What Sutcliffe had said made no sense.

As Ruth passed the village hall, she saw Horgon locking up and preparing to leave. "Mr. Horgon, good day to you." She stopped and got off her bike.

"Why, hello, Gladstone, aren't you the keen one? It's Saturday afternoon. Ready to do some paperwork, then?"

"No, no, I'm here to go to the shops. But I wondered if I could ask you a question. You've been in Martynsborough the whole of your life, have you not?"

"Yes, I'm afraid to say it's true. Why do you ask?"

"I've been talking to . . . someone . . . and they mentioned that Vera's family owned the mill, but my gran doesn't seem to know anything about the mill herself—this all seems very unlikely. You're good friends with my aunt Vera, and I figured this person was just mistaken, and . . ." Ruth trailed off when she saw the obvious change in Horgon's demeanour. He went a little pale and broke eye contact, then cleared his throat and looked at his watch distractedly.

Ruth pressed. "Mr. Horgon? Do you have any idea what this person was talking about?"

"Hmm? No, can't say that I do. Right. Probably mistaken. I'm afraid I was quite young back then, only a boy. Don't really remember much. I ought to be going, though. Door hinges don't oil themselves, you see, and Martha's been on me about the bloody squeaking for ages—promised it would be done today. See you Monday, Gladstone." He turned and walked briskly in the opposite direction, leaving Ruth even more perplexed than before.

Ruth had a lot to think about, and when she got home, she was happy to find that Maude was out somewhere, probably at the pub with Ellen.

Edith and Vera were in the far end of the back allotment with Johnny, their hats on, harvesting a bit of winter green. Ruth crept upstairs into Vera's room and opened the small wooden desk drawer in the corner. She looked through collections of papers, a receipt for a girdle, weigh bills for vegetables Vera had sold to the ministry, some annual statements about land taxes. She needed much older things and opened some cupboards and found a metal box. She took it out and placed it on the quilt. She peered between the curtains to confirm that the two women were still out on the grounds, then opened the box, in which she found papers, legal documents, and other things from the previous century. Near the bottom, she found what she was looking for, from the 1870s—a Certification of an Entry of Birth for one Vera Catchpoole.

Ruth stared at the paper in disbelief. Vera was *not* born in London, nor was she born with Edith's maiden name. And yet they were sisters . . . unless. Ruth thought of the story of Doll and Kate. Perhaps . . . perhaps it didn't just tell the tale of sisters moving to separate bedrooms but of sisters being separated by their father in another way. Vera had said that it was as if she had always lived in the country, at least in spirit. But no, Ruth now knew that Vera *had* always lived in the country, and there was only one explanation for how that could be possible. She carefully put the papers into the box and returned everything to where she found it. She looked out at the garden and saw Edith and Johnny on their way back to the cottage, while Vera remained, filling a basket with green leaves. Ruth got her coat and went out to meet her.

"Can we talk for a moment?" Ruth asked. Vera looked up from her toil, the sun catching her eye, and squinted.

"Hallo, Ruth. Yes, of course, child. What can I do for you?"

"This may be coming from out of nowhere, but I've been thinking about it. From everything I've heard and all the time I've watched you and Gran interact, I think I've figured out that there is something you've not told me. Clearly there is some ancient scandal with the two of you, and without embarrassing Gran too much, I just want to say that I've figured it all out, and it doesn't bother me a fig."

"Oh?" Vera's face went white.

"Yes, but you needn't worry, your secret will be safe with me."

"Secret? I don't know what you're talking about." Vera turned and stumbled a little in a garden furrow.

"A secret, Vera—I know that you and Gran don't have the same mother, and I can see by your reaction that I am right in my assumption."

"What makes you think this?" She still did not turn to face Ruth.

"Clearly my great-grandfather came to Martynsborough in some distant past and had an affair with . . . a woman here, who would be your mother. They had an affair that resulted in a child . . . you."

The air let out of Vera's chest, a sigh that seemed to weigh a thousand stone, and she turned, this time looking Ruth directly in the eye. "Go on, what else do you think?"

"Well . . . that's it: you're half-sisters, one from the city and one from the country, with different mothers. I realized it when I was thinking about Castor and Pollux—the names from myth. They shared a mother and had different fathers, whereas with you and Gran, it was the other way around. I have a great-grandfather with a secret that he seemed to keep, at least for a while. I understand in the past such things were probably much more scandalous than they are now. There'd been no mention of it afterwards—my mum seemed to think that you were sisters in the truest sense; our family never questioned it. People here, perhaps the older ones who were alive then and remember—they would have known about the illegitimacy and have kept this information to themselves as anyone in old-fashioned polite society might. I assume that it was your mother's side of the family that owned the mill. I've learned that you did not take your husband's surname, that Catchpoole is in fact the name of your unmarried mother—I learned this . . . by accident. Your family lost the mill to Wolstenholme. Perhaps my great-grandfather provided money to your mother so that she could raise you.

He brought your sister to see you every summer under the guise of business trips or holidays perhaps. It was those times you played together by the river. The story of you being moved to separate rooms—perhaps that had to do with your inevitable separation, that your rooms in fact were separated not by a hallway, but by many miles of travel—I don't really know the details. It doesn't really matter in the end, I suppose."

"You're right—it doesn't really matter in the end, does it? I am here. You are here. Edith is here. We're together now. But it's best if we don't speak of it, for . . . for Edith's sake. Yes? It was indeed quite the scandal, and for me, too. Back then, to be illegitimate was a horrible thing—but now, ancient history, right? Why should we unearth such things?"

"Of course, I'll not speak of it. I can see that you were once very close, and then over time, through the mores and rules of society, perhaps Gran felt she didn't want to expose the family to scandal when she married my grandfather, and then sadly you parted ways; it all makes sense to me now, and I am so very happy that you've found each other again, even after all these years. I'm also glad that *I've* found you, too, and I don't care what the nature of our relation is—to me, you're my aunt in the fullest sense and always will be."

"You are an exceptional young woman—and very astute," the older woman said, her eyes glistening with tears.

"From bad things sometimes come good—as with this war. No matter what happens, you'll always be my true heart, as real and proper family." Ruth dabbed her eye. "Now, please, please come inside. Let me make you some tea, Aunt Vera. Sit by the fire; you've worked hard enough today."

"Thank you, darling."

They returned to the cottage, and Vera went into the sitting room, where she sank into her favourite chair and closed her eyes, enjoying the warmth of the hearth. She felt a welling of emotion and love—so much love for Ruth—but deep down, somewhere in her heart, in a place she seldom visited, flickered a small, smouldering bit of consternation. Because despite all the love she felt radiating from Ruth, she also knew that there was something she could *not* tell her. No, no—she could never tell her that. Because despite her cleverness and perceptiveness, Ruth was, in fact, dead wrong—so truly and horribly wrong about everything.

Sunday morning, Ruth woke up early, wishing to go shooting alone, and maybe to think. She eased herself out from bed quietly and got dressed in the dark, hoping not to wake Maude. She made herself a cup of tea and opened the kitchen blackouts to reveal the first cold rays of light appearing on the horizon. She hadn't stopped thinking about the mill—she'd dreamt of it. Something was calling to her from some ghostly realm, this building with its locked wheel. She'd generally ignored it, only going there to pick watercress, but now she knew that she had a family connection to the place. The crumbling pink house next to it—did Vera once live in it? She wasn't sure, but as she finished her tea, she realized that a gun would not be required that morning.

She rode her bike along the road, just as the sun crested the horizon, passing the Yellow Rattle, then down the cobblestone grade towards the river and the mill. She leaned her bike against the wall and tried the door, knowing that it would be locked. She peered in a darkened window but could see nothing. She walked around the perimeter, found a second locked door, then discovered a strange, low, hatchlike door on the side wall. She stooped to inspect it and ran her fingers around it, looking for a handle or a way to open it, when her fingers grazed a metal catch up under the jamb. She fiddled at it a little, and with the sound of a click, the door eased inward. She took a small electric torch from her purse. Its war-regulation red beam was meagre, but better than nothing. She bent over and moved into the gloom.

She shone the torch around and saw the large, oily gears, a hay-strewn floor, timber beams, and then, tantalizingly, a ladder leading up into a trapdoor. She started to climb. When she got to the top, the red beam of her torch revealed a small, windowless room, which astonishingly had an actual bed with a hay mattress, an unlit oil lamp, a bookshelf, and a tiny hearth. There was a table and two chairs, and on the table were the remnants of food—bread crusts and a small jar that looked like it once contained jam. She stepped towards the table, and a few mice skittered away under her feet. She moved the beam of the torch around and on the wall at the foot of the bed saw scratchings of graffiti, made by the sooty lumps of coal from the fireplace. The drawings depicted two figures, hand in hand. Another one showed two figures in a boat, what looked like little girls. Then, further over, by a less adept hand, was a crude drawing of a horseshoe and wagon wheel. Then, nearby, a sketch, this one by a different, more artistically inclined hand, of a man and woman and two children. Ruth stepped closer and could see that it was once a rather good rendering, but it had been ruined, smeared by what looked like an angry, frustrated hand, the faces of the figures blurred almost beyond recognition except for the young girl. Ruth could make out some of her features in the gloom, and a familiarity tugged at the back of her brain.

She investigated a low shelf and discovered a mishmash of old and tattered books. She picked up a curious-looking volume, *The Roxburghe Ballads*, and flipped through the Victorian collection of old songs and poems. Judging by some of the tiny woodcut prints, it was meant to be a bit bawdy. Ruth smiled as she riffled through the pages and thought she'd take this one with her. She flipped to the front cover and found a name, her own, *Gladstone*, written in the top corner of the inside front cover. A shiver went down her spine. She slipped the book in her purse and heard a door slam somewhere below her. She stepped quietly back into the shadows and snapped off her electric torch. The ladder trembled as someone began to ascend it.

She crouched in a corner, behind a battered old wardrobe, holding her breath. She could not see who had climbed through the trapdoor; she could only hear the person cough and clear their throat. It sounded like an older woman—her movements slow, panting lightly with each mysterious task she performed out of sight. There was the striking of a match and a change in the lighting that suggested a candle was lit. Ruth moved further back, out of view, and dared not peer out. She heard shuffling and more breaths and sighs, like someone winded from the climb, then the sounds of objects placed on the table, the dragging of a chair, the rustle of fabric. The candle was extinguished, and the ladder creaked as this person descended. Ruth waited until she heard the door on the lower level click shut before she emerged from her hiding place. She snapped on her torch and looked to see that someone had left some apples and a loaf of bread, arranged in a peculiar way, like an offering of some sort. Ruth got down the ladder as fast as she could. She thought to rush home but instead lingered by the mill for some time, trying in vain to understand what had just happened.

SPRING 1941

-26-

At the beginning of March, the air started to warm a little, while small shoots of green thrust out from the soil and appeared on the boughs. England had been at war for a year and a half, and Martynsborough had not heard or seen a single German plane since the night of the Christmas dance.

For many weeks, Ruth patiently concealed her discovery at the mill. She was not certain how it was all connected, but some instinct told her to remain silent, to not even tell Malcolm. Although unspoken, she had written of it, and then re-written it into a story that was starting to resemble a novel. She was very well pleased with it—although there were still some glaring holes in the narrative. She could fill them in with conjecture, but preferred learning the truth—however unpleasant that might be. Ruth's best source of village gossip, Ellen, had told her of a flurry of sightings of the wraith in January and February. However, as of early March, the wraith had not been seen in some weeks. Fear and suspicion still rippled through much of the village, but the arrival of spring had tempered this fear somewhat. Ruth still wondered about Elise. There had been no closure in this regard, as she was none too anxious to raise the issue with Malcolm. Either way, doctor or no doctor, she continued to harbour a suspicion that in the case of Malcolm's peculiar wife, things were not at all as they seemed.

Maude, meanwhile, had made her stay in the village a semi-permanent one. Wearing her pinafore dungarees and Wellington boots, she spent much time afield, walking the moors and roads of the village, with her small mallet and magnifying glass, seeking some elusive truth among the stones at her feet. Her arms became tanned, and her hair became wild—caught in the wind, it unfurled like spring ivy. It seemed that the River Harold now flowed through her veins, and the village of Martynsborough was growing on her skin like so much lush moss.

As time passed, Maude had been spending more time with Ellen, and had even slept occasionally in the small flat above the pub, lingering in the warmth of the Yellow Rattle. On those nights, Ruth stretched out in her bed, enjoying the luxury of space, but she'd be lying to herself if she didn't admit to missing Maude at least a little bit. Alone in bed, she read until dawn. Or she wrote under the glow of a dim lamp with paper propped up on her knees and her hand cramping as the pen flew across the page.

Ruth knew that soon she would have a complete novel, but much of it depended on the envelope she had given Mr. Sutcliffe to deliver to Wolstenholme some weeks before. So, it was with great excitement when, on the second Monday of March, she saw the letter that had arrived at the numbered post box she had rented in Clitheroe.

Dear Dr. Gladstone,

I have read your letter with great interest, and we are indeed honoured to be considered part of your scholarly research. We would be delighted to have Wolstenholme Park included in your guide to Great English Estates, and we ask that you please accept an invitation, along with your assistant, on this fifteenth of March at six o'clock. Please feel free to bring your notes and a photographer if you have one. Mr. Blackwell will meet you at the front gate on the day and at the hour. We look forward to making your acquaintance.
Best,
RMW

Ruth's letter had been too tantalizing for the man to ignore—an updated history, to be written as an addendum to the original fawning volume that she and Malcolm had found in the library. A bit of fudging with the facts of course was required, including Ruth's newfound postdoctoral degree, and a made-up publishing company with offices in both London *and* New York (and the occasional numbered post box). Malcolm was to be her assistant—a designation that worried him, given the old man's likely Victorian attitude towards female scholars, but it was Ruth's novel, so he happily acquiesced to the rather mad adventure they had set out for themselves.

Wolstenholme had taken the bait, and they were going to finally find out what lurked in the conservatory. *Pets*—as Sutcliffe had called them. Ruth and Malcolm had wondered with great delight for more than a month what kind of pets they could be. Or perhaps it was the wraith herself who lurked within the glasshouse, as Malcolm had speculated.

They rode bicycles there, and the warmth and the dust had them looking slightly unkempt as they neared the escarpment. As they rounded the bend, they saw the open gate and a man, shrouded in all black, standing ominously between the palisades. "This will be Blackwell," Malcolm whispered, "He looks like the grim reaper."

". . . or ferryman of the River Styx," said Ruth. They leaned their bikes against the outside wall of the gate and stepped across the threshold of Wolstenholme Park. Blackwell stood, unmoving, like a mythical spectre, colourless, a poisonous lump of black coal. He presented no facial expression, and appeared, for a long, horrible moment, to in fact be dead—propped up by some unseen pole in the ground—until he spoke.

"Welcome to Wolstenholme Park." His voice was the groan of an iron hinge. "Dr. Gladstone, I presume?" He stepped towards Malcolm.

"Actually . . . ," Malcolm mumbled.

"I am Dr. Gladstone," Ruth said, extending her hand. Blackwell looked at Ruth with distaste, and begrudgingly shook her hand—his flesh was as cold as wax. "This is my assistant, Malcolm."

"This way, please." Blackwell closed the gate behind them, turned, and started walking down the path. Malcolm and Ruth lagged. Blackwell stopped a moment to allow them to catch up and said, "Mr. Wolstenholme has asked that you meet in the library, and from there, he wishes to provide a short tour. Do you not have a photographer?"

"No," Ruth said. "There's little in the way of photography on offer as of late—the war, you know."

"Ah yes." Blackwell raised an eyebrow—the closest thing to a facial expression he'd yet displayed. "The war, of course. Sometimes I forget. We were once friends, you know, we English and the Germans." He resumed his forward stride.

After a long walk the house came into view, a large, grey-stoned monolith with a massive double door that looked like the entrance to a fortress. Behind the manor house, they could see the edge of the conservatory, a building that, while past its prime, still appeared to be intact, with steamed-up windows and great iron columns holding up acres of glass.

"This way," Blackwell said. They entered an august foyer of immense scale and grandeur with twin coiling staircases leading to a high-ceilinged mezzanine. And although grand in scope, all seemed so very dark, as if a thin layer of coal dust coated the walls and floor, the draperies and dour portraiture on the wall, the marble step, the oak banisters and newel posts—like all the colour had been siphoned away.

They followed Blackwell along a carpeted corridor that had the same mouldy sense of neglect, at the end of which a doorway led into a dim room; inside, they could see a fire in the hearth, and a large, wingback chair turned towards the mantel. A voice emerged from it. "Ah, you're here. Jolly good. Come, join me by the fire." It was a voice as soft and fragile as cracked vellum. An unimposing white hand slithered out from the side of the chair and gestured towards a sofa nearby.

The room was flanked on all sides by immense bookcases. On the few walls that did not have shelving were hung framed oddities—dead and embalmed butterflies, grotesque exotic insects in keep-safe cabinets lit by small electric lights, along with botanical diagrams and other Victorian curiosities. Malcolm and Ruth approached the sofa, and soon were confronted with the man in the chair; he was small and wrinkled—ancient looking—with wisps of white hair on a mostly bald, mottled scalp. He wore a white suit with black tie in the Edwardian tradition. He did not stand. Instead, he presented a small twist of his hand as way of greeting and said, "Please sit." The sofa he offered, however, was not so much a sofa as a wider-than-normal club chair, forcing the two of them to squeeze into a rather limited space with their thighs crushed against one another. Malcolm, who didn't seem to know what to do with his arm in such a tight arrangement, placed it around Ruth's shoulders like a paramour in a darkened cinema, while she placed her attaché case between her boots and folded her hands in her lap. It was the closest their bodies had ever been, and in such peculiar circumstances, Ruth almost laughed aloud at the absurdity of it.

"You are scholars, so your letter indicates," the man said without taking his gaze from the fire. "What interest do you have in this very old house?"

"We're evacuees, sheltering here because of the war—while helping with the effort, of course—and we've both been quite interested in the history of this place."

". . . the war. Yes, the war. You're here because of the war. Our king has as much German blood in his veins as English. Why do we fight with our friends?"

"Mr. Wolstenholme," Ruth said, slightly too loudly. "I was hoping to write about the estate, about the conservatory, which I've read was once well known in Lancashire."

"*Once* well known, you say." He looked over at them and noted Malcolm's cloudy eye and then glanced down to his missing fingers. "Your assistant doesn't appear to be fully intact."

"A war injury, sir," Malcolm said quietly, "two fingers and one eye."

"Ah. *In regione coecorum rex est luscus.*" He raised a wiry eyebrow. "You are scholars—you should know your Latin. It's Erasmus: *In the land of the blind, the one-eyed man is king.*" Wolstenholme appraised them both cannily while waiting for a reply, a rebuke perhaps, but received none. He then returned to the subject at hand. "So, then, Dr. Gladstone, you're here in Martynsborough, a small village that rarely sees outsiders, to stir up what exactly . . . ghosts? No? To tell a story? Now, what would you and your Polyphemus here like to know about the estate?"

Already deeply disliking their host, Ruth tried to hold her temper, and carefully went through formal introductions, followed by a series of tame, non-challenging questions with a slightly fawning air in hopes of winning the old man's trust. Malcolm meanwhile spoke no more, and dutifully scratched out notes in a small book. "And family? Is it just you?" Ruth asked.

"Hmm? There's Blackwell. Just Blackwell and I here, although I did once have a family. My wife died of dysentery many years ago, probably weakened by grief."

"Grief?" Ruth asked, newly interested.

"Yes, our daughter, Charlotte. She disappeared just before the turn of the century—she was sixteen years old at the time."

"I'm sorry to hear that," Ruth said, recognizing the name from the book she had borrowed from the library. She had to suppress a burning curiosity to pursue the matter too eagerly; she would need to do so delicately, but before she could speak, he did.

"She was obstinate like her mother—like an unbreakable horse, I couldn't contain her. We woke one morning to find her gone. Her mother was convinced she was dead, while I suspect she ran off with a beau, to elope or some other nonsense. She probably spent her finest years in a crumbling cottage full of runny-nosed urchins, living hand to mouth with a ditch-digging drunkard husband, and now—who knows? Dead? Widowed? I don't spend an ordinate amount of time concerning myself with whatever life she chose." He paused; his lips pursed. "I had wanted a son, but it was not to be. I tried to raise her properly, I was stern, but it was for naught. As it is, I've no heir." He looked up at Ruth, his eyes, black and deep set in their sockets, revealed not sadness but rancour. Ruth felt it unwise to pursue the matter, so she changed the topic to the Wolstenholme holdings and the extent of his estate.

". . . and the mill?" Ruth asked nonchalantly. "Is that something you've had interest in?"

"Not *had*—but *have*. I still do."

"Oh. I find that peculiar; the mill does not appear to be an active business, and it looks a little, if you don't my saying so, run-down."

"It is indeed run-down, Dr. Gladstone. As I wish it to be."

"I don't understand."

"The man who originally owned and operated that mill, a man called Catchpoole, had a terrible habit of playing about with the village dam, which resulted in flooded pastureland of a farm that I happen to own. I don't know the mechanics of mills; he told me that such adjustments were required to move his wheel and mill the flax of his clientele. I sent Blackwell to the village early in the morning, with some tinkerer or other, and they fixed the dam higher to drain my land. Catchpoole dropped it once more. We took this disagreement to a magistrate, who, to my chagrin, took the side of Catchpoole. This caused great trouble for me, and being such a pig-headed man, Catchpoole gloated and disparaged my name around the village, crowing of his victory. He was a small and weak man who amplified his voice to appear more than he was—I had to correct that. It was a hostile takeover, as they're called these days, I suppose—some financial and legal sleight of hand, a facile process when one has the means. I was most generous and offered him the opportunity to continue to operate the mill at my behest and my profit, but he refused—predictably proud, in spite of himself, as I knew he would be, and soon enough he was dead of heart attack, and his family penniless. They vacated the property. I've left the mill to fall into ruin, perhaps as reminder to the plebeians not to cross the lord and liege, but more likely, it seemed that no one wished to work for me, and thus the mill is now merely a subject for bad water-colour paintings. As it stands, much grain processing is now done under diesel power—Catchpoole was a dying breed on the way to extinction; I merely helped him along—natural selection, as they call it."

"Right," Ruth said, doing her best to contain a growing anger caught in her throat. "And the conservatory, then?" she asked in hopes of changing the subject. "According to our research, it was quite the local landmark. Tell me about it."

"My glasshouse is a small world unto itself, a world I built. I am fascinated by the diversity of life on this planet. Like that." He pointed at a thick glass frame holding a pinned and mounted specimen of a bright red centipede, like a creature from some primordial mangrove.

"Is this an area of interest for you? Insects?" Ruth asked.

"Moths, specifically, Dr. Gladstone. My obsession is moths. Creatures of the night, frail, dusty, flitting here and there, like a tortured soul leaving the fleshy prison of their caterpillary instar, rising, ethereal—to be exiled below, upon the earth, darkness or aloft, to be drawn to the moon like an ocean tide—like a spirit in a way."

"You see much more in the humble moth than most," Ruth said. "Why not butterflies, or birds?"

"Birds? I have some of those too—colourful things, plumage that only a god could create. I *had* some, I should say, in the past tense. I lost my only remaining peafowl most recently." Ruth felt her neck redden and a flush descend from her fringe.

"Moths then," she said more forcefully than intended. "Beautiful creatures of the night—mysterious, yes. Speaking of creatures of the night, if you don't mind, I'd like to turn your attention to another matter. You've some lime kilns, which have filled with water over the years and, I suppose, have taken on a sort of accidental beauty."

"You've seen them?" There was a whiff of accusation to his tone.

"Well . . . um, no," Ruth stammered a little. "I've only heard of them. Some of the villagers have spoken of them, and now that we're on this topic, I ought to touch at least once on another subject that is of great historic interest to me. It relates to matters that occurred some thirty years prior, in 1910, December, as I've been told."

"The year of the comet. And the last year that the damn gypsy wagons were here. Thankfully, they've never been back."

"Yes, that's right. It was that year. There's been documentation of a strange incident that occurred around that time; a man claimed to have found something . . . a body, a girl's body in the lime-kiln pond. Thereafter, there was some panic in the village—a panic that came from a possible supernatural source. I wonder, Mr. Wolstenholme—I wonder if you've any opinion or knowledge of . . ." The old man snickered under his breath a little, then laughed louder. Ruth continued, "Perhaps, if you've some information about this local peculiarity, I would be most . . . most interested . . ." A peal of laughter erupted from the old man, and he fell into a hacking fit. Ruth looked up by the doorway to find Blackwell standing there in the hall, his own shoulders spasming with ill-concealed amusement. "Clearly something is funny? I'm not sure I follow," she said.

"Dr. Gladstone, I'm sure you speak of a foolish man from my past. He came up to my manor house to ask for a reprieve on his rent—has it been thirty years, Blackwell? Dear God, how quickly it slips away. You see, the entire stretch of terraced cottages in the north end of Martynsborough is owned by me. I knew the man since he was but a boy, he was among a few hired hands in the stables—back when we had horses, that is. Either way, he made nothing of himself as he grew up, but my wife always had a soft spot for him—among her dying wishes was to assure he had a place to live. Not the brightest one he was, but able enough to work—to earn a living as it were. But he hadn't been paying his rent. Seems he was a bit of a gambler and not faring well with his fixed costs. I sent Blackwell around to provide him a notice of eviction and a bit of a fright perhaps. The fool asked to see me, to plead his case, so I invited him around for a *drink*." He put an unusual emphasis on the word *drink* and glanced at Blackwell as he did, who let out a gravelly bit of laughter that was among the ugliest sounds that Ruth had ever heard. "Come, would you like to see what he had to drink?" He stood and shuffled slowly towards a tremendously high wooden cabinet. Ruth and Malcolm awkwardly extracted themselves from the tight-fitting club chair and followed. In the centre of the bookcases, there was a recess, lit dimly with small electric lightbulbs that illuminated exotic crystal decanters, and peculiar bottles. "I might seem a sorcerer with so many potions," the old man said. "Come, have a look at what I have here." Ruth and Malcolm stepped closer. "Now this"—he held up a bottle—"I found this in a tomb in Prague—two hundred years old, an ancient example of wine. Would you like to try some?" He tilted the bottle slightly so that it sloshed about with grit and other detritus floating within the viscous fluid. "No? Not for the faint of heart, these old vintages, I should say." He moved some bottles around and reached towards the back, the glass tinkling softly. "But this, this is the one that has caused the most trouble, my little fairy." He brought out the bottle made of dark brown glass containing a mysterious liquid. "You think absinthe, don't you? A green fairy? Oh no, not this. This fairy is much more special. She's called soma. Have you heard of it?"

"No," Ruth said, hoping she wouldn't be asked to sample the vile-looking fluid.

"It's a Sanskrit word, a ritual drink, from the legends of north India. I spent some time in the colonies on the subcontinent. This elixir was provided to me by a man I met on the edge of the Thar Desert. A drink fit for the gods, he told me, or at least a way to speak to the gods; it's made from the small seed of a rare plant, distilled and fortified, as he told me, and it has incredible properties. They say that such a drink can open the third eye."

"Third eye?" Ruth was perplexed by the direction of the conversation.

"An ancient concept perhaps, but at the very least, to sip from this draught will produce ghosts, or more likely, it produces visions that are windows to the truth—our own truth."

"So, this man Phineas," Ruth said. "That was his name, by the way—Phineas—he drank this, and then . . . then . . ."

"Oh, it was all in a little fun. I wanted to teach the fool a lesson. He took the drink. He went a bit mad. I offered a walk about the conservatory, which seemed to set him off even more—he and the men of the village were quite frightened of my glasshouse." He grinned cunningly. "In any event, the fool quivered and shuddered and jumped at his own shadow and I found it all very amusing. Soon his behaviour became erratic, so I sent him away. He must have passed by the ponds on his way back to Martynsborough, but there was no girl in the water, I can guarantee that. He saw something, yes, but no girl—dead or otherwise."

"You know what he saw?"

"Of course I do." Wolstenholme replaced the bottle and returned to his chair. Ruth and Malcolm glanced at each other and followed.

"So, what was it?" Ruth asked, Malcolm had his notepad at the ready.

"He saw a cat. That is all."

"I don't understand—a cat?"

"Yes, yes, a cat, you know, as in 'meow-meow.' It sometimes happens, we sometimes get unwelcome interlopers in the conservatory such as this. It seemed to come from nowhere—I've no idea how it got in, but it certainly raised a proper ruckus—it's never a good thing when a foreign entity interlopes into a pristine and balanced natural environment. This filthy animal trod over a rare flower from the Amazon jungle that only blooms once a year, and then had the nerve to give birth to kittens right then and there. Revolting. I had Blackwell remove them, and while I sat with this fool—Phineas—and watched him go mad from the soma in my library, I had Blackwell bag up the rotten felines and drown them in the pond, as we've had to do occasionally with other animals that infiltrate my glasshouse."

"Oh. That's quite . . . quite . . ."

"Horrible? Yes, I suppose. But the inhabitants of my glasshouse are fragile. Blackwell told me about it later. That this fool wandered home, and stumbled past the ponds, the mother cat might have fallen from the mouth of the bag, the kittens, perhaps with some life left in them, squirmed within—he somehow misconstrued this assemblage of cat, kitten, white burlap bag, and black water for a drowned girl. It was the soma no doubt infecting his mind, but I didn't catch wind of this till the next day when the villagers came traipsing up the bluff and made a hell of a mess hauling rubbish from the pond and screamed bloody murder about a yellow-haired girl. We realized that the soma gave him this vision—not a yellow-haired girl, but yellow-furred cat—*dead* cat—spilling from a burlap bag. The soma reveals truth, and I think that this man saw some memory or desire for which he was ashamed—some girl to whom he had done wrong perhaps in his past, and then, you know the rest—he careened through the town with accusations of murder and mayhem over what? A dead cat—which by the way, Blackwell had removed long before those cretins made the mess of my ponds that they did the following day. Whatever spectre he dreamt up in the village had nothing to do with the ponds, or a girl or even me, but it all resided neatly within his own troubled brain, and his mania seems to have been contagious among the other men. The wraith—yes, I have heard of the wraith, Dr. Gladstone—she is nothing more than a pub-inspired trifle by local fools with too little work to busy their hands. I hate to spoil such a resplendent story of a ghost, but sometimes inconvenient facts usurp spectacle and fancy."

Ruth sat quietly fuming and confused—and as relieved as she was that no person had died, nor was murdered, she felt a growing distaste for this man. The drowning of kittens was one thing, but Wolstenholme had a repugnant view of all humanity—and life in general, pillaging graves, ensnaring insects and plants, flora, fauna, objects of culture, poisons, and potions. He thought himself better than others, like a small god unto himself, for which all living creatures were merely something to cage in his glasshouse, or to pin and mount like a trophy. His travels to distant places were not for the acquiring of knowledge, but the theft of things. He flung about sacred draughts for his own amusement, a joke—a drink to be offered casually to an oblivious mark. Unlike Maude, who picked up stones by the side of the road, Wolstenholme was a plunderer. Moreover, he had ruined Vera's family—and by proxy, Ruth's own—for pure spite. She wanted no part of it. She rose, and was about to announce that she had all the information she required and declare her intention to leave, when Wolstenholme said, "We'll now go into the conservatory. There are none of your ministry's blackouts there, so we must use a red-light, lest our friends, the Germans, rain bombs on us." He laughed. "Come, don't be frightened. We'll see my pets." Ruth's curiosity overruled everything, and she glanced at Malcolm, who nodded. So, they walked down a long, cavernous corridor replete with various heraldic symbols, coats of arms, and dull, empty suits of armour. At the end was a blackout curtain, hoisted some twenty feet up to the high ceiling. Wolstenholme took two electric torches. He handed one to Ruth. "For you, Dr. Gladstone, so you might find your way." The old man took up the second torch and disappeared between the curtains as if he were stepping on to a theatre stage. Ruth and Malcolm met each other's eyes, and then followed.

The sun had dipped low, and it was quite dark as they stood before a large glass door gauzy and veiled with humidity. Through it, Ruth could just make out shapes, vegetation, trees perhaps. "Shall we?" Wolstenholme opened the glass door, releasing a whoosh of warm air that smelled thick and organic, of damp soil, fermentation. Ruth and Malcolm followed him into a dank world. There were tropical plants in abundance, large palm trees and jungle creepers slithering up the sides of the vast conservatory to the glass ceiling. "It requires four boilers to keep this glasshouse at the optimal temperature—the climate of the equator, Southeast Asia if we're to be exact. I've some plants from the Amazon basin, but mostly French Vietnam."

Along a path of sorts, made from cobbled stone, Wolstenholme walked further into the glasshouse while Ruth and Malcolm followed, looking around warily, wondering what lurked among the trees and foliage. Wolstenholme showed no such concern and continued onward, pointing his red-beamed light at various plants and flowers, commenting keenly here and there. Soon the path led to a central circle, with a small stone column, resembling an altar, on which there was a simple, glass-domed oil lantern. Around this central feature were wooden benches, like the pews of a church. Wolstenholme pointed his red beam at one of the benches. "Please, have a seat. I'll summon them."

"Them?" Ruth asked nervously as she sat.

"The inhabitants of this place." He opened the lantern, struck a match, and lit the wick, then slid the glass dome over the lamp. He turned the wick wheel until a bright glow spread out, illuminating the immediate surroundings.

"Mr. Wolstenholme, there're no blackouts in here." Ruth looked up at the glass ceiling. "We're surrounded by windows." He glanced at her with an annoyed expression, his face glowing eerily in the light of the lamp.

"Do you honestly think there is a German squadron of bombers anywhere near this god-forsaken village?" He sat on a bench next to them. "No, not bombers, but other types of flyers. I chose today for our meeting purposefully; there will be special visitors tonight that are not always here. You'll see."

Almost immediately, they came, landing on the stone table. They were tiny, winged things, like midge-flies; then there followed some beetles, small black ones, followed by rather large, colourful specimens. The air buzzed with various clicks and vibrations, rustlings, like tiny bells and rattles. Then moths came, dozens of small creamy blue things, flitting about erratically, landing on the glass of the lamp, then zigzagging away again. On the table, an enormous centipede crawled around. "Mind that one"—the old man pointed—"she's venomous."

"This is all very fascinating," Ruth said, swatting away the vibrant blue carapace of a rather large beetle that had landed on her arm. "But I think maybe we've seen enough—quite interesting, perhaps we'll get going now."

"Oh, you've not seen the best yet. You know, a long time ago, I brought Charlotte in here. My wife wouldn't set foot in the glasshouse, but Charlotte—well, I thought that if she'd spend a night or two in this place it might enlighten her, to calm her disobedience." He cocked his head in a curious bird-like movement. "Ah, they've arrived." Wolstenholme's gaze fell behind Malcolm and Ruth into the deepest bit of tropical growth. "Here's one right now; he seems to like you, Dr. Gladstone."

Ruth felt something prickly affix to her shoulder like a grasping clawed hand, but she was too seized with fear to look. Something soft brushed her cheek. "Don't be frightened." Wolstenholme stood and approached her. "Dr. Gladstone, if you'd just turn your face a wee bit to the right, you'll see a lovely thing." Ruth turned to find what looked like a large bird, but twitching antennae, massive unblinking eyes, and six white-furred legs proved otherwise. She had an instinct to swat at it, but she did not; instead, not moving, sweating profusely, she asked, "What is it?"

"An atlas moth, my dear," said Wolstenholme. "The largest moth in the world. It won't harm you." The old man took the moth carefully from Ruth's shoulder, and set it on his wrist, like a falconer with his kestrel. It was more bird than insect, its wingspan a foot wide at least. Tangerine-coloured fur covered its body, and its wings shimmered with layers of incandescent crimson, ochre, teal, and gold along with dazzling chevrons of pure white, one for each of the four wings, the edges of which curled in a unique way to resemble the head of a burnished serpent. "One of my larger ones, I'd say. Oh, here's another," said Wolstenholme, and soon, dozens of moths, a flock of flitting, strangely weightless bird-like things, gathered about. Other smaller species joined, some mottled grey-brown, like tree bark and deadfall, others brilliant, buttery yellow, amber, crimson, and sapphire, some with bizarre double tails like Japanese kites, others with gilded, iridescent eyes, their antennae like tufted, emaciated feathers, soft and white, twisting on the wind, tasting the air for the scent of their mate. They floated about, landing on Ruth, snagging on her blouse cuffs, and sweeping by her ears. "Isn't it wonderful?" Wolstenholme said as he launched the atlas moth from his withered hand. The creature took to the wing at once, graceful as a sparrow, but then it dove erratically, and foundered, only to shake away some invisible ballast and flutter back towards the lamp, weightless as a fairy.

"They are indeed beautiful," Ruth said, looking around in wonderment. Malcolm, next to her, inspected a large specimen on the arm of the bench.

"They won't bite, if that's what concerns you; in fact, the atlas moth has no mouth at all."

"How can that be?" Ruth asked. "How would they eat?"

"They don't. They begin life as a caterpillar instar, which *does* indeed eat—quite industriously—for months. It will then shroud itself in a chrysalis and be reborn as this beautiful thing, with no mouth, no stomach, no digestive system, and wings large enough to travel far and wide to find a mate. It will not eat, it will not drink water, it will neither grow nor change tonight—for this is the only night of its life in this form, as a moth. Dr. Gladstone, this creature has one purpose, and one purpose only, and that is to fuck." He chuckled. "If you don't mind my candour to say so in such a coarse way. And they will all be dead in the morning—so there is simply no time to eat. They live like this for one day only, long enough to copulate and for the female to lay her eggs, which will hatch, and themselves, repeat the cycle, emerging once again many weeks from now to play out the same tragic mating ritual."

Ruth wanted to change the subject, feeling like Wolstenholme was using profanity and lingering on the topic of sex to take delight in offending her. She thought of what Sutcliffe had said about the names Castor and Pollux. "Do you name them?" she asked.

"Name them? Yes, I often do—a spur-of-the-moment thing, I suppose—given they only live for a single night, I find a certain pleasurable cruelty in it, to provide a name for something so fleeting and short-lived, a creature who will, if you'll excuse the expression, spend the night fucking, only to drop dead as the sun rises. I've used Greek myth, and other overstated, epic-sounding names to designate these creatures. Just think, for an immortal god of Mount Olympus, our time on earth may seem as fleeting in their perception as these creatures are to us. Zeus—if he were to exist—might look at you and me as colourful, short-lived insects searching for a mate with whom to sexually couple so that we might prolong the misery of our species with offspring. It's a little pathetic really, and in a roundabout sort of way, it brings me great delight. This day, I've named none; it is at my whim to do so or not to do so. Tonight, they will die without the benefit of moniker. To add to this sublime tragedy, I'll also presume that many will not find a mate, and they will die, beautiful, irrelevant, and without a name, to be swept away by Blackwell in the morning like so much dust."

"Your daughter, Mr. Wolstenholme—you said you brought her in here—what do you mean? She stayed in here—slept in here? Why?"

"She was rather obstinate; I'm a believer in firm discipline."

"What are you saying?" Ruth was growing alarmed, wondering what on earth had come to pass in the conservatory.

"Discipline has grown lax in this modern age. Charlotte was frightened of this place, and although the only living thing in here which might present any true danger is the occasional centipede, fear can be a useful component of persuasion, Dr. Gladstone. Fear is a many-faceted, many-layered, most wonderful thing, and it can be employed for a positive outcome. Unfortunately for my daughter, even fear was not enough to calm her wildness." He leaned forward and turned down the lamp until the wick was nothing more than a dull orange spot. "That's all I wish to say this evening. Blackwell will show you out."

-27-

It was dark as they rode home from the manor house. The moon hung low and heavy, and the air was thick with musk and blossom. In the distance, purple-grey clouds gathered against the black sky, threatening a storm. Their minds were alighted with all they had learned, and by some unspoken agreement, they decided that they would need time to digest so much information before they discussed it.

As they approached the lock bridge, Malcolm stopped, looking back towards the church. "Look there," he whispered. Ruth turned and saw a flutter of white in the church yard. Then from the shadows of some trees, a figure stepped out. Wearing a pale shift and a cowl about her head, the spectre seemed to look around, then approached the church. "I can't believe it—there she is. This is our chance," Malcolm said quietly. "We need to go see who she is. Leave these." Malcolm leaned his bike against the bridge rail, and Ruth did the same. They moved towards the church quietly. As they did, the wraith slipped around the back of the building. Malcolm hurried after her. "We'll lose her," he whispered. "Hurry." They arrived to where she had stood, then rounded the corner into the cemetery. As they did, a brilliant flash of lightning appeared over the escarpment, and the wind turned abruptly, rustling the spring branches, and sweeping over the village with an impending sense of the coming gale. Malcolm stopped and pointed. "There, by the wood, she's gone into the wood." They walked quickly, weaving among the gravestones, as the clouds approached, boiling above them like a cauldron. There was another flash, then an angry, distant rumbling of thunder. They reached the edge of the wood and found a worn trail. "She's taken this path," Malcolm said. He turned to Ruth. "Should we continue? We may be caught in a storm. I wonder if she will take shelter from the storm herself somewhere, that is, that is if . . . I'm assuming it's a person we've seen. Right?" Thunder cracked alarmingly close, and Ruth instinctively pushed in close to Malcolm. "Right?" He repeated it with a small amount of fear in his voice.

"Let's not continue." Ruth looked at him, her face fraught with worry. "I think I know where she may be going, and we need not follow. We ought to get home. I can explain later." They turned and headed back as the gale picked up. It blustered and challenged, nipping at their heels, then, as they pushed their bikes across the bridge, the rain came, enveloping them in great curtains of ice-cold water. It came in sheets, transforming rivulets on the ground into raging spates, instantly flooding roads. They splashed through the puddles, pushing their bikes through the mire as fast they could, their shoes becoming thick with mud as thunder crashed around them.

"Drop them, Ruth, we'll get them in the morning." A bolt of lightning struck in the flax field, and the thunder that followed was deafening. Ruth was so startled and blinded by the blazing white light that she almost fell. They left their bikes against a fence post, and Malcolm took Ruth's hand. They fled up the road, which itself was becoming like a torrent, with the ground softening, and sinking. They could just make out Virginia's cottage emerging from the relentless rain. "Let's get out of this now—come inside, we'll wait it out a bit." He led her around the back, and then fumbled with the keys in his wet hands, until he got the door to his studio open. They pushed through the blackout curtain, and pulled the door shut behind them.

Ruth stood in the pitch-dark, soaked to the bone, the rain thrashing the roof above while Malcolm clumsily felt about for the lamp. He snapped it on to reveal two sodden, nearly drowned people, red-faced, bright-eyed with misting breath. Malcolm glanced at Ruth with a wry grin. "You look like hell, Gladstone."

"As do you." Ruth removed her wool jacket to find her white blouse sodden, revealing the lace of her brassiere through the sheer material. "I can't . . . I mean, I'm soaked. Do you have anything I can wear?" Malcolm removed his own jacket and hung it on a hook.

"Yes, I've a paraffin heater here, let me warm it up and we'll see if we can dry some of your clothes. I'll get you something. I've some pyjamas you can wear while we wait. They'll be too large, but at least you'll be dry." He puttered about, while Ruth stood dripping near the door, a puddle forming under her feet. She kicked off her muddy shoes and reached up under her skirt to detach her garter suspenders and then peeled the filthy, wet stockings from her legs. She wrung them out on to the floor.

"Sorry, I had to get those off. I couldn't stand it a moment longer." Malcolm opened a cupboard and produced a towel and a pair of striped flannel pyjamas.

"Here, you can dry off and change into these."

"Where? Right here?"

"No, I suppose not." Malcolm looked around. "But it's best we stay in the studio; I don't think it would be a good idea to . . . to . . ." There was a thump from somewhere within the house. Malcolm didn't seem to notice it.

"Will the thunder frighten Elise? Wake her? Might she come looking for you?"

"She's slept through storms before." He looked around. "I'm sure she and Virginia are sound asleep. Right. I'll turn off the light and you can change over there, I'll change here." Ruth ran the towel through her hair for a moment, then walked over to the other side of the studio, placed the fresh pyjamas on a table, and said, "You can turn it off now—but don't turn it back on till I say so." The room was dark once more, and along with the sound of the hammering rain on the roof, she heard from across the room the rustle of fabric, the heavy drop of wet pants, and clank of a belt buckle on the stone floor. Ruth, herself, clumsily unbuttoned her blouse and slipped from the brassiere, towelled off briefly, and felt about in the dark for the pyjama shirt.

"Are you decent?" he called from across the room.

"Oh, no, sorry, still not ready." She kicked aside her sodden skirt and knickers, towelled off her feet and legs, and then slid into his pyjama trousers, which were, as he had warned, much too large.

"Everything all right over there?"

"Yes. I'm afraid I'll be another moment." She finished with the buttons, and, holding the waist with one hand, she gathered her wet clothing with the other. "Right, I'm decent." The light flickered back on, just as a peal of thunder roared above them. Malcolm's hair was slick, and he wore a loosely closed robe over a pair of silky pyjama bottoms.

"This is a strange situation," he said.

"Yes, indeed it is." She pulled her trousers up a little higher.

"I'll get our clothes hung up around the heater; we'll wait to see how long this rain goes on. I've some vermouth here. Would you like a drink? I certainly could use one."

After sorting out a jury-rigged laundry string, he hung their clothes, including Ruth's brassiere and knickers, where they dripped in full view. She thought ruefully that it was the second time that her undergarments were on display for him. Her stockings had so many ladders and tears, she doubted she could wear them again, but he nevertheless handled them with great care as he laid them gingerly on the line.

Malcolm found another folding cot, and brought it close to his, so that they both had a place to sit. Then, perching chastely, they sipped vermouth from teacups.

"The rain isn't letting up," said Ruth.

"You could stay, you know, worst case." He put down his teacup and stood to rummage around in a cupboard and took out a couple of blankets and pillow. "It's probably best you stayed for a while at least. I know it's only a quarter-mile to Vera's cottage, but the lightning is terrible outside. You shouldn't worry about Virginia or Elise, the door there can be locked from the inside here, they . . . she won't barge in and find you, if that's a worry. I can put the cot over there, on the other side of the room." He placed the blankets and pillow next to her.

"We don't need to be hollering at each other across the room, competing with the drumming rain and thunder. We'll just leave this cot here." She finished her vermouth and put the cup on the floor.

"I've no lavatory. Only a chamber pot," he said.

"It's warm and dry here," she said, feeling light-headed, realizing that she'd drank the vermouth too quickly. "It's perfect. I can only hope that Vera and Maude will quell my gran's inevitable anxieties if I'm not home this evening, I mean . . . I *am* a grown woman, am I not? She need not know about *this*." Ruth waved her hands around, indicating the two sleeping cots. "I've already crafted a story in my head as it is—I've stayed at the pub, as Maude sometimes does. That ought to put Gran's prudishness at ease. I'm sure you'll go along with it, yes?"

"Of course."

Ruth arranged the blanket and pillow with one hand while holding up the waist of her trousers with the other. She then pushed her cot closer to his and slid her feet under the blanket to lie on her side. He did the same on his cot.

"You mentioned something about the wraith earlier—that you knew where she was going," he said.

"I don't want to discuss the wraith anymore tonight. Or the manor house. Or the awful man who inhabits it. Or any of that," Ruth said quietly. "I'd like all those things to remain outside of the blackouts tonight, out of sight, on the other side of darkened glass."

"Darkened glass? I've never heard it quite put that way."

"Well, I haven't told you, but other than a rough manuscript of a novel, I did finally get around to writing a poem, one that I have to admit I'm quite happy with—those words just came to me one night, among others, *through a darkening glass* to be precise."

"Bravo. A poem. 'Through a Darkening Glass,' then?"

"Yes, that's the title. It plays with the idea of the blackouts, you know, and the ponds and . . . well . . . I'll read it to you another time." She reached out and took his hand, the left, and examined it. She held the small stumps of his index and middle fingers.

"You can still move them?"

"Yes, a little."

"What is it like to lose your fingers? What does it feel like to have . . . nothing there?" She turned his hand around, looking at it from different angles, as if it were a strange relic.

"I sometimes still feel my fingers, when I don't think about it too much, it's like they're still there. Sometimes they feel sore—the missing fingers, that is—*phantom pain* is what they call it among amputees. I also got some shrapnel in one of my ribs. That was the lesser of the injuries." He opened his robe, and pointed to the side of his abdomen, to a long pale scar. "A hot bit of metal slashed into me here, but it didn't embed, it seemed to career off my rib." Ruth reached across and ran her finger along the ragged line, and then she slid her open palm along his sternum, feeling the soft crinkle of his chest hair. He took a sharp breath while Ruth smiled coyly.

"I was told . . . once . . . that when men return from battle, they're quite keen to be with a woman—more than normal. You know, like a knight returning bloody from a campaign, trembling with anticipation, hoping to maraud his own concubine. Is this true?"

"I don't know really. I came home to an unfortunate situation that would have made little difference in that regard."

"So, I would think that you and Elise—you . . . you don't . . ."

"No, we don't."

"So, since you've been back, you haven't . . ."

". . . no, I haven't."

Ruth's fingers grazed further down his stomach; his flesh quivered at her touch. "So, you can't do that with her anymore. What will you do now? Will you ever . . . ?" He took her hand and placed it on the cot and held it firmly there.

"Ruth, if it were anyone else asking, I'd probably be irate."

"Oh, I'm sorry, I just thought . . ." She blushed.

"Yes, I know. I know. It's all right."

"Am I that repulsive?" She said it so quietly that he could barely hear her over the sound of the rain.

"No, Ruth, no, please don't think that."

"A man riled up by battle, returned home to find he could not be with his wife, all that time, with no sexual outlet, and I am practically— if clumsily—throwing myself at you, hoping that I might . . . maybe help with *that*. Perhaps we might find comfort in each other, and here you refuse my offer. Is it the way I speak, my strange tongue? I'm horrible, aren't I? I've attempted to draw you into adultery." Ruth withdrew her hand and looked away. "Like Francesca—that's me. I deserve the inferno, but I'll be alone there, not with you—you're innocent. I have to say, your reluctance only makes my desire stronger."

"It's more than that," he whispered. "I've had to put a lot of thought into what my future might look like—whatever remains of the marriage I once knew—if anything. And no, Ruth, you're not repulsive. In fact, I find you very beautiful, I *love* the way you speak—I'm very much drawn to you, and I'll admit it. I think of you endlessly. I would want nothing more . . . nothing more than to . . . to *be* with you right now—but I'm afraid that if we . . . if I were to . . . there would be a risk that things would change irreversibly." He paused as another roar of thunder shook the roof. "I like *wanting*," he said. "I like wanting you. I like coveting but *not* having—it is almost better, more satisfying to . . . to think about how very much I want something, to envision it, to play the scene out safely in my mind but not to do it. At least not yet." He touched her wet hair. "I like knowing you're here, listening to the rain with me. I'd like to sleep close to you, to feel your presence, to hear the rustling of the sheet, your breath, to sense your warmth without the uncertainty of entangling ourselves any further. That would provide me so very much pleasure, that alone, I think for now, at least. I'm sorry, I'm speaking rubbish, aren't I?" He placed a hand on her thigh.

"Just like Paulo and Francesca in *The Kiss*," Ruth murmured, "the hand on the thigh."

"Yes, but our lips—a hair's breadth apart, so very close but not . . . not . . ."

". . . not touching."

"No. Not touching." He grasped her with more firmness, then slid his hand over the pyjamas, along the slope of her thigh, down into the valley of her waist. He grazed the hollows and ridges of her hip, and in his sculptor's mind, he imagined her pelvic bone, its slopes, curves, and recesses. Then up further, now under the fabric of the pyjama shirt, his hand stopped briefly, startled as he discovered the warm, bare skin of her torso. He could feel the ridges and furrows of her ribs. His fingers tentatively ventured further, then stopped where he felt the rise of her breast. Sighing heavily, he slipped his hand from under her shirt and then gently touched her lips with a single finger. He closed his eyes. "No further than this . . . please. Before I change my mind. Not yet." He withdrew his hand and rolled away.

They listened to the patter of rain on the roof for a while, their blood pumping, their hearts fluttering, then he rose slightly and reached over to turn off the lamp; his robe fell open as he did. Ruth looked longingly at his chest, the pelt of fleecy brown hair, his pale stomach, the white line of the scar. He snapped off the light, and the room fell into complete darkness.

"Ruth?" Malcolm whispered after a few moments of silence.

"Yes?"

"I wonder, will you need to do your trick with your hand over your ear, to create your ocean sounds, to help you sleep—given this strange environment?"

"No, not here. I'll not need it tonight." She rolled on to her back, and the room spun a bit; the rain, violent and rhythmic, was the most beautiful sound she'd ever heard. "Goodnight, Malcolm," she whispered.

"Goodnight, Ruth."

She moved about in the dark quietly, trying not to wake him. Her clothing had not fully dried from the night before and it was rather unpleasant pushing her body into her damp knickers and damaged stockings, especially after enjoying the silky warmth of Malcolm's pyjamas against her skin all night. She finished dressing and put on her heavy, wet coat and left through the back door.

The horizon was a clean, indigo line as the dawn was only just starting to break. Looking around, she could see the drain that ran the length of the fields was overflowing and the roads were awash in mud. She slogged back to Vera's cottage and stepped in the door quietly. She removed her shoes and meant to creep up the stairs, when she heard a voice in the kitchen.

"Ruth, is that you?" Vera whispered. "I shut your bedroom door; Maude has spoken for you. Edith does not know you were out. Are you well?" Ruth stood in the kitchen doorway with her rumpled hair and ruined stockings. She felt the urge to weep.

"Confused, perhaps, but I am well. If you were wondering, there was nothing last night that ought to worry you or anyone. I'd just like to have a clean-up. The roads are frightful; it will be trouble getting to church today."

"Close your eyes for a while. It's early yet."

Ruth quietly ascended the stair, went into the bath, and dropped her sodden clothes to the floor in a pile. She wrapped a towel about her body and crept back into her room. She slipped into bed next to a snoring Maude and lay awake for what seemed hours, staring at the ceiling.

In the light of the morning, with the sun properly established in the sky, Ruth awoke, surprised to find herself alone and naked beneath the quilts, tangled up in her damp towel. She thought of her stockings lying in a heap on the bathroom floor. Her last presentable pair had been wrecked escaping from the storm with Malcolm. She couldn't go to church bare-legged, and unless she painted her legs in gravy browning, Maude would have to lend her something—although they would probably be too large. Either way, she was relatively certain at that moment, there was not a single pair of stockings left for her in the whole of England.

Despite a muddled start to her morning, Ruth nevertheless dressed and accompanied Edith and Vera to church, wearing a rather heavy pair of winter knit stockings that she'd forgotten about—a lucky discovery in the bottom of her suitcase. They were hot and itchy for spring weather, but they would have to do. Meanwhile Maude had donned wellies and dungarees and spent that Sunday morning alone out on the moor, hoping the heavy rains would reveal some newly glazed and colourful mineral that she might add to her collection.

After church, the congregants gathered outside. On this morning, they spoke of the storm and the state of the river. The rain, it seemed, had fallen all around the area, pouring into the dales and valleys, transforming the normally placid Harold into a boiling cauldron of silty water; the mill race was a gush, and the wheel rattled in the violent current. Edith and Vera walked home with Virginia, while Ruth lingered outside the church until Malcolm emerged from the door.

"I'd like to have a walk," Ruth said. "Malcolm, you would like to come?" Malcolm had Elise on his arm as was usual, and Ruth felt uncomfortable being in her presence. This time she did not search Elise's eyes for meaning, but looked away, a little frightened. They walked down to the mill and came to a cobbled path that ran along the banks, where they stopped and watched the muddy Harold slither by.

"I feel we ought to talk a little." Ruth looked around, to confirm that no one else was nearby.

"Yes," Malcolm said.

"I can't . . . I don't think we should talk so close to her. I'm sorry. I just can't." Ruth looked at Elise, who showed no expression. "Perhaps to be fair to her, too, we ought to talk in private just for a moment."

"Elise, come sit." Malcolm led his wife to a bench, the same bench that Ruth had sat on to eat her lunch the first day she worked at the hall. "Darling, just stay here a moment, yes?" Elise sat and did not move. She stared straight ahead vacuously, as always. Malcolm and Ruth stepped away, towards the mill shed. He did not take his eyes from his wife. "You left this morning while I slept. I'm glad you're well," he said. "I worried a little when I woke up."

"I'm sorry. With my gran, I was avoiding a potential scandal and thought to sneak in before the birds started singing. You were sleeping." She paused, trying to arrange the words in her head. "I didn't want to leave things hanging from last night. I wanted to make sure that between you and me—that we are all right and not strange."

"We'd had a few drinks. Our emotions were high, I suppose, from the storm and so on."

"Yes, yes—but did you mean what you said? All those things you said to me last night?" Malcolm was silent, his eyes fixed vigilantly on Elise. Ruth continued, "I don't want to be a cause of trouble for you or for your marriage. I only . . . But what you said . . . you said . . ."

"I know what I said." He looked at Ruth quickly, then turned his gaze back to his wife. "And yes, I meant it. Every word. I should not have said it, but now that I have, I don't know what comes next."

"Nor do I. Can we just step over here? Look, here behind this mill shed. I don't want her to see—just for a moment."

"I'm not sure what you're on about," he said as Ruth took his hand and led him around the wall.

"I may never have the courage to do this again," she said. "I don't know what the future holds. I intended to do this while you slept this morning, but I was too frightened I'd wake you." She stood on her toes, grasped his jaw in her hand, and brought her mouth to his; it was gentle, a mere grazing of their lips, and nothing more. Ruth then released his face and stepped back. "That's all I wanted to do. Close the hair's breadth, just once, in case I never get the chance again."

"I'm not sure what to say."

"Don't say anything. Let it be for now. Let's return to how it was. We'll find our way eventually, I reckon. For now, let's finish our work. Let's solve the mystery and write a novel. There's still so much to do, and there are some things that I've discovered that I've not told you about yet."

"Yes, I would like that." They stepped out from behind the shed to find that Elise was not on the bench; she had wandered down near the water's edge. Ruth looked across the expanse to see in the distance a white spot on the green, there in the grassy meadow on the west bank, the ewe. Ruth knew what was about to happen and ran towards Elise, realizing this disaster was of her own making. She didn't look back, even as she heard Malcolm cry out.

Elise was strangely graceful, slipping into the water like a pebble in a pond. Her head immediately disappeared under the churning, lead-coloured water. She came back up a moment later, only the back of her blonde head and a scrap of her red wool coat visible as she moved swiftly with the current. Malcolm had claimed that he was not a strong swimmer. Ruth knew this. If he went in, he would possibly drown trying to save his wife, and she knew he would nevertheless make the attempt unless she did something about it.

Ruth reached the edge, tore off her coat, kicked her shoes away, and dove into the River Harold. The cold took the breath from her, and she flailed, dazed for a moment, before getting her bearings and swimming with the current, surprised by its strength. Ahead she saw a flash of red dip under a boiling torrent and then bob up again. Ruth swam hard, and was gaining on her, but her sodden wool stockings and skirt dragged her down. She could see a stone bridge looming ahead; large tangles of broken tree branches were piling around the columns. Elise would be smashed against them. With her muscles aching, the water freezing, Ruth came within reach, but Elise sank under the water once more. Ruth dove, her hands flailing in the murk, and then grasped something—Elise's red coat. She pulled the woman to the surface. Elise's face was a rictus of confusion, but she was conscious, sputtering, breathing. Ruth grasped her tighter and kicked towards the shore where the ewe had been, a safer place with rushes and cattails. With one last push, she managed to get them into the marsh, and she continued until she had Elise in a small, shallow inlet. They leaned against the muddy shore to catch their breath, then Ruth dragged Elise up on to the grassy bank. She was coughing and gasping, and her teeth were chattering, but she appeared to have escaped major injury. Ruth sat her up and knelt by her side.

"Elise?" She shook her by the shoulders, knowing she wouldn't speak, knowing—now—that Elise was not play-acting; how could she be? To risk her life, to drown, to die so as to stay in character? No, Ruth had been incorrect all along. Elise was innocent, no malice, no forethought, a tragically injured woman whose true nature and spirit had sunk deep into the ether of her broken mind. Ruth had probably projected onto Elise her *own* fears, her own insecurities, her own deficiencies and saw on the woman's face and in her veiled eyes what she wished to see instead of what actually was there. Over the previous months, Ruth had wavered in her suspicions of Elise, at times convinced that she was out in the fields at night, faking her injury, and then there were other moments when Ruth wasn't so sure, but now—*now*—she knew for certain: Elise never left her home at night—she couldn't—which meant that the wraith was out there still, the *real* wraith.

Ruth examined Elise carefully; it was the most physically close she'd ever been to her. She was indeed beautiful, even soaked and ravaged by the river. She had a delicate, pale face, flawless, with high, proud

Gallic cheekbones and eyes of the lightest, taffeta blue. Even her sodden hair shimmered like burnished gold—her brow, eyelashes too, all
luminous and glittering—maddeningly so. Elise met Ruth's eyes, her
breath rattled; her lips were the colour of a bruise.

"I'm sorry," Ruth whispered. "I'm sorry for thinking that you were
jealous of me or were play-acting. I'm sorry for everything that's happened to you; I'm sorry your parents died. I'm sorry you were hurt, that
you've lost your ability to speak. You've lost everything, haven't you?
You've even lost yourself. I don't know if you understand or if you can
hear me, but I promise you that I'll never take him away from you. In
a way—just now—I realized that you've got nothing left but him. It
was wrong of me to . . . I should never have considered the possibility.
I shouldn't have . . ." Ruth's voice cracked, and her eyes gleamed with
stubborn tears. "I have to say, I must tell someone at least—seeing that
it doesn't really matter anymore." She lowered her voice to a bare whisper. "I love him. I do. I didn't mean for that to happen; I didn't mean to
feel this way. After all the poems and romances I've read, you'd think I'd
have known a thing or two about love, but I didn't. I had no idea that
such an enormous feeling could just happen like that. It comes from
nowhere . . . and also it comes from *everywhere*. I've seen it in other
people's lives, and now it is here in mine. I had no plans, no notion
that I would feel this way until it was too late. Either way, Elise, it's
happened. But don't worry—I'll be firm with myself. I'll swallow it all
down, and I'll push it all away. I'll never take him from you. That is my
promise." Ruth searched the woman's eyes, looking for some flicker of
understanding, but saw none—only the same empty blue gaze as before.

Then Elise did something unexpected; she reached out and touched
Ruth's hair, grasping the barrette, which hung loosely by only a few
strands; she tugged it lightly and it came free. She examined it closely
and turned it over in her hand a few times, then stuffed it into the
pocket of her wet red coat and sighed audibly, a soft hush that almost
sounded like satisfaction.

"A gift." Ruth smiled, and a single, determined tear slid down her cheek.

Elise's teeth still chattered a little, and so Ruth wrapped her arms around the shivering woman, hoping to provide her with some elusive warmth, and perhaps take some back for herself. Neither woman noticed Malcolm as he came running across the bridge, shouting frantically, calling out both their names, asking if they were well.

Neither Malcolm nor Ruth went to work at the hall for the next week. Elise took ill with a fever. There were a few days of worry, but it appeared to be no more than a cold caught from being in the river. Ruth visited often, and for the first time, Malcolm allowed her upstairs, into Elise's room. There, she helped nurse Elise back to health by bringing tepid tea, and even some spring flowers that she thought might brighten her room. Ruth's hair barrette sat on the bedside table next to Elise, like a favourite object, and Ruth watched as Elise often picked it up and examined it closely, grasping it and turning it over in her hand.

For a few days, Ruth became a common sight in the cottage, putting on the kettle and helping Virginia here and there. A place that Ruth had once crept around in stockinged feet now felt as much a home as Vera's cottage.

Given all that had happened, Ruth and Malcolm did not discuss the nature of their own relationship that week. They fell back into their previous patterns with much unsaid, but the warm amity between them had not faded in the least. If anything, their friendship grew stronger, a new affection had come to them, and in one quiet moment, whilst sitting on a cot in his studio, Malcolm said, "Why don't you recite that poem you spoke of, the one about the darkening glass?"

"I'm afraid I've not memorized it. The page is at home."

"Do you remember even a little?"

"Well, there is the final stanza," Ruth took a deep breath. "I do hope you like it."

> *Through a darkening glass, none can see*
> *We blunder forth in callow*
> *For dusk and starless our eyes be*
> *Reflecting our own shadow.*

Malcolm turned towards Ruth and touched her jaw, drawing her close, he gently kissed her on the mouth, briefly, just once. "That was beautiful. You are surely talented." He looked at her squarely. "There's something else I've wanted to say, and it is simply this: *thank you*. Thank you for what you did for Elise—I haven't really had the opportunity to put it into words." So, he went on. He thanked Ruth for saving Elise's life, and in a way, sparing his own, as he would have likely drowned trying to save her; a debt that he could never fully repay. As much as Ruth wanted to contest his sentiment and claim her own responsibility for leaving Elise alone on the bench, she let it be. His hand lingered on her shoulder after he had kissed her, their bodies growing accustomed to being in the space of the other. And although Ruth certainly dared not say it, or even think it, and as much as she tried to bury it very deep within herself, the truth was, she loved him.

As if she were falling backwards from a precipice, arms flailing, the ground rushing up to shatter her body and bones, the love had struck her, broken her, and infected her with a mystical sense of vertigo. All the sonnets that she had read, and all the poems, and tragedies and romances—they all took on a new colour, a new shade of light, a new clarity and poignancy. Everything made sense because she loved him, and within the space between their bodies, between their lips, the agonizing, most minute hair's breadth that separated them, there lurked a multitude, there lurked a thousand years of time and a limitless space, there lurked Truth. She loved him. That was all. She loved him but could do nothing about it.

Ruth sat across from Malcolm on the train as the countryside slipped by. "My gran would go mad if she knew we were on a trip together. I'm glad that Vera and Maude can vouch for my absence." Dappled sunlight fell on her face as she spoke, and Malcolm watched her intently. The journey from Clitheroe to Blackburn was not long, but with the wartime schedules, they would be gone all day. Of course, the previous week, whilst quietly planning the trip, Maude had suggested to Ruth a multitude of sordid possibilities that might occur with all the time that Ruth and Malcolm would be spending alone together. Ruth had to shush her, lest her gran hear them giggling. Either way, Ruth had tried to explain to Maude that she had no intention of entangling herself with a married man, despite the fact she very much wanted to.

"No scandals to worry about," Malcolm said. "Just boring research."

This trip was a follow-up to their strange evening spent in the manor house. The visit with Wolstenholme and his conservatory had provided much information, including the final identification of the "pets"—large moths and nothing more. Frightening to look at perhaps, especially for a village in which the largest insect might be a grasshopper. Either way, both Ruth and Malcolm felt there was so much more to learn. According to Wolstenholme, the wraith of 1910 had only ever been a figment of Phineas's imagination, and perhaps the other sightings had been the result of a short-lived collective mania among the villagers. No girl had ever drowned in the pond. The rest of the village had been storytelling, passing yarns around the pub, tall tales that activated some deep fear among the people—people with a long history of witch-fearing going back to the Pendle witch trials.

But why had he seen a girl where there was none? Was this hallucination, brought on by the strange soma drink, that of a specific person? What had convinced him so thoroughly of his vision? How could so many people see the same vision? Ruth wasn't ready to relinquish the legend to Wolstenholme's theory of mass hysteria quite yet. It was far too convenient. It nagged at her consciousness and felt like a loose end, and more critically, it did nothing to explain the current woman in white roaming Martynsborough, a figure that Ruth had seen with her own eyes. So, the most logical thing to do was to talk to Phineas himself. It wasn't hard to determine his location. Ellen knew most things about the village, including the asylum in Blackburn where Phineas resided.

It was late in the afternoon when they finally arrived at the Woolery Sanatorium. Walking briskly down a quiet street, they worried they had missed the hours of visiting. They rushed through a large double door and down a corridor that looked more like a hospital than a residence. A nurse cheerfully informed them that they had thirty minutes to meet with the patient before he was to be taken for his tea. "He doesn't often receive family," said the rotund woman as she tapped her clipboard. "In fact, I've been in this particular institution for many years, and you're the first visitors he's ever had during that time."

"I am only a distant cousin, but I've learned about Phineas through my mother, and I'm eager to meet him—if only to put a face to the name," Ruth said casually. "I'm Ruth, this is . . ." She paused momentarily. "This is my husband, Malcolm."

Malcolm seemed to choke; clearing his throat, he said, "Nice to meet you."

The woman shook Malcolm's hand. "Mr. Greenwich is not always talkative. He suffers from various mental deficiencies, and requires medical intervention, so he will be extraordinarily calm. Do not be alarmed by his demeanour. Visiting hours are until half-past four." The nurse looked once at her clipboard, and then strode away in her thick-soled white shoes, along with smart stockings that Ruth appraised enviously.

Ruth and Malcolm stood in a doorway peering into a room bathed in sunlight. A man sat in a chair, his back to them. Ruth rapped lightly on the door. "Mr. Greenwich? Phineas? Hallo?" The man turned his head slightly, a look of puzzlement on his face.

"Aye?"

"Phineas." Ruth took up another chair and placed it near to him. Malcolm stood behind her. "I'm called Ruth, pleased to meet you." Phineas assessed the woman sitting in front of him.

"What's this all about?" According to Ellen, he was barely sixty, he looked twenty years older than that, emaciated and bony. He had a large, beaked nose and thin lips. His hair was cropped short, and white. He wore a threadbare dressing robe. "Who are you?" he asked.

"As I said, I am Ruth from Martynsborough. I would like to ask you a few questions."

"Martynsborough?" His expression changed immediately from a languid confusion to alertness.

"Well, I wasn't born there," Ruth added. "No, no—we've been evacuated there on account of the bombing."

"Bombing?"

"Well, let's not concern ourselves with that. I am writing a book about Martynsborough, your home, and I've learned of something that happened in 1910, about the lime-kiln ponds." Ruth watched his expression carefully, worried she might set him off.

"Aye, the year of the comet. The lime-kiln ponds, it's where I saw her, I did."

"Oh. Who did you see?"

"Aye, a girl. And I thought . . . I thought, well, she reminded me of . . . someone." He trailed off.

"Reminded you of whom?"

"Why are you asking such things?" Phineas looked at her; the sun caught the brown of his eyes and turned them to gold.

"There was a wraith," Ruth said quietly. "People in the village spoke of her. Albert, your friend, he spoke of it haunting the village, connected in some way to what you saw in the pond." Phineas did not respond, and a long moment of silence stretched out agonizingly. Finally, he spoke.

"Albert. I've not seen him in a long time. Is he well?"

"Yes, very well." Ruth paused. "And the lime kiln?"

"Aye, I saw a girl in the kiln who reminded me of my sweetheart. Dead she was."

Ruth took a deep breath. "Who was your sweetheart, Phineas?"

"Lottie was my sweetheart."

"You mean Charlotte Wolstenholme?" Ruth glanced back at Malcolm, surprised. "You knew her?"

"Yes—more than knew her—I loved her from the moment I seen her. I worked in the stables when I was fifteen years old. She would have been around sixteen herself. Wolstenholme only had the one daughter— no sisters or brothers. Lottie loved to roam about the fields, had brambles in her hair, burrs on her stockings. She was different than other girls, a little wild, didn't like being corralled between four walls, you know?"

"We've spoken to Mr. Wolstenholme; he said that his daughter disappeared around the turn of the century."

Phineas gazed out the window, his hands bunching into fists. "Aye." He turned back to Ruth, his eyes limpid and pleading. "She did disappear, she did indeed."

"You seem to know something," Ruth said.

"Aye." There was another long pause, and as Ruth looked at the clock on the wall nervously, he spoke again. "One day, she come running out to me, along the sheep path, met me by the stables just at daybreak—her feet bare and dirty, wearing only her nightclothes, properly upset, she was. She told me her papa had locked her up in the glasshouse that night, trying to scare some sense into her. She told me that there were things in there, awful things—dangerous animals. She told me to warn the other boys to never go near the glasshouse. And I did. I told them that, and we stayed away ever since." He paused for a long moment, then said, "She told me she's running away. I loved Lottie, so very much, and I'd have done anything for her. I said I'd help. We hid in the woods of the estate in a small place I built from tangles of willow branches, we stayed there all day—unsure what to do. We heard people calling for her, the stable hands, and even that horrible Blackwell out looking for her. Then it got dark, and it was cold—so cold, so we went around to the kilns. In those days, they were left to burn overnight, a-glowing and warm they were—they'd burn for many days back then, when they still used them, that is. 'Let us sleep here for a spell,' she said, just to be warm. She had no coat nor hat. She said if she could only sleep a bit, by the morning, we'd go, we'd find some warm things and run away to another village, but she was so tired, having spent a sleepless night in the glasshouse. She was like a bird, happier to be out of the cage, to be free, even at night. 'Just let me close my eyes for a moment,' she said, so we crouched as close as we dared to the mouth of the kiln to stay warm."

He stopped speaking and pulled a handkerchief from a pocket and dabbed at his eye. "We shouldn't have done that, though," he whispered. "Oh, no sir, we should *not* have stayed there. You see . . ." His voice became so quiet that Ruth had to lean in to hear him. "I'd never noticed till much later that the workers of the kiln, the fellows with the shovels and such, down at the bottom o' the bluff when the fire's a-going, they wore some heavy mufflers over their mouths and noses, and special spectacles over their eyes . . . heavy gloves. Something's not right about the air in those kilns when the lime fire's a-going—not right at all—a little like the mustard gas in the Great War, I reckon. So, sometime in the dead o' night, the wind must have changed, I don't really know, but I awoke coughing and gasping for air. I shook Charlotte, to get her awake and to move away from the smoke, but she didn't wake. Even though she slept near the fire, her body had gone cold and stiff. I shook her and slapped her face, whispered, then shouted, but she did not wake. I held my ear against her chest and her heart did not beat, I put my cheek by her sweet mouth, and no air came from it. The sun was coming up, and I was already in trouble for not coming to work at the stables. I couldn't just leave her there, she was dead . . . if they found her, they might come back to me and . . . and . . . there was me mum to think about, and . . ." His voice trailed off.

"And what?" Ruth asked.

"I kissed her, I did, on her cold lips, and I pushed her body into the kiln. She fell into the lime fires and disappeared, burnt up, fires as hot as hell—an inferno—so hot that when it's done, all's left is the white crumbly bits that they spread on the fields in the springtime to help the crops grow. That was all that was left. I came around two days later when the fires were done, and they were shovelling out the quicklime into great barrels, wearing the mufflers over their mouths. There was nothing but the white dust, I say, even her bones I reckon, mixed up with the quicklime. They'd never find her because there was nothing left of her. No one ever knew . . . no one would find her. Some said she'd run away, but she hadn't ever left Martynsborough, no, she was not just there, but *everywhere*—all around, spread on the fields, out for the crops, scattered to the farms all around Martynsborough. Everywhere."

Ruth shook her head in amazement. "All these years you've never said anything. And so then in 1910, ten years later, you're near the kilns, which had since filled with water . . ."

"Aye, many years later, I saw that girl in the pond, at first I thought it Lottie, but I knew it couldn't be. It was some other girl—maybe Wolstenholme or Blackwell had done some ill to another poor girl. I couldn't stand for it. I wanted to punish him, but I knew it couldn't be Lottie. I'd seen her tumble down into the fire all those years before. It wasn't her floating there in the pond, but my, how it did look like her. After that, I saw her everywhere, floating about the fields. I thought that perhaps Wolstenholme or Blackwell had murdered some other young girl, a girl who looked like his daughter. I don't know, it was a muddle, such a horrible muddle, and I do remember that I wasn't quite right in the head that night, nor any night thereafter—not sure why. I take three tablets a day, I do, the doctor here gives 'em to me, so that I'm not so awful, not so shook up. I'd not be able to talk like this, no sir."

"So, you were saying, you saw her everywhere, but also Albert, your friend, he says he saw her too—others did. Who? Who did *they* see? Are you saying this was a ghost . . . a wraith they were seeing? Who did they see?"

"Aye, some of us saw her, after a few nights, but I think now, looking back to then, maybe. I don't know. It's a muddle, I tell you, a muddle. But there she was."

"Who?"

"Lottie? Couldn't be. Another girl? It's a muddle, a terrible muddle."

"Could it have been something else you saw in the kiln pond?" Ruth asked. "Perhaps you were mistaken and saw something you thought was a girl in the water, but it was something else altogether?"

"Something else? What? I don't understand." Phineas was growing agitated, and Ruth decided that there was no point pursuing the question or telling him about the drowned cat. She was certain that he was haunted by the tragic story of Charlotte, and Ruth recalled that Wolstenholme had said the soma elixir would often make people see their own truth.

No, Ruth was now certain there was never a girl in the kiln pond that night. The girl that Phineas envisioned existed only in his memory, a tragic figure named Charlotte. Unbeknownst to the lord of the manor house, Wolstenholme's own daughter was the impetus of Phineas's vision and maybe everyone's collective mania thereafter. Charlotte: vanished, immolated, ten years dead the night of the kiln ponds but very much alive in Phineas's confused brain—the original Wraith of Martynsborough.

-30-

On the Friday afternoon following the river incident, Ruth was riding her bicycle into the village to have her ration book stamped when she saw Mr. Horgon calling to her from the hall's front door. "Ruth, are you well? Recovered from your daring rescue?" Ruth got off her bike and walked it over to him. He kissed her on the cheek. "You'll be returning to work soon, I trust?"

"Yes, I'm well, and Elise is on the mend. Malcolm and I'll return Monday to work, I think."

"You're a hero, the talk of the village."

"Oh, it was nothing."

"So modest. Now Ruth, there's something else; I'm glad to catch up with you today. I've something important I'd like to discuss with you. I've received an important letter this morning. It's to do with our young Johnny. It seems I've got some information about his brother, Jude."

"Oh, that's wonderful!" Ruth said, and she threw her arms around Horgon impulsively. "I can't wait to tell him!"

"Now, now, let's just hold on for a moment first. I have to say, it took some confusing back-and-forth with the ministry for me to get a grasp on things, which explains why the process has taken so long. Please come into the hall for a moment if you don't mind. There's much to discuss. It's . . . how can I say this delicately—an *unusual* situation."

-31-

Maude couldn't calm her mind. She knew what Ruth planned to do that night and had offered to come with her. The whole prospect was terrifying and maybe a little unhinged, but Ruth, being Ruth, insisted on doing it alone. So, with the blackouts thrown open and the silver moonlight pouring in, Maude lingered alone in their room, gazing out at the fields. She looked to the spire of the church protruding from the trees, knowing that the Yellow Rattle was nearby. She wondered what Ellen might be doing at that very moment, and her thoughts turned wistful. But she also felt restless and frightened and maybe even nostalgic for those first days when she had arrived, fresh-faced in Martynsborough—such an adventure it had been!

She got up from the window and paced around the room, worrying for her friend, wondering about her own future in this strange little town. Should she stay? Should she return to Scarborough? Or Cambridge? Would the bombs stop eventually? She got into the bed and closed her eyes, hoping sleep would come, but she couldn't stop thinking, thinking, thinking. She got out of bed and put on her robe. A cup of tea might calm her nerves. She stepped quietly into the hall and saw light seeping from under Vera's door. Of course, it must be insomnia. They were up late reading, no doubt. She'd offer them a cup of tea, yes—she could just envision it—the three ladies, restless and pacing about with their steaming mugs, worrying about the war, about their dear Ruth, about the future, calming their collective anxieties through companionship.

She tapped on their door lightly, but there was no answer. The women's sense of hearing was not as good as it once was; they'd both admitted to it. So, Maude grasped the doorknob and turned it, expecting to find two cherubic ladies with frilly sleeping caps, romance novels in hand.

She found something altogether different.

The two women did not notice her in the doorway at first. Then Vera looked up and leapt like a startled cat. Edith, in turn, scuttled across the mattress; there followed a small commotion of quilts and rustling nightgowns until each woman was huddled on opposite ends of the bed, their breath rattling in their throats, their faces ashen. A grave moment of silence fell. Then, Vera whispered, "You must know, we are not actually sisters." Maude stepped further into the room, a small grin forming on her lips.

"Well, well, well. By the pricking of my thumbs, what black deeds are these? I've always wondered about you two, and now I know why— quite the ruse you've pulled. You needn't concern yourself; your secret is safe with me. There is extraordinarily little in heaven and earth that I have not already seen." She lingered there with a playful smile on her face. "Tea? I was on my way to start the kettle."

At that very moment, Ruth hoped to test her theory, or more precisely, to confirm her suspicion, a suspicion that she had rolled about in her head but had never thought possible. It would require some hazard. Yes, it was the loneliest hour of the night as she crouched in the secret room in the mill, a dark and windowless cell with mice skittering about in the shadows. She was relatively certain that this small, unassuming space was the lair of the wraith. She was also relatively certain that she knew the identity of the being who would eventually climb the ladder and find her waiting there, although she had moments of doubt— and quaking fear—that someone, or some*thing* altogether unexpected might emerge through the trapdoor. She would be cornered if she had it wrong, and if this mysterious being proved hostile, there was no escape.

She held her red-glass electric torch so that only a whisper of light fell in the room. Having grown accustomed to the dark, she could see relatively well, while not producing so much light as to scare away the resident of the lair.

Ruth heard the door creak below, and then the ladder shook as someone mounted it. She crouched further behind the wardrobe and waited. She heard the sound of someone creeping into the room, towards the bed. Ruth stepped out and pointed the dull red light.

"Don't be frightened," she said gently. The figure stumbled backwards into the bed, startled, then crouched forward for a moment, seeming to consider dashing for the trapdoor, but Ruth stood in the way. The white dress rustled, the figure crawled frantically across the mattress and against the wall, animal like, and took a defensive posture. In the dim ruby glow, Ruth could see a frock that was likely once Elise's, under which were trousers. The face was shrouded by a simple pale woman's scarf, oversized—it had slipped down a little to reveal tattered blonde hair, dishevelled and uneven.

"Who are you?" a frightened voice asked.

"I'm here to help." Ruth approached the figure and reached out to take her hand. "Please come here, sit with me. I'll put on the lamp." Ruth struck a match and lit the lamp, bathing the room in a warm glow. "Let me have a closer look at you, to make sure you're well." Ruth pulled the scarf from the girl's head and touched her cheek. She was skinny, probably starving, twelve years old or so. She recognized the face from the family portrait etched on the wall. Ruth pointed to it. "You're quite the artist. It's a very good likeness of yourself. Did the other pictures on the wall inspire you?" The girl did not respond. "It's a shame that you've almost completely smudged the picture. I can no longer see your brother's face, but you're there; you look a little like him, and your parents are all smudged up, except a bit of your mum, who also looks a lot like you. My suspicion was hard to grasp," Ruth continued, "because I'd thought we were looking for a boy. You are clearly not a boy in this picture, and when I learned some new information just yesterday, a lot of things suddenly made sense. It's Judith, isn't it?"

"Yes. He cut my hair when I was sleeping," she said. "I was so very cross with him. Although now . . . I know why he did it. Perhaps, now that so much time has passed, I understand he meant well, but I was so angry at the time. I—I ran, and when I came back, he was gone."

"Tell me," said Ruth.

Judith then started speaking, her voice dry and laborious from having spent so long being silent.

At their first billet of the evacuation, Judith had been accused of stealing money and threatened with juvenile hall or even prison. It was a false accusation, of course. She had not stolen anything, but it had been apparent from the start that the older couple who had accommodated them preferred boys and were looking for a way to remove the girl from their house, separating her from Johnny. When the situation became unbearable, Johnny and Judith ran away in the dead of the night. They wandered from the outskirts of Blackburn from village to village, looking like two poor Traveller children. Sometimes they resorted to begging, some villagers treating them like urchins, other times, the Home Guard chased them off.

Eventually Johnny met an old woman, a widow, outside a shop who was looking for some boys to billet with her. She wanted hands in the garden, to clean and do a lot of dusty work—not so much evacuees, but labourers. Judith would not be welcome, and with truant officers on the lookout for a boy and a girl, they had to come up with a solution. Judith tied her hair up and hid it under a cap. She was wiry and thin and quite tall. At twelve she could still pass as a boy, at least for a while. Johnny, being clever and well-read, produced papers that transformed Judith into Jude and provided them to the woman. Johnny had to get used to calling Jude a brother, using *he* instead of *she*. They would be sent back to the original billet if they were discovered, to face the theft accusation, maybe sent to a horrible prison, separated indefinitely. For some time, the ruse worked.

On a very windy day in late July, while working in the garden, the wind grabbed hold of Judith's hat, causing her long blonde hair to spill out. The old woman witnessed this and was irate. She poked and prodded the girl, trying to see what she had under her trousers. When the woman asked to see Judith's papers once more, the brother and sister collected their things and ran.

The two arrived in Bolton, and again, they fell into some begging, and with their being so dirty, these villagers too, thought them errant Travellers and hurled abuse at them. Eventually a ministry official acting as a truant officer took Johnny and Judith to a temporary institution until they could figure out what to do with them. He looked at the papers that Johnny had doctored. With Judith's hair tucked up in a cap, he believed them to be two boys. They were to be billeted in another village, further up the River Harold. It had a major flax interest and a labour shortage. They could earn a small bit of pay. Only boys who had reached the age of thirteen could miss school for work. The man raised an eyebrow at Judith's birthdate, but allowed her to stay, thinking she was a boy, and knowing she would turn thirteen soon enough.

The night before they planned to leave, fearing for her safety, Johnny cut Judith's hair while she slept. In the morning, she discovered it. Distraught and angry, she ran away into the wood, tears flowing. The arrangements had already been made—cars were in short supply and the driver couldn't wait, so Johnny was sent alone to Martynsborough, to live in the church basement and earn his small stipend on the flax farm. The ministry man could not find his "brother" but said they would inform Father Tweedsmuir of any new information as it became available. Many volunteers searched for a boy, in the wood and valley, but found no trace of the lad.

Judith had hidden herself well, and with her anger cooled and her stomach rumbling, she returned to town to find her brother gone. She turned to true theft now. She stole a scarf to hide her butchered hair, then followed the River Harold for two days, hoping to locate the village where the ministry man had sent Johnny. She arrived at Martynsborough and wandered that first night, looking for a place to hide, and found the mill. She stayed there, venturing out to steal once more, now a necessity for survival. She stole a white nightdress and wore it over her boy's trousers along with woollen socks for warmth. Villagers spotted her here and there wandering about, but no one confronted her. No, quite the opposite, in fact. Villagers would turn and flee in the other direction at the sight of this starving refugee—as if a nightmare from the past had been awakened.

Judith learned that most of the billetees were staying in the church basement. Twice she attempted to find her brother there. She had tried to peer in windows at night, but they were blacked out, and once when she could see in by chance, she did not find him there with the other boys. Of course, by that point, Johnny had moved to Vera's cottage.

She was too frightened to come out in the day, so she rarely did. She gave up on finding her brother, convinced that she was in the wrong village. But with winter setting in, she could do nothing but try to stay warm and fed until the weather allowed her to follow the river further come spring. She lived like this over the entire winter, she said. Sometimes she found food and such left for her in the room in the mill. One time she'd been in the mill when the person came by. Judith hid, and a woman spoke in the dark, telling her not to be frightened. She never learned the woman's identity. Ruth wondered about this helpful woman, but did not spend too much time on it, given it was merely a footnote to an incredible story.

By the time Judith had finished recounting her tale, she was overwhelmed and exhausted. "We've a home for you now with your brother," Ruth said. "You needn't pretend to be a boy. A good friend of mine has been quite thorough and has found the original papers. We've tracked down all the billets, that's how I learned you were a girl. No police will bother you for anything you've done—you're safe now. Come, Judith, let's go home."

As the sun was coming up, Johnny readied himself for work. His head was a muddle, and he was a bit tired, having heard Maude or Vera or someone making a minor commotion in the middle of the night. Moreover, he had the strangest dreams, and couldn't seem to shake the dust from his brain that morning. He passed Maude in the hall, who presented a knowing grin but said nothing but a whispered "good morning."

He crept down the stairs, and heard the familiar sounds of the kettle, eggs rattling in a pot of boiling water, and Vera preparing tea for their usual morning ritual. He stepped into the dim kitchen, and Vera turned to face him with a smile on her face as broad as he had ever seen. "Johnny," she whispered. "Please, go into the sitting room, you'll be quite pleased." Edith sat at the table, also grinning stupidly.

"What's going on?" Johnny asked.

"Just go, just look."

Johnny walked along the short corridor and peered into the sitting room and saw Ruth sitting next to a small figure in white on the sofa. He could not bring himself to say a word, and tears filled his eyes. "I'm not cross with you any more, Jon-Jon," Judith said. "See, my hair's grown in a bit. Ruth has said she can fix it." She rose and approached her brother.

"B-b-b-but Judy, how . . . where?" Johnny stammered and touched her hair. "Are you . . . are you for real?"

"Silly, yes, of course. You've got lovely people here, they've all helped me, and I can stay here with you now. We've no need to hide who I am any longer. I don't need to wear that horrible cap anymore!" She threw her arms around her brother. "I'm so glad you're all right, I've been looking for you for ages."

"Where were you? Oh my, you're so skinny . . . I wasn't sure what I was going to tell Mum and Dad—I thought I'd lost you. Oh, I'm so happy you're well!"

"It's all a long story, but I'm so hungry, can you not smell that? Hot toast with real butter! Vera says I can have all the jam I like—I can hardly wait!"

-32-

Two days later, Ruth gathered Maude, and then Malcolm, and they walked down the road sometime after the dinner hour, with the low sun stretching their shadows well out in front of them. They crossed the lock bridge, and like an unruly gang of rogues, they piled into the Yellow Rattle.

"Well, the three of you look quite pleased with yourself," said Ellen as the trio approached the bar.

"We're celebrating," said Ruth. "I've got a book that's almost finished." She lowered her voice a bit. "And we're relatively sure we know who the infamous wraith is—we don't wish to draw too much attention to it, though."

"I can't wait to hear—do tell," Ellen whispered.

"Not a ghost, a real live girl, a lost evacuee, hidden in the village trying to find Johnny, her brother, who she is now reunited with. She wandered the night, cold and hungry and to those who saw her, this child was a frightening wraith."

"A happy ending then." Ellen poured their usual pints. "And to think of the fuss in the village with talks of deadly wraiths. Just a young girl. But then . . . not the same as the wraith of 1910. What of the original legend?"

"In some ways still a mystery," Ruth said, "but we've learned a lot. From what we can tell, we believe the legend originated in the imagination of a man with a tragic secret. From there it grew into a collective mania among people with a history of witch-fearing—at least that's as close to an answer as we can reach."

"But you can't be sure?"

"I'm afraid we can only speculate," Ruth confessed.

The pub was quiet that night with only the village's resident singer, Cora Dunn, sitting quietly alone by the hearth, lost in her own thoughts. Ruth said hello to her, and then the three friends took a table nearby.

"Johnny's sister is settling in well?" Malcolm asked.

"Oh yes," said Ruth.

"Will there be room for her? It's getting quite crowded in the Catchpoole cottage."

". . . a little less actually." Maude glanced over at Ellen, then added, "Soon enough, I will be giving Ruth room to stretch her legs in the bed and read her books well past a proper bedtime. I'll be taking myself and my collection of stones to live right here in the Yellow Rattle. There's room upstairs, and Ellen has shown such enthusiasm in my geological pursuits, while I must admit, with the war and all, I've taken quite a liking to beer. I'll be just as happy pouring it as drinking it."

"You wish to stay in Martynsborough longer then?" Malcolm asked.

"Yes." Maude smiled quietly, as if she were remembering something. "It was only just recently that I felt the courage to inquire about such an arrangement. It seems that the war is making for interesting bedfellows. Of course, on a more practical note, this will free up some space for young Judith, who needs all the care she can get right now."

"Well, that's all quite good then, I guess." Malcolm sipped from his glass and looked back at Ruth. "And I have to wonder, how did the poor thing survive for so long on her own?"

"She mentioned that someone had helped her," Ruth said.

"It was me; I helped her," said Cora from the table nearby, startling the others. "Sorry, I couldn't help but listen in on your conversation, and I suppose I should admit to it. I've heard that the girl has been discovered, but I was never aware that her brother was here."

"You?" Ruth was shocked.

"Aye. I've been looking after her . . . just like the other lost soul that haunted the streets some thirty years ago." Ruth nearly knocked her glass over in surprise.

"So, there *was* an original wraith! Please, join us. Tell me," Ruth cried.

Cora brought her glass over to their table and sat. "I've never spoken a word of this before. Perhaps it's best it doesn't go beyond this table—if it can be helped."

"Of course," Ruth said.

Cora took a deep breath and began. "In 1910, she was a girl, lost, looking for her parents—two women had stumbled on her in the mill, found her there hiding, and they told me she needed caring for."

"Women? Who?" Ruth asked, thinking perhaps she could follow up with another interview.

Cora raised an eyebrow. "Long gone, I'm afraid, can't say I recall. They weren't local as far as I know, crossed paths with me by happenstance. Anyway, seems some other villagers had seen the girl wandering the streets, and the fear had spread through Martynsborough that there was a wraith about. I found the girl in the hidden room in the mill. I took her to a children's home in Bolton. The girl was a Traveller by birth; she spoke with a different accent, sometimes using words that didn't always sound like English to me. She'd been left behind when Wolstenholme banished the wagons from the meadow with threats of death. Her parents didn't return, or if they did, I never heard about it—quite tragic. Before that, while she wandered the streets and fields, perhaps looking for food, I figured that Phineas saw her, as did Albert, and soon others did. Their heads were so filled with dread of some story of a body in the pond, a day spent dredging it, the appearance of the steward, Blackwell. Some contagious notion of gothic horror must have infected their brains, and then they see a young yellow-haired girl lit by moonlight in a tattered white dress roaming the fields not twenty-four hours since their misadventure by the pond. Thereafter, a mania seemed to take the village. The whole mess eventually became a sort of folklore to the men of the pub. I was happy enough to let them believe what they wished." She stopped and sighed, rubbing her temples as if exhausted. "So, no. She was no wraith. No ghost of a murder victim, just a girl, lost and hungry. After we took her to a safe place, the mania died down. Sightings still happen now and again, but it's mostly the men, usually after time spent with pint glasses if you know what I mean."

"I can't believe it," said Ruth.

"So, this new girl now—the one with the badly cut hair. I noticed her one night when I was on my way home from the pub, followed her to the mill. I figured that's where she hid, just like the last one, so I provided things for her secretly. She seemed intent on not being found, so I treaded lightly. I worried with the new wraith panic that some harm might come to her, and so I kept an eye on her all winter, hoping that she wouldn't wander in the light too much. The blackouts helped this time. I figured her for a runaway, or another Traveller. I'm glad to hear she's found a safe place. I wonder, what's her name? I never learned it."

"It's Judith," Ruth said. "And you've known all along? Both times the village was haunted by the wraith—thirty years apart—why didn't you say something?"

"I didn't wish for them to be discovered. I could just envision the village men scrambling into the mill and tearing the place apart, looking for some crime or other. They were girls, lost and frightened—displaced children—a tragedy under any circumstances. Such creatures aren't new to our village or any village really, whether stray Travellers ripped from their kin or children evacuated from the foolish wars of small-minded men. We treat them poorly, like a near-invisible insect to be swatted away or worse, they metamorphosize into a frightening spectre, something to hide from or banish . . . or exorcise. I chose not to tell anyone, because I think we should occasionally be haunted by those ills that we create ourselves—for when we peer into strange and darkening windows, we see not monsters, but often our own reflection. Perhaps we shrink in fear of our own sins and shame. And the room in the mill, beyond this table, I don't wish for anyone to know. Some instinct tells me to leave it be—it serves some purpose or other."

"You've a lot of wisdom," said Ruth.

"I just do what is right."

With Ruth and Maude out at the pub that night, the cottage was quieter than usual. Edith checked in briefly on Johnny and Judith—both slept soundly—then she went to her bedroom, closed the door, and hung up her robe. She got into bed with Vera and said, "At least we know that Maude will not barge in on us this evening. What a fright."

"We needn't worry," Vera said. "I've spoken to her, she . . . understands. Perhaps more than understands. I'd an instinct she would."

"You've told her everything?"

"Yes, I had to, maybe for my own sanity, for one other person to hear, someone who seems to know our struggles."

"Really? It's good to know we're not alone." She noticed Vera had a large book on her lap.

"What on earth have you got there?" Edith asked.

"You should recognize this, given it was once your father's." Vera turned the book to reveal the cover. "See? *The Roxburghe Ballads.*"

"My God. Where did you get that? Did you . . . did you go there? Did you climb the ladder?"

"Like my scarf, this had found its way back to me all on its own. Our things have a habit of returning to us, don't they? Although at least we now know there's nothing nefarious about it."

"How?"

"Judith presumably had my handkerchief, picked up in the mill where I dropped it after discovering the raspberry jam on the ladder. On one of her night-time wanders, she left it in Jeffrey's garden, where Ruth retrieved it. As for the book—it was also Ruth—she went *in* there. She's held on to it for some time and had temporarily forgotten about it with all the other excitement. She handed it to me this evening before leaving for the pub." Edith reached out and took the book, turning it over in her hand, her eyes glistened. "Go ahead, dear," Vera whispered. "Do you remember the page number?" Edith flipped through the book knowingly and stopped. She opened it and placed it on top of the quilt. "You go first," said Vera. Edith placed her forefinger at the top of the page and read:

> *"The Bloody Battle of Billingsgate,*
> *beginning with a scolding between two fish women,*
> *Doll and Kate."*

"And there we are, Doll and Kate." Vera brought her finger down on the woodcut print under the title. A rough and slightly faded image of two women in an alcove bed. "Fish women" as the ballad described them, having fought in the streets, and later, with much drink in them, to make peace in bed. One woman reclined on the pillow, bare breasted, while the second lay nestled to her side, her hand slipped around the belly of her bedmate, their faces close, and their lips nearly touching, only a hair's breadth separating them.

"Yes," Edith said quietly. "There we are—at least a silly picture that we thought looked like us. I would hope you wouldn't tell Ruth."

"Ruth? Of course not, that's not even an option. Instead, I told her that we played in the mill room as 'sisters' when we were young, that we had nicked the books from our 'father' and left them there. But she's smart and hopelessly curious. I knew she'd start to piece something together. Her research led her to the mill and some public records pertaining to my birth, but she's gone another direction. She's deduced that we're half-sisters and that your father had a tawdry affair resulting in me, a bastard child, and my unwed mother and I lived with an uncle in the mill until it was sold. Which is really rather interesting and slightly ironic, given it is generally the story that I've quietly mentioned to our village elders to explain *you*—that it was *my* father who had a bastard child with whom I had reunited after leaving Martynsborough all those years ago. I think Ruth may have tried to pry some information from Walter, as curious as she is. He had mentioned it to me that she was asking questions and he did not indulge her. But for those still alive who were here in Martynsborough back in those times, they are thankfully old-fashioned in their views and know well enough not to speak of *your* illegitimacy, or anyone's really. For the rest, I believe they simply don't remember. It's been a bit of a tangled web we've woven, I'm afraid, but I figure, all's well now, and we need not worry about our stories being straight."

"Well, I would hope not. You assured me over and over before I dared step foot back in this village that all was explained as to why no one knew of your sister when you were a child. How interesting that Ruth would produce a story so similar to what you've concocted—I can only hope that the few who are old enough to remember you and your family half a century ago will not speak too much of it, lest it reignites Ruth's hopeless curiosity. God forbid she cross-reference the many fibs required to keep us safe."

"You've my word. We're but two old women, why would anyone care about the details of our youth now? There are probably only a dozen people left in this village who knew me back then, and I trust that none of them will ever feel the need to mention any of this. We *are* sisters, and that is how we shall be perceived." Vera squeezed Edith's hand for reassurance.

"You know it can never be uttered, never." Edith sighed, then said, "Read me a little, the bit at the end, that's the best bit." Vera took up the book and put on her reading glasses; she read a few lines, then pointed at the woodcut print. "Just like our bed in the mill, and you know, it's curious, Judith—she herself had hidden there too—in *our* bed, probably reading *our* books by oil lamp. I'd like to think that we helped make that room for her, a safe place for a girl to go, to get out of the cold and weather a storm"—she arched an eyebrow with a determined pause—"you know, just like the other one who walked in on us all those years ago."

"Yes, like the last one. I wonder where she is now," Edith said. "I've always worried that she would remember . . . that it would come back to trouble us eventually. I must admit, before Judith was discovered, I started to think—that she *had* come back, that this wraith as Ruth described her was in fact *our* yellow-haired girl, returned to haunt us. It would be a thing far more dangerous to us than any actual ghost. I really wished that Ruth wouldn't pursue the matter."

"She'd be a grown woman today. She couldn't possibly return in the way you imagine. Perhaps she's the same age now, as we were then, you know, when . . . when she saw us."

"And to think"—Edith smiled ruefully—"the villagers were all hiding in their homes, terrified of this thing, when it was really you and I who should've been frightened. She could harm us much more than any of them."

"Yes, 1910, the year of Halley's Comet, my God, has it been that long?" Vera sighed. "I missed you terribly. To think that small girl would separate us for decades. You realize that for all those years, I only saw you one other time after that, when I met Ruth as a child, and that was a strained meeting to say the least. No, not like the year of the comet—up until we were caught, that was so very lovely."

"Yes, but it was foolish for us to come back here after that time in Cornwall. Halley's Comet was so beautiful, so sublime. I wonder if there'd been no comet, what would have become of us? Was that not a reckless lark? To spend a night in that long-abandoned mill room—two women in middle age? One, a childless widow, the other a mother on a made-up vacation to visit a fictitious sister? The comet led us to that room, on that day, in that year." She paused with a thoughtful expression. "After the girl saw us, the fear haunted me—I worried for my family, my future. I'm sorry that I avoided you after that. It was that kiss, stolen in front of our yellow-haired witness, that undid all we had."

"Yes, but truly, it was *we* who undid everything. Our own fear." Vera glanced at the book on her lap and thought of all they had been through—how they had met as children when Edith came to the village for holiday and returned each summer. As small girls they became the best of friends. As they got older and became young women, the friendship blossomed into something else. When strangers asked then, they would always proclaim that they were sisters, and people who didn't know them generally believed it. Then Wolstenholme had thrown her family out of the mill, and her mum and dad died. Vera was only seventeen years old, but she was resourceful and tenacious—she had built the room for them in the empty mill so they could continue their summer trysts. Vera had provided a straw bed; Edith had provided the food and books. They drew their lives in coal dust on the wall.

They grew into women, and eventually they moved on with their lives, following those rules prescribed by society, to marry men and keep a home. Edith left for London to marry a man met by happenstance on a train—a man who seemed to have little interest in her extended family, so he never seemed to think twice that there might be a sister he didn't know about and never thought to cross-reference this information with any of Edith's other relatives. He was a quiet man, an heir to a modest estate, and he often spent time out in the fields, and he was kind. Edith could have done much worse. Vera, meanwhile, left Martynsborough behind and moved on to another village and married a man who was more friend than husband. Even still, the two women found ways to see each other from time to time, carefully building an alternate history of their kinship, their sisterhood, so that their husbands would never know otherwise, and as parents and aunts and uncles died off, so too did any knowledge that they were not truly sisters. It was not as hard as one would think to do, really. For many years, they managed in this precarious way, stolen moments here and there, then pining over longer periods of time, their bittersweet ardour: delicious, forbidden.

Then that year of the comet, 1910, they had met in Cornwall to watch the skies. It inspired them to return to where it all began as grown women; the love within them had never stopped smouldering. How were they to know that their hiding place would be discovered? How were they to know the villagers hid in their homes because of a girl wandering about? It seemed the safest place at the time. It was their sanctuary. It was just bad luck that they'd been discovered. After that day, it would never be the same. Edith returned to London and did not correspond. Vera eventually returned permanently to Martynsborough, alone, shortly after her husband died of the Spanish flu, and she generally kept to herself. A few remembered her from the past, but not many.

"But she saw us." Edith interrupted Vera's thoughts. "She saw us kiss—the kind of kiss in which two women should never indulge. Half borne through that trapdoor, she was the most terrifying thing I'd ever witnessed."

". . . and she was so young a child, no more than twelve years old, how would she know what it meant? In any event, the girl was taken far away, Cora saw to it."

"Cora—she is another loose end that often frightens me. She knows even more than the rest, beyond our fictitious sisterhood."

"We can trust her. And we can trust that our yellow-haired girl is long gone and forgotten."

"I know we've been avoiding the topic, perhaps it's too strange to consider, but have you wondered why this would all happen again?" Edith asked. "I feel as if I may have brought it on myself by coming to Martynsborough. I was here the last time when . . . when she found us, and now, all these years later, there's once more a girl hiding in the mill room? And Ruth, bless her, chasing after these things. Now Maude walking in on us. What strange divine providence has led to this?

Perhaps someone else has seen us, witnessed us like that girl did. Then what? They'll inform my family. Scandal, divorce. I know my husband and I don't spend much time together these days—as is the case with many marriages in the later years, however, it must remain intact in whatever form it has. Without my marriage, I'll lose everything—what prospects does an old woman have to feed and clothe herself without money? I couldn't bear it. I feel as if a divine hand wishes for our sin to be discovered, that it might have been best if I'd stayed in London."

"Sin? Please don't say that. No, there's no providence behind any of this. It is a coincidence and nothing more. I should say much good has come of it all. A girl has found her brother. I've met Ruth, she's like a daughter to me now. And *we*, we've found each other once more. If there is any providence, it's of the good kind."

"Hmm. I'll not argue, I do prefer the sound of that." Edith smiled sadly. "I have to say, that story you told Ruth, about us being sent to separate beds with our dollies, was wonderful. Very creative. I believe you made up another story some twenty-five years ago; this one involved a litter of kittens, if I recall." Edith laughed.

"Ah yes, the twin kittens named Doll and Kate given to us by our 'father.' That was a lovely little story as well."

"We've had to tell a lot of stories, long and creative tales, so that we might hide our secret, haven't we? I think we've become quite good at it—storytelling."

"Indeed."

"We'll probably have to tell more stories if we hope to continue with . . . *this*."

"Yes, but who doesn't love a good story?" Vera smiled.

"Yes. Yes. And as you know, since Raymond has grown up and become a father himself to Ruth, my husband spends more time in Scotland with his beloved dogs than in our house in London; he certainly didn't have any interest in accompanying me to this little village. I've written him, and he seems quite agreeable to my spending summers here when the war is over. I can maybe stay longer than the summer months . . . much longer." Edith placed a hand over Vera's, and they were silent for a moment. Their attention returned to the woodcut print of the two women in bed.

"I never thought I'd see this book again," Edith said.

"Nor did I." Vera closed *The Roxburghe Ballads* and placed the tome on her bedside table. She turned off the lamp, and in the dark, she embraced the woman whom she'd been in love with for the better part of a lifetime.

It was approaching closing time at the pub and the table of friends lingered over their last pint, when Cora looked up to see someone step through the blackout curtain. "Well, here's someone who doesn't often darken a pub's door."

"Mr. Horgon!" Ruth stood. "You're not one for pints."

"Yes, well, even I need to steady my hand now and then. The truth is, I've some paperwork I'm trying to clear out. I thought I'd come around to Vera's cottage to discuss something with you, and she's sent me here to find you."

"The paperwork is chasing us home now," Malcolm said.

"No, no, not weigh bills in this case. You see, with all the other things happening over the course of this winter, I've let some things fall behind. Tonight, I thought that I ought to do my due diligence and inform you about a certain investigation that has been languishing on my desk for some weeks, something to do with a missing peacock."

Ruth blushed. "Peacock? I'm not sure what you're talking about?" She glanced at Maude, who looked away guiltily.

"Yes, apparently there had been some poachers wandering the escarpment some weeks ago who took the last ornamental bird of the estate. The gamekeeper there seems to think it was women who were doing the shooting."

"Women?" Ellen placed a pint down in front of Horgon. "Women hunting for peacock. Now that's a story."

"Yes, indeed," he said. "I'll be truthful, I'm not so concerned about a peacock. So, I'll just say that I've no eyewitness of this crime, nor will I spend too much of my time pursuing it. I'll simply leave warnings, to all people who might take up a gun, that they stay within the rules of law, war or no war." Horgon retrieved the hair clip from his pocket and placed it on the table. "I suppose this belongs to you, Gladstone."

"Oh, no, actually, I don't think so—not mine," she said. "It's made from jet, I see." She turned to Maude with expectant eyes.

"No, can't say that's mine," said Maude. Ellen reached across and picked up the hair clip.

"This is mine. I've not seen this since I was a wee girl. I've the mate for it back in me jewellery box. Where on earth did you find this?"

"Blackwell found it, actually." Horgon cleared his throat. "Found it on the lands of the estate, on the sheep path near to the kiln ponds; he assumed that the poachers dropped it." He looked around in confusion. "Ellen, you say you lost this when you were a young girl—not recently?"

"Not recent. No, many, many years ago, I lost it, but I wasn't living in . . . wait . . . I don't think . . ." Ellen seemed to consider something. She started to speak, but stopped herself, a great confusion passing over her face. "Wait . . . wait, this is curious," she mumbled quietly.

Ruth had a revelation then, a revelation so shocking she nearly blurted it aloud. Martynsborough was *the* village, the village that Ellen had been in when she lost her cat, as she had mentioned during Maude's first visit to the pub. She had searched for it for days, she had said. Her father moved the family around a lot for his job. How could she have searched for *days*?

She had been left behind.

After travelling about so much as a child, each village would look the same to her, even the one in which she lost her cat. So, on returning, all those years later, Martynsborough was not familiar to her, just another village. And Ruth was now certain Ellen's father wasn't some travelling sundries man or other. Ellen had not been completely forthcoming; she spoke in a particular way, quickly, with a cadence that was reminiscent of Travellers.

She *was* a Traveller, at least born to them, but knowing the dim view that villagers tend to have for them, Ellen did not speak of it. She had been evasive about her youth.

The group of wagons had scrambled away with the threats of law and village justice at the end of an elephant gun while Ellen, oblivious, looked for her pet on the escarpment. Ellen's family, whoever they were, fine people or bad, Ruth could not know, they must have left her behind and did not come back for her, or came back after she'd left. With her cat drowned by Blackwell in the kiln pond, Ellen had nothing left. She would have wandered the escarpment and the streets to find food. Phineas witnessed her that first night. His head was clouded by the soma, a yellow cat in the pond became a yellow-haired girl—imaginings of his long-dead sweetheart whirling about in his confused mind. He saw Ellen wandering in her white dress. Only when Albert and others witnessed Ellen did they believe him. Word spread of the body in the pond, a mysterious girl drifting about the fields, a mania began. Who could say how many sightings were of a real girl wandering the streets, and how many were delusions born from superstition and an ancient and collective fear of witches?

Cora took the girl away. The sightings ended, but as some had said, Phineas never stopped seeing the figure of his lost love, Charlotte, haunting the fields on which her bone dust had been spread far and wide. His grief perhaps fell to madness. Then amazingly, decades later, by some strange providence, Ruth and Maude, whilst tumbling down the sheep path, must have unearthed the wayward hair clip themselves. As she thought all these things silently, she glanced at Ellen's dark-brown hair. She was once blonde when she was young. It was the name of the pub, the Yellow Rattle, named for a small yellow-haired girl: the original Wraith of Martynsborough.

It was a remarkable discovery no doubt, seemingly on the tip of everyone's tongue, ready to be recounted that night in the pub, except . . . the conversation never did happen. Ellen claimed the hair clip, her face distraught, and seemed reluctant to speak further of it. Ruth, herself, said nothing, unsure how or even if she should broach it—how many more secrets might it reveal? Ellen had not been altogether honest about her past, and perhaps she wished to keep it that way. Ruth looked over at Cora, thinking that this village elder might offer some answers, but she also did not speak; she seemed to know too, and perhaps like Ruth, Cora felt some deep instinct that the truth ought to remain concealed. Maude and Malcolm felt the peculiar change of energy in the room, and they too chose not to pursue this most unlikely of conclusions.

So, after a small murmur of confusion passed among the friends gathered at the table, Ruth cheerfully led the conversation away to other things. Soon they took up their pint glasses and spoke of the war and how hopes of it ending any time soon were dwindling, then the prospect of a spring dance, and the military commandeering of the Wolstenholme estate and what was to be done with the conservatory and the strange creatures within it.

And many hours later, deep into the night after her friends had gone home, Ellen examined the hair clip in the dim light of the pub. Martynsborough *was* the village, the place she was left behind by her Da, the place where she wandered, cold, looking for her cat. In these woods she lost her hair clip, tumbling down the sheep path, and muddying her already dirty white dress. The night was cold, and when she found her way back to the meadow, her Da was gone. The wagons, all of it gone. They'd return surely—her Da always came back. She waited there that first night, on the edge of the meadow, straining to hear the wagons, shivering in the cold, but heard nothing.

Why would he leave? That part, she now knew, from the stories of Albert. They were driven away with threat of violence. Why did she not make a connection when she heard the story in the pub that night? She could not be sure. Her memories of that time were hazy, but she recalled in a misty kind of way how she wandered the fields aimlessly, giving up on her cat. To think that she so frightened the men of the village when they saw her.

After two nights in the cold, she saw two women slip into the small door of a house by the river, which she now knew was the mill. She followed, not quite knowing what she would find, but some deep instinct told her that the women would lead her to safety. She hid for a while on the ground floor and listened as the women moved about in the place at the top of the ladder. She worked up some courage and started to climb. She poked her head through the trapdoor. They didn't notice her. Ellen watched as the women sipped from cups, like a tea party, with a pretty table, all set with wine and candles and a fat earthen vase bursting with wildflowers. It was like a dream, to come into this dark and frightful mill to find such a lovely sight. The two women smiled and laughed and looked happy. She didn't rightly recall their faces all these years later, only that one of the women had fiery red hair.

She watched as they leaned into each other, quite close, perhaps to whisper a secret, but their faces disappeared behind the rotund vase with its great bundle of flowers, and they lingered there for some time. Ellen could no longer see them. Frustrated, wanting to see more, she climbed up another rung, but her foot slipped, she gasped, and slapped her elbow against wood. The women sat up, emerging from the shadow of the blooms, and now visible, they looked her way, their faces pale, as if they'd seen the most monstrously frightening thing.

After an agonizing moment of silence, the woman with the red hair offered Ellen something to eat. They were sisters, the lady said, her face fraught and anxious, eyes darting here and there. Ellen could never figure why the women were so nervous, but she did indeed take their help, and stayed there that night on a hay-mattress bed, and as she fell asleep, she heard one woman say quietly "we've been seen, whatever shall we do." Ellen never understood what she meant by that and drifted off to sleep soon enough.

The next day, they said they had to leave, but they provided her food and said they would find a way to help her. A day later, another woman came, a woman she now knew as Cora. How could she not have known? How could Cora not have recognized her after all these years pouring her pints? Yes, Ellen's blonde hair had darkened to mahogany, she had grown tall and looked different—but then why had *Ellen* not recognized *Cora*? Perhaps memory is a fleeting thing; we don't see what we remember unless we wish to. Or maybe . . . maybe Cora had known all along, all these years drinking pints in the pub with the child she had rescued, and not said a thing. With what Ellen had learned that night, she knew that Cora was good at keeping secrets; perhaps she carried many more. Either way, Ellen remembered being taken to another village. A family of dairy farmers took her in. They were good people, and although for many nights she cried about her Da, she eventually settled into her new home. She grew up, and as a young woman, she moved about in different villages, restless, perhaps hoping to cross paths with the wagons once more, but she never did. On her travels, she met a man, and together they came to Martynsborough to pull pints, but she had never recognized the river, or the mill or the village.

She turned down the lights of the Yellow Rattle and went up the stairs to her bed, wondering where her husband was, wondering too, where her Da was. Did he think of her? Did he miss his yellow rattle? She was certain he did, and tears threatened. To think, she had returned all these years later, and only now, with her hair clip found, did she know that Martynsborough *was* the village . . . and without ever realizing it, she was its wraith.

The sun was low in the sky, bleeding gold into pink as Ruth pushed her hands into her pockets and walked under the ebbing light. Although nearly April, the air was still rather cool, but by lucky fortune, her last pair of intact heavy knit winter stockings had survived her adventure in the river. Now dry and clean, they were doing a fine job keeping her legs warm, and she was quite content to linger outside with her thoughts.

An odd thing weighed on her mind. For some reason, she couldn't seem to forget the fact that the ewe was alone the day that Elise fell in the river. Then, as she tried to articulate this fact, it occurred to her that the sheep had been named Castor and Pollux. They were both male gendered names, and neither name had ever been affixed to one or the other individual animal. No, they were known by the double moniker—inseparable by name—but now seemingly separated in physicality. How could she refer to the ewe alone? And what had happened to the ram? Had he been swept up in the flooded Harold during the storm? Or had he simply left, moved on to greener pastures, seeking another mate? Ruth couldn't be sure, but she decided to go to that place where she last saw the ewe.

She crossed the stone bridge on the far side of the village and walked past the marsh where she had pulled Elise to safety. Then as the sun dipped below the tree line, she stepped into the meadow, where the dandelions had turned to feather, and the yellow rattles were starting to bloom. The mist captured the amber glow of the sinking sun and filled Ruth with wonder.

"No Dandelions tell the time, although they turn to clocks,
Cat's-cradle does not hold the cat, nor foxglove fit the fox."

Ruth recited the verse to no one in particular, then, ahead in the tall grass, she saw something rustle the blades. Then she saw another erratic movement, like the flit of a butterfly, but no—something different altogether. A small white creature leapt, and Ruth saw the downy head of a lamb crown the green, with creamy fleece and bright black eyes, then another in chase. They tumbled on to each other among the tall blades of grass, shaking the rattles, cow's clover, and primrose. Ruth watched with delight as they danced and frolicked in the meadow. The ewe appeared—the nameless, doting mother, moving out among the wildflower to check on her little ones. Then, the ram stepped from a tangle of bracken at the edge of the wood; his handsome horns spiralled crookedly, his black face appraising his children. They were together again, in name *and* in form. Ruth smiled, and turned away, letting them be.

She stepped out to the middle of the stone bridge and watched as the Harold flowed beneath her. The water had calmed since the storm and had once again become the languid, passive river that she had grown to love. She stayed that way for some time, lost in thought, until she realized the sun had slipped below the horizon and only a dull azure glow seeped between the ragged black trees. The swaying spring grass took on deeper shades of blue, and the fallow fields undulated lazily this way and that. She looked back once more for Castor and Pollux, but they had vanished; instead, she saw something else, beyond the meadow, at the periphery of a newly ploughed field. She blinked in disbelief.

It was a girl in white. Ruth brought a hand to her mouth, thinking she had conjured this apparition from her weary, writerly brain. But no, the figure remained, lit by the moon with yellow hair and a white dress, no, not a dress, a nightgown, the type worn at the turn of the century. The girl looked back at Ruth, and for a moment, they studied each other silently. The figure then turned and disappeared into the twilit mist, drifting over the rich and fecund soil of the Martynsborough fields. Ruth's fear melted away, and instead, she was glad of what she had seen, happy in a way for Phineas too, feeling she now shared something special with this misunderstood man who had never stopped seeing his sweetheart.

Ruth turned, crossed the bridge, and retraced her steps back through the high street of Martynsborough, then on to the cottage that she now considered her home.

It was to be a novel. A great gothic tome, loved, savoured, read slowly, and consumed greedily by the light of a low-wattage bulb, deep into the early hours of a delicious night.

But Ruth changed her mind and decided that she was *not* going to tell a ghost story; she would not share the Wraith of Martynsborough, at least not yet. It needed to age a little longer. Like the rabbits that Vera hung in her shed, something so fresh might taste too much of blood.

She would tell some other story, for her head was now filled with them. Perhaps a story about two sisters reunited after a lifetime separated, or a story about a girl who disguised herself as a boy and followed a river in search of her lost brother, or a story of a young stable-hand whose sweetheart died tragically and had her ashes spread on the fields so that the crops might grow high and strong, or a story of the last two sheep who hid from a storm and emerged with lambs.

For each story could be wrapped and woven within others, and not exhaustively cross-checked like some textbook or other, nor history, no—facts be damned—these tales would all be fanciful and gilded, beautiful and tragic or heart-rending, or revelatory. Facts aren't required for these tales. No, facts are not necessary to tell *any* story at all, that is, as long as somewhere among all the embellishments, within the spaces—between the hair's breadth—there might lurk one small and stalwart bit of Truth.

SUMMER 1945

-34-

As much as Ruth hated the typewriter—noisy, clacking away—she nevertheless accepted its practicality. She had nearly finished her second novel, and she wanted to get it in the post and to her editor in London as soon as possible. She could then put up her feet and rest for what felt like the first time in a long time.

A year before, her debut novel was published in New York, where resources were not stretched so thin from the war, and it sold well in America for several months before she saw it, much later, in print in her own country. She remembered the giddy, dreamlike feeling when she received a box of proofed and bound copies at the village hall as VE celebrations were being planned. It seemed so long ago and far away—for now it was the sunny back end of August, the war in Europe over, and she, on the verge of finishing book number two, bathed in the light of her window, which overlooked the rolling hills of central France.

There was a soft knock on the door. "Ruth, are you busy?"

"Malcolm, you needn't knock—you know that. This is your house." He opened the door, an envelope in his hand.

"*Our* house." He handed her the letter. "You've got something in the post. From Martynsborough." He smiled sheepishly. "Sorry, I think I've got a bit of clay smudged on it—I need to do a better job washing up."

"From Maude." Ruth beamed. "I can't wait to read it. And how is your monstrously large sculpture? Can I see it yet?"

"No, not yet, I'm afraid. Good art takes time. It's half-past four; come have a drink, in the garden." He massaged her shoulders gently. "You've worked hard enough today, darling." She reached around to touch his hand.

"Yes, so true. I've got nothing left in me to write this day. The sun is beautiful, I should get outside. I should also abandon this wretched machine—pen and paper in the garden, that's how it should be done." She stood and stretched out her arms and bent her neck to the side, producing an audible crack. "I'll be right there, give me a moment to arrange my things here." Malcolm left the room, and she heard the creak of the step as he descended.

She looked around and her gaze fell on the two rifles hanging on the wall. Perhaps she should head to the valley for some shooting tomorrow. The ducks in France were so much better than in England. She'd never admit it aloud—especially not to Aunt Vera—but it was true.

She went down the stairs, through the kitchen, and stepped out into the garden to see that Malcolm had arranged a table with a vase with flowers, some lovely things to eat, and a bottle of Champagne. "What's all this?" she asked. "Are you flaunting the cornucopia of France to this malnourished English girl?"

"No, it's to mark an anniversary. It's today. Do you recall?"

"No, actually . . . what is this?"

"Five years ago, today, we crossed paths on a dusty road in a tiny village in northern England. We didn't know each other's names, and if I recall correctly, I had my shirt thrown open and perhaps was frowny and a bit terse, and you . . . well, you had a basket filled with poisonous leaves with which you were about to make a salad for your family."

"Oh, Malcolm . . ."

"Five whole years." He glanced at the double doors leading from the kitchen. "Oh, and look here, the lovely lady who helped arrange these

flowers, up from her siesta. Come join us for our celebration, Elise."
He pulled a chair out for her. "Here's to victory." He popped the cork.

In the dark of the garden, with the flicker of oil lantern as her only light,
Ruth, sitting alone, opened her letter. She unfolded the pages, took a
sip from her wine, and began to read.

Dearest Shakespeare's sister,

*First let me say how quiet this village is without you here
stirring up endless trouble. No robberies, no air raids,
no peacock hunts . . . yes, quieter, although strangely,
the wraith is still occasionally seen, at least that is what
I sometimes hear whispered within the walls of the pub.
The mystery lives on, I suppose.*

*I miss you so very dearly, but alas, I remain here.
Why do I linger? Why do I not return to Cambridge, to
teach young girls about sedimentary layers? Why do I find
so much happiness pulling pints with a woman ten years
my senior? It's a mystery more profound and perplexing
than your wraith.*

*I'll say, it has not been easy since Ellen learned of
her husband's fate. The hardest part is having nothing to
bury, so we've decided at some point in the future, when
things have settled, we'll take a cruise across the Bay of
Biscay and we'll salute him, from above, while he lies
somewhere below. She'll never marry again, she says. I'm
of a like mind, so I hate to say it, Gladstone, but I've a
new bedmate who is almost as good at keeping me warm
on a cold night as you.*

Shall I catch you up? Of course. First, the best thing:

Judith caught her train just this morning—going home—Johnny landed safely at Portsmouth two weeks ago and is on his way to Sheffield—both mum and dad await them—the happiest of endings.

The estate and all its crumbling palisades have housed those fresh-faced officers now for a few years, and the lands of Wolstenholme continue to abound with swaying sweet corn. There appears to be no rush for the men in uniform to leave anytime soon. The original ancient residents of that place have had their living space shrunk ever more, and they are now ensconced in a tiny apartment in the east wing, and after the generals learned of all their shenanigans with contraband, they will likely be living under the strictest of rationing till the ends of their lives.

Also, not that you're interested in livestock, but it seems that much of the roaming sheep of the village—how many were there last we checked? Dozens? Well, a great many of them are back on the grazing land, flocking nicely with the help of those handsome herding dogs. We'll all have mutton on the menu again, it seems. But our Castor and Pollux—the original Adam and Eve—remain hidden, location unknown. It seems they've showered us with offspring galore, and then fled towards the sunset, to put their hooves up and have a cigarette perhaps?

Oh, and I loved your book, and I look forward to the next. I know which character was me—I do, but I won't say, in case I'm wrong—but yes . . . oh so good, Ruth. Top form. Bravo. And what of your poem, "Through a Darkening Glass"? I fondly remember it. So lovely. Make sure you get that wedged into some famous literary anthology or other!

By the by, I would like to say this, if I might draw back my visage of thick-skinned trouser-wearer for a moment to say, with sincerity, that as much as you are a fierce hunter with your gun, beguiler of all the men—a breaker of hearts, and a hero, saving the lives of desperate women caught in raging torrents, and an intellectual, writing best-selling novels, a thinker, an artist, a renaissance woman well beyond her time, and so many other great things that I could barely comprehend, above all, I really, really would hate for you to change. Stay as sweet as you are, Gladstone, don't ever lose your earnestness, humility, your curiosity, that natural . . . I don't even know what to call it . . . goodness? Yes, goodness. Ruth, you are a good person. Stay that way. Please do. After everything we've been through in the last six years, the world needs good people.

I hope you're enjoying France, and I'm sure Ellen and I will very soon be coming to sully up your castle or villa or whatever it is you're living in, and definitely drink away whatever French plonk your one-eyed friend has lying about.

On the subject, I do have to wonder about your living arrangement—it is unique to say the least—what is it you French say? "À chacun son gout"—that's it.
Stay true, Ruth,
Your best mate,
M.

P.S. I wasn't going to write this, but I've just knocked back another pint as I reread the first bit, and now I have no impulse control. I just wanted to say, for the record, I did see that peacock well and clear—I was fully aware it was a peacock, but we needed a bird, so I delivered—I made it look like an accident for your benefit—you're so moral—you'd never live with yourself if you knew I shot such a colourful boy purposefully—and then where would we be? We needed that peacock, Gladstone—we really did. Or at least I did. It was one of the finest moments of my life, taking down that pretty cock.

ACKNOWLEDGMENTS AND

AUTHOR'S NOTE

When I wrote "facts are not necessary to tell *any* story" in chapter thirty-three of this book, it was not just to provide the reader with a notion of Ruth Gladstone's ethos on writing. I also included it as a small insurance policy for my guilty habit of sometimes playing fast and loose with historical fact. As much as I like the idea of artistic license (I wield it regularly), I also agree with Horace, who wrote of poetry that it ought *to instruct and delight*. I would hate to think the "instruction" component of this novel might be lacking, so I would like to set the record straight on a few items.

Many breeds of sheep have horned males and non-horned females, but in the case of Lancashire Lonk mules, *both* male and female are horned. In order to easily tell them apart in the story, I took the ewe's horns away. My apologies to all the Lonk breeders out there.

Green uncensored letters were more a thing of the first world war than the second, and although during WWII there were indeed envelopes for which an enlisted signatory could avoid censorship (for the most part) by providing an "honour pledge" to include only personal and family-related material, these envelopes were not usually coloured green. I liked the visual effect, so I muddled the two versions together in this sense.

Girton College never saw a bomb during the summer of 1940, but the wider city of Cambridge *did*. In fact, it was among the earliest raids of the war, when Vicarage Terrace was hit on June 18, 1940, resulting in what were possibly the war's first civilian casualties from German air raids. The deaths included children.

Homes in small English villages would not likely have enjoyed dedicated electricity in the 1940s; in fact, many places had to wait until the 1970s to be connected. Amazingly, the last British village to get electricity was just connected in 2008. I gave Martynsborough electricity so that the blackouts would be more meaningful, and Vera could enjoy listening to the wireless.

Auguste Rodin's famous sculpture *The Kiss* exists in several forms, including the bronze relief on a door called *The Gates of Hell*. Some versions have the figures' lips touching, while some don't. As Malcolm speaks of the sculpture in the story, he is in fact describing a mash-up of several different versions of *The Kiss*.

Atlas moths can live more than one night, but rarely longer than five days. I kept it to one night for the sheer tragedy of it all.

Elise's medical condition is fictitious but based in fact. Brain injury and related conditions are unpredictable and difficult to diagnose then, as now. Those who suffer brain injuries can have personality changes and lose the ability to live independently. Some become non-verbal and lose certain motor functions. Sometimes their behaviour is puzzling to their loved ones. I have based some of her condition on my real-life observations and experiences with a family member who suffered a permanently brain-altering stroke. The terminology used by the characters in this book, of course, is in keeping with a time when the layperson did not understand much about brain injury and they misused terms such as *catatonic* or applied anachronistic words such as *invalid* and *deficient,* which by today's standards are considered pejorative and ableist.

The use of the small-g *gypsy* in the text by Wolstenholme and some other characters is keeping with the nomenclature of the time and how

Irish Travellers may have been identified in the 1940s. It is a word with a long and complicated (and often ugly) history and is used here in a historic context only. In modern Britain, *gypsy* continues to be an accepted legal term used to describe Travellers, who are not to be confused with the Romani people, with whom Irish Travellers share no genetic relation.

Martynsborough is an imaginary place on an imaginary river that exists somewhere north of Clitheroe and south of the Bowland forests. And despite only one encounter with airplanes during the story, such a place could very well have been on a flight path of either the RAF or raiding Luftwaffe, but information remains elusive on such things, so I will leave it at that.

I would like to acknowledge some important resources that helped me write *Through a Darkening Glass*. This includes the BBC's *People's War Archive*. It is a veritable treasure trove of real diaries, letters, and first-person verbatim accounts from the time of the war. I found myself regularly losing any sense of time while perusing these precious archives.

As much as I'm a bit sheepish to include a television program as part of my research, I have to acknowledge Ruth Goodman, Alex Langlands, and Peter Ginn, whose documentary series *Wartime Farm* was not just terribly instructive (and entertaining), but also the source of my inspiration for an agrarian village called Martynsborough.

I would also like to credit a lovely bit of writing by E. Joan Wilson, a geography student enrolled at Girton College during the war. Her personal essay, "An English Geographer Remembers," follows her journey from public school to Girton in 1939 and then on to become a teacher herself. She later became a well-known geography professor and finished her career in America. She died in 2015. I'd like to think that Maude Sedgwick would have been one of her contemporaries and drinking mates. I picture them sipping sherry and comparing stone collections at Girton College.

I was also inspired by a January 2012 *Washington Post* piece titled "A family learns the true meaning of the vow 'in sickness and in health,'" written by Susan Baer. It tells the heart-breaking story of Page and Robert Melton, in which a brain injury challenges their vows of marriage. This article helped me to understand and explore the ethics and obligations of Malcolm and Elise's marriage and the unique ways in which married couples learn to navigate these life-changing injuries while still retaining some sense of a loving relationship.

Finally, on to the people.

I'd like to thank my amazing agent, April Eberhardt. She believed in me, even when I did not believe in myself.

And my deepest gratitude to my editor, Jodi Warshaw, who helped me take my first tentative steps into the labyrinth that is modern publishing. She has been calm, affable, knowledgeable, and patient. I am blessed to have her as my guide.

I couldn't have completed this project without the help from my small but mighty writing circle who gave me a place at the table—J. Gregory, I. Herman, M. Johnson, S. McGreeghan, S. Seymour, M. Summers.

And of course, thanks to Dorothy, Isabelle, and Juliet. You know why.

R. S. Maxwell
Toronto
November 2021

ABOUT THE AUTHOR

Having earned an arts degree from York University many moons ago, R. S. Maxwell continues to read and study voraciously across multiple subjects that include cookery, gardening, English literature, music, art, and art history. Maxwell, who resides in Toronto, can typically be found working on another novel.